About the

New York Times and *USA T~~...~~g author*
Katee Robert learned to tell her stories at her grandfather's knee. Her 2015 title, *The Marriage Contract*, was a *RITA®* finalist, and RT Book Reviews named it 'a compulsively readable book.' When not writing sexy contemporary or romantic suspense, she spends her time playing imaginary games with her children, driving her husband batty with what-if questions, and planning for the inevitable zombie apocalypse.

Dare Me

April 2023
To Want You

April 2023
To Need You

May 2023
To Crave You

Dare Me
to Want You

KATEE ROBERT

MILLS & BOON

First Published in Great Britain 2023
by Mills & Boon, an imprint of HarperCollins*Publishers* Ltd,
1 London Bridge Street, London, SE1 9GF

www.harpercollins.co.uk

HarperCollins*Publishers*
Macken House, 39/40 Mayor Street Upper,
Dublin 1, D01 C9W8, Ireland

Dare Me to Want You © 2023 Harlequin Enterprises ULC.

Make Me Want © 2018 Katee Hird
Make Me Need © 2019 Katee Hird
Make Me Yours © 2019 Katee Hird

ISBN: 978-0-263-31900-2

This book is produced from independently certified FSC™ paper
to ensure responsible forest management.

For more information visit: www.harpercollins.co.uk/green

Printed and Bound in the UK using 100% Renewable Electricity
at CPI Group (UK) Ltd, Croydon, CR0 4YY

MAKE ME WANT

To Tim.

Second chances make for the best stories.

CHAPTER ONE

GIDEON NOVAK had almost canceled the meeting. He would have if he'd possessed even a shred of honor. Some things in this world were just too damn good for him to be associated with and Lucy Baudin topped that list. To hear from her now, two years after...

Focus on the facts.

She'd called. He'd answered. It was as simple as that.

The law office of Parker and Jones was the same as it had been the last time he'd walked through the doors. The small army of defense attorneys took on mostly white-collar crimes—specifically the ones that paid well—and that showed in every element of the interior. Soothing colors and bold lines projected confidence and created a calming effect.

Pale blue walls and good lines didn't do a single damn thing to dial back the pressure building in his chest with each step.

He usually didn't contract out with law offices. As a headhunter, Gideon preferred to stick to tech companies, various start-up corporations or, literally, anyone except lawyers. They were too controlling and wanted their hands on every detail, every step of the way. It was a pain in the ass.

This is for Lucy.

He kept his expression schooled on the elevator ride up. When he'd known her, she was somewhere around floor six, proving herself by working cases not big enough for the lawyers with seniority to want but that were too big to turn down. Now she was on floor nineteen, only a couple below Parker and Jones themselves. She'd done well for herself in the two years since he'd seen her last. Really well.

The elevator opened into a large waiting room that didn't look anything like an actual waiting room. The more money people had, the more care was required in handling them, and the coffee bar and scattering of couches and trade magazines reflected that. The hallway was guarded by a large desk and an older woman with tasteful gray shot through her dark hair. Surprising. He'd expected a bottle-blond receptionist—or perhaps a brunette if they were feeling adventurous.

But then the woman looked up and he got the impression of a general surveying her domain. *Ah.* They'd chosen someone who couldn't be bulldozed, if he didn't miss his guess. Useful to keep unruly clients in line.

Gideon stopped in front of the desk and did his best to appear nonthreatening. "I'm here to see Lucy Baudin."

"She's expecting you." She turned back to her computer, effectively dismissing him.

He spent half a second wondering at her qualifications—and if she was amiable to being poached for a different company—before he set it aside. Stepping on Lucy's toes by stealing her receptionist wasn't a good way to start off this meeting.

He'd spent the last week trying to figure out why the hell Lucy would seek *him* out. New York was rife with headhunters. Gideon was good—better than good—but considering their history, there had to be someone better suited for the job.

You could have said no.

Yeah, he could have.

But he owed Lucy Baudin. A single meeting wasn't much in the face of the fact that he'd more or less single-handedly brought her engagement down in flames.

He knocked on the dark wooden door as he opened it. The office was bright and airy, big windows overlooking New York, the only furniture a large L-shaped desk and two comfortable-looking chairs arranged in front of it. Gideon took in the room in a single sweep and then focused on the woman behind the desk.

Lucy sat straight, her narrow shoulders tense, as if she was about to step onto a battlefield. Her long dark hair was pinned back into some style that looked effortless but probably took a significant amount of time to accomplish. She raised her pointed chin, which drew his attention to her mouth. Lucy's features were a little too sharp to pass for traditional beauty—she would have made a killing on a runway—but her mouth was full and generous and had always been inclined to smile.

There were no smiles today.

"Lucy." He shut the door behind him, holding his place to let her guide the interaction. She was the one who'd called him here. It didn't feel natural to take his lead from someone else, but for her he'd make an effort.

At least until he heard her out.

"Gideon. Sit, please." She motioned at the chairs in front of the desk.

Maybe she could pretend this was like any other job interview, but he couldn't stop staring at her. She wore a dark gray dress that set off her pale skin and dark hair, leaving the only color present in her blue eyes and red lips. It created a striking picture. The woman was a goddamn gift. She always had been.

Jeff, you fucked things up beyond all recognition when you threw her away.

Focus.

She hadn't arranged this meeting because of their past. If she could be professional, then he'd manage, as well. It was the least he could do.

Gideon sank into the chair and leaned forward, bracing his elbows on his knees. "You said this was about a job."

"Yes." A faint blush colored her pale cheeks, highlighting the smattering of freckles there. "This is confidential, of course."

It wasn't quite a question, but he answered it anyway. "I didn't put together a nondisclosure, but I can do that if you need to make it official."

"That won't be necessary. Your word that it stays between us will be enough."

Curiosity curled through him. He'd had clients insist on confidentiality in the past—it was more the rule than the exception—but this felt different. He set the thought aside and focused on the job. "It would help if you'd describe the position you want filled. It gives me a general idea of what you're looking for, and we can narrow it down from there."

She met his gaze directly, her blue eyes startling. "The position I need filled is a husband."

Gideon shook his head, sure he'd heard her wrong. "Excuse me?"

"A husband." She held up her left hand and wiggled her ring finger. "Before you get that look on your face, let me explain."

He didn't have any *look* on his face. *A husband. Where the fuck does she think I'm going to find a husband?* He opened his mouth to ask exactly that, but Lucy beat him there. "The timing isn't ideal, but gossip has come down the grapevine that I'm being considered for partner at the end of the year. While that would normally be a cause for celebration, some of the old guard have very strong beliefs about single women." She rolled her eyes, the first *Lucy* thing he'd seen her do since he'd arrived. "It would be laughable if it wasn't standing in the way of what I want, but I watched Georgia get passed over for a promotion last year for this exact reason. She wouldn't bend and they chose her male competition instead."

She was dead serious.

Gideon took a breath, trying to approach this logically. Obviously she'd put a lot of thought into the idea, and if she was misguided, that didn't mean he had to verbally slap her down. *This* Lucy, put-together and in control, was a far cry from when he'd seen her last, sobbing and broken. But that didn't change the fact that they were one and the same. He could handle this calmly and get her to see reason.

But calm and reasonable wasn't what came out of his mouth. "Are you out of your goddamn mind, Lucy? I'm a headhunter—not a matchmaker. Even if I was, getting married to secure a promotion is bullshit."

"Is it?" She shrugged. "People get married for much less valid reasons. *I* almost married for love before, and we both know how that ended. There's nothing wrong with handling marriage like a business arrangement—plenty of cultures do exactly that."

"We aren't talking about other cultures. We're talking about *you*."

Another shrug. As if it didn't matter to her one way or another. He *loathed* that feigned indifference, but he didn't have a goddamn right to challenge her on it.

She met his gaze directly. "This is important to me, Gideon. I don't know about kids—I love my job, and having babies would potentially interfere with that—but I'm lonely. It wouldn't be so bad to have someone to come home to, even if it wasn't a love for the ages. *Especially* if it's not a love for the ages."

"Lucy, that's crazy." Every word out of her mouth cut into the barrier of professionalism he fought so hard to maintain. "Where the hell would I find you a husband?"

"The same place you find people to fill the positions normally. Interview. We're in New York—if *you* can't find a single man who's willing to at least consider this, then no one can."

Gideon started to tell her exactly how impossible it was, but guilt rose and choked the words off. He thought this plan was bat-shit crazy, and the thought of Lucy in some loveless marriage irritated him like sandpaper beneath his skin, scratching until he might go mad from it.

But it wasn't his call to make.

And he was partially to blame for her single status right now.

Fuck.

Gideon straightened. No matter what he thought of this plan, when it came right down to the wire, he owed Lucy. He knew that piece of shit Jeff had cheated on her, and Gideon had kept his mouth shut for a full month before he'd told her the truth. That kind of debt didn't just go away. If she was coming to him now, it was because she'd exhausted all other options, and his saying no wasn't going to deter her in the least— she'd find a different way.

Really, he had no option. It might have been two years since he'd seen Lucy Baudin, but that didn't change the fact that he considered her a friend, and he'd never leave a friend hanging out to dry when they needed him. Gideon might have questionable morals about most things, but loyalty wasn't one of them.

She needed him. He'd have found a way to help her even if he didn't owe her.

At least if he was in the midst of this madness, he'd

have some ability to keep her as safe as possible. He could protect her now like he hadn't been able to protect her from the hurt Jeff had caused.

If she was crazy for coming up with the plan in the first place, he was even crazier for agreeing to it. "I'll do it."

Lucy couldn't believe the words that had just come out of his mouth. It was too good to be true. Attempting to rope Gideon Novak into this scheme had been her Hail Mary. She was desperate and he was the only one she trusted enough to even attempt something like a search for a husband. But she hadn't thought he'd actually agree to it.

He said he'd help. Shock stole her ability to speak for a full five seconds. *Say something. You know the drill—fake it until you make it. This is just another trial. Focus.* She cleared her throat. "I'm sorry—did you just say yes?"

"Yes." He studied her face with dark eyes lined with thick lashes, which she secretly envied. Gideon had always been too attractive for Lucy's state of mind. His dark hair was always styled in what she could only call "rakish," and his strong jaw and firm mouth would have kept her up at night if he wasn't firmly in the friend zone.

At least, he used to be.

She set the thought aside because going down the rabbit hole of despair that was her relationship with Jeff Larsson was out of the question. It had ended, and her friendship with Gideon had been a casualty of war.

Until now.

Gideon shifted, bringing her back to the present. "How exactly were you planning on going about this?"

This, at least, she had an answer for. Lucy had spent entirely too much time reviewing the steps required to get to her goal with minimum fuss—a husband and her promotion. "I thought you could come up with a list of suitable candidates, I could have a date or two with each, and then we could narrow the list down from there."

"Mmm-hmm." He tapped his fingers on his knee, dragging her attention south of his face. He wore a three-piece suit, which should have been too formal for this meeting, but Gideon managed to pull it off all the same. The pin-striped gray-on-gray gave him an old-world kind of feel, like something out of *Mad Men*.

Thankfully for Lucy, he had better morals than Don Draper.

She fought not to squirm in her seat under the weight of his attention. It was easy enough to be distanced and professional when she'd laid out her proposal—she'd practiced it the same way she practiced opening and closing statements before a trial. Getting into the nitty-gritty of the actual planning and actions was something else altogether.

"I'm open to suggestions, of course." *There—look at me, being reasonable.*

"Of course." He nodded as if deciding something. "We do this, we do it on my terms. I pick the men. I supervise the dates. And if I don't like the look of any of them, I have veto rights."

Veto rights? That wasn't part of the plan. She shook her head. "No. Absolutely not."

"You came to me, Lucy. That means you trust my judgment." He gave her an intense look that made her skin feel too tight. "Those are the terms."

Terms. Damn, she'd forgotten the most important thing.

It doesn't have to be the most important thing. He doesn't know it was part of the plan, so it's not too late to back out.

But if she backed out, the deep-rooted fear from her time with her ex would never be exorcised. She'd spend the rest of her life—and her prospective marriage— second-guessing herself and her husband. It would drive her crazy and ultimately poison everything.

She couldn't let it happen, no matter how humiliating she found asking for Gideon's help with this.

Lucy managed to drag her gaze away from his. She pulled at the hem of her skirt. "There's one more thing."

"I'm listening."

She smoothed her suddenly sweating palms over her desk. "Are you seeing anyone?"

"What the hell does that have to do with anything?"

It had everything to do with things. She'd never known Gideon to hold down a relationship longer than a few weeks, but that didn't mean he hadn't somehow changed in the last two years. The entire second part of her plan leaned heavily on the assumption that he *hadn't* changed.

The Gideon she'd known before had been her friend,

yes, but he'd also been a playboy to the very definition of the word. He hadn't dated seriously. He'd never
mistreated women, but he hadn't kept them around for
long, either. Lucy had heard the whispers in college
about his expertise in the bedroom—it was legendary
enough that most women ignored the fact they had an
expiration date from the moment he showed an interest in them.

To put it simply, he was *perfect* for her current situation.

She just had to find the strength to speak the damn
words. She forced her hands still. "I'm going to need…
lessons."

"Lucy, look at me."

Helpless, she obeyed. He frowned at her like he was
trying to read her mind. "You're going to have to explain what the hell you're talking about."

It was so much harder to get it out while looking at him. She pressed her lips together. She'd faced
down some of the most vicious prosecutors New York
had to offer. She could damn well face Gideon Novak
down, too.

*You know these words. You've practiced them often
enough.*

"I need lessons of the sexual nature." He went so
still, he might as well have turned to stone, so she
charged on. "This might be an arranged marriage, so
to speak, but it would be a true marriage. And, as I
don't cherish the idea of being cheated on by yet another fiancé, that means sex needs to be part of the

bargain. It's been a long time for me, and I have to brush up on my skill set."

Not to mention the only man I ever slept with was Jeff, and he never missed an opportunity to tell me how uninspiring he found our sex life.

Or that he blamed his cheating on my being unable to meet his needs.

She didn't let what Jeff thought dictate her life anymore, but Lucy would be lying if she pretended his words didn't haunt her—that they hadn't been instrumental in her two-year celibate streak. She'd enjoyed sex. She'd thought Jeff had enjoyed it, as well. If she could be so terribly wrong on such a fundamental level before, what was to stop her from failing at it again?

No, she couldn't allow it. If she trusted Gideon enough to secure his help finding a husband, then she trusted him enough to create a safe space to teach her something she obviously needed to know to be an effective wife. His rumored sex prowess just sweetened the bargain, because he was more than experienced enough to walk her through a crash course in seduction.

He still hadn't said anything.

She sighed. "I know it's a lot to ask—"

"I'm going to stop you right there." He stood and adjusted his jacket as he buttoned it. "I will charge you for the husband hunting—the same rates of a normal client. I'm not a sex worker, Lucy. You can't wave a magic wand and acquire lessons in fucking."

She did her best not to wilt.

You knew it was a long shot.

"I understand."

"That said…" He shook his head like he couldn't believe the words coming out of his mouth any more than she could. "Come by my place tonight. We'll talk. After that, we'll see."

That…wasn't a no. It wasn't a yes. But it most definitely wasn't a no.

"Okay." She didn't dare say anything more in fear that he'd change his mind. *I can't believe this is happening.* He didn't look happy to have offered the invitation. In fact, Gideon looked downright furious.

He pinned her with a look. "Seven. You remember the address."

It wasn't a question but she still nodded all the same. "I'll be there."

"Don't be late." He turned and stalked out of her office, leaving her staring after him.

What just happened?

A thrill coursed through her. What just happened was that Gideon Novak had agreed to help her. Professionally he had a reputation for always getting his man and, personally, he had everything required to get her pending marriage off to the right start.

He said yes.

With him in her corner, there was no way she'd fail.

The promotion was hers. She could feel it.

CHAPTER TWO

GIDEON SWAM LAPS until every muscle in his body shook with exhaustion. It didn't help. All he could see was Lucy's earnest expression as those sinful lips spoke words he would have killed to hear before. *Teach me.* His attraction for that woman had never brought him anything but trouble, and apparently he was doubling down because he hadn't told her no like he damn well should have. Instead he'd told her to come to his place.

So they could talk.

About him giving her lessons in fucking.

He pulled himself out of the pool and climbed to his feet. He'd been prepared to tell her no—to both the husband hunt and the lessons. Instead he'd invited her over tonight. What the hell was that about?

You know what that's about.

Gideon wanted Lucy.

He'd wanted her from the moment he'd seen her across that crowded bar in Queens six years ago. She'd been so fresh-faced and, even too many shots in, he'd known there was something special about her.

Unfortunately so had Jeff Larsson, and that bastard had beaten him to the punch—meeting Lucy, dating Lucy, proposing to Lucy.

Gideon had tried his damnedest to be happy for his best friend—and to table his desire for his best friend's woman—but it had never quite gone away. It didn't matter how many girls he'd dated, because his heart had never been in it. When Jeff had made a passing remark on Gideon's tendency to find willowy brunettes with freckles, he'd shelved dating completely and restricted his interactions to one night.

He showered and dressed quickly. It would be tricky getting back to his place before she arrived, but he'd had to do something to take the edge off or he was in danger of throwing caution to the wind. The temptation of Lucy in his bed, even for such a shitty reason…

He'd be a bastard and a half to do it.

No, Gideon would grab takeout, sit her down to her favorite Chinese and explain all the reasons why sex between them wasn't an option. He'd be calm and reasonable and use whatever arguments he had to get his point across. She didn't need *lessons*. No man with a pulse and a working cock was going to have a problem with anything Lucy had to offer.

His step hitched at the thought of someone else waking up next to her every morning. Of the long nights buried between her thighs and the friction of sweat-slicked skin and—

Fuck.

He glanced back at the gym, seriously considering calling the whole thing off and spending the next three hours back in the pool. Maybe if he was too exhausted to move, his fury at the thought of her with another man would subside.

He knew better.

If he hadn't been happy that his best friend was with her—even before the idiot had started fucking around—he wasn't going to be pleased with a stranger. There was no help for it. Lucy would charge ahead with this plan of hers whether he agreed to it or not. He might be able to talk her out of the sex bit, but he wouldn't be able to convince her that she didn't need a husband.

He'd failed her when it came to Jeff. Even as his best friend, Gideon had missed the warning signs until it was almost too late—and then he'd hesitated a full month before breaking the news to her. He'd well and truly fucked up across the board and it had cost him her friendship—something he'd valued more than he could have dreamed.

He wouldn't fuck up again.

She wanted a husband? Well, then, Gideon was going to find her the most honorable man he could to make her happy. He owed it to her to do so.

He barely had time to drop the takeout on the kitchen counter when a knock sounded. He skirted the couch and opened the door. "You're early."

"I hope you don't mind. Your doorman remembered me, so he didn't bother to buzz you." She gave a tentative smile that pulled at him despite his determination to do the right thing.

Lucy must have made it home because she'd changed into a pair of black leggings and a lightweight slouchy shirt that seemed determined to slide off one shoulder. She saw him looking and bit her bottom lip. "I know we talked about lessons, and this isn't exactly seduction personified, but I went through my closet and, aside from work clothes, I don't think I *own* anything that's 'seduction personified.'"

For fuck's sake, she was killing him. Gideon stepped back and held the door open. "You look fine."

"Fine." She frowned. "I know you're cranky about being cornered with this whole thing, but you don't have to damn me with faint praise. I asked you to do this because I trust you to tell me the truth. I've always trusted you to tell me the truth."

If she'd taken out a knife and stabbed him in the heart, it would have stung less. Gideon closed the door carefully behind her, trying to maintain his control. It didn't matter how honest she thought he was, he wouldn't agree to take her to bed. He couldn't. "This won't work if you're going to jump down my throat every time I say something. I said you look fine. You do. I didn't tell you to dress for seduction, Lucy. I said to get your ass over here so we can talk. That—" he motioned at her clothes "—is perfectly adequate for a conversation between two friends."

"Right. Okay. I'm sorry. I'm nervous." She pulled at her shirt, which caused it to drop another inch down her arm.

Gideon had never found shoulders particularly provocative before but he wanted to drag his mouth over the line of her collarbone. *Keep it together, asshole.* He cleared his throat and looked away. "You don't need lessons, Lucy. Not from me. Not from anyone. You're beautiful and any man would be lucky to have you in his bed."

"If you don't want to teach me, that's fine. I did say that this morning." She wandered farther into his apartment and circled the couch he'd bought six months ago. It was slate gray with dark blue accents, and the saleswoman had insisted it would pull the room together in a way he'd love. He was still waiting to love it. Lucy picked up one of the ridiculous blue throw pillows and hugged it to her chest. "I'm not fishing for a compliment, by the way, but thank you. Though, beauty only goes so far. Since you haven't… We haven't…" She huffed out a breath. "Can I be perfectly frank?"

"You weren't before now?" If she was franker, she might actually kill him.

"Jeff might be a cheating bastard, but that doesn't change the fact that even before he started sleeping around, he was never…satisfied. Since he obviously found that satisfaction with those other women, it's impossible to blame the entire problem on him."

Gideon watched her pick at the tassels on the pillow while he dissected what she'd just said.

"You've been with other men since him."

"No." She still wouldn't look up. "I almost did once. But I kept hearing *his* voice in my head with those nasty little comments that he always wrote off as a joke and

I just couldn't. I know that's pathetic, but after a while, the risk of finding out that Jeff was really right all along wasn't worth the potential pleasure. So I focused on work instead of dating—and now here we are."

Gideon wished he could go back in time and deliver a few more punches to Jeff's perfect face. He'd known things weren't perfect with Jeff and Lucy, but he hadn't realized just how much of a dick his friend had been. "He's a piece of shit."

"I'm not arguing that, believe me." She gave a faint smile. "Thank you again for saving me from marrying him. I don't know if I ever said it before, but it couldn't have been easy to say something. You two had been friends for so long."

Gideon scrubbed a hand over his face. He read people for a living—both his clients and the people he found to fill the open positions. He was damn good at it, too. That skill made him the best in the business and ensured that he almost always got the secondary bonus for the position still being filled for a year after the initial contract.

Every instinct he had was insisting that Lucy's sheepish smile covered up a soul wound. If he was a good man, he'd let someone else help her heal from that—someone who'd be there for the long term. Likely that theoretical husband he was supposed to find her. But Gideon wasn't a good man.

He didn't want it to be anyone else.

He wanted it to be *him*.

"Sit down."

She dropped onto the couch, still clinging to the pillow. "Okay."

There wasn't a convenient playbook for how to go about this, but they *did* need to have a conversation before it went any further. "I will give you...lessons. On two conditions."

"Agreed."

He shot her a look. "Hear the conditions first and then decide if you're good with them. First—you communicate with me. You like something? Tell me. You aren't into it? You need to speak up. You fake anything and we call the whole thing off. I can't help you if you aren't honest with both yourself and me."

She wrinkled her nose. "Fine. I'm an adult. I can talk about sex."

He didn't comment on the fact she seemed to be trying to convince herself. The confidence and ice queen bit she'd played in the office was nowhere to be seen now, which made him wonder who was the real Lucy—the cold and professional lawyer or the unsure woman sitting in front of him now.

Gideon leaned forward. "Second condition is that you're not with anyone else for the duration."

"Why?" She held up a hand. "I have no intention of being with anyone else, but I'm curious."

"It's respect." *Liar. It's jealousy.* He smothered the snide little voice and kept his tone even. "We're exclusive—both of us—until the expiration date."

"Exclusive." She said the word as if tasting it. "When's the expiration date?"

Never. Fuck, he was already in over his head and

sinking fast and he hadn't even touched her. "When you decide on a candidate for a husband, we end it."

Lucy nodded. "That seems reasonable. Should we start now?" She reached for her shirt.

"Holy fuck, slow down." He made an effort to lower his voice and held out a hand. "You want lessons? We start with the basics. Come here."

She reluctantly let go of the pillow and rose to cross over to his chair. Lucy eyed his hand, but ultimately placed hers in it. Gideon drew her down slowly, giving her plenty of time to see where things were going. She obliged him by climbing into his lap, though she held herself so stiffly she felt downright brittle.

He kept hold of her hand and set his other on her hip. It would have been innocent if not for the fact that she was straddling him and his cock had not gotten the memo about moving slow.

She shifted, her eyes going wide. "Ah…"

"Are you uncomfortable?" He spoke before she could think too hard.

"No…" She bit her lip. "Right. Honesty. Okay, yes, this feels weird. Awkward. I don't know where to put my hands and I can feel you, and it's making me nervous."

She was right. It was awkward as fuck. But Gideon wasn't going to throw her off the deep end on the first night, no matter how surreal this whole thing was. She trusted him to take care of her and he'd do whatever it took to be worthy of that trust. *Do whatever it took to keep her from changing her mind.* He kept his voice low so as not to startle her. "I'm going to kiss you now."

"Okay." She licked her lips and carefully tilted forward.

Gideon moved his hand from her hip to cup her jaw, guiding her down as he leaned up to brush his mouth against hers. She smelled of citrus and he had to fight to keep a growl internal. *Nice and easy.* He nipped her bottom lip and then soothed it with his tongue. She placed her hands on his biceps and relaxed against him, bit by bit. Gideon took it slow. He kissed her, keeping it light, until she shifted restlessly against him.

Then, and only then, did he slip his tongue into her mouth.

His first taste of Lucy went straight to his head. He used his hand on her jaw to angle her to allow him deeper and stroked his tongue against hers. Slow and steady was the name of the game.

Lucy whimpered and went soft against him. Her body melded to his, her breasts dragging against his chest with each inhalation. She shifted her grip and tentatively sifted her fingers through his hair. As if she wasn't sure of her welcome.

He wanted her sure.

Gideon shifted back to lean against the chair. The move settled her tighter against him as her knees sank into the cushion on either side of his hips. She gasped into his mouth and he ate the sound. He kissed her like he'd wanted to since that first night, when he'd heard her infectious laugh across a crowded bar. She tasted just as sunny as she smelled, as addicting as a summer's day in the midst of winter.

He couldn't get enough.

CHAPTER THREE

LUCY'S AWKWARDNESS WENT up in smoke the second Gideon kissed her. She'd expected... Well, she wasn't sure what she'd expected. For him to take her into the bedroom and strip them down and just go for it. Preferably with the lights turned off to hide her mortification.

He stroked his hands up the sides of her face and tangled his fingers in her hair. The move pulled her out of their kiss, but Gideon didn't let the distance stand. He dragged his mouth down the line of her neck, raising goose bumps in his wake.

A deep, hidden ember inside her burst into flame.

She was doing this. She was straddling Gideon Novak with his mouth on her skin and his hands on her body. Something she'd never even allowed herself to *think* about until she'd come up with this plan.

"You're thinking too hard."

"I can't believe this is happening."

He set his teeth against her collarbone. "If you change your mind—"

"I won't." She'd never dared fantasize about him—

she hadn't let herself cross that line, even in her mind—but she wasn't missing this opportunity for the world. Warmth flared with each breath, the heat centered at her core, where she could feel his cock lining up right where she wanted it.

I want it.

The realization startled her, though it shouldn't have. Gideon was sex personified and having all his considerable attention focused solely on her was a heady feeling. She wanted... More. All of it. Everything he could give her. She moaned. "More."

Gideon took her mouth. There was no other way to put it. He claimed her, establishing dominance with a stroke of his tongue, engulfing her entire world in that single contact. He tasted like peppermint—a shocking sensation against her tongue. Unexpected.

Just like the man himself.

It wasn't enough. There were too many clothes between them. She could feel his broad shoulders flexing, could test the definition of his muscles as she slid her hands down his chest, but his button-up shirt barred her from the skin-to-skin contact she craved.

Her breasts felt too tight, her nipples pebbling until they almost hurt. At least her yoga pants didn't offer much in the way of a barrier as she rocked her hips against him. His slacks did little to hide the size of his cock, and that little movement felt deliciously good. Intoxicating. So she did it again.

Gideon dropped one hand to her hip. For one horrifying moment she thought he'd stop her—maybe tell her that grown adults did not dry hump in the middle of one's living room—but he just urged her on. He never stopped kissing her, never stopped exploring her mouth. As if kissing was his be-all and end-all rather than just the first step to get to sex.

God, I am so messed up.

He squeezed her ass and nipped her bottom lip. "How we doing?"

"Good." Was that her voice? She sounded like she was doing something requiring a whole lot more exertion than kissing Gideon Novak. *If this is what kissing is like, am I going to survive actual sex?*

Who cares? It'd be a glorious way to go.

He used his grip on her hip to pull her closer yet, lining up his cock with her clit. "And now?"

She hissed out a breath. *Please don't stop.* She could come like this if they kept it up. "Really good. But—" She didn't want to talk about it, didn't want to do anything to make this stop, so she went in for another kiss.

Gideon tightened his hold on her hair just enough to prevent her from moving. "But?"

His insistence on honesty had seemed like a good idea at the time—how could she improve if she didn't know what she was doing wrong?—but in practice it felt like he was stripping her bare in a way that had nothing to do with sex. She closed her eyes, because it was easier to answer when she wasn't meeting his gaze. "Isn't dry humping kind of juvenile?" *Are you going to mock me if I orgasm from this? Maybe make a joke about cobwebs or how long it's been for me?*

His chuckle pulled at things low in her stomach. "Does this feel juvenile to you?"

"No." It felt hotter than it should have and even a little dirty. She wanted it too much, and that was the problem. She forced herself to open her eyes and found him watching her with a contemplative expression. "What?"

"Pleasure isn't something you can put limits on, Lucy. There isn't a right way to go about it. Would you tell someone who was eating one of those double-chocolate-death desserts you love so much that they were eating it wrong if they did it differently than you?"

"Of course not." She blinked. How had he possibly remembered her favorite dessert?

"Then why is *this* wrong?" He urged her to rock against him again. "Feels good to me. Feels good to you. No reason to overthink it."

When Gideon put it like that, it sounded so simple. Deceptively simple. She started to ask another question but forced herself to silence it. This insecurity wasn't her. This was the ghost of her relationship with Jeff coloring the current interaction.

Exactly what she'd been afraid would happen.

"Thank you for agreeing to this, Gideon. You didn't have to and—"

"Lucy." He framed her face with his big hands, preventing her from looking away. Those dark eyes were so incredibly serious. "Stop thanking me for this. The matchmaking shit? Sure. Not this. You're crazy if you think I'm not getting something out of it—same as you. Enjoy it. Enjoy *me*. It's as simple as that."

Easier said than done. The malicious voice that had spent far too many years lurking in the back of her

mind wouldn't be silenced. Not completely. *Pity fuck.*
She pressed her lips together. "I want to have sex now."

"No."

She frowned. "What?"

"No." He sat up, forcing her to grab his shoulders to stabilize herself, and then stood, taking her with him. "You want me to teach you? Then we're doing this on my terms. You were enjoying the hell out of this and something tripped you up." He laid them down on his ridiculously comfortable couch. She sank into the cushions as his weight settled over her. It felt good. Right.

It scared the shit out of her.

"Gideon."

"My terms, Lucy." He kissed her again. Before it had been sweet, and then intense, but she hadn't realized he was holding back until that moment. Gideon kissed her like he owned her. He took her mouth, urging her to meet him halfway.

She held back for all of one second; it was impossible to maintain distance with his very presence overwhelming her. So she let go, tangling her tongue with his. The second she did, he started to move.

It had felt good when she was on top, but it was nothing compared to him pressing her into the couch as he stroked his cock against her clit. One long slide up and then another back down. The desire that had been put on hold while she'd let her insecurities get the best of her seared her—with interest. As if it'd been waiting for her to just let go and enjoy this moment for what it was. *Pleasure. No questions asked.*

She arched up to meet him. "That feels good."

Gideon hitched a hand beneath her knee and drew her leg up and out, opening her farther. He kissed her again and kept up that slow drag that had sparks dancing at her nerve endings. Her body wound tighter and tighter with each stroke until she teetered on the brink. Lucy writhed against him, trying to get closer, to get him where she needed him, to do whatever it took to reach that edge. "Gideon, *please*."

He shifted back and she sobbed out a breath at the loss of him. But he didn't make her wait long. He slid a hand beneath the waistband of her yoga pants and into her panties. His rough curse would have made her smile under other circumstances, but she was too busy holding her breath. *So close. Please just touch me.*

He did.

He made a V with his fingers and slid it over her clit in the exact same motion he'd been doing with his cock before. She lasted three strokes before she came apart in his arms, her pleasure drawing a cry from her lips and blanking out her mind into delicious static. He softened their kiss to the barest brushing of lips and then shifted to the side so his weight wasn't completely on her.

Lucy blinked at the pale gray ceiling and tried to reconcile what had just happened with reality. *I just came. Without pressure. Without having to force it or fake it.* A world-ending orgasm and *Gideon* was the one who'd coaxed it from her. "Wow." As soon as the word popped out of her mouth, she cringed. *What a stupid thing to say.* She was hardly a virgin and she wasn't an idiot teenager, no matter what they'd just done.

Gideon gave another of those low laughs. "All flavors, Lucy."

Against her better judgment, she couldn't help comparing what they'd just done to her experiences with Jeff when they'd first started dating. Night and day. Even though it'd taken her and Jeff a bit to work up to sex, he'd always had an air of impatience about him when they were intimate—like he couldn't wait to get to the next step. Add that to his competitive need to make her come multiple times every time they were together and the pressure had twisted with the desire until it made her jumpy every time they'd been alone together. Things had changed a little once they'd finally had sex, but then other elements had come into play.

Boring.

Uninspired.

Like fucking a doll.

"Lucy, look at me." Gideon's voice drew her out of the horror show that was her past.

She shook her head. *God, I can't even do this right.* What they'd just done was so incredibly perfect and she'd had to go and ruin it by letting her issues with her ex creep in. "I'm sorry."

"No, I'm sorry." He stroked a hand through her hair, the move so tender, her stomach tried to tie itself in knots. His dark eyes took on a distance as he looked at something she couldn't see. "I knew Jeff was an asshole, but if I'd known what a piece of shit he was, I would have warned you off before he got his hooks into you."

"It wouldn't have mattered." Six years ago, in the midst of her headlong rush into adulthood, she was so sure that she knew better, she hadn't listened to anyone. Not her sister, not her friends, not her fledgling instincts. As nice as it was to think otherwise, she wouldn't have listened to Gideon, either.

Being this close to him, talking like this while her body still sang from the pleasure he'd given her… It was too intimate. Too revealing. Just plain too much.

She slid off the couch and stood. A quick look at the front of his slacks confirmed that he was still, in fact, painfully hard. *Nice job, Lucy. Bask in your post-orgasmic bliss and ignore the fact he's still in need.* "Do you want me to…?"

"These lessons aren't about me." He sat up. "They're about you. And you need space."

Yeah, she did. His airy living room was suddenly too small, the walls closing in even as her heart beat too fast. "I asked for this."

"You don't have to explain." He gave her a half smile that didn't reach his eyes. "We poked at some old wounds tonight. If that means you need some distance from the whole thing, then so be it. You're being honest, and fuck if I'm going to punish you for that." He grabbed his phone off the coffee table. "But if you're headed home, I'm calling you a cab."

She should push back. She was more than capable of calling her own damn cab and the subway would be running for hours yet. But if Gideon could respect her need to flee without his pride being injured and throwing a fit, she could respect his need to get her home safe. "Okay."

He made the call quickly and set the phone down. "What's your schedule look like tomorrow?"

The change in subject left her discombobulated. "I have court in the afternoon, so I'll be doing last-minute preparations beforehand." It was as close to an open-and-shut case as such things got. The cops had mishandled the evidence and the lead detective had an established vendetta against her client. She had every intention of getting the whole damn thing thrown out.

"I know that look on your face. You have this one in the bag."

Her stomach gave another of those flutters that wasn't altogether uncomfortable. He'd said that with such confidence, as if there wasn't a single doubt in his mind that she would win. Lucy tucked a strand of hair behind her ear. "I should be free in the evening." *For another lesson?* She didn't know if she'd look forward to it or dread it. *Liar. You haven't even left yet and you're already craving another hit.*

"Good." He stood, suddenly taking up too much space. She tensed, half expecting him to touch her. But Gideon headed for the door. "I'll have a list of preliminary candidates ready for you, and we'll go over them at dinner."

"That I'll pay for." She cast a pointed look at the way his jaw tensed at her words. "Don't be like that. If I was a normal client, I'd pay and you wouldn't blink because that's how things are done."

"You aren't a normal client, Lucy. There's nothing *normal* about this." He motioned between them.

She couldn't really argue that, but that didn't mean he'd win this battle. "I'll handle the reservations and text you the details."

"Stubborn."

The twisting in her stomach took on a sour edge. Jeff had thrown that word at her like a curse more often than she could count. *Stop it. Oh, my God,* stop. *He's in the past and he's staying there.* "It's my best trait."

"I wouldn't dream of arguing that." He held the door open for her. "Until tomorrow."

"See you then."

She headed for the elevator, stopping several steps down the hallway and leaning against the wall as she tried to calm her racing heart. She hadn't known it could be like this. He'd just…taken care of her. Both physically and emotionally. Bringing her to orgasm and recognizing and respecting the panic driving her to leave. Lucy hadn't expected that. She didn't know what to do with a version of Gideon who was different than she'd expected.

What did I get myself into?

CHAPTER FOUR

"YOU'RE FUCKING CRAZY."

Gideon didn't look up from his computer. "You don't have to tell me that."

"And yet I'm telling you all the same. What the hell are you doing? *Matchmaker?* For *Lucy Baudin*?" Roman Bassani paced from one side of the room to the other, his restless energy irritating as fuck.

"I know we're supposed to have lunch, but this came up and can't wait. I'm going to have to take a rain check." Gideon wrote down another name and moved to the next candidate on his preliminary list. When Roman paced another lap around the office, he cursed. "Sit down or get out. You're distracting me."

"You need the distraction. Hell, you need a god-damn intervention." Roman threw himself into the chair across from the desk and slouched. He would have been at home in some artsy perfume ad with his brooding good looks and the way he seemed to pose without noticing he was doing it. On any other man, the affected attitude would have pissed Gideon off, but with Roman it was just… Roman. He was too honest, too brash, too comfortable in any space. It was part of what made him so good at his job—he had never met a challenge he wasn't fully confident he could tackle.

Whether his confidence was misplaced or not was an argument for another day.

"Gideon, why are you doing this? Wait—don't tell me. You're not still feeling guilty because you didn't tell her what a douche Jeff was immediately? Look, we all fucked up. You're the only one who stepped in, and that's something I have to live with." He made a face. "I convinced myself that it wasn't my place or my business."

"Jeff's good at spinning any situation to benefit him." He'd sure as hell laid on the guilt and idiotic bro code heavy enough to give even Gideon pause at the time.

"Changes nothing." Roman shrugged. "Including the fact that you are not qualified to be a matchmaker, let alone for Lucy. She's a good girl and, damn it, she deserves a professional. I know a few in the city. I can call in a favor and get her shoved to the top of the list and wrap this whole thing up without anyone crossing any lines."

He tried to be rational and actually consider it. He fucking failed. The line had been crossed last night and there was no going back now. "No. She asked me, so I'm the one who'll do it. And don't get any funny ideas, Roman. You meddle in enough people's lives. I have no interest in being added to the list."

"As if you'd let me." Roman affected a sigh. "You're as mean as a junkyard dog."

"And you're wasting my time. Unless you have something worthwhile to add to the search, get out."

He realized his mistake the second his friend perked up. "Who's on the list?"

Fuck me. "No."

"Come on." Roman shot to his feet, towering over the desk, and snatched the paper from beneath Gideon's hand. His hazel eyes went wide. "Shit, Gideon. You put Aaron Livingston on here. Shooting for the stars, aren't you?"

"She's worth it." He grabbed the paper.

Roman studied him for a long moment. "Interesting."

"For fuck's sake, Roman, don't you have some business to buy up or small children to terrify?" He still had several hours' worth of work to do before he met up with Lucy tonight. The address she'd texted him wasn't far, but rush hour would be a bitch to navigate, so he'd scheduled in extra time. That didn't mean he was going to dick around with this damn list.

His friend pointed to two names on the list. "Take Travis and David off the list. They're fuckheads with women, though they both hide it well."

Gideon crossed out their names. "I hadn't heard."

"Why would you? You don't date, and that handsome mug of yours might have people intrigued, but it's from a distance. People aren't rushing to confide in you because there's a solid chance you'll rip them a new one for wasting your time."

Gideon glared. "Are you finished?"

"Not yet." Roman gave a lazy grin. "My point is that people talk to me, so using that as a resource is a smart thing to do. Aaron Livingston is as straight as they come. If that guy has any skeletons in his closet, they're buried deep. The other two left on the list are up in the air. I'll find out what I can and let you know."

He fought down the need to snap back. The truth was that Roman was right. People didn't open up to Gideon. His clients only cared that he got the job done and had one of the highest ratings in the industry. The people he placed for his clients only cared about their endgame in a company that would pay them well to do what they loved. Friends? He had them. He just preferred them at a distance.

Roman had never been able to take that hint.

"Fine. Look into them."

"It's charming that you think I need your permission." Roman grinned. "I'll come by in the next few days and let you know what I dig up."

A call would have been preferable, but Gideon knew Roman well enough to know that arguing was pointless. His friend did what he wanted, when he wanted. He sighed. "Fine."

"Chin up, Novak." Roman paused. "All joking aside, if you're going to do this, do it right. I know your history with Lucy is complicated, but playing this straight is the only way. Otherwise, there are a lot of potential complications that could arise."

Last night had been nothing if not one long, agonizingly good complication. Even almost twenty-four hours later, he could still taste her in his mouth. It made him crave more, which was a dangerous path to walk.

Lucy wasn't for him.

He had to remember that.

If she'd wanted *him*, she would have said so. Even this almost-timid version of her wouldn't have balked at putting it out there. She was direct, as evidenced by her plan existing in the first place. But she hadn't brought him into her office to ask *him* to step into the role of husband.

Husband.

What would that even look like?

Gideon shook his head and focused on his friend. "I have it under control."

"Keep telling yourself that." Roman headed for the door. "I'll check in tomorrow, but in case I don't see you before then, we still on for Friday?"

"Yeah." They had a standing reservation in Vortex's VIP lounge on Friday nights. It was one of the only social appointments he held consistently, despite occasionally running into Jeff there. But that asshole had started coming less and less in the years since he and Lucy had broken off their engagement. People had started to see through his charming act and called him out when he was acting like a douchebag—which was often.

"See you then." Roman opened the door and paused. "You should bring her."

Gideon tore his gaze away from the list of names yet again. "What?"

"You should bring Lucy on Friday. I know Aaron Livingston since we worked together last year. We can orchestrate a non-pressure meeting. You're on your own with the other two, but I don't think Aaron would agree to a blind date for shits and giggles."

Since Gideon had only met him in passing, he couldn't argue that. "Do it." He spoke before he had a chance to think up half a dozen reasons why it was a bad idea. It *wasn't* a bad idea. It was his issue if he didn't want to see her with someone else—not hers.

He waited for Roman to shut the door behind him before he grabbed his phone. Both Mark and Liam were acquaintances he'd come across in the last few years who had seemed like upstanding guys. He'd feel them out for interest and then take the list to Lucy to see where she stood with all of it.

The knowledge that she'd likely end up with one of these men sat in his stomach like a rock. He hesitated, his contact list staring back at him. It would be the easiest thing in the world to sabotage this. All he had to do was feed some false information about Lucy and they'd say no. Or feed her false information about *them* to prove New York had a shitty dating scene.

"No." He'd promised her to do his best and he'd damn well do his best. Gideon had lied to her once before and it had almost destroyed them both. He wasn't going to do that to her again.

Fuck, he was in this situation *because* of what happened before.

Gideon would do right by Lucy. He'd have to be a heartless bastard to do anything else. The only option was to find her a damn husband.

No matter what it cost him to do it.

Lucy was on her second glass of wine by the time she caught sight of Gideon's familiar form moving toward her table through the darkened room. He towered over the tiny host and the poor man kept shooting looks over his shoulder as if he expected Gideon to club him over the head. The thought made her smile and was almost enough to distract her from her nervousness.

She'd woken up this morning from the single hottest dream of her life, starring none other than Gideon Novak. It started identical to their encounter last night, but they hadn't stopped until they were naked and in his bed, both shaking from their respective orgasms. Her body flushed at the memory and she took a shaky sip of wine.

What was the protocol for greeting a man who'd used his fingers to make her come on his couch the night before? They weren't dating, so a kiss seemed inappropriate. They weren't even really friends anymore, so a hug was likely presumptuous. A handshake was just absurd.

Gideon saved her from having to decide by sitting before she had a chance to stand. He shot a look at the host. He probably meant it as a polite dismissal, but it actually looked scathing. Lucy watched the man nearly run from the table. "You really have to work on your attitude."

"My attitude is fine."

"Without a doubt, but you have a very intimidating persona. You know most women judge a man by how he treats the waitstaff on their first date—and you would have just nixed the possibility of a second date and we haven't even had appetizers yet."

Gideon raised his eyebrows. "Good day in court, I take it."

"We're not talking about me." She leaned forward and lowered her voice. Enjoying poking at him a little. "Though that was a very smooth change of subject."

The corners of his lips twitched upward. "Yes, it was. We're not here to talk about my dating prospects. We're here to talk about yours." He looked up as a waiter approached and she actually saw the effort he put into forcing a smile. It looked downright pained, but it was better than nothing. "I'll have a seven and seven." He glanced at her half-full wineglass. "Another?"

"Sure." She didn't drink more than two glasses often, but she'd busted her ass on today's case and the judge had been persuaded to dismiss the entire thing. It was a coup that should have been the tipping point for her promotion, but when Rick Parker had come by her office to congratulate her, he'd made a comment about the big, broody man who'd been in to see her yesterday. Because, of course, who she was or wasn't dating was just as important as her professional skill set.

Well, damn it, Parker's crappy attitude wasn't going to ruin her night.

"Tell me about the case."

She almost refocused the conversation, but the truth was that she didn't have anyone to talk to about it. Her sister was supportive and wonderful, but Becka had her own thing going on and couldn't be less interested in law. Get together for drinks and chat about life and what their parents were up to? Sure. Hash out the details of whatever case Lucy was working on? Not a chance. And Gideon actually looked interested.

She picked up her wineglass. "I got the entire case thrown out today. All they had was circumstantial evidence and a bad attitude about my guy's priors. They were so certain he did the crime, they didn't look at anyone else. Anyone on the outside would have come to the same conclusion, but it's always a crapshoot with Judge Jones."

"That's great, Lucy. Congrats."

"Thanks." She smiled and then took a drink. "How was your day?"

"Productive." He leaned over and pulled a tablet out of his briefcase. "I have some things to show you."

Disappointment coated her tongue when he slid the tablet across the table to her. They'd barely gotten their conversation started and now they were back to business. *You hired him as a business decision. You don't get to have it both ways.* It wasn't fair to ask him to go back to being her friend along with her being his client.

She picked up the tablet and found pictures of three men. She clicked on the first one—a blond guy with a close-cropped beard and a seriously expensive suit—and found a file. "'Aaron Livingston, born May thirteenth...'" He'd compiled a list of information ranging from where Aaron was born to where he graduated high school and college—and his GPA at both. There was also a notification about possible likes and dislikes. "Wow, Gideon. You really don't do anything halfway, do you?"

He had compiled the same information for each of the other two men. Interestingly enough, all three of them were local and had gone to prestigious business colleges, graduating close to the top of their class. All three had moved on to respected companies and seemed to be doing well for themselves.

Using their information and ignoring their pictures, she wouldn't have been able to pick any of them out of a lineup. "This... Wow."

"You said that already." He frowned. "Is something wrong? I assumed that you were looking for someone in the same financial class as you, and leaning toward white-collar businessmen. That *is* why you came to me, correct?"

Yes, at least in theory. In reality, this whole thing was playing out much differently than she'd expected. It didn't make a bit of sense, especially because it was proceeding *exactly* how she'd hoped. "No, it's fine. They're excellent candidates."

Seeing them laid out like this, the situation just became so much more real. In a very short period of time she'd be sitting across the table from one of these men, rather than Gideon. She'd be torturing herself with wondering if they'd kiss her after dinner—if maybe they'd expect more to happen.

I'm not ready.

She took a gulp of her wine. "Can we get dinner to go?"

CHAPTER FIVE

NERVES STOLE LUCY'S voice as she and Gideon walked to her apartment. She'd intentionally picked a restaurant close to her place so that they wouldn't have to worry about a cab ride to get from point A to point B. She nodded at the doorman as he held open the door for them and then she strode to the elevator and pushed the button.

Gideon followed her inside and leaned against the elevator wall. The food in the paper bag smelled divine, but her craving was solely for the man holding it. She clasped her hands together to keep from touching him. "I want to progress tonight."

He raised his eyebrows. "I'm listening."

Why was it so challenging to say these things aloud? She was an adult. She should be able to express her needs honestly without fear of being laughed out of the building—or rejected. Lucy fisted her hands and raised her chin. The mirrors in the elevator walls and door reflected a version of her that looked ready to go several rounds on the courthouse floor. "I don't want to wait anymore. I want everything."

That predatory stillness rolled over him and his eyes seemed to flare with barely banked heat. "Bite-size steps are the smart option."

"Nothing about *this* is smart, and I think we both know that." Last night had made her skittish in a way she hadn't expected, and if she was shrewder and less stubborn, she would have called the whole thing off as a result. Instead she was pushing them toward something neither could take back.

The elevator door opened and she wasted no time walking into the hall and down to her door. There were only four apartments on this floor, each occupying their respective corner of the building. Hers faced southeast, so she often woke to the early morning sunlight streaming through her windows. At least on the days she wasn't up before dawn.

She unlocked the door and held it open for Gideon. He stopped just inside the entranceway, barely leaving room for her to slide inside behind him. She tried to see the place through his eyes. The open floor plan showcased the big floor-to-ceiling windows. The kitchen lay just to the right of the front hall, the white cabinets set off with little turquoise handles she'd found online. The living room contained a decent-size TV that she rarely used and two short couches arranged in a loose V. Her cat, Garfunkel, lifted his head and gave Gideon a death stare.

Gideon moved to the kitchen counter—white marble shot through with pale gray—and set the bag of food on it. He turned and crossed his arms over his chest. "Why the change of pace?"

"Maybe I just want you." It was the truth, but not the full truth.

He shook his head. "Honesty, Lucy."

Why had she agreed to that particular term? She pulled at the hem of her fitted blue dress. "I'm nervous. Last night was good, but I didn't expect that level of reaction, and I'm afraid if we don't get it over with, I'm going to change my mind."

"Get it over with," Gideon murmured. "Sex isn't something you 'get over with.' If you think of it that way, there's a problem somewhere."

A problem he was determined to fix if the expression on his face was anything to go by. She sliced her hand through the air. "No problem. That's not what I meant at all. My issue is that the anticipation, the will-we-or-won't-we, is driving me nuts. I want to rip it off right now—like a Band-Aid."

He stared at her for a long moment and then burst out laughing. "A Band-Aid. Fuck, woman, you really are going to kill me." He ran a hand over his face. "The anticipation is meant to be enjoyed."

She could think of a lot of words to describe how she felt standing in her apartment with Gideon and knowing they were alone and could do what they wanted for hours. *Enjoyment* didn't top the list. Her body was too hot, her lungs too tight, her core aching from need. But she knew that look on his face. If she didn't do something rash, he was going to put the brakes on and sit her down and coax her to talk through it. For someone with such a ruthless reputation, Gideon was overwhelmingly careful with her.

She knew why—he had residual guilt over not telling her immediately about Jeff's cheating ways. But she didn't care about any of that right now.

All she cared about was getting through this interaction so she could go back to breathing normally again.

Before she could talk herself out of it, Lucy unzipped the side of her dress and slid it off. She didn't look at him as she kicked the silky fabric to the side. If she thought too hard about the fact that she stood in front of him in only a pair of nude-lace panties, she might die on the spot.

A second passed. Another.

Still, he didn't say anything.

What is he doing?

Probably looking for a way to gracefully exit that wouldn't have her throwing herself from the nearest window. *Stop that right now.* She was stronger than this. Lucy looked good. She ate relatively well and hit the gym at least three times a week. Last night Gideon's physical reaction had proved that he'd wanted her. He might not have taken his release, but he wasn't remotely unaffected.

So why was he standing there without saying a word?

Stop waiting for him to make the first move.

Do it yourself.

Gathering her courage, she lifted her head and looked at him. Her first step took more effort than she could have dreamed, and the intense look on his face didn't help her any. He held himself perfectly still, every muscle coiled. Though, for the life of her, she couldn't tell if it was to keep from jumping her or to stop himself from fleeing.

Only one way to find out.

She took the last few steps that brought her close enough to touch. Tentatively she reached out and laid her hands on his chest. *Why isn't he saying anything?* She waited another few seconds but the only sound in her kitchen was the soft rush of their quickened breathing.

Maybe she'd misjudged the situation. *Oh, God, what did I do?* "If you've changed your mind, just tell me. We can pretend this whole thing never happened."

Gideon couldn't look away from Lucy. She was fucking perfect. He'd known that, of course, but seeing it without clothes barring his vision was something else altogether. Her breasts were small and high, capped with dark rose nipples. He forced himself not to reach for her as she stroked her hands down his chest and back up again.

"Gideon?"

She'd asked a question, hadn't she?

"What?" His gaze snagged on her narrow waist and the nude-lace panties that were so sheer, he could see a shadow of her slit beneath them. He cleared his throat and jerked his attention back to her face.

She frowned a little. "Did you change your mind?"

"No." He finally allowed himself to move, reaching up and covering her hands with his. "Fuck me, but you can't expect a man to be faced with the sight of you naked and still be able to hold down a conversation."

"That's sweet."

But she thought he was lying. He could read it all over her face.

It struck Gideon that he'd been playing this wrong. He'd known Jeff had hurt Lucy with his actions, and then she'd told him that she hadn't been with anyone since, and he'd gone straight to treating her like an innocent virgin. She was innocent in some ways, but by being so careful with her, he'd created room for her to doubt herself—and him.

Fuck that.

He guided her hands to his shoulders and then started unbuttoning his shirt. "You don't believe the words, and I don't blame you for that. But if you won't listen to me when I tell you that you're a fucking goddess personified, then I'll show you."

She kneaded his shoulders slightly, her eyes glued to his hands as he finished with his shirt and started on the front of his slacks. "I believe you."

"You don't." He kicked off his shoes and shoved down his pants. Lucy shook her head as if fighting off a daze and pushed his shirt off his shoulders. He let it fall to the floor and then the only barriers were their respective underwear. He snagged the lace with a single finger. "These have to go."

"Yours, too."

He took a step back and hooked his thumbs in his boxer briefs. A single, smooth movement and he stood before her naked. Watching Lucy's jaw drop was ridiculously gratifying. She took in each part of his body, starting with his head and moving over his neck, his shoulders, his chest, his stomach and, finally, settling on his cock. He grew harder in response to her hungry expression.

Gideon had never had a woman look at him the way Lucy did. As if he was a present she'd found under the Christmas tree—just for her. It threatened to turn this interaction into something it could never be, so he smothered the thought. She wanted him physically. End of story.

"Gideon, you're beautiful." She shucked off her panties, never taking her gaze from him. "I mean, I'd seen you in a swimsuit, but this is different." She closed the distance between them once more, a small line appearing between her brows. "Is it weird, though? I never considered you a brother or anything like that, but you were family."

Family.

He'd forced himself to forget that feeling of belonging that Lucy seemed to extend wherever she went. When he'd hung out with her and Jeff, he'd never felt like a third wheel—he'd just been part of the unit. Of all the things he'd missed when she'd cut off communication between them, that might be the highest on the list. "I never saw you as a sister."

"I know." She laughed softly. "I'd catch you watching me sometimes—not often—and you never made it weird. But... I know."

He thought he'd hid it better than that. Gideon shoved the past away just like he shoved aside so many inconvenient feelings that seemed to arise the more time he spent with Lucy. "It's not weird."

"I guess it's not." She carefully slid her hands up his chest and around his neck, taking that last step to bring them chest to chest. He rested his hands on her waist, but she felt too good to limit the contact. Gideon stroked up her back and down again to cup her ass.

There was nothing left to say. They'd reached the point of no return the second Lucy's dress had hit the floor. Gideon lifted his head. "Bedroom."

"This way— *Oh!*"

He swept her into his arms and strode across the living room to the door she'd indicated. Her bedroom was purely Lucy: a pretty wood headboard, more pillows than one woman should require, and a bright yellow floral bedspread that brightened the room even in the low light of the single lamp she must have left on.

He laid her on the bed and settled between her thighs. Gideon had every intention of slowing things down and having a very specific conversation about how this would proceed.

Every. Intention.

But Lucy wrapped her legs around his waist and arched up to meet him, and that honorable plan disappeared as if it'd never existed. Maybe it hadn't and he'd just been lying to himself all along. It didn't matter. There was only her soft skin beneath his palms, her body sliding against his and her mouth on his neck.

He kissed her. Gideon might never get enough of her sunny taste, and he wasn't about to miss a chance to immerse himself in the feel of her. This was happening. They would cross the line he'd never once considered anything other than insurmountable.

He stroked a hand down her waist to squeeze her ass and hitch her up to fit tighter against him. The temptation to sink into her was almost too much, but this wasn't about him, his wants, his needs.

This was about Lucy.

Gideon hadn't leashed himself and his desire for her this long to skip over for anything less than the full experience. He didn't want to miss a single thing. He kissed down and across her collarbone and palmed her breasts. "Perfect. Every single thing about you is fucking perfect."

She laughed a little nervously. "You said that before."

"I'll say it again." He tongued one nipple. "Pretty and pink and...fuck. Just fucking perfect."

"Don't stop." She laced her fingers through his hair and drew him back down. "Harder."

He set his teeth gently against her nipple and then increased the pressure slightly when she went wild beneath him. Through it all, he kept his eyes open. Gideon wanted it all, every nuance of expression, every reaction. All of it.

A flush stole across her freckled cheeks and over her chest, and her small breasts heaved with each sobbed breath. He moved to give her other nipple the same treatment but kept stroking the first, pinching it with the same amount of pressure he'd applied with his mouth.

She shuddered against him, her hips grinding. "Gideon. Oh, God. I think I could come from this alone."

"I'm not done yet." He pressed one last kiss to each

nipple and then slid back until he knelt on the floor next to the bed. He grabbed her hips and jerked her to the edge. This close, he could see every part of her. Gideon drew his thumb over her slit. "You need more."

"Yes."

He used his thumbs to part her. "Next time, you'll tell me exactly what you want."

"Next time?" She lifted her head to give him a dazed look. "Why next time?"

"Because I'm a selfish bastard." His mouth actually watered being this close to the most private part of Lucy. Her pussy was as flushed as the rest of her skin, wet and wanting and practically begging for his tongue. There wasn't a single damn reason *not* to give her exactly what he wanted. "I hope you're ready."

CHAPTER SIX

LUCY HAD NEVER enjoyed oral. Not really. It was yet another area where Jeff's competitiveness soured any inkling of pleasure she might get from the act. He had a series of moves he'd go through, the goal being to get her wet enough for sex. Truth be told, she'd always suspected he didn't like the act any more than she did, but the one time she'd brought it up, it had been one of the worst fights they'd ever had.

The first rasp of whiskers against Lucy's inner thigh drove thoughts of her ex right out of her head. Gideon didn't immediately go for her clit. Instead he dragged his cheek against her other thigh, using the motion to spread her legs farther.

She lifted her head just as he dipped down and drew his tongue over her in one long lick. Then he did it again—as if she was his favorite flavor of ice cream. Considering their frenzied making out, she'd expected this to be just as quick...

Should have known better than to make assumptions about Gideon.

Especially after last time.

He spread her folds and thrust his tongue into her, his low growl making the act unbearably erotic. Lucy's thoughts slammed to a halt and her mind went gloriously blank. "Holy shit."

He didn't appear to hear her. Gideon fucked her pussy with his tongue as if he couldn't get enough of her taste. He gripped her thighs with his big hands, holding her open to his ministrations even when her muscles shook with the effort to react, to move, to do *something*.

She thrashed her head from one side to the other, the sensations too much and not enough—and she didn't know how to put it into words. *Honesty.* Words crowded in her throat, too raw and vulnerable to give voice, but then she felt his teeth and they burst forth in a rush. "My clit. Gideon, suck on my clit. Use your teeth." Like he had with her nipples. Like he was doing right now with her labia.

Her entire body coiled at the thought, and the feeling intensified when he did exactly as she asked. There was no macho posturing or telling her that he was more than capable of pleasing her without an instruction manual. Gideon just…listened.

He sucked her clit into his mouth and set his teeth against the sensitive bundle of nerve endings. She arched almost completely off the bed, and he used the move to slide his hands under her ass and lift her so he could feast more effectively.

Because that was exactly what he was doing— feasting.

There was nothing gentle or teasing about his touch

now. He went after her clit in a way that was just shy of pain, sending little zings of pure bliss through her. Her body coiled tighter yet, so close to the edge, she didn't know how much longer she could hold out.

Gideon lifted his head just enough to speak, his lips brushing her heated flesh with every word. "Do you want to come like this?"

Asking that question was the single sexiest thing anyone had ever done to her. Choice. Control. Who knew it could be such a turn-on?

She almost said yes. Lucy was so close to orgasm, she shook with need and had to focus entirely too hard to create verbal words beyond *yesyesyesyesyes*. Did she want him to keep doing what he'd been doing? Hell, yes.

But she wanted him inside her more.

She licked her lips. "I want..." How did she want him?

Every way.

Right now, though? "I want to ride you."

A muscle in his jaw ticked and his grip on her thighs twitched. "You have condoms."

"Yes." She pointed a shaking finger at her nightstand.

The ones she'd bought after her breakup had expired ages ago, victim of her self-esteem issues, so she'd picked up a new box this morning. She'd also unwrapped the box so they could save time. It had felt presumptuous in the extreme when she'd been sitting alone on her bed, Garfunkel staring at her in feline judgment. Now she wished she'd already had one of them on Gideon.

He slowly released her, as if it pained him to move away. She sat up and scooted back so she could watch him pull open the top drawer. It wasn't until his dark eyes flashed that she remembered what *else* was in the drawer. "Ah…"

He held up her pink vibrator. "We'll talk about this later." He dropped it back in the drawer and pulled out a condom. "Scratch that. We're not going to talk. I'm going to stroke myself while I watch you use it."

Her eyes went wide at the image his words painted. Him, sitting against the headboard with his cock in his hand. Her on her back with her legs spread, using her toy. Her core clenched. "I want that. Later."

"Later," he agreed. He ripped the wrapper open and proceeded to roll the condom down his length.

She stood and pushed him to sit on the edge of the bed. "Like this." Lucy climbed into his lap and reached between them to notch his cock at her entrance. With her desire driving her, it was easy to speak things that would have stoppered her words with embarrassment in any other situation. "Kiss me while I ride you."

"You have no idea how fucking sexy it is that you know exactly what you want." He scooted back enough that she could brace her knees on the mattress. Then he hooked one arm around her waist while he dug his other hand into her hair. He tugged a little. "Yes?"

She moaned. "Yes." She loved when Gideon didn't treat her like she was breakable. He didn't so much as hesitate when she urged him to bite her harder, to grab her tighter. Things she hadn't even known she craved until he gave them to her.

Lucy slid down until he was completely sheathed inside her. She had to pause to adjust to the almost uncomfortable fullness. The sensation passed quickly, dissipating to sheer pleasure as her body accommodated his size. She wrapped her arms around his shoulders and kissed him as she started to move. Their position had him rubbing against her clit with every stroke and, despite trying to hold out, her orgasm loomed all too soon.

Her strokes went choppy. *"Gideon."*

He shifted his hands to her hips, helping her maintain the rhythm that would get her where she needed to go. "You feel so fucking good."

"You…too." She opened her eyes, not sure when she'd closed them, and the expression on his face stilled her breath in her lungs. *Possession. Desire. Need.* It was too much.

Lucy cried out his name as she came. He kept her moving, kept the orgasm going, until her muscles gave out and she slumped against him.

He carefully pulled out of her and shifted them back onto the bed. Gideon spooned her, lightly stroking her arm, her hip, her stomach. She stared at the art print on the wall next to her bed for several long moments while she relearned how to breathe. Gradually she became aware of a very specific part of him pressed against her ass. "You didn't come."

"Not yet."

Not yet.

Who knew those two little words would be the sexiest thing she'd ever heard?

Gideon kept up his light touching until Lucy arched back against him. Judging her to be recovered enough, he hooked one knee and lifted her leg up and over his legs, leaving her open to him. He slid a hand carefully between her thighs, testing her tenderness. "Tell me what you want."

"You."

He kissed the back of her neck. "You have me." *For now.* "Tell me what other fantasies you've been harboring." The image of her using that toy on herself would be enough to keep him up at night for the foreseeable future. He was a goddamn idiot for feeding his imagination more images, but he craved them the same way he craved her.

"You want my sexual bucket list?" Her amused tone turned into a gasp as he idly stroked her clit. "You can't expect me to think when you're doing *that*."

"Consider it inspiration." He liked the idea of being the one who helped her cross items off that type of list. Fuck, he liked the thought that he was in her bed right now and would be for as long as she felt he had something to teach her.

Lucy reached back to sift her fingers through his hair. "I haven't really thought about it."

"Liar." He took the move for an invitation and slid his other arm beneath her so he could palm her breasts. "There's at least a few things you have lurking in the back of your mind about this—something you've always wanted to try." Something he could be the only one to ever give to her.

At least for now.

She hesitated and he could practically hear her thinking it over and considering laying herself bare in this way. Gideon could have pointed out that they were already bared to each other, but this was different.

He stilled his hands, waiting for her answer.

"Don't stop." She covered the hand between her legs with one of her own, guiding him back to her clit and then lower, to push a finger inside her. Lucy moaned. "High-end dressing room. I've always wanted to have sex in a high-end dressing room—lingerie, maybe, if that's not super cliché." She tensed. "Crap. I'm doing it again. God, it's so hard to turn *off*."

"I think we could make that happen." He kissed along her neck to growl in her ear. "I want to see you in green—that bright jewel tone."

She tilted her head forward, giving him better access. "I think we could make that happen." She echoed his words back to him.

"Charitable of you." He paused his stroking long enough to guide his cock into her. She clamped tight around him and he barely bit back a curse.

As many times as he'd slipped and imagined what it would be like to have Lucy in his bed, his fantasies hadn't come close to the bliss of reality. She was fucking perfection. Every move, every word, every gasp—Gideon stored them all away in his memory. He only had a limited time to accumulate enough to last him a lifetime.

A worry for another day.

Tonight he was inside Lucy.

Tomorrow could wait until tomorrow.

Gideon sat in Lucy's living room and ate reheated leftovers. She had a bright throw wrapped around her shoulders and her cat in her lap as she tried to arrange her food in an order that she could actually eat. He reached over and plucked the cat out of her lap.

Or he tried.

In reality, Garfunkel had no intention of going anywhere against his will. He let loose a yowl that raised the small hairs on the back of Gideon's neck. Before he could react, the cat hissed and swiped claws across his forearm. He cursed but managed not to chuck the horrid little beast. Instead he dropped the animal the short distance to the floor.

"Oh, my God!" Lucy shoved her food containers to the side and grabbed his wrist. "What were you thinking?"

He gritted his teeth as she dabbed at the blood welling in the scratches with a napkin. "I was thinking you'd have an easier time eating if he wasn't taking up so much space on your lap."

"You weren't wrong." She dabbed a little harder. "But if you haven't noticed, Garfunkel is territorial. And he doesn't like men much."

"You think?" He took the napkin from her and pressed it hard against his arm. "It's fine. I should have known better." His lifestyle wasn't one that allowed for a pet, but if it had, Gideon would definitely be a dog person. Cats seemed to be little assholes as a general rule, and he had a feeling if he tried to adopt one, he'd pick the biggest asshole of them all through sheer karma.

Though Garfunkel has a solid running for that title.

"I'm really sorry."

"Lucy, it's fine." He grabbed his food and joined her on the couch. "How are you feeling?"

"Unwound." She leaned her head against the back of the couch and gave him a sleepy smile. "I'd forgotten how relaxing good sex could be."

Good doesn't begin to cover it.

He bit the comment back. It was sheer pride that made him want to say it and he didn't have a right. Not in the current situation. He was here for a specific purpose and he couldn't afford to forget that even for a moment. Lucy wasn't for him in any permanent way. This was a window into the world of what could have been in another life, if things had fallen out in a different sequence of events.

But they hadn't. So here he and Lucy were.

"What made you pick those particular men?"

It took him a few seconds too long to make the subject change with her. He didn't want to talk about other men while he still had the memory of her body against his and the smell of her on his skin. It felt wrong on a whole hell of a lot of different levels. An intrusion.

Except it wasn't.

Lucy had asked him for a specific set of things, and sex had been an afterthought. Just because it wasn't an afterthought for Gideon didn't mean he could snap at her for keeping her head in the game. So he did his best to do the same.

"They're all ambitious men who have reputations for being honest and are old enough that they're likely thinking about settling down with one person. I've personally placed both Mark and Liam in jobs, so I did all the research and then some. They have solid histories. Neither has any record of being a cheater or abusive in any way. They're good guys—as good as anyone is." And he'd checked. Even with only twenty-four hours at his disposal, he'd done extensive research and even gone so far as to call a few of their exes, though Gideon wasn't about to admit that to Lucy. None of the women had said anything to raise red flags.

She speared a green bean with her fork. "And Aaron?"

"He's the best of the best. I actually tried to poach him for a client last year and he wouldn't give me the time of day." When she raised her eyebrows, he shifted, something like embarrassment sifting through him. "There's more to it than that, of course. He's got an excellent reputation, and Roman is actually friends with him."

"Your pitch is overwhelming." She laughed softly. "But then, this is what I asked for, isn't it?"

He didn't like seeing that look on her face, as if she was resigning herself to a life half lived. "Lucy, if you want to change directions on this thing, we can do that. Even if you go on dates with these guys, nothing is set in stone."

"I know you mean well, but I would very much appreciate it if you'd stop trying to talk me out of this."

He tried to rein in his temper, but he'd held himself too tightly under control the last two days. Too careful. It wasn't Gideon's natural default, and it had started to wear on him. He glared. "I'm not trying to talk you out of shit. I'm giving you options. You want this to have a chance in hell of working, you need to stop being so goddamn defensive. I'm helping you with this bat-shit-crazy plan, so I need you to throw me a bone once in a while."

She set down her fork. "I think you should leave."

Fuck. He started to apologize but stopped. Lucy might be fragile in some ways, but she wasn't broken. He had to remember that and stop treating her with kid gloves. And yet letting her make what might be the biggest mistake of her life because he felt guilty over her last relationship was a shitty thing to do.

He wasn't sure what his other options were, but he'd have to figure it out. Fast.

In the meantime he needed to get the hell out of there before he said something they'd both regret. Gideon stood and buttoned the last few buttons on his shirt. "I'll email you the details tomorrow."

"Okay." She still wouldn't look at him.

He hesitated, but there was nothing left to say. Sex had changed things. Having concrete proof of how deep the connection ran between them was enough to set him back on his heels. She felt it, too. There was no way she didn't.

Now he just needed her to actually admit it.

CHAPTER SEVEN

"I'M SORRY—did you just say that you have a *date*?"

Lucy swirled her white wine, not looking at her little sister. "You don't have to sound so shocked by it." She hadn't wanted to confess her plan, but it twisted her up inside not to be able to talk about it with at least one person. Gideon hardly counted, especially since his reactions were hardly consistent with what she'd expected—and *her* reactions weren't cooperating, either.

"I *am* shocked. You've been all work, work, work. When did you have time to set up a date?" Becka leaned over and snagged a chip from the plate in the middle of the table. "That's not a dig, by the way. That's just facts. I'm on three freaking dating websites and *I* have trouble finding dates who aren't candidates for 'but he seemed so nice.'"

Lucy sighed. "They can't all be serial killers, Becka."

"It only takes one." Becka frowned. "Besides, we aren't talking about me. We're talking about you."

Now that push came to shove, she didn't know where to start. Or if she even should confess any of it. In truth, if she hadn't had these drinks set up with Becka already, she'd be at home, moping. It had been two days since she'd seen Gideon and, aside from a few emails confirming her first date, they hadn't talked, either. She knew she'd been an ass, but it wasn't like Gideon to avoid a conflict.

Not that there had to be a conflict. There didn't. She just didn't want him to think that their having sex meant he could push her into not going through with her plan. She'd made the decision. He had to respect that. If that meant he didn't want to continue with their lessons… Well, that was something she'd just have to deal with.

Unless he doesn't want to continue for a different reason…

"You okay?"

She blinked and tried to focus on her sister's face. Becka changed her hair color with the seasons and today it was a bright blue that was the exact shade of her eyes. Her lip piercing glinted in the light of the little hipster bar where they always met up. She had the cute-alternative look down to a science. *She* never had problems with men, despite her lamenting about dating.

Lucy tried to smile. "Just a crisis of faith. You know, the usual."

"Don't do that. If you don't want to tell me, that's cool, but don't pat me on the head. You don't have to protect me anymore, Lucy. You know that, right?"

"It's not about protecting you." And it wasn't. They'd had a fine upbringing. Decent—if distant—

parents. A solid middle-class lifestyle. Nothing traumatic happening to make waves in their lives.

But Becka was still her little sister. When they were growing up, Becka had been the shy one, the bookworm who was a little too odd to fit in with the rest of the kids in her grade. It led to bullying and, when their parents had failed to notice, Lucy had taken care of it.

She'd been taking care of her little sister ever since.

Though these days, Becka fought her own battles.

But her sister had a point. Holding on to the turmoil inside her wasn't doing Lucy any favors. She'd talked about it to Gideon, but he wasn't exactly a neutral party. Neither was Becka, for that matter. "I just… I know it's been two years, but I still have Jeff's comments rattling around in my brain. It's pathetic and I should be over it by now, and I *am* over *him*. I don't know what's wrong with me."

"Nothing's wrong with you." Becka grabbed the wine bottle on the table and refilled her glass. "It's not like you had a monthlong relationship and turned around and let it mess you up for the rest of your life. You and Jeff were together for…what, like four years? You were going to marry him." She narrowed her blue eyes. "Though he better hope we never cross paths, because I'm going to kick his ass one of these days."

"Becka."

"Lucy." She mimicked her voice perfectly. "But that day is not today. Either way, I'd say you were having a normal reaction and that's that. Why's this coming up now? The whole matchmaking thing is kind of out there, but it's not like you're jumping into bed with these guys to give them a trial run." Becka grinned. "Though *there's* an idea."

She tried to imagine it—taking a single night with each of the guys on Gideon's list—and instantly rejected the idea. "No way." It felt wrong and she didn't want to spend too much time thinking about why. *I promised Gideon to be exclusive.* Sure, that was it. Definitely.

"Worth a shot." Becka ate a few more chips. "You'll be fine, Lucy. I promise. Dating is weird and it's hard to get to know people, but you have a matchmaker in your corner. It'll all work out."

She couldn't tell her sister that Gideon Novak was the so-called matchmaker in question. Becka had met him on several occasions and she'd lose her shit if she knew. Since they'd managed to get through this conversation without her thinking Lucy was out of her mind, she'd like to keep it that way. "I'm sure you're right."

"I am."

Lucy's phone rang and her heart leaped in her throat at the sight of Gideon's name on the screen. "Hello?"

"I'll meet you there ten minutes early, so be ready."

She blinked. "I'm sorry—what?"

"The date, Lucy. Please tell me you haven't forgotten about it."

She bristled at the irritation in his voice. "Of course I haven't forgotten. But I was not expecting you to be attending." She was nervous enough about going out with Mark Williams without having to do it under the watchful eye of Gideon. "That's unacceptable."

"My rules. Be there ten minutes early." He hung up.

Lucy set her phone carefully on the table and looked up to find her sister watching her. "What?"

"I know that move. The 'gently set your phone down so you don't chuck it across the room' one. Who pissed you off?"

"It's a long story and, unfortunately, I have to leave in order not to be late." *Not to be late to being early. I'm going to kill him.* She dug out her wallet and flagged down the waitress. "Same time next week?"

"Sure. You're the one with the crazy schedule." Becka finished her drink and set it on the table. She grinned. "And whoever that was that just called you, give 'em hell, sis."

"I plan on it." She set the appropriate amount of cash on the table under the ticket and rose. She accepted Gideon's direction in the bedroom because that was exactly what she'd asked for. She accepted his list of men for the same reason.

She refused to accept him taking control of every aspect of this matchmaking situation.

He vetted and picked the candidates, yes, but ultimately it was up to her and the individual men to see if it was something that could actually work. Gideon's role in this ended the second she and one of the men came to an agreement. She tried very hard not to focus on the way her stomach dropped at that thought.

It didn't matter.

What mattered was his trying to steamroll her on

this. She had to have some freedom to figure out if she could stomach the thought of spending her life with the man across the table from her, and she couldn't do that with Gideon standing at her shoulder.

If he did, she couldn't shake the feeling that she'd compare every man to him and it would skew her perception.

Against Gideon Novak, who could compare?

Gideon checked his watch for the third time in as many minutes. Where the hell was she? He turned to look down the street again just as Lucy walked around the corner. She didn't seem particularly concerned to be running late—or happy to see him. He motioned to his watch. "We had an understanding."

"Wrong. You told me something. I disagreed." She crossed her arms over her chest, which drew his attention to her dress.

"What are you wearing?" It was a pale blue lacy thing that gave the illusion of showing more than it actually did. It clung to her body, the gaps in the lace showing a nude lining the exact same shade as her skin. At a glance, she might as well have been naked beneath it.

He loved it.

He fucking hated it.

"A dress." She touched it, a frown drawing a line between her brows. "Don't take that overprotective tone with me, Gideon. It's a good dress."

"It's inappropriate for a first date. He's going to sit

across that table and spend the whole time thinking about fucking you."

Lucy gave him a brilliant grin, her plum-colored lips mirroring the darkness of her hair, which she'd left in waves down around her shoulders. "Then it's doing its job. Now, if you'd please get out of my way, I can take it from here." She strode past him and through the door to the restaurant.

Jealousy flared, hot and poisonous, down the back of his throat. He didn't have a right to it any more now than he had before, but it was a thousand times more powerful now that they'd put sex on the table. Gideon followed her inside and hooked a hand around her elbow, towing her sideways into a small hallway that led to the coat check.

It was dimmer there than in the main entrance—more intimate. He pressed his hands to the wall on either side of her shoulders. "You make me fucking crazy."

"That makes two of us." She poked him in the chest. "You might be calling the shots in some things, but you have to give me enough space to breathe. The compressed timeline is already going to play havoc on my instincts—I don't need your constant presence doing the same."

He'd think about how his presence affected her later. Right now all he could focus on was the first part of the sentence. "If the timeline is too tight, then extend it. The only person who put this deadline in place was *you*."

"And it stands." She lifted her chin. "I'm already

late for this date. I don't want to have this conversation for the seventh time. Just give me some space to breathe."

He pushed off the wall even though it was the last thing he wanted to do. The truth was that he wanted Lucy, and it was fucking up his head space and messing with *his* instincts. He knew better than to push her, but he couldn't help doing it all the same. He wanted her and she wanted him—at least physically.

What if it could be more than just physical?
What if I actually played for keeps?
The thought stopped him in his tracks.

He watched Lucy greet the hostess and follow her deeper into the restaurant, but he couldn't move. This whole time, he had been letting Lucy take the wheel and guide things—at least to some extent. Gideon had handled her so goddamn carefully because he was well aware of the damage Jeff had caused her and he blamed himself, at least a little, because of it. That guilt was the same reason he hadn't pushed her to face the fact that there was more than just friendship between them.

But what if he did?

He couldn't hit this head-on—Lucy would tell him to get lost, and with good reason. She had her eye on the prize and she wouldn't be deterred by an outside force, even if it was Gideon.

If he could get her to change her mind, that would be a different story.

Gideon smiled.

Let her have her date with Mark. The guy was nice

enough, but Gideon fully intended to take her to bed until she was so wrapped up in him that she forgot Mark's fucking name.

A man looked up as Lucy approached the table the hostess had indicated. He was cute in a hipster sort of way, his close-cropped beard and glasses a combination that would have been strange five years before. Now it seemed like everyone had them. The only thing missing was suspenders or a bow tie. Instead, he wore a nice button-up shirt and a pair of slacks. When he rose to pull her chair out for her, she got an eyeful of his broad shoulders and clearly outlined muscles.

Too many muscles. Too much facial hair.

Oh, my God, stop. *What is wrong with me?*

He resumed his place and grinned at her, his teeth white and straight. "Lucy, I presume. Otherwise, this is about to get incredibly awkward."

That startled a laugh out of her. "Yes, I'm Lucy." She extended her hand. "That would make you Mark."

"The very one." He gave her a firm handshake, which she appreciated. Too many men—especially men who worked in corporate jobs—tended to give handshakes like they thought they'd break her. It drove her crazy.

Mark leaned back, his gaze roaming over her face.

Another mark in his favor—not ogling my chest. Lucy gave herself a shake. She had to stop overanalyzing every second of this date. Mark was most definitely not Gideon, and that didn't have to be a tally in the negative column.

It was just hard to focus when she could still smell Gideon's cologne from where he'd pressed her against the wall a few short minutes ago. It wasn't musky and strong like so many men she knew—it was light and clean and reminded her of… She couldn't place it.

Focus.

She gave a polite smile. "Thank you for agreeing to the date."

"When Gideon called me and explained the situation, I'll admit I didn't believe him." The corner of his mouth hitched up. "And then I asked him what was wrong with you."

She tensed and then admonished herself for doing so. He was joking. He didn't really think there was something wrong with her. "As you can see, I'm in possession of all my teeth."

"Not to mention beautiful and successful." Mark's easy smile made the words fact rather than a throwaway compliment. "I've heard of marriages of convenience, but I assumed they were the stuff of fiction. This whole situation is kind of strange."

"I can't argue that." She'd known it was a reach the second she'd called Gideon to put the plan into action. That didn't change the fact that she had no other option. "But I have to ask. If you think it's so strange, why are you here?"

He sighed. "I'm fucking up this small talk, aren't I? That was way too heavy to start in on."

"I don't mind. This isn't exactly the most conventional situation." She appreciated the frankness, even if there was something missing from this interaction that she couldn't quite put her finger on. Mark was attractive—there was no denying that—but... Lucy didn't know. It was off.

"In that case, I agreed to this because I've worked eighty-hour weeks for several years and that won't be stopping anytime soon. I don't know if you've been to a bar lately, but meeting people there is a joke. Everyone is on their phones or with their friends or not interested. Dating apps are even worse, in large part because women have so many nightmare encounters that they're edgy and distant. It makes it hard to really get to know a person when they're sure that you're going to turn on a dime and send a dick pic or freak out because they cancel the date." He shrugged. "It comes down to time. I don't have much of it to meet new people and jump through the hoops of first dates and second dates—and balancing the knife edge of showing that I'm interested without being too goddamn pushy." Mark sighed. "Sorry. It's a sore spot for me."

There was a story there—perhaps several.

The waitress appeared to take their order and then disappeared as quickly. Lucy leaned forward. "Tell me some of your dating stories."

He raised his eyebrows. "If there was a playbook for first dates, I'm one hundred percent sure it wouldn't include recalling dates with other women."

"This is hardly your textbook first date." She smiled. "My little sister runs the gauntlet of online dating, and some of her stories defy belief."

"I wish I could say she was making it all up." Mark relaxed a little, just the slight loosening in his shoulders. She hadn't realized he was tense until it disappeared. He grinned. "If she's half as beautiful as you, she's seen more than her fair share of crazy on those sites."

"I'm sure she has." Lucy knew all too well that Becka had kept plenty of it back, sharing only the funny stories. That was what gave her away—there only seemed to be funny stories. Nothing dark, nothing worrisome. Nothing indicating she'd met anyone she had more than a passing interest for. "Tell me about them."

He hesitated, surveying her expression, but he must have seen only the interest she felt there because he chuckled. "I'd rather know more about you. Gideon said you're a lawyer."

"I'm a defense attorney." She had to wonder what else Gideon had told Mark and the other men he'd managed to get to agree to meet her. Lucy looked good on paper. She was confident in that, even if she wasn't in any other romantic aspect of her life.

But a lot of women looked good on paper and weren't going about marriage in such an odd way.

Mark leaned forward, expression attentive. "Do you like it? I've been fascinated with the court system since I was a kid. Too many *Law & Order* marathons, you know."

"It's not much like that in real life. There's a truly unglamorous amount of paperwork, and research can be tedious to the point where I've believed more than once that it might kill me." She forced herself to relax a little. "But actually being in court is exhilarating. It's like a game of chess but with higher stakes. I wouldn't trade it for the world."

Their food arrived and the conversation proceeded easily, her work moving into his work as cybersecurity expert, and then sharing a bit about their childhoods. Mark was as nice as he was handsome and Lucy waited through the entire meal for her heartbeat to pick up at the sight of his smile, or for her mind to leapfrog into what it would be like to get naked with him.

There was nothing but a vague pleasant feeling of spending her time in friendly conversation.

No sizzle whatsoever.

She'd asked for that, but she couldn't help comparing him to Gideon. They were different in so many ways. Mark was built lean like a blade—a very well-muscled blade—whereas Gideon looked like a Viking who had decided he'd bring his pillaging to the corporate world. His broad shoulders created a V that tapered down to a narrow waist and there was no way he'd be able to buy a suit off the rack with those powerful thighs.

Mark was attractive but missing a vital component she couldn't put her finger on. A sizzle. A flair. Something that screamed *life*.

I've been reading too many romance novels.

Or maybe she was trying to rationalize something that couldn't be rationalized. She didn't have a connection with Mark. That didn't mean there was something wrong with her—or with him. It just wasn't there.

Mark seemed to notice it, as well. He paid for their meal and sat back with a rueful smile. "This has been fun, but I won't be hearing from you for a second date, will I?"

She liked his frankness. She just wished she felt some kind of pull to the match.

Lucy pressed her lips together. "I can't say for certain."

"I get it." He stood and moved around the table to pull out her chair. "I'd love to get to know you better—as friends."

That was exactly it. She'd enjoyed the dinner. She wouldn't mind spending more time with him. She just couldn't imagine walking down the aisle to him, even in an arranged setting. "Thank you for a wonderful evening."

Mark pressed a quick kiss to her cheek. "You're something special, Lucy Baudin. I hope you get what you're looking for."

"You, too. She's out there. Don't give up yet."

He squeezed her hand. "Good night, Lucy."

She followed him to the door and allowed him to hail her a cab. It was only when she was on her way back to her apartment that she took out her phone and texted Gideon.

Heading home.

I'll be there in thirty.

Her stomach dipped pleasantly and she clenched her thighs together. There was no mistaking what would happen the second he walked through her door, and her skin heated just thinking about it.

She couldn't wait.

CHAPTER EIGHT

GIDEON STORMED THROUGH Lucy's door without knocking. He found her pacing nervously around her living room, practically wringing her hands, and stopped short. "What did he do?"

Her blue eyes went wide. "Excuse me?"

"Mark. Obviously he did something." He sliced his hand through the air to indicate her current state. "Tell me what it was and I'll take care of it." He'd thought Mark was a safe enough bet for the first date, but Gideon shouldn't have taken it for granted. If he'd stayed, he could've stepped in.

Lucy was still blinking at him. She burst out laughing. "Mark was a perfect gentleman."

"You don't have to smooth it over. It's my job to ensure you have solid dates, and if something went wrong, I need to know." He very pointedly ignored the fact that he almost hoped something had ruined the night. Mark was fucking perfect. If he wasn't essentially married to his job, he would have found a girl, gotten married and had a couple of kids by now.

She crossed to him and put a hand on his chest.

"Gideon, stop. Nothing happened. We had a nice conversation and decided to leave things at that."

Leave things at that.

Call him crazy, but he hadn't spent much time dwelling on what would transpire during—and after—the dates. Jealousy reared its ugly head and, even as he fought for control, his words got away from him. "Did he hold your hand?"

She blinked. "I don't know if I'd call it handholding—"

"Help you into your coat?" He took a step closer to her, crowding her and unable to stop. "Kiss you?" The thought of Mark in Gideon's current position, leaning down to take Lucy's mouth, made him crazy.

And, damn it, she saw it.

Lucy frowned. "What's wrong?"

"Nothing." *Fucking everything.* He kissed her to keep from saying anything else. Lucy responded instantly, her hands sliding up his chest to loop her arms around his neck, her body melting into his. Her instant yielding should have soothed him.

There were far too many "shoulds" when it came to Lucy Baudin.

He grabbed the hem of her dress and yanked it up as he tumbled her back onto the couch. Gideon had the presence of mind to catch himself so she didn't bear the full brunt of his weight. The break in their kiss gave him the chance to say, "You want this."

"That wasn't a question. But yes." She jerked his shirt out of his pants and went to work on the buttons. "I want to feel you."

He palmed her pussy. "Then feel me." He spread her and pushed a single finger into her. Lucy made one of those sexy fucking whimpers that he couldn't get enough of and yanked his shirt apart, sending the last few buttons flying.

She shoved the shirt down his shoulders. "I need you, Gideon."

He'd give every single dollar he owned to hear her say those words every single day of his life. It wasn't his destiny, but he sure as hell planned to coax her to say it as often as he could during their time together. "Tell me. Guide me."

"I, uh…" Her eyes shut for a split second as he circled her clit with his thumb. When she opened them again, there was new purpose there. "I want you in my mouth."

He froze. "Lucy—" *Fuck me, it's like she pulled a fantasy right out of my goddamn head.* He saw the exact moment her confidence wavered and bit back a curse. He was so determined to give her everything, he was missing signs.

Gideon shifted to sit next to her on the couch. He stopped her from going to the floor with a hand on her shoulder. "Open my pants."

She didn't hesitate. Lucy undid the front of his slacks and withdrew his cock. She stroked him once and then sucked him into her mouth. Gideon had expected some sort of cautious exploration, but she went after it like she was desperate for him.

As desperate for him as he was for her. He pulled her hair back so he could see his cock disappear between her deep purple lips. A sight he never thought he'd stand witness to. She opened her eyes and pinned him with a pleased look, and he couldn't stand it a second longer. Keeping one hand holding her hair back, Gideon pulled her dress higher, baring her ass completely. He squeezed her ass and then ran his hand down until he could push two fingers into her.

Her eyes went wide then slid shut and she sucked him harder, faster.

"You like that? You like me playing with your pretty pussy while you have my cock in your mouth." It wasn't enough. He was so goddamn desperate for her that feeling her come on his fingers wouldn't do a thing to take the edge off. He kept thinking about her wearing that peekaboo dress across the table from Mark and laughing at that fucker's jokes, and inspiring a lifetime of filthy fantasies. "Give me a taste."

He grabbed her around the hips and lifted her until her knees rested on the back of the couch on either side of his head. Gideon waited for her to start sucking his cock again before he ran his cheek up her thigh to her pussy. "So beautiful." He licked her, teasing.

Or at least that was the plan.

She was so fucking drenched and tasted so fucking sweet, he lost his precarious hold on his control and gripped her thighs where they met her hips, raising her to his mouth and spreading her wider in the same move. She moaned around his cock and the sound drove him wilder. He licked and sucked her folds, growling against her hot skin. *I've got my face bur-*

ied in her pussy. Me. *Not that asshole she went to dinner with.*

Lucy reached between his thighs and cupped his balls, slamming him back into the present. She twisted up off his cock enough to say, "You like this?"

"Hell, yes, I do. I like every single thing you do to me." His world narrowed down to the taste of her on his tongue and the feel of her mouth wrapped around him. Her whimpers and moans drove him on, leaching every bit of rational thought from Gideon's head. He needed her to orgasm.

Needed to claim her.

Lucy couldn't tell which way was up—and not just because Gideon had her in the most impossible and erotic position. She'd barely made it home before him and now he had her upside down on the couch with his face buried between her legs as she sucked his cock. She took him deeper. He made her so damn crazy.

For once, she wanted to return the favor.

She shifted her hold of his balls, squeezing lightly. He made a sound she felt all the way to the back of her throat. Nothing mattered but the next slide of his tongue over her clit and the way his fingers dug into her hips, effortlessly holding her in place.

Her orgasm rolled over her from one breath to the next, and she sucked him with unmatched desperation, needing Gideon with her every step of the way. She could *feel* him holding back, trying to outlast her just like he had every other time since they'd started.

If she didn't do something drastic right this second, he'd move them somewhere else and she wouldn't get a chance to finish him like this.

So she played dirty.

Lucy pressed two fingers to his perineum. She'd read in so many books that it was a hot spot for men as well as women, but she'd never had the courage to try.

Gideon's response made the risk worth it many times over.

His back arched and his balls drew up. He hissed out a breath that made her clit tingle. "Fuck. I can't hold out."

She sucked harder, not willing to lift her head to tell him to go for it. She wanted this. She *needed* this.

He hesitated but she circled her middle finger against him and that was all it took. Gideon cursed long and hard against her skin, his grip spasming as his hips bucked up to meet her mouth. She took him as deep as was comfortable and then took him deeper yet. He growled her name as he came. Lucy drank him down, sucking him until he shuddered and gently lowered her to the couch.

Only then did she raise her head.

The look on Gideon's face could only be described as shell-shocked. He opened his mouth, closed it and shook his head. "Come here." Without waiting for a response, he pulled her onto his lap and tucked her against him.

She settled her head onto his shoulder. "That was…"

"Yeah."

How to put it into words? She might not be the more experienced of the two of them, but she wasn't stupid. That hadn't been like the other times. There was no lesson here that Gideon wanted to teach her. He'd come through her door like a jealous boyfriend and then delivered one of the most devastating orgasms of her life and now he was holding her like he…cared.

Of course he cares. He wouldn't have agreed to this if he didn't.

Just because he considered her a friend didn't mean the lines had blurred for him.

She clung to the thought with a stubbornness born of desperation. Lucy had a plan and she knew better by now than to deviate from it. The last time she'd done that, she'd ended up with Jeff, and that entire experience had screwed her up, at least emotionally.

It would have screwed her up professionally, too, if she processed pain in any other way than powering through it out of spite.

Gideon stroked a hand down her back. "Did I hurt you?"

"What? No." She leaned back to look at him. Not as shell-shocked now and the thread of guilt in his dark eyes made her heart hurt.

That was the other reason she couldn't allow the lines between them to blur. Gideon might be someone she cared about, and he might make her body sing, but he would never forgive himself for his role in Jeff's shitty choices.

He'd never be able to look at her without seeing his

friend's ex-fiancée. The one *he'd* had to take aside to let know she was being cheated on—and everyone knew.

Gideon frowned. "Tell me what put that look on your face."

"It's nothing." The very *last* thing she wanted to do was to bring Jeff into the room with them. It was hard enough to banish the memory of him without inviting him in. She almost settled back against Gideon, but the moment had passed. Cuddling and soft words wasn't what this was.

Lucy climbed to her feet on shaking legs. "Give me a few minutes to change."

"Sure."

She retreated to her bedroom and threw on a pair of leggings and one of her knitted sweaters. It felt too comfortable, but as he'd been quick to point out before, this wasn't about seduction. If he wanted her to dress the part, he would request it so he could help her strike the right note. She closed her bedroom door behind her and made her way back into the main room. "I need to go shopping."

"This instant?"

"Don't be silly. Of course not." Her laugh felt forced, mostly because it was. Lucy pulled a newly purchased bottle of wine out of her cabinet and took out two glasses. "Wine?"

"Yeah."

She poured them, still not looking at him. "The date with Mark was nice enough, but I think it's best I meet the rest of your list. That said, I'd like to be as prepared as possible, and I think I mentioned before that I have nothing in the way of seduction clothing."

Gideon snorted. "*You* are seduction enough, Lucy."

He didn't get it. But then, she didn't expect him to. She turned and offered his glass then took a sip of her own. "This may sound strange, but I dress well."

"I noticed."

She ignored that. "Walking out to face a judge or jury—or both—is terrifying. It's exhilarating, too, but taking that first step is like jumping out of a plane and hoping you remembered your parachute. Or, more accurately maybe, it's like stepping onto the dueling grounds and hoping like hell you prepared your weapons and they won't malfunction. I know that sounds dramatic, but it's what it feels like for me. My clothing is both armor and weapons combined. It allows me to take that first step without fear crippling me. I'm going to need that in the bedroom, as well."

There. He might laugh in her face, but at least she was being honest.

Gideon didn't laugh. He studied her with those dark eyes, mulling over what she said and the implications behind it, no doubt. She'd revealed far more of herself in that little tidbit than she had in a long while. Becka knew, of course—she was the one Lucy always dragged along on her shopping trips—but everyone at the office assumed that Lucy was just extremely into fashion and expensive clothing.

Finally he took a drink of his wine. "Do you have free time next weekend?"

Next weekend? It was Thursday. "That's eight days from now."

"I'm more than capable of counting, Lucy." He set the glass down. "Tomorrow, you'll meet Aaron Livingston at the weekly event Roman puts together. I'll be out of town most of next week meeting with several potential fits for a client."

Disappointment soured her stomach but she did her best not to show it. Of course Gideon wasn't exclusively focused on her predicament. From what she remembered, he usually had multiple clients at any given time and there was no reason to expect to be the exception to the rule.

It also meant almost a full week that she wouldn't see him.

No lessons for seven days.

Stop it.

She managed a smile. "I'm free next weekend, aside from a lunch date with Becka."

"We'll go shopping afterward."

Which would give her a chance to imbibe enough alcohol to feel a little fearless at the thought of picking lingerie with Gideon. Lucy wasn't feeling anything resembling fearless at the moment. She swallowed hard. "Okay."

His gaze sharpened on her face. "Tomorrow, wear something appropriate."

Just like that, her nerves disappeared. She drew herself up straight. "Excuse me?"

"You know damn well that you were playing with fire with that dress tonight. I don't know how the fuck

Mark kept his hands to himself, but it's a small miracle. No other man would."

Meaning *he* wouldn't, which he'd more than proved by walking through the door and ravishing her right there in her living room. *I did a bit of ravishing myself.*

That wasn't what they were discussing, though, and she didn't appreciate his attitude. The whole point of this was to market her—for lack of a better word—to these men, and he was acting like she'd been out of line. It wasn't a dress she would have worn for work, but it was a far cry from indecent. He was acting like she'd shown up in a minidress with all her goods on display. Lucy glared. "I'll wear whatever I please."

"Wrong. You'll wear something that doesn't project sex."

"You can't be serious." She threw up a hand. "I am more than capable of dressing myself. The lingerie excepting, I don't need or want your opinion."

Gideon set the wineglass down and advanced on her, a forbidding expression on his handsome face. A muscle in his jaw jumped and her stomach leaped in response. He stopped mere inches away. "You wear some shit like you wore tonight and you won't like the results."

She could barely catch her breath with him so close. "What are you going to do, Gideon? Put me over your knee? I don't think so."

"Put you over my knee." His hands came down on either side of her, bracketing her in. Still, he didn't touch her. "Yes, Lucy, that's exactly what I'll do. And after I've spanked your pert little ass red, I'll bend you over the nearest surface and fuck you, date with another man or no."

CHAPTER NINE

"YOU KEEP STARING at the door like that, you're going to start scaring guests away."

Gideon didn't look away from the door. He couldn't relax. Truth be told, he hadn't managed to relax since he'd walked out of Lucy's apartment last night, his words ringing in his ears. They hadn't talked today, other than his text with the address and time to be here and her reply that she would show up.

The question of *how* she would show up was driving him crazy.

He didn't know which outcome he wanted. It would be best if Lucy listened to him and dressed in something that was less of a goddamn tease.

But a part of him wanted her to challenge him—to push him to follow through on his threat. It crossed the line and he knew it, but he was past caring. If Lucy's date with Mark had made anything clear, it was that Gideon couldn't stand the thought of her with another man.

He'd stepped aside for Jeff.

He wasn't about to step aside now. Not again.

None of those other fuckers would care about her the way he would. Their chemistry about set the apartment on fire, and they had a history of genuine caring between them—all of which Lucy said she wanted with whatever husband she picked.

He was the right choice.

He just had to find a way to make Lucy see that.

"Shit," Roman muttered. He stepped to the side, blocking Gideon's view of the door. "Don't make a scene. I invited Aaron here in good faith and you look like you're about to rip someone's head off if they glance at you wrong."

"I'm not going to make a scene." As long as Lucy didn't test him.

He hoped like hell she *did* test him.

"The expression on your face is about to make a liar out of you." Roman slid his hands into his pockets, still looking on edge. "You've already crossed the line with Lucy, haven't you?"

He'd crossed so many lines, he'd lost count. But Roman wasn't bringing this up now just for shits and giggles. Gideon jerked his chin to the side. "Get out of the way."

"No. Scene."

Roman stepped out of the way and Gideon went still. Lucy made her way through the tables toward the VIP section, drawing stares in her wake. She had on a little black dress, but to call it that didn't do it justice. It was so short, it made her already long legs look even longer. It was also strapless, the heart-shaped bodice adding extra curves to her body. Her hair was down in a carefully messy wave that made him think of fucking, and her bloodred mouth only drove the image of hot sex home. She nodded at the guy manning the entrance to the VIP section and then strode straight to Gideon. Closer, he realized there were little beads sewn into the skirt of the dress, giving an extra shift of movement with each step.

Without looking away from Lucy, he handed Roman his beer. "We'll be right back."

Roman cursed. "Whatever you're going to say to her, make it quick. Aaron will be here in thirty."

Thirty minutes was more than enough time to thoroughly make his point. He stood and prowled the last few steps to her. "Follow me. Now."

She wet her lips, her eyes already a little hazy. "And if I don't want to?"

"You do." He turned and stalked back through the VIP section to the hallway that led to bathrooms and two rooms for meetings or private parties. One held a table and chairs and Gideon had used it on more than one occasion. The other had several couches for a more informal touch.

He chose the boardroom.

He opened the door and walked in, Lucy on his heels. She shut the door behind her and glared. "This is ridiculous."

"If you really thought that, you wouldn't be here right now." He grabbed her hips and pulled her against him. She instantly went soft, even as her blue eyes sparked. Gideon dipped his hands beneath her dress and froze. "What the fuck, Lucy?"

"Hmm?"

"You know exactly what I'm talking about." He pulled her dress up, though he didn't need the confirmation. "You come in here with that cock tease of a dress and you aren't wearing panties." Jealousy and desire twisted viciously through him. "Were you going to give Aaron a little show?"

"Oh, please. Give me a little credit." She lifted her chin. "I'm proving a point. You, Gideon Novak, don't get to make my decisions for me. I appreciate your help, but that's where it ends."

She didn't want him.

He was good enough to fuck but not good enough to listen to.

He kept a white-knuckled grip on his temper because having a knock-down, drag-out fight here and now wasn't an option for either of them. Not to mention the fact that he didn't have a *right* to be pissed. She'd laid out the terms that first day, and if he chose to ignore them, that was on him—not on Lucy.

It didn't make how shitty this situation was any easier to swallow.

Gideon stepped back. "The table. Bend over it."

Her eyebrows inched up. "You can't be serious."

"As a fucking heart attack. I told you what would happen if you showed up like that, and you were all too eager to pick up that gauntlet. Choices have consequences, Lucy. This is one of them."

She backed toward the table. One step. Two. "The consequences being that you'll spank my ass red and then fuck me right here."

She wants it.

It didn't soothe his temper. If anything, it ratcheted it up a notch. She might want *it* but she didn't want *him.* "The table."

Lucy turned and, prim as a princess, bent over the table. She seemed to consider and then lowered her chest farther until the top half of her body was flush against the polished wood. The position left her ass in the air and had her skirt riding up so he could *see* how turned on she was by this.

"Which part is getting you?" He stood between her and the door and pushed her dress the last few inches to bare her completely. "The spanking, the defiance, or the fact that we're in an unlocked room where anyone could walk in—including your fucking date?"

She tilted her ass up, just a little, an offer that made his mouth water. But it was her words that sealed her fate. "All of the above."

Fuck me.

He placed a steadying hand on the now-bare small of her back. "Brace yourself." Gideon wasn't into pain play, and he didn't think Lucy craved more than some rough-and-tumble shit, so he delivered a smack to her ass designed to sting without any lasting pain once they were through. Her gasp was almost a moan.

Gideon alternated smacks, giving each of her perfect fucking cheeks three. Enough to redden them as promised, but not more than that. He slipped a hand between her legs and groaned when he found her drenched. "You're going to fucking kill me."

He pulled out his wallet and retrieved the condom

he'd stashed there this morning. The crinkle of the wrapper sounded unnatural in the silence of the room, but he could barely hear it over the roaring in his ears. He nudged her legs wider and notched his cock at her entrance. "Next time, obey."

"Not likely." She used her forearm to muffle a moan when he shoved all the way into her.

Damn him to hell, but he loved that she pushed back. She'd been so timid in some ways their first couple of times together, and this defiance was more like the Lucy he used to know. He gripped her hips and pulled almost all the way out before he slammed back into her again. It was good—so fucking good— but it didn't satisfy the feral edge of rage he'd been riding for damn near twenty-four hours.

Gideon pulled out of her and flipped her around. She barely caught herself on his shoulders when he hooked the back of her thighs and lifted her onto the edge of the table. *Better.* But not enough. He yanked down her dress, baring her breasts. "Fucking *hell*, Lucy." He spread her legs wide and shoved into her, his gaze glued to the way her small breasts bounced with each thrust.

It wasn't enough to erase the image of her wearing that dress while chatting up Aaron.

Don't have a right to be jealous.

Don't give a damn if I have a right or not.

"Touch yourself. I want to feel you coming around my cock." He maintained his hold on her hips as she reached between her thighs and stroked her clit. Every thrust ground him against her fingers, the sensation as unbearably erotic as the sight of her touching herself while he fucked her.

Her body tightened around him and she cried out as she came. Gideon tried to hold out, but there was no fighting against the intoxication that was Lucy. He came with a curse. His breath tore from his lungs and he had to keep a death grip on the table to keep from hitting his knees.

It had never been like this for him before. He'd cared about women—even loved them—but the insanity Lucy drew out of him without seeming to try all that hard blew his fucking mind.

He stared into her bright blue eyes and wondered how the hell he was supposed to go back out into that club and pretend like he hadn't just been inside her.

As soon as she had control of her legs again, Lucy climbed off the table and fixed her dress. She could feel Gideon watching her, but she ignored him and pulled a pair of panties she'd stashed earlier out of her purse. She slipped them on and double-checked to make sure she wasn't in danger of indecent exposure. She straightened and froze. "What?"

"You just pulled panties out of your purse."

Heat flared over her exposed skin, but she forced herself to meet his gaze. "Yes, I did."

He didn't move, but he seemed closer. "I don't know whether to be impressed or pissed the fuck off. You baited me on purpose."

"Yes, I did," she repeated. "I was also proving a point. I won't allow you to control every aspect of these dates, but this thing between us is separate from that. For the duration, I'm yours." The words felt funny, as if she was declaring more than she intended, but she couldn't take them back without sounding ridiculous and giving them more weight than they deserved. *It's the truth. We're exclusive.*

But only sexually. There wasn't—couldn't—be anything more between them. She had her plan and Gideon hadn't held down a relationship for longer than two weeks the entire six years she'd known him. Even if Lucy was willing to bend on this—and she couldn't afford to be—Gideon would lose interest right around the time she needed him the most.

There would be no change of plans. They might fit better sexually than she could have dreamed, but that didn't mean anything in the grand scheme of things. She'd let good chemistry sideline her before—or what she'd *thought* was good chemistry. She wouldn't do it again, even if this felt as different from that as night to day.

"Mine for the duration." It sounded funny coming from him, too. Or maybe those were the butterflies erupting in her stomach.

She couldn't manage a smile, so she nodded. "Now, can we please go out there and meet this guy? Not to mention I haven't seen Roman in years and you hustled me past him so fast, I didn't even get to say hello." As ridiculous as it was, the thing she'd ended up missing most about being with Jeff was his friends.

Gideon had disappeared the second she'd broken up with Jeff and the rest of that group hadn't put up more than a token effort to keep in touch. To be fair, she hadn't tried, either. It was hard to look them in the face and know that they'd all had at least some idea of Jeff's extracurricular activities well before she had.

It doesn't matter anymore. I won't let *it matter.*

She didn't wait for Gideon to answer before she marched to the door and back the way they'd come. There was no helping her flushed cheeks, but she'd purposefully styled her hair a little wild in the event that Gideon was good on his threats. She might not be willing to admit it aloud—to him—but she was so very glad he had. The first two times with him had been wonderful beyond measure, but last night and tonight felt like the *real* Gideon. The man beneath the carefully controlled exterior.

She wanted more.

In fact, the last thing she wanted to do was exactly what she was doing—walking back into the VIP section. Much more enjoyable to slip out the back door with Gideon and go to one of their apartments to relieve the tension that only continued to rise the longer they were sleeping together.

It wasn't an option.

She ignored the way Roman glanced over her shoulder to where Gideon had no doubt just stepped into the room, speculation in his hazel eyes. Lucy gave him a big smile. "Roman, how have you been?"

"Well. Really well." He took her hand and stepped a little too close to be comfortable, his handsome face severe. She tensed and his next words did nothing to dispel the feeling. He kept his tone barely above a whisper. "I'm so sorry. If I'd have known he was going to be here, I would have passed on the information."

It took her pleasure-drugged brain several seconds to catch up. He wasn't talking about Aaron.

He was talking about Jeff.

She turned horror-movie slow toward the sound of a painfully familiar laugh. Jeff sat next to a pretty redhead and the entirety of his attention appeared to be on her. Lucy hadn't seen him in nearly two years—not since she'd thrown every single item he'd owned out their second-story apartment window—and she hated that he looked good. There was no extra weight, no puffy face that would indicate alcoholism, no slovenly appearance.

In fact, Jeff looked better than ever.

Lucy, no doubt, looked like she'd just been up to illicit activities in the back room—because she had been.

She looked up at Roman and didn't know what she was supposed to say or do. Jeff hadn't seen her yet, but it was just a matter of time before he did. She wasn't ready. She'd fought long and hard to get past the damage he'd done to her, but occupying the same space as him was enough to bring the truth flashing in front of her eyes.

She was still making her choices because of Jeff.

A hand pressed against the small of her back and Gideon's crisp scent wrapped around her. He stepped into view, blocking Jeff from her sight—or her from Jeff's. If Lucy felt off center, Gideon looked ready to shoot fire out of his eyes at Roman.

"Hey, man, like I just told Lucy—I didn't know he'd be here or I'd have let *you* know. He just showed up."

She pressed a hand to her chest. *I can't breathe.* An invisible band closed around her, tightening with each exhalation until black dots danced across her vision. Two years later and he still had so much power over her. She hated it. She hated *him*.

"Holy shit. Look what the cat dragged in." Jeff's voice came from directly behind Gideon.

Roman and Gideon looked at her, identical expressions on their faces. Asking how she wanted to handle this. If Lucy so much as blinked, she had a feeling Gideon would sweep her out of there without hesitation—and Roman would block Jeff from following if he tried.

But that was what she was so very tired of—letting Jeff's bullshit dictate how she handled any given situation.

Lucy lifted her chin, giving a slight nod. Gideon frowned, but he and Roman parted, taking up positions facing Jeff and only leaving a small sliver of a gap between them—standing sentry between her and her ex.

For all his pleased tone, Jeff's blue eyes were cold. The redhead on his arm didn't seem particularly happy, either, and Lucy spent a worthless few seconds wondering what he'd told her about this encounter. It didn't matter. *Jeff* didn't matter.

Or at least, he shouldn't.

She put all of her not inconsiderable willpower into appearing surprised. "Jeff. I had no idea you came here anymore."

"Not often." The look he shot the men in front of her was downright lethal.

Apparently his friendship with them hadn't lasted any longer than hers had. Lucy had known that about Gideon, but it comforted her to think of Jeff feeling just as abandoned as she had, even on that small scale.

He didn't jump in to say anything else, so she went with the first thing that popped into her mind. "You look well." *Meaningless chitchat.*

"I am well. Better than ever, really." His gaze jumped between her and Roman and Gideon. "You three look cozy." There was no mistaking the undertone of the statement. *Which one are you fucking?*

Looking too much into this. Get hold of yourself.

Gideon surprised her by taking a step back and pressing his hand to the small of her back. "We were just leaving."

At that, Jeff's mask slipped. His brows dropped, the first indication of what had always turned into a huge fight—one she had no chance of winning. Jeff seemed to take in her dress for the first time, his gaze leisurely raking over her body, pausing at her breasts and her bruised-feeling lips. "You and Gideon, huh? You took a pretty high-and-mighty stance with me when you broke off our engagement, and now you're fucking my best friend. Classy, Lucy, really classy."

No matter how much she told herself that his opinion didn't matter, it still felt like he'd sucker punched her. "It's not like that."

"It's exactly like that." Gideon spoke over her. He slipped his arm around her waist, pulling her against his side. "You fucked up and lost her. That's not on anyone but you, so don't start spouting that bullshit." He looked down at her, his expression hard. "You ready to go?"

"Please." She didn't want to stand there any longer than strictly necessary. The fact she hadn't sprinted for the exit was a win, as far as Lucy was concerned. Asking anything more of herself was out of the question.

Gideon nodded and glanced at Roman. "Next time."

"For sure."

He didn't give her a chance to say anything further before he steered them out of the VIP section and through to the front door. But what else was there to say? Anything she could come up with on that short walk sounded defensive, as if they'd done something wrong.

Well, I am *sleeping with him.*

But not dating him. Even if I was—it's been two years.

Two incredibly long and lonely years.

Lucy couldn't stop her shoulders from sagging the second they turned the corner away from the club. "That was terrible."

"I'm sorry, Lucy." His hand on her hip tensed, as if he wasn't sure whether he should pull her closer or release her. "I didn't know he'd show up. If I'd thought for a second it was a possibility, I wouldn't have taken you there."

"It's fine." It wasn't, but she should be stronger than this. Being brought to her knees emotionally just from running into her ex was inexcusably weak.

It wasn't even *Jeff* that was the problem. It was the fact that with one look, one carefully worded sentence, he could trigger every insecurity she fought so hard to banish. *He* wasn't the issue.

She was.

"It's not fine." Gideon stepped to the curb and flagged down a cab. "Your place or mine?"

If she let him, he'd talk through this with her. Gideon might be gloriously rough around the edges with a temper that would do a Viking proud, but he never failed to be careful around her.

Except when she pushed him hard enough that he forgot he was supposed to handle her with kid gloves.

There'd be no pushing him tonight. He'd pour her a glass of something alcoholic, sit her down and demand nothing but perfect honesty about how screwed up she was in her head. He'd pull out her issues and do his damnedest to fix them. Or, worse in some ways, he'd be wonderfully understanding and tell her it was okay.

She just…couldn't.

So incredibly weak.

Lucy didn't look at him as he pulled open the back door of the cab. "If it's all the same, I'd like to go home alone."

Gideon tensed and, out of the corner of her eye, she watched him fight an internal battle. Finally he shook his head. "If that's what you want."

It's not. "It is." Maybe if she got some distance, she could get her head on straight again. It was so hard to think with Gideon so close, his presence overwhelming her in every way. She couldn't handle it.

Lucy just needed time.

He stepped back, releasing her from her internal debate over whether she'd like him to force the issue or not. "Text me when you get back to your place."

"I will."

He waited until she slipped into the cab to say, "See you Saturday, Lucy."

CHAPTER TEN

GIDEON MADE IT until Wednesday. Three long-ass days in Seattle while he met with the first of the prospective fits he had for one of his clients. The guy was an advertising genius, though he was a little too free spirit for Gideon's straight-edged client. It might not be a deal-breaker, but it was something to take into account.

He shrugged out of his suit jacket and stared at his phone. Lucy hadn't called and she hadn't texted after the one letting him know that she was safely home. He had left New York with every intention of giving her the space she obviously wanted, but three days out of town had given him clarity.

She was running scared.

Seeing Jeff had screwed her up, and Gideon understood that. She hadn't wanted to further break herself open for *him*, and he respected that.

But she was closing him out.

He tossed his jacket on the bed and dialed her before he could think of all the reasons it was a bad idea. She hadn't brought him into this to work her shit out—she just wanted a husband and sex lessons. *Too damn bad. She signed up for* me—*and that's what she's going to get.*

"Lucy Baudin," she answered.

"Hey."

A long pause. "Hello, Gideon."

He hated the awkwardness seeping into this conversation before they'd exchanged half a dozen words. If he let it, it would become downright painful. Unacceptable. Gideon had never met a challenge he wasn't willing to go around, over or through, and a simple conversation wouldn't be the thing that stopped him in his tracks. "How's your week going?"

"Long, and it's only Wednesday. One of my clients is being difficult, and I'm having to work around her just to help her, which makes everything twice as challenging."

"You'll figure it out."

"I always do."

He dropped into the chair next to the desk. This wasn't working. Lucy held herself distant—polite—but there was none of the intimacy they'd started building. He hadn't even realized it was happening until that softness disappeared. *One way to put them back on solid ground.* "You home?"

"Yes. Hanging out with Garfunkel and wading through some old accounts for my current case—and drinking wine. This kind of investigating always requires wine."

"Naturally." He settled back into the chair and kicked off his shoes. "What are you wearing?"

Her surprised laugh was music to his ears. "Phone sex? Really, Gideon? Isn't that a bit juvenile?"

"We already had this discussion."

The amusement faded from her voice. "I suppose we did."

"On second thought, don't tell me what you're wearing. Show me. You by your computer?"

"Always."

"Give me two seconds." He grabbed his laptop and brought it online. A few button pushes later and he had a video call going through to Lucy.

She answered, looking unsure. "I guess I can hang up now."

"Yeah." He set down the phone and shifted to get comfortable. She looked good. She sat on her couch in the middle of several stacks of files, one housing her cat, and wore a fitted tank top and sleep shorts. Her shirt was thin enough that he could see the faintest outline of her nipples through the white fabric, and her sleep shorts gapped around her upper thighs in a way that made his mouth water. "Hey."

"Hey." She spoke just as softly. "Nice shirt."

"Thanks." He pulled his tie loose and tossed it onto the bed. "Have to look the part, though this guy isn't formal at all. He's a big fan of flannel, hair gel and skinny jeans."

She laughed softly. "Poor Gideon. You'd look downright fetching in flannel, but I like you without a beard. I'll hold out judgment on the skinny jeans, though they present some interesting possibilities."

His cock went rock-hard at the desire warming her

expression, but he kept his tone light. "I'll be sure to pick up something while I'm here."

"You don't have to."

"I know." But he wanted to show her that he valued her opinions. Gideon had never owned a piece of flannel clothing in his life, but if Lucy thought she'd like the look, he'd give it a shot. He noted the hesitance in her body language and refocused. "You always lounge in that sort of thing?" He waved to her clothing.

"This? Yes, I guess so." She shrugged. "It's comfortable."

"It's sexy as hell." He set his computer on the desk and leaned forward. "Let those thin little straps slide off your shoulders. I want to see you."

"Right now?" She looked around as if expecting him to jump out of a closet and tell her it was a joke. Lucy tucked a strand of her dark hair behind her ear. "I don't know if I'm ready for this."

She might very well not be, but if she didn't want to talk to him, then he'd keep them in the roles she'd set out for them. "Close your eyes." He waited for her to obey. "How do you feel when you take everything you think you *should* be feeling out of the equation?"

"Warm. Turned on." She hesitated. "A little intimidated. It's different when you're here with me, touching me. There's no room for being self-conscious."

"I've been thinking about you for five long-ass days and thinking about all the things I want to do to you when we're alone again."

"Things…" She licked her lips, one of her tells. Oh,

yeah, she liked this when she stopped remembering the reasons she shouldn't.

He kept going, pitching his voice low and intimate. "That lingerie shopping date we have? I've been thinking about sitting there and watching you come out of that room wearing one of those getups. Maybe you'll tease me, make me wait for it."

"Like this." She used a single finger to inch first one strap off her shoulder and then the other. The upper curve of her breasts caught the fitted fabric and he had to bite back a curse.

"Exactly like that. You know how bad I want it— want you—but I think you've got a little sadist in you because you like pushing my buttons. Making me crazy."

"I do." Her lips quirked up in a smile. "You're so controlled all the time. I like seeing what happens when the leash snaps."

He liked that she liked it. Gideon spent most of his days aware of how he presented himself and how everything from his tone to his appearance to his walk could be interpreted by clients and prospectives alike. He never let himself relax, because even in a social setting, there was no telling who was around.

There wasn't anyone around now—no one but him and Lucy.

"If I was there, I'd tug that top of yours a little lower. Yeah, like that." He watched, mouth dry, as she inched it down, stopping just below her nipples and then baring her breasts completely. "Exactly like that."

"This feels so dirty." She opened her eyes and pressed her lips together. "Would you…?"

"Tell me what you want and it's yours." He craved her words as much as he craved her touch. One was out of the question for the next few days—the other she gave him after the briefest hesitation.

"Unbutton your shirt." She leaned forward, the move making her breasts bounce a little. "I love your shoulders. Your suits have this way of masking how muscled they are, and seeing you shirtless makes me feel like it's my birthday."

He straightened so he could slip his shirt off and drop it on the floor. They stared at each other for a few seconds, Gideon drinking in the sight of her while she appeared to give him the same treatment. He spoke the second he saw doubt start creeping into her blue eyes. "Your breasts look like they ache. Palm them for me."

She instantly obeyed and then took it a step further and lightly pinched her nipples. This time he couldn't hold back his low curse. "Yeah, just like that."

"Are you…? Will you…?"

He instantly understood what she meant. "You want my cock?"

"Yes. Show me." She writhed a little, her hands moving with more purpose on her breasts.

He tilted his computer screen so the camera took in his lower half. He moved slowly, teasing her, and undid his slacks to withdraw his cock. He gave himself a long stroke and was rewarded with Lucy's moan. "You like that."

"I like that a lot."

"Take off your shorts. I want to see you stroking that pretty pussy until you come for me."

She barely hesitated this time before she released her breasts and lifted her hips to slide the shorts off.

He stroked himself again idly. "Spread your legs—yes, like that. Show me how you like it the same way you did that first time."

She slipped her hand between her thighs, parting her folds to draw a single finger over her clit. It was the single most devastating thing he'd ever seen.

Gideon watched avidly, taking in every detail and imprinting it into his memory. It was shitty not being able to be there and touch her, but it allowed him a perfect view and the distance to appreciate it in a new way.

Lucy was fucking magnificent.

After the first halting touches, she gave herself over to her pleasure—to both their pleasure—and stroked faster. Her head fell back against the couch and her body bowed as she pushed two fingers into her pussy. "I wish you were here."

"Saturday. I'll make it worth the wait."

"I don't know if anything is worth the wait." Her words were breathy and her breasts quivered with each exhalation. She managed to open her eyes. "I'm close, Gideon. Are you close?"

He'd been teetering on the edge the second she'd taken off her shorts, holding on through sheer force of will. "I'm close." He spoke through gritted teeth. Pressure built in his spine and his balls drew up, his cock swelling at the sight of her stroking herself to orgasm.

Lucy let her head hit the back of the couch again, but she kept her eyes open and on him as she fucked herself with her fingers. Her breath turned even choppier.

"Next time…" He had to stop and restart the sentence when she gasped. "Next time, you'll bring out that toy of yours. I want to see it sliding into you, vibrating and making you crazy."

"*You* make me crazy." Her back arched and every line of her body stood out as she came with his name on her lips.

Gideon couldn't hold on after that. He stroked faster, harder. She lifted her head in time to see him come in several spurts onto his stomach. He stared down at it marking his body and wondered when the hell his life had taken a hard right turn. A month ago he would have laughed someone out of the room for suggesting he'd be participating in a video call with mutual masturbation, let alone with Lucy Baudin.

And yet…here they were.

He reached down to grab his shirt and wipe himself off, and checked on her. Lucy had slid down to lie on the couch, and she watched him with a sleepy smile. "You've got that look on your face."

Her smile widened. "What look is that?"

"One that says you're thinking filthy thoughts." He liked that look. A lot.

She swept her hair off one shoulder and it pooled around her head on the cushion. "That's because I *am* thinking filthy thoughts." She bit her lip and then rushed on. "What time do you fly in Friday?"

"Our appointment is…" He stopped short. A slow tendril of pleasure that had nothing to do with sex rolled through him. "You want to see me Friday night."

"If that's okay. I know you'll be tired."

"It would take a whole hell of a lot more than a few hours' plane ride to make me too tired to see you. Though I don't fly in until after eleven."

She smiled. "I'll leave the key with the doorman."

Fuck yes. He damn well knew he was reading more into that choice than he should be, but it was hard not to. That simple sentence, more than anything else they'd done to this point, signaled her trust in him. "I'll stop by my place to drop my shit and then I'll be there."

"Perfect." She stretched. "Thank you for this, Gideon. All of it."

Strangely enough, he felt like *he* should be thanking *her*. He'd spent a long time just going through the motions and, for better or worse, Lucy had woken him up. He wanted to keep talking to her, but a quick glance at his phone showed that it was well past ten on the East Coast. "Don't let those files keep you up too late."

"I think I'm done for the night." She pulled on her shorts and resumed her comfortable-looking spot. "I had this really gorgeous guy call and talk me to orgasm just now, and I'm feeling all loose and relaxed, so I'm going to jump in the shower and head to bed to read for a bit. One of my favorite authors has a book out and I've been dying to start it."

I wish I was there. He didn't say it again. It was one thing to put those words out there when talking about sex—it was entirely another to do it now that the desire had cooled.

It was the truth, though.

He wanted to be there to pull her into a relaxing shower, to exchange small talk about nothing important while they got ready for bed, to settle in while she read her book and he finished answering the last few emails of the day. Gideon wanted it so bad, he could barely breathe past the need.

He couldn't say any of that now without scaring the shit out of Lucy.

But he managed a smile. "You'll have to tell me about it when I see you."

Lucy gave him a strange look. "You want to hear about my book?"

"Sure." If only because it was something she was interested in and obviously passionate about—and had been for as long as he'd known her, though she used to hide them under a pillow when he and Jeff would walk into the room. Jeff had always made snide comments that he covered up as joking, and Gideon should have paid more attention to Lucy's reaction to those comments. He'd known his friend was a jackass, but he hadn't realized the depth of the damage Jeff was dealing her.

"That's nice of you to say, but we really don't have to talk about my romance novel addiction."

Damn it, she was doing it again. He leaned forward until his face filled the video screen. "I wouldn't ask if I didn't want to know. Nothing but honesty between us, remember? It interests you, so I want to know more. It's as simple as that."

She opened her mouth, seemed to reconsider arguing with him and shut it. "That makes sense."

"Because it's the truth." He stomped down on his anger. Hard. It wasn't directed at Lucy, and it wasn't fair to take his fury at himself and Jeff out on *her*. Gideon kept his tone low and even. "Enjoy the rest of your night, Lucy."

"You, too." She looked away and then back at the camera. "If you change your mind about Friday, I'll understand."

God, she was fucking killing him. "I'll see you Friday night."

CHAPTER ELEVEN

LUCY HAD EVERY intention of staying awake to greet Gideon. If nothing else, she was sure nerves would keep her alert until he arrived. She hadn't counted on the long day.

It had started at 5:00 a.m. when she'd gotten a call from the office that there was a new client on retainer and that Lucy was needed at the woman's home immediately. Things had only gone downhill from there. The client—accused of money laundering—was as high maintenance as they came, so Lucy'd had her work cut out for her.

Throw in the partners dragging her into a boardroom for a progress report the second she'd set foot in the office, and she was exhausted. Her other clients couldn't be shoved to the back burner, no matter how important the new one was, so she'd worked late to ensure she was ready for court on Monday.

All of it had added up to an exhaustion she couldn't fight, no matter how entertaining the newest episode of her favorite medical drama. Her blinks became longer and longer, and the next thing she knew, she roused to the feeling of strong hands sliding up her thighs.

That alone should have scared the crap out of her, but Gideon's scent wrapped around her, setting her at ease even before she was fully awake. She blinked down at him as he hooked his arms beneath her and lifted her off the couch. "I can walk."

"Humor me." He strode down her hallway without turning on any lights and toed open the door to her bedroom. She hadn't bothered leaving lights on in her room and Lucy regretted that when Gideon set her on the bed and stripped in quick, efficient movements. She moved to do the same, but he beat her there, carefully pulling her oversize T-shirt off. Since Lucy had been expecting him, she hadn't worn anything else.

His quick intake of breath was a reward in and of itself. She ran her hand up his chest. "Hey."

"Hey." He guided her to lie on the bed, quickly put on a condom and covered her with his body. "You looked comfortable on the couch."

"I was." She wrapped her legs around his waist and arched up to kiss his throat. "This is better."

"Agreed." He laced his fingers through her hair and guided her mouth to his, kissing her lazily, as if he had no idea of the need already building in her core. Need that only Gideon seemed to be able to sate. He took his time reacquainting himself with her mouth before he moved to her neck and collarbone. "I was going to wake you up in a very specific way."

"Mmm." She reached between them to stroke him.

"This is better." She notched his cock at her entrance. "I need you."

He slid into her in a single move and kissed her again with them sealed as closely as two people could be. Pressure built between them, but his big body kept Lucy pinned in place so she couldn't do anything more than shake. Even that tiny movement ratcheted up her desire until she couldn't stop a whimper of need from escaping. "Gideon, stop teasing me."

"I know I'm not supposed to say it, but I missed the fuck out of you this week."

Her breath got tangled somewhere between her lungs and throat. The words she was supposed to say lingered on the wrong side of her lips. *That's not what we are.* It might be the correct thing to say, but it wasn't the *right* thing to say—or the truth. "I missed you, too."

He finally moved, rocking against her. It wasn't enough, but that made it all the hotter. She did her best to arch, fighting against the weight of his body and loving every second of it. "More."

"Demanding," he murmured against her lips. "I waited seven fucking days to be inside you again, and I'm going to take my time and enjoy it." He dragged his mouth down her throat, his whiskers rasping against her sensitized skin. "I like having you like this."

"Furious?"

He chuckled, the low sound vibrating through her. "Needy. Wanting. As close as you'll ever come to begging."

"Would begging make a difference?"

His lips brushed the shell of her ear. "No."

Lucy shivered, her breath releasing in a sob. It felt too good and she needed more. But he was right—she loved every second of this. Their bodies slicked with sweat as he kept up those slight rocking movements, every single one inching her closer to oblivion. His pelvis created delicious friction against her clit, and she found herself talking without having any intention of doing so. "That feels so good, Gideon. Don't stop. Never stop." She dug her fingers into his ass, loving the way he growled against her neck. "I love this."

"I know." He slipped one arm beneath the small of her back and the other up her spine to cup her head. She'd thought they were as close as two people could be. He proved her wrong. Lucy slid her feet down to hook around his calves, grinding against him. Gideon kissed her as if he couldn't help himself. His tongue stroked hers, plunging deep, the way she wanted him to elsewhere. Right when she caught his rhythm, he withdrew and then stroked deep again, starting the process over. It made her crazy—crazier.

He knew. He always seemed to know exactly how close to the edge she was.

Gideon began to move. His hips mirrored the movements his tongue had made, stroking deep and then withdrawing before slamming home again.

Lucy couldn't think, couldn't move, couldn't even breathe. Her entire existence boiled down to the places Gideon touched her and his cock between her thighs. Pressure wound tighter and tighter, turning her into a wild creature with no thought but her own pending orgasm.

It hit her like a freight train and she let loose a keening cry that didn't sound human to her ears. Lucy couldn't do more than cling to Gideon as his strokes became more and more ragged and rough until he orgasmed with a curse. He dropped slightly to the side of her, but shifted to pull her leg up and over his hip, keeping them close.

She tried to get her racing heart under control. "That was some wake-up."

"It's good to see you, Lucy." Such a polite thing to say considering their current position.

I think I prefer hearing that you missed me.

With the post-orgasm bliss numbing her common sense, she couldn't quite shut that thought down. She crossed the line they'd drawn in the sand. "Stay."

"What?"

She ran her hand up his arm. "Stay. It's almost morning and there's no point in you cabbing back to your place and turning around to do it again in a few hours. Just…stay here with me."

"You sure that's what you want?" There wasn't a single thing in his voice to indicate what *he* wanted.

"Yes. If you want to, of course." *Maybe I misheard him and I'm wrong about this entire situation.*

Gideon delivered a devastating kiss and climbed off the bed. "Give me a few."

"Sure." She waited for him to walk into her bathroom and shut the door before she relaxed and sighed, staring at the ceiling. *What am I doing?*

He was back before she could muster the energy to second-guess herself. Gideon pulled down the comforter and waited for her to climb beneath it before he followed suit. She tensed, waiting for the inevitable awkwardness, but he just slipped in behind her and guided her so he could spoon her. He kissed the back of her neck. "Sleep."

Lucy thought it impossible, but the heat of him and the feel of safety being tucked against his big body lulled her circling thoughts to a standstill. Between one breath and the next, she slipped into a deep sleep.

Gideon woke to the smell of bacon. For one disorientating moment he didn't know where he was, but then the events of the night came rushing back to him. Lucy. Her apartment. Sleeping here. He sat up and scrubbed a hand over his face. *I told her I missed her and then I stayed the night.* For all his intentions of respecting *her* intentions, Gideon was doing a piss-poor job of following through.

Worse, he'd been so focused on himself, he hadn't stopped to ask her how she was doing after seeing Jeff again—a week ago. *Fuck me.* He stopped in the bathroom to brush his teeth as best he could with a finger and pulled on his pants.

He found Lucy in the kitchen, opening a series of take-out containers. She looked fresh and happy, her hair back in a low-key ponytail, and wore black leggings and a blue sweater that matched her eyes. She smiled when she saw him. "Morning."

"Morning." He took in the spread. "What's all this?"

"I think we can both agree that cooking isn't one of my strengths, so I popped out and grabbed something edible." She grabbed two mugs from one of her cabinets. "Coffee, however, I am capable of throwing together."

"Survival skill."

"Exactly." She passed him a full cup and her expression turned serious. "Can we have today?"

Gideon took a careful drink of the scalding liquid and contemplated her. For all that she appeared relaxed on the surface, there was an underlying tension there. "And after today?"

"I figure we're due a conversation, but we have plans today and I don't want to ruin them by talking this to death. I'm happy and I want to hold on to that."

Meaning that this talk wouldn't make her feel happy— or him, for that matter. Gideon already knew what was coming. He'd muddied the waters by showing up last night, and taken it a step further by staying and holding her while they'd slept. They hadn't talked about lessons after that first time they'd had sex, which was supposed to be the whole purpose of this exercise. She'd also been on exactly one date.

He had to fix that.

He would rather chew off his own arm than set her up on any more dates, but that was what he'd given his word he'd do. Lucy trusted him and he couldn't betray that trust. *Not again.*

Gideon forced an easy smile onto his face. "Sure, we can have today." He didn't want to have that talk any more than she appeared to want it, so he wasn't going to worry about a few hours spent without over-thinking things. "I thought you had lunch with your sister?"

"She got called in to cover a class and had to cancel." Lucy gave him a small smile. "I know we had planned for this afternoon, but I'm free all day if you are."

"I'm free." Gideon had been looking forward to this date all damn week, so he hadn't put anything else on his schedule.

Because that was exactly what this was, even if Lucy didn't realize it. A date.

Maybe she does realize it and that's why she's asking to shelve the conversation we obviously need to have until tonight.

She gave him a sunny smile. "Good. In that case, eat up while I jump in the shower." She pushed the food toward him, grabbed her mug and strolled out of the kitchen.

He spent half a second considering following her and making the shower one to remember, but if Gideon read the signs correctly, Lucy needed time. It had been that way with them from the start of this—she'd take a step forward and need time to acclimate. He could respect that. He *would* respect that. If he pushed too hard, too fast, she'd bolt, and this time he'd never hear from her again. It wasn't a risk he was willing to take, especially now when it felt like they were close to something that could actually be real.

If she'd take that leap of faith with him.

He ate quickly and cleaned up the containers. By

that time, the shower had turned off, so Gideon grabbed the bag he'd brought in the night before and hauled it into her room.

Lucy glanced over from where she'd just walked through the bathroom door. She had a fluffy towel wrapped around her, and though it hid her curves, the exposed skin of her shoulders and calves had him craving the feel of her. She narrowed her eyes. "You didn't go home last night, did you?"

There was no use in denying it. "Nope." He'd wanted to see her—had *needed* to see her—and the extra forty minutes it would have taken were forty minutes too many. He nodded at the bathroom door. "Mind if I use your shower?"

"Of course not. Go for it."

He didn't need to be told twice. Gideon showered quickly, pausing long enough to wish he had time to shave, but he wasn't likely to see anyone he knew professionally today. He paused in front of his suitcase. Lucy had been wearing casual clothes earlier, and it might make her uncomfortable if he used his last suit. The other option wasn't as comfortable for *him*, but he'd make do.

He had promised her, after all.

When he walked out of the bathroom, she froze. "You…" She gave herself a shake. "Sorry, I don't think I've ever seen you rumpled-looking before—not even in college."

He glanced down at his designer jeans and the flannel shirt he'd thrown over a white T-shirt. "I'm not rumpled."

"You are most definitely rumpled." She moved closer, taking him in as a small smile pulled at the edges of her lips. "You look like you should be standing on a porch on some mountainside, a steaming cup of coffee in hand while you contemplate whatever it is that lumberjacks contemplate." She ran her hands up his chest and over his shoulders. "I like it."

"Rumpled suits me."

"You don't have to sound so cranky when you say it." She smoothed down his shirt, actually leaning forward a few inches before she seemed to remember herself and took several steps back. "I'm ready when you are."

She wore a different variation of what she'd had on earlier: dark leggings, a long black T-shirt and a slouchy knitted cardigan thing. Her pants were tucked into a sleek pair of knee-high boots. *Rumpled* was not a word he'd use to describe her, but with her hair falling in careless waves to her shoulders, she looked relaxed. Almost peaceful.

He liked it.

Gideon pulled on his shoes and then they headed down to the street. Lucy paused on the sidewalk. "It's such a nice day."

He could pick up a clue as obvious as that one. "We could walk. It's only a handful of blocks."

"Are you sure? We didn't really talk about what your other plans are for the day and—"

"There are no other plans." He cut in before she could talk herself out of the whole day. "I worked all week. I cleared today for you, Lucy."

"Oh. Well…oh." She managed to look everywhere but at him. "I'm sorry—is this weird? It didn't feel all that strange when I suggested it earlier, but I think common sense has taken hold."

"More like nerves." He pressed his hand to the small of her back. "Walk with me, Lucy. What's the harm that could come of it?"

CHAPTER TWELVE

WHAT'S THE HARM that could come of it?

Lucy forced herself to look at Gideon. His expression was as open as she'd ever seen it, inviting her to take this first step with him. First step into *what*, though? It had been an off-the-cuff thing to tell him that she wanted today, but through her shower and then his, the importance of that statement—this plan—had grown to epic proportions.

It felt like a date.

Except she wasn't supposed to be dating Gideon. She was supposed to be dating the men Gideon set her up with.

He didn't look particularly concerned that they had left the boundary of their agreed-upon relationship in the rearview. He offered his arm, the old-world gesture so very Gideon.

She slipped her hand onto his arm and fell into step with him as if it was the most natural thing in the world. Maybe it was. She didn't know anymore. These days, it felt like up was down and down was up, and Lucy was bouncing somewhere in the middle.

"How was your trip? Other than having to fend off a city full of free spirits." She injected false sympathy into her tone. "You poor thing."

Gideon shook his head. "You mock me while you were here, safe in New York. The people on that coast aren't anything like *our* people. They chat." He gave a mock shudder. "You wouldn't last two days."

"On the contrary, I'm not nearly as cranky and anti-social as you are. I'd be fine."

"There is that." He pulled her to a stop at the curb as cars whizzed past. "It was a productive trip. One of my prospective fits looks like she'll work out, and I managed to source a secondary backup in Portland. Those two cities are filled to the brim with tech geniuses, so if I can lure either woman over here, they'll have jobs waiting."

A barb of something like jealousy embedded itself in Lucy's throat. He'd spent a full week in endless meetings between Seattle and Portland, and a few of the people he'd met with had been women. It shouldn't matter. Lucy had no claim on Gideon. Not really. They might be exclusive for the time being, but there was a looming expiration date. He could have plans to hook up with one of those women—or both—and Lucy didn't have the right to be upset about it.

That didn't change the fact that her chest ached at the very thought.

"Maisey Graham has been married to her high school sweetheart since the month after graduation, and he owns his own business, so relocation isn't out of the question." Gideon spoke low enough that she had to lean in to hear his words, very carefully not looking at him. "Jericha Hurley will be eighteen in two months, though she's damn near a certified genius and she's got her pick of companies vying for her attention."

He knew.

The ache in her chest got worse. She managed to breathe past it—barely. "It's none of my business."

"Honesty, Lucy."

She didn't want to be honest. She wanted to shove her head in the sand. They crossed the road and kept going down the block. She tried to pinpoint exactly what the problem was. *Easy enough—I'm jealous of the thought of Gideon spending time with other women.* Not just spending time, though. Having long meetings, likely alone, on the other side of the country. "It's not that I think you'd do that after you told me we were exclusive."

"The fear is there all the same." He set his free hand over hers and squeezed. "That's not something you just get over."

Maybe she would have. If she'd put half the effort into dating that she'd put into her career, she'd have worked through what was apparently a hair trigger. *Or maybe it wouldn't have mattered.* There was no way to tell, and it was a moot point. "We have to fix this."

"What?"

"This is another issue. I can't very well marry someone if the thought of them being alone in a room with a woman is going to send me into a jealous spiral. They're all businessmen, and so that sort of thing will pop up. There's no avoiding it." She latched on to the idea, turning it over in her mind. "We can start at the lingerie shop."

Gideon pulled them out of the path of foot traffic and guided her to the brick wall of a nearby storefront. He let go and took her by the shoulders. "Lucy, stop."

"Don't take that tone with me. I'm not being crazy."

"Everything about this situation is crazy. No, don't get your back up. It is and you know it, and I'm here willingly, taking part in it." He looked like he wanted to shake some sense into her. "You're asking me to… What? Flirt with someone in front of you? More?"

More?

Her entire body clenched as if trying to reject the very idea of Gideon doing *more* with someone else. *I am out of control.* "If that's what it takes."

A muscle jumped in his jaw. "No."

"Excuse me?"

He shook his head. "Absolutely not. You pick one of these assholes and he flirts with another woman in front of you—or at all—and you get out, Lucy. You hear me? That is not normal, and no man who respects his partner would put them in that situation where they have to wonder if something more is going on. I would never so much as look at another woman if I was with you—in your presence or not."

"But—"

"But nothing. There are a lot of gray areas in relationships. This isn't one of them. Short of there being extenuating circumstances that are agreed upon by both parties, there is a clear line and no one should be crossing it."

She stared. This was supposed to be all in theory—a test run of sorts—but Gideon spoke like it was a personal attack on him. *Because it is.* She didn't know what to do, so she slipped her arms around his waist and pulled him in for a hug. "I'm sorry."

He cursed, but he wrapped his arms around her. "You have nothing to be sorry for."

"I'm blurring the lines." She wasn't even sure where the lines were at this point. Having sex was one thing, though they hadn't even done *that* right because she was too busy enjoying herself to pay attention to whatever he tried to teach her. On what was supposed to be her second date, she was more excited about pushing Gideon's buttons than she was about meeting her actual date.

And now she was getting jealous.

He pulled her tighter against him. "We'll talk about it tonight." He stepped back and reclaimed her hand. "Come on."

Lucy didn't know whether to look forward to the conversation or to dread it. When she'd initially brought it up, she'd deluded herself with the falsity that she had everything under control. Twenty minutes into this day and she'd proved herself wrong half a dozen times. Gideon was probably going to sit her down and explain how out of line she'd been lately.

Let it go. You can obsess about every word and touch and meaning once he's left tonight.

Strangely enough, that made her feel better. Or

maybe it was his fingers laced through hers as they walked down the street. Two blocks later, he pulled her to a stop in front of a boutique lingerie shop. "Yes?"

She took in the window display, a perfect blend of tasteful and risqué. The mannequins reclined on a lounging sofa, both wearing jewel-toned bustiers, ruffled boy-short panties, with garters and thigh-highs. One had on a lace shrug that looked like something out of an old black-and-white movie. "Yes."

She couldn't wait to get into that dressing room with Gideon.

One minute Gideon was leading Lucy into the lingerie boutique, the next, a whirlwind of a saleswoman had stationed him in one of the private change areas and led Lucy away. He blinked at the opening leading into the rest of the store but didn't move from his assigned spot. *That was smoothly done.*

Content to leave Lucy at the mercy of the woman, he surveyed the changing area. It was a clever design, each of the three doorways leading to a small sitting area and an individual change room. The whole setup created the feeling of an intimate environment for shopping for the most intimate of clothing. He approved.

Gideon hadn't decided whether now was the time to play on Lucy's fantasy of change room sex. He'd intended it initially, but their conversation on the walk over had put things up in the air. He'd already pressed her hard just by staying last night. Her showing signs of jealousy was a sign that she felt more than just sexual attraction, but it obviously set her off balance and made her uncomfortable.

He sat back and scrubbed a hand over his face. The truth was, he didn't know how to play this. He'd made his career on being able to read people and find good fits, but he was fumbling around in the dark when it came to Lucy. He felt like he was back in high school, trying to express interest without hanging himself out to dry and becoming the laughingstock of the school.

Except the stakes were a whole hell of a lot higher now.

The saleswoman had hustled Lucy into the change room so fast, he hadn't seen more than a flash of bright colors attached to hangers before the door shut. The saleswoman—a little Goth woman who stood five feet tall, if that—emerged a few seconds later. She had purple streaks in her black hair and a lip ring. She winked at him and raised her voice. "You let me know if you need any different sizes or want to try something else. There's a button in there that will ding me, but otherwise, I'll leave you to it."

"Thank you." Lucy's voice was muffled.

The saleswoman stopped next to him. "Special lady you have there."

"Yes." She wasn't telling him anything he didn't know. She lingered for a second, something obviously on her mind, but he didn't have the patience to deal with it when he could hear the slide of cloth against skin in the dressing room. "Thank you."

"Let me know if you need anything. We have coffee and water." She waited half a beat and then was gone, striding out the door and into the main boutique.

Gideon drummed his fingers on his knee and waited.

Then waited some more.

Five minutes later his frayed patience gave out. He rose and stalked to the dressing room door. "Lucy."

"Yes?" She sounded small and unsure.

"Do you need assistance?"

"No."

He stared at the door, willing her to open it. She didn't. Gideon sighed. "Is there a problem?"

"No. Yes. I don't know. I just feel absolutely ridiculous."

He considered and discarded several responses to that. None of them was worth the breath it would take to give them voice. "Open the door."

"It's fine, Gideon. This was a silly idea. Just give me a minute to change back into my clothes and we can find something else to do today."

"Open the door," he repeated.

Her bare feet padded over the tiled floor and he held his breath as they approached the door. And then it was open and a vision from every one of his fantasies stood in front of him. Lucy wore nude-colored thigh-highs, held up by an emerald garter belt. Its decorative lace almost hid the fact that her panties barely hid anything at all. And the bustier was a work of art, offering her breasts with peekaboo lace that showcased her nipples apparently by accident. The whole thing was a goddamn tease and he loved it. "You look ravishing."

She put her hands on her hips, at her sides, and then finally crossed them over her chest. "*Ravishing* is a strong word."

"It fits." He stepped into the dressing room and shut the door behind him, unable to take his eyes off her. "If you don't like it, *divine*, *exquisite* and *breathtaking* are also accurate."

Her eyebrows inched up. "Do you have a thesaurus tucked into your back pocket?"

"Don't need one." He stopped in front of her and uncrossed her arms so he could see her. As with all things Lucy, both she and the lingerie were even better up close. Gideon stroked his hands down her sides and ran his thumb over the garter belt. What he found had him going to his knees in front of her. "Your panties are on top."

"Well, yes." A blush spread over her pale cheeks and down her chest. "I'd already decided to buy it based on the color, so I wanted the full effect."

There was only one reason to wear panties over the garter belt; they could be removed while leaving the rest of the lingerie on.

Gideon hooked the side of the thong with his thumbs and looked up her body to her face. "Yes?"

"Yes." The word was barely more than a stirring of the air between them.

He slid her panties down her legs, taking his time. "I'm buying this for you. Don't argue. This isn't a disagreement that you'll win."

"This getup is incredibly expensive." As he crouched, she lifted first one foot and then the other so he could remove the thong completely.

"Worth every penny." The garter belt framed her pussy to perfection, an offering he couldn't have resisted if he'd tried—and Gideon wasn't interested in trying. He guided one of her legs over his shoulder, a position that left her completely at his mercy. "Just a taste."

CHAPTER THIRTEEN

AT THE FIRST stroke of Gideon's tongue, Lucy forgot all the reasons this was a questionable idea. She didn't care. The only thing that mattered was his tongue lazily circling her clit. As if he had all the time in the world and they weren't in a public place.

A public place where every moan and sound could be heard by someone on the other side of the dressing room door.

She shivered, heat cascading through her body at the thought of someone listening. Someone knowing what they were doing. Someone thinking Gideon was so turned on by the lingerie that he couldn't wait for the time it'd take them to get home.

He'd had to have her right then and there.

His dark gaze met hers as he licked her again. "What are you thinking?"

She was thinking she wanted more. To be dirty. To break the rules.

Lucy reached down and tugged on his shoulders. Without saying another word, Gideon rose and let her guide him to sit on the bench that ran along the wall in the changing room. He watched her through hooded eyes as she undid the front of his jeans and climbed onto his lap. After a quick detour to her purse for a condom, she rolled it onto his length. He opened his mouth but Lucy pressed a single finger to his lips.

His eyes flashed in understanding and his lazy grin made her pussy clench. Lucy guided him inside her and sealed them together. She leaned forward until her lips brushed his ear. "Someone could hear."

"Yes." The word was barely more than a whisper. He reached up and pulled her bustier down to bare her breasts. "Hope you locked the door. She knocks on it and it'll swing right open. Give the woman the sight of a lifetime."

Her nipples tightened at the image his low words painted. It didn't matter that she knew for a fact the door was locked. It *could* be unlocked. Lucy held on to Gideon's shoulders and started to move. Each time she lifted almost all the way off his cock, her breasts brushed against his mouth and he kissed first one and then the other.

Thrust. Kiss. Thrust.

"Look at how beautiful you are." He gripped her chin and turned her face to the full-length mirror.

What a picture they made. Him fully clothed except for his cock disappearing and reappearing between her legs. Her mostly naked and riding him, her pale skin flushed with desire. Lucy couldn't take her gaze away from where one of his big hands held her hip while the other maintained its grip on her chin, to the look on his face as he stared at her in the mirror. She licked her lips. "*We* are beautiful."

He guided her back to face him. "Fuck me. Come on my cock. But be quiet or Agnes will hear."

The words unleashed the orgasm that had been building from the moment he'd slipped off her panties. Lucy buried her face in his neck and tried to muffle her cry as she came. Gideon looped an arm around her waist and lifted her to reverse their positions, sitting her on the bench with him kneeling between her thighs, his cock still buried inside her.

He held her thighs wide and proceeded to fuck her. She had to cling to the edge of the bench to keep from smacking against the wall with the strength of his thrusts. Through it all, his dark eyes swallowed her up, so full of things she couldn't put a name to. An expression almost like pain flickered over his face as he came with a muffled curse, hips still thrusting as if he never wanted to stop.

Lucy slumped back onto the bench and blinked at the reflection of herself. Gideon crouched in front of her, his dark eyes wild. He started to reach for her and stopped. "Your place. Now."

"We could…" She trailed off. *My place.* Despite the outstanding and filthy sex, she wanted more. She wanted skin on skin and Gideon's taste in her mouth. She wanted it all.

She nodded. "My place." She lifted her shaking hands to finish undoing her bustier, but Gideon beat her there. He undid the tiny clasps carefully, the delicate lace looking strange against his massive hands.

He slid it off her arms and folded it neatly on the bench next to her before giving the garter belt and stockings the same treatment. The panties finished off the pile.

He ran his hands up her legs. Lucy held her breath and arched her back a little. His pupils dilated, which was a reward in and of itself, but Gideon stood. "Get dressed." Then he was gone, snatching the lingerie off the bench and striding out the door, careful to not let it open too much.

She stared after him for a long moment before she dredged up the ambition to move. It was just as well he'd shown a little restraint or she had a feeling they wouldn't have left this dressing room for several hours. She wasn't sure if she was disappointed that he'd walked out or excited for what was to come.

Excited. Definitely excited.

She dressed quickly and paused to check her appearance in the mirror. Flushed cheeks, slightly wild eyes, skin a little too glowy. It was a good look, but there was no mistaking that she and Gideon had been up to no good behind the closed door. It was becoming a habit of theirs, though Lucy couldn't say she was sad about it. She liked the thrill of knowing there were people within hearing distance.

She liked that she was experiencing it with Gideon even more.

Lucy stopped short.

There it was. The thing she'd been doing her best not to think too hard about since their first time— since *before* their first time, if she was being honest. There'd always been an attraction simmering between her and Gideon, even when she'd been with Jeff. She'd gone out of her way to ensure she'd never given him any sign of it, because she'd been in a relationship.

Because she cared about Gideon as a friend, and if something had happened between them, she'd lose him.

There was no Jeff standing between them now, and her feelings for Gideon were significantly more complicated. There was lust, definitely. Her body craved his like she'd never craved anything—anyone—before.

But there were…feelings.

She gave herself a shake. It didn't matter if there were feelings or not. She'd set out the terms and Gideon had agreed to them. Changing the rules without notice meant she really *would* lose him and she hadn't come all this way to falter now. She'd missed him terribly these last couple of years, and the thought of going back to her life without him in it felt like she had a gaping hole in her chest.

Gideon wasn't the keeping kind. A lot had changed, but she couldn't afford to believe *that* had. He'd settle down someday, with the right woman, but he wasn't there yet. Even if he tried to give them a shot for her sake, it would self-destruct sooner rather than later.

No matter which way she looked at the situation, the end result was the same—if she changed the rules now, she would lose him. If she saw her original plan through to the end, she retained the chance to keep Gideon in her life.

Lucy would fight for that, even if it meant hurting herself to do so.

She took a deep breath and straightened her shoulders. *I can do this.* Lucy opened the change room door and marched out. Gideon stood by the entrance to the boutique and she headed his way, very carefully not looking for Agnes. They might be the only people in the shop, but they'd been in that room far too long to be doing anything but exactly what they'd been doing. *Focus, Lucy.* She licked her lips as she stopped next to Gideon. "My place?"

"I changed my mind."

She braced herself. "Oh?"

"That meal might have been sweet, but it won't sustain us for what I have in mind for later." He gave her a wolfish grin that had her warming even as she tried not to read into his words too much.

It won't sustain us.

He didn't mean anything by it—of that, Lucy was sure—but it served as yet another reminder that this was temporary and any effort to make it permanent would backfire spectacularly. She put on her best smile. "What's the plan, then?"

Gideon's grin dropped away and he studied her for a long moment, seeming to see through her façade. Finally he nodded, almost to himself. "Lunch. Then we'll head back to your place to finish what we started."

Not a brush-off, then, but a detour. She kept her shoulders from sagging through sheer stubbornness. "I could eat."

"Good." He touched the small of her back and ushered her out of the building. He didn't say anything as they walked down the street, and she was too twisted up inside her own head to try for conversation. Nothing she said right now would change the truth, and the weight of it threatened to send her scurrying back to her place to barricade herself in with Garfunkel and the work files she still had to find time for this weekend.

Their destination was a little restaurant on the second floor of a converted apartment building. They'd left most of the interior walls up and designed low lighting so that even in the middle of the afternoon, it gave the illusion of a night tucked away. The hostess led them to a room that might have been a closet at one point, though it had two doorways now and space for a little booth for two.

Gideon waited for her to slide in and then took the spot next to her. The hostess left and Lucy became aware of a low jazz song playing in the background. She ran her finger over the rough tabletop. "I didn't even know this place existed."

"It's new. A friend of mine bought the building a couple years back and construction just wrapped up a few months ago. The bottom floor is split into a clothing boutique and shoe store, and the third floor is privately owned."

She'd definitely come down here to check out the shoe store in the future. She twisted to face him, but he spoke before she could. "What happened back there?"

"Excuse me?"

"You know exactly what I'm talking about. You

were fine in the dressing room, and when you walked out, you'd put a wall up between us."

She desperately didn't want to talk about this, but his jaw was set in an all-too-familiar way. There would be no getting out of this conversation, short of crawling over the table and making a run for it. Since that was beneath Lucy's dignity—and she didn't know for certain that Gideon wouldn't just chase her down—she sighed. "We have clear boundaries."

"Mmm-hmm."

That response gave her no indication of what he thought of that, so she hedged. "Very clear boundaries."

Gideon drummed his fingers on the table. "Is the problem that you feel that I'm threatening the boundaries or that the boundaries themselves are the problem?"

Trust the man to just lay it out there with no qualms. She fought not to fidget. "I value our friendship. I know it may not seem like that after not speaking for two years, but I missed you terribly during that time and I feel like we're almost starting to reclaim that lost ground."

The guarded look on his face cleared. "You don't want to jeopardize our friendship."

"Exactly." She didn't mention the theoretical pending marriage or what their friendship might look like once she'd picked a man and followed through on that. The marriage might have sex included in the bargain, but it would still be a marriage without love. Having

Gideon in her life, even on the outskirts, wasn't something she was willing to give up.

Not now that she'd just gotten him back.

The waiter brought their waters and took their drink orders. Once the man disappeared through the doorway, Gideon turned back to her. "That gap in communication was as much my fault as it was yours. I let guilt get the better of me and figured that you didn't want to see my face any more than you wanted to see Jeff's."

"You…weren't wrong—at least, not at first." She'd been so hurt and angry and embarrassed that she hadn't wanted to see *anyone* for months after she'd broken off her engagement. The only person who'd ignored that was Becka, and even she'd had to come to Lucy. If Gideon had tried during that time, she would have slammed the door in his face.

By the time she'd gathered the strength to get back out into the world again, it was to find that her former friends had moved on without her. It made sense, in a way. She'd lost most of her good friends when she and Jeff had started dating—a sign she should have paid more attention to. He hadn't missed a beat after their breakup, and most of their friends had been his first, so they'd moved along with him.

It was Gideon's steady presence that she'd missed the most, but she hadn't known how to reach out to him.

Or if she even should.

I'm here now. We are here now.

She held herself steady. "Regardless, I feel like I just found you again."

"And you don't want to lose that." He said it almost as if musing to himself. When she tensed, he leaned back and slung an arm over the back of the booth. "I don't want to lose it, either, Lucy. I missed you, too. I'm still missing you, if we're going to be perfectly honest."

Her jaw dropped. "What are you talking about? I'm right here."

"Yes, you are." He pulled her closer, tucking her against his body. "But we haven't stopped to have a real conversation since you sat me down in your office and told me you wanted me to help you find a husband."

Lucy opened her mouth to say he was wrong, but stopped and thought hard about it. Was he? "We've... talked." But not like they used to. There had been nights where Jeff had passed out, or was occupied playing whatever his video game of the week was, and she and Gideon had sat and just talked. Shared things about themselves, about their dreams. She'd always chalked it up to being good friends—family, even—but even if they'd restarted their acquaintance, they hadn't reestablished the intimacy they'd once had.

Sex, yes.

Intimacy, no.

She frowned. "I guess you're right. God, I'm sorry, Gideon. I've been treating you like a prize stud."

He chuckled. "I haven't exactly complained. But

I do miss us, Lucy. Whatever version of your future you're aiming for, make room for me."

That startled a laugh out of her. "You're just as confident now as you were back then."

"Two years can change a person, but it can't *change* a person."

That was what she was afraid of. Lucy had fought hard to shed the timid woman she'd become while dating Jeff. She'd even mostly succeeded, if one didn't look too closely at her lack of dating. But she couldn't shake the fear that, deep down, she was still that mouse of a person who'd let her boyfriend say such horrible things to her—worse, who'd believed him when he did.

"I should have known." He spoke softly in the tiny space between them. "I said it before and I'll say it again—I knew Jeff was an asshole, but I didn't know the extent of it. I would have stepped in."

Her heart surged even as she shook her head. "If anyone should have seen the signs and stepped in, it was me. I let myself get taken in by him, and I almost married him because I was too stubborn and too naive to see him for what he was. If we're going to lay blame, there's plenty to go around." She covered his hand with hers. "I don't want to talk about Jeff anymore. He's taken up enough of both of our lives, and I don't want to give him even another second."

"I won't argue that." Gideon nudged her closer yet, until she was almost sitting in his lap. "I have the prettiest woman in all NYC sitting with me in a dark restaurant. I can think of a thousand things I'd rather say and do than talk about a piece of shit that we share a mutual history with."

She laid her hand on his thigh, enjoying the way the muscle clenched beneath his jeans. "I can think of a few things to add to the list." They were alone in this mini room within the restaurant. They could do anything they wanted to beneath the table and no one would be the wiser. "Gideon..." She slid her hand higher.

"Yeah?"

"What have you been up to since I saw you last?"

He blinked down at her as if he couldn't reconcile her ever-sliding hand with her words. Finally he relaxed, muscle by individual muscle. "After you and..." He looked away and back. "Two years ago, I looked at my life and decided I was done dicking around. I went after the biggest accounts I could find and went head-to-head with companies that had reputations stretching back before we were born." He laughed. "I figured I had nothing to lose, so I might as well aim for the stars."

"You've made quite the name for yourself." Even if her company didn't make a habit of contracting head-hunters to fill positions, Lucy would've had to be living under a rock not to hear news of Gideon. He'd beaten out several more well-known headhunters and developed an excellent reputation in the process. He always got his man—or woman, as it were.

God help the woman he finally sets his sights on. She won't stand a chance.

The thought was bittersweet in the extreme. Lucy

cared about him. She wanted him happy…but contemplating him with another woman made her want to throw things. *Stop that.*

He's yours for the duration.

That will have to be enough.

But what if it wasn't?

CHAPTER FOURTEEN

GIDEON INSISTED ON DESSERT, if only to keep things going for a little bit longer. Lucy must have felt the same way because she didn't hesitate before she picked a particularly delicious-sounding apple cobbler to his cheesecake. The waiter—who was getting a significant tip since he'd made himself scarce in between checking on them—took their order and hurried off. The restaurant had filled up, though the only evidence of it they had was a low murmur of conversation by people they couldn't see.

He curled a strand of Lucy's hair around his finger. "You said we needed to talk."

"Don't we?"

He'd always liked Lucy's directness. Even when she was highly uncomfortable with the subject— like sex—she still made an effort to cut through the bullshit and be as honest as possible. Now he almost wished that she was willing to let the slow slide of afternoon into evening go on without following through on her words this morning. Gideon should have known better. "Yeah, we do."

She met his gaze directly, never one to shy away from a potential confrontation. "Shall I go first or shall you?"

Though he was tempted to let her take the lead, that was the coward's way out. Gideon knew what he wanted and the only way to give him a snowball's chance in hell was to go for it without reservation. So he let go of her hair and sat back. "Pick me."

She blinked and then blinked again. "I'm sorry?"

"Screw the others guys and screw the list I put together. They won't make you happy like I can, and you know it. I know you as well as anyone, and we match up in the bedroom and out of it. Pick me." *I love you. I've always loved you.* He didn't say it. He'd already pressed his luck by putting his cards on the table. If he threw that at her, she'd be gone before he finished the sentence.

She leaned forward and then shook her head. "What are you saying?"

"You know what I'm saying. I want you. You want me. We fit, Lucy. You can't deny that it's true." He held himself still in an effort to keep from reaching for her. Crowding her now was a mistake and using sex to cloud her judgment was a dick move. Not one that he was above, but if he wanted a chance—a real chance—with her, he had to do this right.

As right as he could do it when they'd started this thing with her dating another guy and then restarted it by bargaining for sex lessons in addition to her attempting to marry another man.

When you put it like that...

Lucy put her hand to her mouth and dropped it as quickly. "I don't know what to say."

Hell, he really had overplayed it. He didn't retreat farther physically, though he wanted to. Instead, Gideon gave her an easy smile. "It's fine. We're fine."

"No, I don't think we are." She rubbed her hands over her face and looked at him, her blue eyes so bleak, it broke his fucking heart. "Gideon, even with all the crap in our history and the two-year separation, you're one of the closest friends I have. I *care* about you. I don't know what I'd do if I lost our friendship again and…" Her hands fluttered between them. "We have irreconcilable differences."

"What are you talking about?" He reined in his reaction until she could tell him exactly what the hell she meant by that. *I was never on that goddamn list.*

"When's the last time you dated someone for longer than a few weeks?"

He froze. "That's the measuring stick you're going to use against me? Fine, Lucy. I haven't dated anyone for longer than a few weeks. I've been focusing on my career, and before that, it was school." He shook his head, frustration reaching a boiling point. "It's pretty rich that you expect me to roll with your limited dating history, but mine is the reason you won't consider me."

"That's not what I meant." She tucked her hair behind her ear. "Okay, it's a little what I meant, but the core concept is still the same. What happens when I throw all my other options out the window and say yes to you? Are you planning on marrying me? Because that's still the endgame, and rather quickly. Even if you *are* willing to take that step, what happens in a few weeks, months, however long, when you get bored—or, heaven forbid, you meet someone who you might actually love?" Lucy slumped in the booth. "No, it's not worth the risk. You'd realize that if you took emotion out of your reaction."

That was the problem—Gideon couldn't take emotion out of the equation when it came to Lucy. He'd never been able to. "I wouldn't do that to you."

"Maybe not intentionally. But eventually you'd resent me for pushing you into this choice."

He took a calming breath and then another. "You're not giving me much credit here, Lucy." She thought she had it all figured out, and he couldn't say a damn thing to dissuade her because it'd just be used as evidence of either how unready he was for that kind of commitment, or how much she valued their friendship. *Struck down because she cares about me.*

That brought him up short.

He was being greedy, but hell. The thought of her with someone else when they *fit* drove Gideon out of his goddamn mind. He took her hand, noting the tension there. "You've given me the worst-case scenario, and I respect that. Let me paint you a different picture."

Lucy hesitated. "Okay."

"You pick me. We get married, figure out living arrangements. Nothing bad happens. In fact, our quality of life improves exponentially. We force ourselves to take a few breaks from work a year and travel a bit. We start working through that list I know you've put together. We make our house a home. Fuck, maybe we have some kids, too. And every night, it's just us. You and me."

Her lips curved in a faint smile. "I like how you added in my sexual bucket list."

"It's important." He ran his thumb over her knuckles. Gideon wanted the life he'd just described. He wanted to be able to shoot Lucy a text and meet her after work for dinner and then walk home together and make love on every goddamn surface of the place they shared. He wanted the lazy Sunday mornings and the long weekends away. He wanted to be able to call her when he nailed an account or to get her calls when she was victorious in court.

He wanted it all.

Lucy pressed her lips together. "What if it blows apart in our face?"

"What if it doesn't?" He kept stroking her knuckles as she relaxed against him, bit by bit. "But let's talk this out your way. You pick someone else. We stop sleeping together, but that tension isn't going to disappear. Your new husband—" the term soured his stomach "—picks up on the tension and it makes him uncomfortable. Because it will, Lucy. Even if the guy is interested in marriage in name only, he'll have a problem with it."

"But—"

"Trust me. He will draw the line in the sand, and you'll have to choose which side of it you're going to be on." Gideon hated seeing the worry all over her face, but if they were being real, it had to be said. "You'll pick him. You'll have to."

The waiter walked in carrying their desserts. He set them on the table, took one look at Gideon's and Lucy's faces and stepped back. "Let me know if you need anything. Enjoy." He dashed out of the room.

"I don't... This is too much." She picked up a fork and poked at her apple cobbler. "You just dropped a serious information bomb on me and I don't even know how to wrap my head around it."

"Then don't."

She twisted to look at him. "What are you talking about?"

"I'm not saying you need to make the decision this second." He nudged his dessert away. "But you need to stop thinking that I'm not an option. I am. Fuck, I'm the best option."

"Arrogant to the very end."

"I'm sure of my worth. I'm even surer of how good we'd be. We've more than proved it over the last two weeks."

"One of which you weren't even on the same side of the country." But she relaxed against him and allowed him to tuck her head against his shoulder. "I'll think about it, Gideon. I don't... I don't know if I can promise more than that."

"Don't let fear win, Lucy. You've gone down that road before and you already know how it ends."

The walk back to Lucy's place happened in a blur. She couldn't get Gideon's words out of her head and his big presence at her side eclipsed all else. He made it sound so simple—the easiest thing in the world. *Pick me.*

It wasn't that easy.

The picture he painted was an attractive one. More than attractive. She craved that life, craved the connection already strung between her and Gideon. But Lucy had seen firsthand how bad things could get when she let someone close and they turned on her. Gideon would never cheat on her—of that, she was certain—but there were so many ways a person could hurt someone they cared about. Most of the time, it was even unintentional.

If she married some near stranger and they did something careless or cruel, she could respond without missing a beat. They weren't close enough to hurt her. Gideon, though? He could cut her to the bone.

Aren't you tired of living in fear?

The voice in her head sounded a whole lot like his. She nodded absently at the doorman and led the way into her building. Fear had controlled every choice she'd made since she'd found out Jeff had been sleeping around on her. Fear that she'd never get out had prompted her to end things in a rather remarkable fight. Fear of failure had thrust her into a career that she might love but which she'd chosen for its earning potential. Fear of being hurt again kept her from giving dating more than a token effort.

What if she just…jumped?

Lucy unlocked her door and turned to him. "Come in?"

"Sure."

His presence filled her apartment, giving it a life that it seemed to miss when it was just her and Garfunkel there. The feline in question meandered up as if he just happened to be in the room at the same time they were. She bent to pick him up and turned to face Gideon. "What if we do a trial run?"

"Trial run." Neither his tone nor his body language gave even the slightest indication of what was going on in that beautiful head of his.

"Yes, a trial run." She warmed to the idea as she spoke. "I have a few months before I'll be down to the wire on this marriage business. A week or two shouldn't make much difference."

His eyebrows rose. "What do you think you'll know in two weeks that you don't know now?"

He had a point, but she wasn't about to admit it. Making any kind of decision right that second felt like too much too soon. She'd know in a week or two. She'd be *sure*—or as sure as Lucy ever was these days about things outside of the office. "What do you say?"

"Yes." He carefully extracted Garfunkel from her arms and set the cat free. Then he set his hands on her hips and pulled her slowly toward him until they stood bare inches apart. "I say yes, Lucy. If you need two weeks to figure this out one way or another, that's what you'll have."

Her throat tightened. "You're too good to me."

"You've got that backward." He sifted his fingers through her hair, tilting her head back so she lifted her face to him. "I'm taking you to bed now."

She blinked at the change in subject. But was it really

a change at all? Anything left to say would just be re-hashing what they'd already gone over. Left to her own devices, she'd drive them both crazy with her doubts. Better to let their obvious physical connection take over and push her worries to the back seat than to sabotage things before they had a chance to get started.

Gideon didn't wait for a response before sweeping her into his arms and striding back to her room. He carefully kicked the door shut, his gaze on the floor. "Woke up this morning to the damn cat watching me."

"He does that." She dragged her fingers through his hair and kissed his neck. "In his defense, you look absolutely marvelous while you sleep."

"You watched me while I slept?" He set her on the bed and backed up enough to pull her boots off, quickly followed by her leggings. "That's very creepy of you."

"You're in my apartment—that means I'm not creepy." She pulled her shirt off and tossed it away. "If I was standing on the fire escape outside your window and doing it, *that* would be creepy."

"A fair point." He nudged her onto her back and stripped slowly.

Lucy propped herself on her elbows. "Have I mentioned lately how much I enjoy you in flannel?"

"It might have come up once or twice." He dropped the shirt onto the floor and started on his jeans. "Careful there, or you might look up one day and realize I've grown a beard and started wearing thick-rimmed black glasses."

She laughed. "You don't even need glasses."

"My point stands." He hooked the back of her thighs and slid her farther onto the bed. She expected him to follow her to the mattress, but Gideon stepped back. He pointed at her. "Don't move."

"Okay…" She froze when he went to her nightstand and unerringly opened the bottom drawer. When he straightened, he had her pink vibrator in his hand. She shivered. "Oh."

He examined it. "This isn't a design I'm familiar with."

"You—"

He chuckled. "Give me some credit. I can figure out how it works." He thumbed it on, his grin widening. "Brilliant." He joined her on the bed and took up a position next to her with his head propped on his hand. "Spread your legs."

"This feels…" When he didn't immediately jump in, she had to search for something to fill the space. "Naughty." It wasn't quite the right word, but it fit.

"More or less than bending over that table and offering your ass to me?"

Her entire body went hot at both the memory and his words. "I'm not sure. It's not the same thing." There was no one here except them. No one to potentially walk in or witness. It didn't make the encounter less hot, but it had a different flavor as a result.

Gideon traced her puckered nipples with his gaze. "More or less than stroking yourself on a video chat with me?"

She gave a mock frown even as her breathing picked up. "You've made your point."

"Have I?" He ran his thumb over the circular silicone portion of the vibrator. "I still have a few points to make. Spread your legs wider."

She paused just long enough to have his brows slant down—the reaction she was aiming for—and then obeyed. The heat in his dark eyes was nothing compared to the inferno blasting into existence beneath her skin. *What if it was always like this?* He pressed the vibrator to her clit before the thought could take root. The silicone perfectly circled her clit, the vibrations drawing a moan from her lips. The fact that it was *Gideon* wielding it only made the entire situation that much hotter.

"How often do you use this on yourself?"

She arched half off the bed when he lifted it away. "Often. Don't tease me. I was so close."

He grinned wickedly. "I know."

"Gideon." She couldn't stand the teasing even as she loved it.

"Next time we go out—" he touched the vibrator to her clit long enough to have pleasure almost cresting and then took it away again "—wear what I bought you today under your dress. Halfway through dinner, I'm going to tell you to take off your panties and slip them into my pocket."

She couldn't catch her breath. "Tricky."

"I have a better idea." He set the toy aside and idly stroked her with his fingers. "There's a blackout restaurant I've been interested in trying."

How he could talk so calmly when she was in

danger of going out of her skin was beyond her. "Gideon—"

He shoved two fingers into her, drawing a cry from her lips. "I'll spend the entire dinner fucking you with my fingers right there at the table. You'll have to be quiet or the other diners will hear you." He stroked her and slid her wetness up to circle her clit before pushing back into her again. "Though, if *they're* too quiet, they'll be able to hear exactly what I'm doing to you."

She reached for him, only to have him use his free hand to press the vibrator into hers. "Show me."

It took three tries to get her shaking fingers to operate it while he kept fucking her with his fingers the same way he'd described. She could picture exactly how it would feel to sit in perfect darkness, her dress up around the tops of her thighs, Gideon's big hand palming her pussy as he gave the waiter their order with none the wiser. She froze. "Don't the waitstaff have night-vision goggles?"

He guided her hand with the vibrator to her clit, waiting until she'd placed it perfectly to respond. "Yes. They'll be able to see every single thing I'm doing to you."

Her orgasm exploded through her. Lucy's back bowed and she fumbled the toy, but Gideon was there, his fingers still inside her as he repositioned it and sent another wave of pure bliss through her. "Oh, my God." She thrashed, though she couldn't say if she was trying to get away from him or closer. "Oh, God. Gideon. Please. Stop. Don't stop."

A thunk sounded as the vibrator hit the floor and

then his mouth was there, soothing her oversensitized clit in long strokes. She laced her fingers through his hair, riding his face. "What are you doing to me? I don't… I feel completely out of control."

He lifted his head just enough to say, "I have no control with you, either, Lucy. I feel like a fucking animal. I can't get enough of you."

"Then get up here." She tugged on his hair. "You want me? Then take me."

Gideon hadn't bothered with a plan when it came to seducing Lucy into seeing things his way. All his damn plans went right out the window the second their clothes came off. Now, looking up her body into those blue eyes demanding he take her, he wished for a plan. This whole day was special. The start of their trial run. But more than that, it was the first time they'd spent time together without someone else between them.

Just Gideon and Lucy.

He wanted her to know how important that was to him, how close to perfect today had been. How much he cared about her. How much he wanted her in every way, body and soul.

In the end, Gideon did the only thing he could do. He crawled up her body and kissed her. She met him eagerly, her body already shifting to accommodate his, her legs wrapping around his waist and her hands coasting down his back to dig her fingers into his ass. As if they'd done this a thousand times before and would do it another thousand times.

"Condom," he rasped.

"I'm clean." Her lips brushed his with every word. "And…well, I'm on birth control."

He went still. "What are you saying?" There was no room for misunderstanding—not here, not now.

Lucy kissed one side of his mouth and then the other. "If…"

"I'm clean. I haven't been with anyone since the last time I was tested." He hadn't done anything to disabuse her of the notion since it'd be wasted breath, but Gideon hadn't had much interest in sleeping around in the last couple of years. He hadn't been celibate, but the demon driving him had disappeared right around the time Lucy had vanished from his life.

"I don't want barriers between us. I want you—all of you."

He wanted that, too. So bad, he could fucking taste it. "You're sure."

She wedged her hand between them and stroked his cock once, twice, before guiding him to her entrance. "I'm sure."

He didn't ask again. Gideon kissed her as he slid into her, inch by inch. There were no words to express his feelings at her trust in him. From the very beginning, she'd trusted him, but this was something else entirely. He kissed her with everything he had, everything he couldn't say. And then he began to move.

She rose to meet each thrust, their bodies moving in a dance as old as time, neither of them willing to break the kiss. He laced his fingers through her hair to tip her face for a better angle. She raked her nails over his ass, urging him to move faster, harder.

It was like flipping a switch.

He froze for one eternal second. Lucy nipped his bottom lip. "Stop being so careful with me. I can take it."

He knew that. Of course he knew that. Gideon tightened his grip on her hair with one hand, tilting her head to the side so he had access to her neck. He dragged his mouth down the line and then bit her shoulder. "Teeth?"

"Yes." She let loose a shaky laugh. "Just don't mark up where anyone can see."

Which was as good as saying that she *did* want him to mark her somewhere.

Gideon rolled onto his back, taking her with him, and slammed her down onto his cock. "Fuck me." He sat up enough to palm her breasts as she did what he commanded. Gideon sucked her nipple hard, urged on by her fingers in his hair and her hips slamming down onto him again and again. He took as much of her breast into his mouth as he could and bit her. Lucy cried out, her pussy squeezing him as she came.

He wasn't through.

He flopped her onto her stomach and yanked her to the edge of the bed. Gideon guided his cock back into her, paused to kick her feet a little wider and press his hand to the small of her back, and then he started to move.

He fucked her. There was no other word for it. She wanted it hard, and her hands fisting her comforter and the cries slipping from her lips only drove him on. He became a wild thing, slamming into her over and over again, driven toward a release he couldn't have stopped if he'd tried.

It wasn't enough. He was so damn close, and it wasn't enough.

Gideon covered her with his body, reaching around to bracket her throat with one hand while he slipped the other between her thighs and pinched her clit. "You're mine, Lucy. *Mine*." The move bent her backward and she twisted to give him her mouth.

"Yes, yes." She bucked against him, grinding herself against his hand. "Yours. Always. God, Gideon, don't stop."

"Never. I'll never fucking stop."

CHAPTER FIFTEEN

A LAZY SUNDAY morning was the only thing Gideon wanted, but he'd agreed to breakfast with Roman weeks ago. He left Lucy a note and brewed her a pot of coffee before heading out. An hour—two, tops— and he'd be back with her. Simple.

He still had to talk himself out of turning around seven different times during the cab ride—and again when he climbed out onto the sidewalk. The limited timeline Lucy gave him rattled around in his head, and he had the irrational fear that if he didn't spend every second with her that he could scrape out, it wouldn't be enough and she'd leave.

She's not leaving yet. I have time.

Not enough. Never enough.

Roman stood outside the little hole-in-the-wall place, staring at a pair of guys smoking just down the way. Gideon stopped next to him. "You quit."

"I know that. Doesn't mean I don't miss it sometimes."

"Miss the ability to breathe a whole lot more when you end up with lung cancer."

Roman rolled his hazel eyes. "Yeah, got it. Thanks, Mom."

"How's your mother doing?"

"Same as always. *Just swimmingly, darling.*" He gave a spot-on impression of his mother's breathy, high voice. Roman opened the door. "She and my old man are on that goddamn yacht somewhere. The Caribbean this week—either Saint Lucia or Jamaica."

"Worse ways to spend your retirement." He followed his friend into the brightly lit restaurant. If one could call Frank's a restaurant. There were exactly two tables and three chairs, and in all Gideon's time of coming here, he'd never seen them empty. Most people took their food to go, which was what he and Roman did. They turned left without bothering to talk about it—it was always the direction they took when they managed to carve time out of their schedules for this sort of thing.

They both finished their breakfast sandwiches by the end of the first block. Roman barely waited for them to cross the street before he started in. "What are you doing with Lucy?"

"None of your damn business."

"No, it's not, but you know me well enough to know that I'm not going to leave it alone. Explain. Now."

Gideon stopped walking and turned to face his friend. He didn't like the set of Roman's jaw or the tight way he held himself. "Why are you pissed?"

"Everyone with eyes in their head has seen the way you've watched her since she came into our group.

You've had a thing for her for as long as we've known her."

He crossed his arms over his chest. "You have a point. Get to it."

"My point is that you agreed to find her a husband—that's it. A husband that is from the agreed-upon list that I helped you put together." When he didn't immediately jump in, Roman glared. "I may be pretty, but I'm not stupid. You dragged her into the back room at Vortex and you two had sex, which means you've crossed so many damn lines, you're too deep into it to realize exactly how much you're fucking up."

He wasn't fucking up. He might have changed the rules with her, but she was on the same page he was. *More or less.* It was the "less" that worried Gideon. Lucy had put it all out there yesterday—her fears about the future and what it might mean for them—and he'd essentially steamrolled her.

Admitting that to himself and admitting it to Roman were two very different things.

Roman, damn him, knew it. He shook his head. "She gave you an opening and you just went for it, didn't you? Didn't bother to stop and think about the damage you were dealing because you were too busy thinking with your cock."

Enough was enough. "I would never hurt Lucy."

"You're hurting her *right now.*" Roman raked his hand through his hair. "We all stood by while that piece of shit ran around on her, and we have to live with that. There's no making it right—not really—but she came to you for help, Gideon. You do anything else than give her exactly the help she wanted and you're just as bad as he is."

No need to clarify the "he" Roman meant. Gideon gave his head a sharp shake. "It's not the same."

"Isn't it? You and me—and even him, though I hate to include Jeff in anything—are not good men. We're just not. We never have been—you don't get as far in the world as we've gotten without throwing people under the bus along the way. I've made my peace with that, and I thought you had, too, but you've always had a white knight complex when it came to Lucy. *She* is good—as good as anyone is. She deserves a hell of a lot better than she's gotten up to this point, and that means we owe her."

"Fuck, will you listen to yourself?" Gideon knew all that. How could he not, when he'd thought it himself over and over again for years? But hearing Roman say it felt different. Real. As if Gideon really had been deluding himself all this time by thinking things could work out between him and Lucy. "She and I just work."

Roman's eyes didn't hold a shred of sympathy. "For how long? How long until she wakes up one morning and realizes you pulled one over on her? She asked you for help, and instead of doing what you promised, you used her needing you to leverage a place in her life. That's shitty, Gideon. If our positions were reversed, you'd tell me the same thing."

He started to react, but stopped short. If Roman had come to him with news that Lucy had approached him for help, and he'd ended up sleeping with her and sabotaging her matchmaking plans… "I would have punched you in those perfect teeth."

Roman rubbed his jaw. "You have a wicked right hook."

He didn't smile, though it couldn't be more obvious that his friend was trying to lighten the mood.

Gideon tossed his garbage into a trash can and stared at the street. "I didn't set out to do this." *I love her.* But what did his feelings matter when he hadn't taken hers into account? Lucy'd had years of playing second fiddle to some asshole—she didn't need Gideon coming in and starting a replay, regardless of his intentions. He'd never cheat on her, would do everything in his power to make her happy.

She didn't choose me.

That was what it came down to. If she'd given him any indication that she had started this process with some sort of feelings for him beyond friendship, he would have a right to ask for more. Yesterday she'd even gone so far as to try to explain that she didn't want to lose him as a friend, and he'd leveraged that fear into getting her to agree to give them a trial run.

His shoulders slumped. "Fuck me, you're right."

"I'm not saying it to be a dick." For once, Roman sounded downright apologetic. "You're my friend, and if she was any other woman, I'd say to hell with her plans—play dirty. But this isn't any other woman. This is Lucy we're talking about."

And, because it was Lucy, that changed everything. Gideon took out his phone and stared at it for a few moments. He knew what he had to do. The honorable thing—the thing he'd promised to do.

He had to set her up with another man.

Lucy woke up disorientated. The day before had been an emotional roller coaster, and she'd seriously looked forward to spending a lazy Sunday with Gideon, letting their time together ease her concerns over the whole thing.

Then she'd woken up alone.

She touched the side of the bed Gideon had slept on, but it was long since cold. Telling herself there was nothing to worry about, she went through her morning routine and then headed into the kitchen. A full pot of coffee sat waiting, along with a sticky note with a hastily written explanation. "Breakfast with Roman. Back soon." Lucy smiled a little and poured herself a cup of coffee. If he was occupied for a little bit, it wouldn't hurt to check her emails and make sure there was nothing requiring her immediate attention.

He still hadn't arrived by the time she was done with that, so she scrambled up a pair of eggs and went back to work on her files. Normally she had no problem losing herself in the facts she was compiling, but Lucy couldn't help keeping one eye on the clock as an hour stretched into two.

Did Gideon feel as strangely about what happened yesterday as she did?

Maybe he had regrets.

She wished he was there so his presence could keep her from second-guessing every single thing she'd said or done yesterday. Had she been too honest at dinner? He'd said he wanted honesty, but there was honesty and *honesty.* The sex had been even more outstanding than she'd come to expect, both the tender touches and murmured words and the rough and possessive…

"Stop it." She poured herself a third cup of coffee and headed for her living room. Obsessing over what Gideon did or did not regret would only drive her crazy. *Crazier.*

Work would steady her. Work *always* steadied her. It was her job that had gotten her through the worst times of her life, the ability to lose herself in the facts and how to use them to create the story she wanted the judge or jury to believe.

Except this time it didn't work.

Lucy kept glancing at her phone, waiting for a call or a text or, hell, a smoke signal. Something from Gideon. Something to prove that he didn't think this whole thing was a terrible mistake. Something to reassure *her* from deciding she needed to find a different way to accomplish her aims.

When her phone finally buzzed, she dropped the paper she'd been staring at for five minutes without reading and snatched it up. It was from Gideon, but only a few words.

The Blue Lagoon 7pm.

She hesitated, wondering if she'd missed something, and typed out a quick reply.

Dinner?

Yes. Wear something nice.

Lucy waited, but no information was forthcoming. She glanced at the clock. Two hours until he wanted her there. *Where has the day gone?* She could keep pretending to work, but the nerves bouncing in her stomach spoke of the futility of it. Something had changed with Gideon, and she wasn't sure it was a good sign.

Yesterday he'd been almost in her face with how much he wanted her—wanted *this*—and now he was playing least-in-sight. She'd thought Gideon was too direct a man to ever disappear on a woman, but she should have known better.

She'd watched him do it before, hadn't she?

She and Jeff even used to joke about the Gideon Special. He'd grow distant from whoever he was dating, showing up more and more at their place, and if the woman didn't allow him to fade gracefully away, he'd take her out for dinner and cut it off.

Kind of like the dinner he had planned with Lucy tonight.

She shot to her feet. "No. I'm being paranoid." Gideon wouldn't have said the things he'd said if he was planning on turning around and dumping her on her ass. He wouldn't have changed the perfectly good set of rules to push her to put her heart on the line.

Oh, my God. My heart is on the line.

She sat down heavily. She'd known she cared about

him, of course—hard to be friends and not care about someone—but her heart being in danger had nothing to do with friendship and everything to do with deeper feelings.

Real feelings.

The same kinds of feelings that made a person blind to another's faults and left them emotionally bloodied and bruised. She didn't want that. She'd actively worked to *avoid* that.

And yet here she was.

She got ready, mostly to escape the doubt plaguing her. It was fear talking—it had to be. Having a meltdown about their first speed bump during this trial dating thing they had going was just going to prove how unready to date or marry Lucy really was.

Obviously something had come up with Gideon that required his attention and prevented him from coming back to spend the day with her. Just as obviously, if it was important enough to need his presence then it would make his sending her a bunch of texts impossible. He'd arranged dinner tonight and paused in whatever he was doing long enough to let her know that they had plans, and *that* was a good sign.

She was overreacting.

Simple.

But she didn't feel any better two hours later when she stood in front of the Blue Lagoon, shivering in the cold beneath her thick coat. *This is fine. Everything is fine.* She walked inside and gave Gideon's name. The host smiled welcomingly and led her to a semi-private corner.

Lucy caught sight of a man sitting there already, but her steps stuttered when she realized he wasn't Gideon. *What the hell?* There was nothing to do but keep following the host. She started to reach for his arm to let him know that there had been some mistake, but as they came even with the table, she recognized the man. *Aaron Livingston.*

No. Oh, Gideon. Why?

She had to fight to keep her expression neutral as Aaron rose and smiled. "Lucy, it's been a while."

"I'm surprised you remember." She let him pull out her chair, her mind racing a million miles a minute. Gideon had set this up. It should have gone without saying, but she still couldn't wrap her mind around it. Twelve hours ago he'd told her that he wanted her to pick him—only him—and now he'd set her up with another man.

Aaron resumed his seat. "It's been a few years, but you're not a woman one forgets." He smiled charmingly, and though she could recognize why *BuzzFeed* had labeled him one of the hottest bachelors in NYC, his perfect features did nothing for her.

They also did nothing to explain why he was *here*.

You know why he's here, just like you know what it means.

If she was a better person, she'd sit and make small talk with Aaron and keep her eye on the prize—the whole reason she'd put this plan into motion in the first place. A husband.

But Lucy couldn't focus on anything beyond the fact that Gideon had set her up. She lasted a full thirty seconds before she pushed back her chair and rose. "I am so sorry, Aaron, but I've got to go."

"Go...?" Those keen dark eyes took her in. "You didn't realize you were meeting me, did you?"

"I'm really very sorry." She headed for the exit as quickly as she could without actually running. Lucy made it onto the street before she found her phone at the bottom of her purse. She dialed Gideon's number and listened to it ring and ring and ring before clicking over to voice mail. She hung up without leaving a message.

That was the moment she should have stopped. It was clear Gideon didn't want her, that he'd misled her horribly. She didn't give a flying fuck. He didn't get to put her in this position and then avoid dealing with the fallout.

She scrolled through her contacts to find Roman's number. It wasn't one she'd used more than once, and that was years ago when she'd planned Jeff's surprise birthday party. *I was such an idiot. Apparently, I am still an idiot.* She dialed, holding her breath as it rang. He'd probably changed his number by now—most people did at one time or another.

But she recognized the cultured, masculine voice that answered. "Lucy?"

She lifted her arm to hail a cab. "You're going to tell me where he is, Roman, and you're going to tell me right this instant."

CHAPTER SIXTEEN

THE SECOND GIDEON heard the buzzer being pressed repeatedly, he knew it was Lucy. He hadn't even tried to hide. He'd known what he was doing today and, as sick to his stomach as it made him, Roman was right—it was the right thing to do. Hurt her a little now and set her back on the path she'd carved out for herself.

Knowing that did nothing to prepare him for the fury on her face when he opened the door. "Lucy."

"No, you do not get to *Lucy* me as if nothing's changed." She pushed into the apartment and spun to face him. "What the hell was that tonight, Gideon?"

He kept his expression stoic, knowing it would make everything worse. "I'm just doing what you contracted me for."

She actually took a step back. "You've got to be kidding me. You're going to take that stance now? What happened to you wanting me to pick *you*?"

"I was wrong." It actually hurt to say the words aloud, and it hurt more to see the naked pain on her face. He forced himself to keep talking. *A little hurt now, rather than a big hurt later.* "This was fun, but you were right when you pointed out that I'm not the keeping kind." She'd survived her breakup with Jeff. She'd bounce back even faster from this mistake with him.

Because that was how she'd see it in a few weeks—a mistake, a bullet dodged.

"You're serious." Lucy shook her head. "What happened between leaving my bed and writing me a note and…" She trailed off. "What did Roman say to you?"

She always had been smart. He let nothing show on his face. "He didn't have to say anything. A little distance was all I needed to realize that we aren't suited."

"Aren't suited." She pressed a hand to her chest as if he'd reached out and hit her there. Gideon felt like he had. She finally took a deep breath and lifted her chin. "You're a coward, Gideon Novak."

He flinched. "What the hell are you talking about?"

"You. Are. A. Coward." He could actually see her putting the pieces of herself back into place, though her bottom lip quivered, just a little. "Last night was too good and, I'll be honest—it scared me, too. But the difference between you and me is that *I* fought that fear and focused on how good it could be." She raked him with her gaze. "I'm not fighting for this. I spent too long fighting to be with someone who didn't even try. I won't do that again, Gideon. This was barely a bump in the road and you've already jumped ship. Fine. So be it." Her lower lip quivered again, but she made an obvious effort to still it. "I chose you, and you didn't choose me."

It felt like she'd stabbed him and twisted the blade. "Lucy—"

"No. Your actions speak just as clearly as your words and I'm not stupid. I understand." She drew herself up. "Consider our contract terminated. Keep the fee for all I care, as long as I never see you again."

Gideon watched her walk out of his apartment—and out of his life. He shut the door softly behind her and walked to his kitchen and stared blankly out the window. *It's done.* Something that took so much effort to coax into being, decimated in the course of a single day.

He braced his hands on the edge of the counter, an anchor to keep from chasing her down and trying to explain. There was no explaining this in a way that accomplished the severing of their relationship and left her pissed off enough to leave him behind for good. As much as he'd hated hearing it, Roman was right. Gideon hadn't been thinking straight from the second Lucy contacted him. If he had been, he would have set her up with someone else for her matchmaking needs. He wasn't qualified for either of the things she needed from him, and he sure as fuck wasn't an unbiased party.

Letting his own selfish needs overshadow hers, and then convincing her to see things his way…

Yeah, there was no explaining that away. Cutting Lucy loose was the best thing he could have done for her.

He let his head drop between his shoulders. The best thing for Lucy, but he'd be riding this wave of pain for the foreseeable future. Getting out of town might help, but the memories of what they'd done here and elsewhere would still be waiting to ambush him when he returned.

No, better to stay and push through the worst of it.

A band around his chest formed, blisteringly hot and so tight he exhaled in a rush. He'd just ended things with Lucy.

Ended for good.

Gideon slumped against the counter. He'd known that woman for six damn years. Had been respectful of her relationship with Jeff and never said so much as a word out of line. Had backed the fuck off and left her alone after things had imploded so she wouldn't have to look at his face and see a constant reminder of the lies she'd fielded.

Through it all, a small part of him had been sure that it would work out. One way or another, he'd find a path to Lucy. That he'd win her if he was just patient enough.

He huffed out a pained laugh. He should have known better. He'd been so busy putting her on a pedestal, he hadn't stopped to ask what *she* wanted. Worse. He'd ignored what she'd wanted in favor of his own desires being met.

She hadn't picked him.

If he hadn't forced the issue, if he'd just stayed in the place she'd designated for him, he could have maintained their friendship. Would it be painful watching her marry another man? Fuck yes. It would have ripped his still-beating heart out of his chest to smile and congratulate her on picking a man who'd do as a husband.

But less painful than standing there, realizing he was never going to see her again.

Lucy wandered the streets for hours. She'd intended to go home, but the thought of four walls closing her in was too much to bear. It wasn't any better on the street—the city itself boxed her into place, preventing her from running until she couldn't breathe, couldn't think, was too tired to process the level of Gideon's betrayal.

He blamed himself for not telling her about Jeff's cheating sooner. She knew that. She'd even used that to ensure he wouldn't say no to helping her.

She'd also foolishly assumed that, when push came to shove, he'd get over it.

Lucy looked up and breathed a sigh that wasn't quite relief. She dug out her phone and called. Her sister answered on the first ring. "What's up?"

"I don't suppose you're home?"

All joking disappeared from Becka's voice. "Yes. What's wrong? What happened?"

Burning started in her throat, making it hard to swallow. "Buzz me up?"

"Yeah, right away."

She hung up before her sister's concern had her breaking down in the street. The walk up the rickety stairs to the tiny apartment Becka insisted she loved was a lesson in torture. As if her body knew she was almost safe and had decided now was the perfect time to break down completely.

Becka opened the door as she lifted her hand to knock. Her sister wore a pair of brightly printed work-out pants and a sports bra with more straps than was strictly necessary. Lucy stopped short. "You have class."

"I already got someone to cover for me, so don't even think of turning around." She stepped back. "Now, get in here and tell me everything while I make some tea I threw together this weekend."

That almost brought a smile to Lucy's face. "Is it better than the last batch?"

"The last batch was the exception to the rule, though thank you very much for reminding me of it." She made a face. "I couldn't get the taste of licorice out of my mouth for days, no matter how many times I brushed my teeth and drowned myself in mouthwash."

"Live and learn." Her voice caught, because living and learning was exactly what Lucy *hadn't* done. She'd been so sure she knew her path, and yet the first chance she had to take a detour that would ruin everything, she'd jumped in headfirst.

"Sit. Immediately." Becka took her coat and purse and tossed them onto the threadbare couch. Then she guided Lucy into a chair at the small dining room table and headed for the stove. The loft apartment meant Lucy only had to rotate a little to keep her sister in view.

Becka got hot water going in an ancient-looking kettle and doled out loose leaf tea into two wire tea steepers. The few minutes it took to get the water boiling was enough to calm Lucy's racing thoughts a little. "I'm sorry to drop in like this."

"What are sisters for if not to be there when you need them?" Becka poured the hot water into two mugs and brought them to the table. "This is about Gideon."

She started to deny it, but what was the point? She'd locked down everything after the Jeff fiasco, and all it had done was completely isolate her from the world. Maybe talking through it with her sister was the right choice.

"I... He changed the rules on me. I had a fully fleshed-out plan, and every intention of following through on it, but I didn't anticipate *him*. Our connection. He showed every evidence of wanting more with me—we even talked about it and he said so in as many words—and then I wake up this morning to find him gone." She had to stop and focus on breathing for several moments. Even with the break, when she spoke again, her voice was strained. "I thought we were meeting tonight, but when I showed up to dinner, he'd set me up with another man."

Becka's blue eyes, so like Lucy's, went wide. "I think you're going to have to rewind to the part when you woke up alone. You had *sex* with Gideon?"

She'd left out that part of the plan, hadn't she? Lucy cleared her throat and stared at the ever-darkening water of her tea. "We've been sleeping together since the initial agreement. It started out as a way to get my confidence back sexually, but things...changed."

"They'll do that when sex is involved." She shot her sister a look, and Becka gave her wide eyes. "Not that I would know, of course. Your dear little sister is most definitely one hundred percent a virgin."

She snorted. "I'd believe that if I hadn't caught you and…what was his name?"

"Johnny Cash." Becka laughed. "Don't look at me like that. I know it wasn't his real name, but I was eighteen and he was hot." Her smile fell away. "So Gideon pulled a bait and switch on you? That's seriously shitty, Lucy. I never pegged him for the type to play games like that, but I've been wrong before."

"We Baudin women don't have the best of tastes in men."

"You can say that again."

She was tempted to let them skirt into safer territory, but the raw feeling inside her only got worse with each minute that passed.

Lucy pulled her mug closer. "I promised myself that I wouldn't fall in love again—that I wouldn't even put myself in the position to do so. Feelings and caring on that depth only cause pain. I didn't expect him. I couldn't fight against the connection or the way he made me feel." The burning in her throat got worse. "I thought we had a chance, Becka. A real chance. That maybe I didn't miss my chance at a happily-ever-after, and maybe it could be with Gideon."

"Oh, Lucy."

She laughed, the sound vaguely liquid with unshed tears. "That's very foolish, isn't it?"

"It's hopeful. There's nothing wrong with hope."

Except it was hope that had gotten her into this situation. It was because of hope that every beat of her heart felt as if someone were stabbing her. Hope had driven her to lay her heart bare for Gideon, and it'd gotten crushed in the process.

She took a drink, ignoring the way the hot water scalded her mouth. A small pain compared to her emotional wounds. "Screw hope. I want nothing to do with it anymore."

CHAPTER SEVENTEEN

Gideon didn't look up as the door to his office slammed open. "Whatever it is, I don't want to hear about it." Keeping the damn door shut in the first place should have been enough to discourage anyone from coming in—anyone except Roman, that was.

But when he finally looked up, it wasn't Roman kicking the door shut behind him.

It was Becka Baudin.

He stared for a long moment and shook his head. "No. Whatever you have to say to me has already been said, so get out."

"It might have been said, but it wasn't said by me." She ignored his command and marched over to drop into the chair across the desk. She wore tennis shoes and neon-green workout shorts tiny enough to have him concerned about frostbite. When she shrugged out of her huge coat, she revealed a fitted tank top in an equally eye-searing pink. How it managed not to clash with her bright blue hair was beyond him.

"What the hell are you doing, walking around New

York in *January* wearing that? You're going to freeze your ass off."

She blinked and then shook her head. "You have a lot of nerve. I could appreciate that if you weren't such an overbearing, selfish asshole." Becka jumped back to her feet. Gideon caught several of the men from the cubicles gravitating toward the windows of his office and stalked over to close the blinds.

"Put on some damn clothes."

She pointed at him. "Sit your ass down and listen to what I have to say, and then I'll leave and take my apparently inadequately clothed body with me." Becka pulled her ponytail tighter. "What the hell are you doing with my sister?"

"Nothing."

"No, shit." She looked like she wanted to throw something at him. "You know, Lucy doesn't get why you pulled that sneaky little trick with the date."

"I—"

"But *I* do." Becka paced from one side of his office to the other. "I might not have been around her and Jeff as much as you were, but I was around enough. I know you've been holding a flame for my big sister for years, and I know *you* were the one who broke the news to her about Jeff being a cheating bastard."

He started to cut in, but she spoke over him. Again. "That must have been a head trip for you, huh? Hard to break up their relationship, even if it was the right thing to do, because you were in love with your cheating best friend's girl. That muddies the waters."

"Actually—"

"I am not through." She glared, her blue eyes practically luminescent. "When I'm done talking, then you get to talk. Until then, sit down and shut up."

He didn't sit, but he did give her a short nod. Obviously she wasn't going to be deterred from whatever she was trying to accomplish. After what he'd done to Lucy, the least he could do was stand here and take a verbal lashing from her sister. "Fine."

"Good." She took another lap from one side of his office to the other. "So, you're carrying around a boatload of guilt, and playing the martyr and letting her try to move on with her life." She shot him a look. "Martyrs aren't sexy, by the way."

She sure as hell wasn't holding back. "Noted."

"So, as my sister is telling me the insane deal she put together with you, I can't help wondering what your motivation was. For screwing her, I get that—it was fulfilling a lifelong dream."

He couldn't let that stand. "No."

She stopped. "No? Which part? Screwing my sister being a lifelong dream or—"

"Stop saying that. Fuck, Becka. I didn't manipulate your sister into bed with me. *She* came to *me*."

She propped her hands on her hips. "Aha. It wasn't the sex, then. It's the guilt." She pursed her lips. "Guilt isn't any sexier than martyrdom."

"Why are you here, Becka?" He needed her to get to the point of this verbal thrashing so she'd leave. She wasn't saying anything Gideon hadn't already gone over more times than he could count. He'd replayed every step and second-guessed every action. It all added up to a mistake he couldn't take back.

He still wasn't sure if the mistake was agreeing to help Lucy—or leaving her.

"My point is that you love the shit out of my sister and have for years, but you decided to be the guilty martyr and make an executive decision about what she *should* have." She stared him down. "Tell me I'm wrong."

"She should—"

"Sweet baby Jesus." Becka rolled her eyes. "Here's a tip—take 'should' out of your vocabulary when you talk about my sister and her future. You might care about her, but ultimately, you don't get a vote. She's an adult. She can make her own choices. And she chose *you*, you asshat." She shook her head. "The question is whether *you* are willing to choose her instead of your idealized version of her." She snatched up her coat. "If I had a mic, I'd drop it, but you get the picture. Woman up or don't, but unless you have a good grovel prepared, I don't want to ever hear about you contacting my sister again." She strode out the door, leaving a trail of startled and appreciative gazes behind her.

Gideon dropped into the chair behind his desk and stared at his dark monitor. Becka hadn't said anything he didn't already know. And yet...

And yet.

He drummed his fingers on the desk. The last twenty-four hours since the fallout with Lucy had been the worst of his life. He hadn't slept. Food wasn't of interest. He hadn't even been able to work up the resolve to get good and drunk. Every time he turned around, he caught a trail of her summery scent, and the few times he'd been on the street, he'd looked for her distinctive stride even though he knew better.

He'd had his dream in the flesh—Lucy in his bed and in his life—and it'd been better than he could have imagined. He already knew she was driven and kind and had a sense of humor. He knew she loved Chinese takeout and discovering little hole-in-the-wall restaurants no one had ever heard of. He knew her parents were MIA, but she had a wonderful relationship with her sister.

He couldn't have anticipated the passion that flared between them. Hoped, yes, but even that hadn't encompassed reality. Lucy met him every step of the way, *challenged* him every step of the way. She brought fun into the bedroom even as she made him crazy in the best way possible.

And now he'd never touch her again. He'd never be able to show her a new place that he discovered. Never call just to chat with her because he was thinking of her. Never spend those fantasy lazy Sundays they kept talking about.

He'd done that.

There's no one to blame here but me. I had it all and I shit it away.

Even if he tried to make things right, Lucy would likely tell him to get lost. She *should* tell him…

He went still. *Fuck me, Becka is right.* He and Lucy had been doing just fine before he'd started obsessing over what *should* happen rather than what *was* happening.

He'd done this. He'd ruined it.

Gideon had known that, but the truth drove home hard enough to have him rubbing the back of his hand across his mouth. He felt like the biggest piece of shit in existence to have been so close to everything he'd ever dreamed of romantically and for *him* to have been the one that made it combust.

He drummed his fingers faster.

Could he fix this?

Should—

No. There was no more room for *should*. He was head over heels in love with Lucy. If she'd have him— if she'd forgive him once again—he'd do everything in his power to ensure that he never hurt her again. Not like this. Never like this.

He straightened. He'd fix it. Tonight.

Right now.

CHAPTER EIGHTEEN

LUCY CRASHED AND burned in court. There was no other way to describe it. She'd bungled the opening statement and then made an ass of herself getting into it with the prosecuting attorney until the judge called a recess until the following day. She strode out of the courtroom, her throat tight with shame and her skin hot. *I screwed up.*

No matter how frustrating or crazy her personal life got, she had always—*always*—found refuge in work. With her clients, the world made sense. It didn't matter what case they had leveled against them, she had a knack for finding the right facts to turn things in their favor. That click was her favorite thing in the world.

She'd lost it.

Two days since Gideon had unceremoniously dumped her, and she'd spent the entire time going through too many boxes of Kleenex and watching movie after movie while clutching Garfunkel. She hadn't touched her files. She hadn't checked her email. She hadn't done anything other than sit there and feel sorry for herself.

It didn't make *sense*. Work was her everything.

Work was the reason she had contacted Gideon to begin with. Dropping the ball there was inexcusable.

Why? Why can't I focus?

She knew the answer. She didn't want to face it.

But Lucy couldn't keep on like this indefinitely. If she didn't recover tonight and fix the mess she'd made today, she could kiss her promotion goodbye and it would all be for nothing. Facing down the ugly truth required more courage than she thought she had.

She hit the street and turned a direction at random, needing the movement to untangle her thoughts. Three blocks later and she was no closer to unveiling the truth.

Coward. Just like you called him.

Damn it. Lucy stopped short. "I love him." The comment earned her a few looks from people walking around her, but she started moving again before anyone could get pissed about her being a human roadblock. *I love him.*

She'd loved Jeff, but it was…different. Even if they'd been planning their wedding when she'd found out that he'd cheated on her, her connection with Jeff had never come close to what she felt for Gideon. Her heartbreak at the time hadn't made her miss a step at work. If anything, without the stress of trying to juggle her emotions over Jeff's nasty comments, she'd been free to focus solely on what was most important—her job.

The only problem? Her job didn't hold up against what she felt for Gideon. Every time she tried to work, she caught herself wondering where he was or what he was doing—or who he might be with.

The last was her own personal demon. Lucy didn't think for a minute that Gideon had dropped her on her ass and gone off to hook up with someone else. No matter what he'd said about not being the keeping kind, it was his fear talking—not reality.

He cared about her. He wouldn't have taken the noble route if he hadn't. It was a stupid choice, to be sure, but she understood that he was trying to protect her. He just wasn't giving her the benefit of making her own choices.

That was the problem.

That was the thing she didn't know if she could get over.

Liar.

Gideon might have pulled the trigger on ending things, but only because he'd beaten Lucy to it. She hadn't fought for him—for them. He'd tried to do the noble thing and, instead of telling him where to stick his high-handed attitude, she'd just walked away. So much easier to retreat than to put herself on the line and be rejected by him.

Lucy wove through the crowd of people on the corner and stopped next to the building, staring at the stream of yellow taxicabs. She'd projected herself. She couldn't even blame her history on her reaction. What she felt for Gideon scared the hell out of her. She *knew* he cared about her—loved her, even. They hadn't shared so much for it to be anything less than love. He wouldn't have told her to pick him unless he was one hundred percent serious. That wasn't how Gideon operated. He didn't play games.

Honesty. He demanded perfect honesty—and he'd given it, as well. She mentally played back everything he'd said to her. Nowhere in there was him telling her that all he'd wanted was sex. No, he didn't think he was good enough for her, so he'd cut her loose. *High-handed, but so very Gideon.* He'd chosen *her* happiness over *his*.

She needed to put herself out there. To tell him that *he* was her happiness. Lucy had lived a decent life the last couple of years. She'd been perfectly content, but she'd also cut herself off from anyone that would make her feel deeply enough to hurt her. She'd barely tried to date and hadn't attempted to reach out to friends she'd lost touch with.

She'd been the coward.

That stopped now. If Gideon didn't want her—didn't love her—he could damn well tell her to her face. That was the only acceptable reason for him dumping her. Anything else they could work past as long as they were together. Lucy would make him see that. The man might make her fumble her words a bit, but she'd power through it to get the truth out.

Her phone vibrated and she almost ignored it, but the only way to make her Dumpster fire of a day in court worse was to ignore a call from her client or one of the partners. But when she dug it out of her purse, it was the last number she expected to see there. *Roman?*

Lucy frowned and answered. "Hello?"

"I owe you an apology."

She blinked. This situation kept getting weirder and weirder. Roman had never called her before, and she couldn't think of a single reason he'd have to call her now. Unless… Her heart lodged in her throat. "Is Gideon okay?"

"What?" His shock seemed genuine and then he laughed, breaking her tension. "Shit, I guess I owe you two apologies. Gideon is fine last I saw him, which was yesterday. I should have realized you'd think the worst."

Lucy let loose the breath she'd been holding. "Okay. Sorry. I just thought…"

"Logical. I should have considered it." He cleared his throat. "Look, I fucked up, Lucy. I never asked your forgiveness for not telling you about Jeff, and then I went and compounded the issue by letting my guilt prod me to give Gideon some truly shitty advice."

She'd known that something had happened while Gideon was with Roman to push him into action, but she didn't hold it against him. Any of it. "Gideon's strong-willed. He wouldn't have been pushed into doing something he wasn't already considering doing."

"Still."

She smiled at the stubbornness in that single word. It was no wonder the two men got along so well. They were cut from the same kind of cloth. "Consider yourself forgiven."

"I'd actually like to make it up to you. Before you tell me it's not necessary, know that I realize it's not necessary and that's how good apologies work."

Amusement curled through her, though she wished he'd get to the point so she could hang up and call Gideon. "What did you have in mind?"

"What are you doing right now? A friend is doing a soft opening of his restaurant and I have a table reserved so we can talk."

"Right now?" She looked around. "I guess that works." Damn it, she wanted Gideon, but if she was going to get him to come around, it wouldn't hurt to have Roman on her side. Maybe she could use the lunch to mine for information. The thought buoyed her disappointment a bit. "Text me the address, please."

"Will do. I'll meet you there." He hung up before she could ask him any further questions.

Lucy frowned. *Strange.* Her phone pinged almost immediately and she frowned harder because she recognized the address. It overlooked Central Park, though it used to be owned by someone else. It must have cost a small fortune—or large one—to purchase. She set the information aside and stepped to the curb to flag down a cab.

The ride was blessedly short, all things considered. Lucy kept looking at her phone, but now that she was going to meet Roman, she didn't want to call Gideon until afterward. Just in case he wanted to talk immediately. Her stomach did a slow flip-flop. *Please be willing to meet with me.*

To her surprise, the restaurant was actually the top floor of the building. After getting off the elevator, Lucy stood in the entranceway for a solid thirty seconds, just taking in the opulence of the place. It screamed wealth with its polished white-marble floors and subtle gold accents. Nothing déclassé, but there all the same.

A well-dressed man strode over, a practiced smile on his handsome face. "You must be Lucy. This way, please."

She followed, taking in empty table after empty table. "I thought this was a soft opening?" Surely there should be *some* people there. *Good Lord, did Roman invite me here to shove me out a window?* She pushed the thought away. Hysterical was what it was.

"It is." He chuckled. "Just a *very* soft opening."

That wasn't an answer at all, but she allowed him to lead her into what appeared to be a greenhouse. The air warmed enough that she unzipped her jacket. Flowers of every color and shape lined the walls. There were even trees in the corners, which made her smile despite everything.

She was so busy looking at the foliage that she didn't realize the man had left—or that she wasn't alone—until she turned around and found Gideon standing in the doorway. Lucy froze. "But—"

"I'm sorry for the cheap trick. I wasn't sure if you'd agree to see me if I called." His dark eyes drank her in and she actually felt his longing even across the space between them.

Lucy shook her head. "Gideon, you have to *stop.* If you want to see me, call me and say so yourself instead of trying to manipulate things into a perfect setup." Now that she had him here, though, she was just glad she didn't have to have this conversation over the phone. She lifted her chin. "And if you love me, you stay. You don't choose the self-sacrificing route because you think you know what's best for me. You sit down and have a damn conversation where we talk it out."

His smile wasn't all that happy. "I fucked up."

"Yes, you did." She wasn't about to let him off easily, no matter how much she wanted to cross the distance between them and feel his strong arms wrap around her.

"I'm sorry. There's no good reason to explain why I freaked out, but guilt makes people do crazy things— like walk away from the woman they love because they think it's what's best for her."

"*I* decide what's best for me."

His dark eyes took on a tinge of sorrow. "I know. And we both know that I don't deserve to kiss the ground you walk on. Not because I love some idealized version of you, but because you're *you*. You're a good person, Lucy. The best kind of person. You are funny and kind and sexy as fuck, and I might not deserve you..." He took a step forward and then another. "No, I *know* I don't deserve you."

"Stop saying that," she whispered.

"Maybe we both fucked up. Fear makes for all kinds of mistakes, and what we have between us is wildfire." Gideon stopped in front of her and went down on one knee. "But, Lucy, I'd gladly spend the rest of my life burning for you." He withdrew a ring box from the inner pocket of his suit jacket. "I love you. I've loved you for six goddamn years, and I convinced myself that the right thing to do was to stand back and let you be with someone you deserved. I fought every single damn day not to pull some underhanded shit and steal you from that douche."

She reached out with shaking hands and touched the ring box. "Gideon—"

"I know you wanted a safe and pat marriage to some guy you don't give two fucks about. I can't offer you that, Lucy. But I can offer you a husband who will love you beyond all reason, even if he occasionally screws up. I can offer you a safe harbor, a full life and more sex than you know what to do with. I *am* offering you that."

She couldn't catch her breath. In all the scenarios she'd played out over the last few days, she'd never once imagined Gideon, down on one knee, offering her everything she'd spent two years being too terrified to admit she wanted. "Gideon."

"Yes?" He didn't look scared while he waited for her answer. He looked totally and completely at peace for the first time in as long as she could remember. As if he was exactly where he wanted to be—where he was meant to be.

Lucy stepped forward and tangled her fingers in his hair. "Steal me."

His dark eyes went wide. "That's a yes."

It wasn't a question but she answered anyway. "That's a hell yes."

He gave a whoop and shot to his feet, sweeping her off hers in the process. "I love the shit out of you, Lucy. I'll spend the rest of our life making up for six years of missed opportunity."

She kissed him with everything she had. "Maybe it

was good that it took us six years to get here and more than a few missteps along the way. There's a right time and place. This is *our* time and *our* place." Lucy kissed him again. "I love you, Gideon. So, so much."

He stepped back enough to slip the ring out of the box and onto her finger. It was…perfect. The simple silver ban framed a princess-cut diamond that was big enough to have her shooting a look at him. "Wow."

"Funny, that's what I say every time I see you." He pulled her back into his arms. "Wow. This woman is mine. And I'm hers."

"Yes and yes and yes." She smiled up at him. "Always."

* * * * *

MAKE ME NEED

To Hilary

CHAPTER ONE

Trish Livingston didn't do sad. Life was too short to focus on the negative crap. No matter how bad things got, it could always be worse.

Granted, she wasn't exactly sure how much worse *her* life could get. She was drowning in student loans, living with her wonderfully understanding but ultimately smothering parents and the only job she could get was one with her older brother's cybersecurity company.

Positive, Trish. You could be homeless. Your parents could be awful people—or gone completely. You could have as few job prospects as you did two weeks ago.

She smoothed a shaking hand down her skirt and squared her shoulders. Maybe this wouldn't be so unnerving if Aaron was actually here to introduce her to his partner and walk her through her responsibilities. But his fiancée had had their baby a week earlier than expected, so he was currently playing the doting father. He'd offered to slip away for a few hours, of course. That was what her brother did—took care of everyone around him. She'd declined because that was what *she* did—smoothed waves and gave people what they really wanted.

The elevator shuddered to a stop and the door slid open, removing any chance she had to change her mind. Trish smoothed her hair back as best she could, pasted a bright smile on her face and stepped out.

From what Aaron said, this entire floor was Tandem Security offices, which seemed a little strange since it was the two of them, but who was she to complain? Trish eyed the front office. *Not the most welcoming first impression.* A layer of dust covered the desk and she'd been under the impression that plastic plants couldn't actually die, but the teetering tree in the corner threatened to make a liar of her. Even the chairs were eyesores, a perfectly functional beige…that belonged in a hospital waiting room somewhere.

She walked over and sank into one and grimaced. *Thought so.* Whoever had designed these chairs didn't want the occupants to spend any amount of time in them. She shook her head and muttered under her breath, "Well, this is what Aaron hired you for. Apparently he actually *does* need someone—desperately."

"What do you want?"

She jumped to her feet and teetered in her cotton candy–pink heels. "Sorry, I was just trying out the chairs and..." She trailed off as she caught sight of the guy who'd snarled at her. He wore a pair of faded blue jeans and a white T-shirt that stretched tight across his impressive chest and set off his dark brown skin to perfection. A chiseled jaw and shaved head completed the picture and made her mouth water.

At least right up until she registered who this must be.

Trish turned her smile up to an eleven and stepped forward. "Cameron O'Clery? I'm Trish Livingston. Aaron was understandably occupied, so he said I should just head over here and make myself at home." She held out a hand until it became clear he had no intention of shaking it. Undeterred, she dropped it and smoothed a nonexistent wrinkle from her skirt. "I know he mentioned this place needed a bit of a face-lift, but I never realized my brother had quite such a gift for understatement."

He stared and finally shook his head. "Info is in the top drawer of the desk. Do what you want."

Cameron turned and stalked down the hallway and out of sight.

Trish frowned. She rounded the desk and pulled open the creaky drawer. The only things in it were a credit card with Tandem Security's name on it and a paper with account names and passwords written out in neat block lettering. A little more snooping found a brand-new laptop tucked in the next drawer down. Trish shot a look down the hall, but since Cameron hadn't made an appearance, she shrugged and booted it up. Typing in the websites listed brought up accounting software, an email address and the company software itself. She scrolled through the list of clients—past and present—and sighed. *This would be a lot easier if I had a little guidance.*

Chin up, Trish. You know how to make the best of any situation. This is no different.

She stood and propped her hands on her hips. Since she had to start somewhere, the waiting room was the way to go. Aaron had hired her to redesign the office space, liaise with incoming clients and provide general support to him and Cameron. She turned in a slow circle again, mentally tallying everything she needed to accomplish her first goal. No reason to pay top dollar for everything. It didn't matter if the company could afford it or not. Even bargain shopping, it would be a chunk of change to do it all at once, so she'd roll up her sleeves and save costs wherever she could.

She palmed the credit card and headed into the back offices. There were no plaques or signs to indicate where anything was, but only one door had light coming from beneath it, so she headed in.

"I'm busy." Cameron didn't even bother to look up from his monitor.

Good grief. If this is his attitude, I can see why Aaron needed someone to handle clients. She didn't let her smile slip, though. "I can see that, so I won't take much of your time." Trish held up the credit card. "Just let me know the budget for the front office and I'll be out of your hair. Or, well, you have a shaved head so..." She smiled harder. "Sorry, I'm wasting time with babbling. Budget, please."

His dark brows drew together and he finally deigned to look directly at her. "What?"

"A budget. For the front office." The urge to keep talking bubbled up, but she pressed her lips together to prevent the words from escaping. Call it a hunch, but Cameron O'Clery didn't seem the type of man to appreciate small talk or meandering conversational threads.

His frown didn't clear. "Spend whatever you want."

Lord, grant me patience. She crossed her arms

over her chest. "With respect, I do better when I have clear guidelines. A budget would be helpful."

Cameron cursed, as if this two-minute conversation had taxed what little patience he had. "Spend what you need to. If I think you're out of line, I'll tell you."

Of that, she had no doubt.

Recognizing this was a losing battle, Trish edged back out of the office. "I'll just get started, then."

"Do that." He turned back to his monitor, and it was as if he'd forgotten she was in the room.

She'd never been so summarily dismissed in her life, and Trish couldn't deny that it rankled. She opened her mouth, but common sense got the best of her. As satisfying as it would be to pester one half of her new bosses, it was her first day. Better to set a precedent of doing her job well before she started pressing Sir Crankypants to hold down an actual conversation.

She headed back to her desk and considered. It was Friday, which gave her today and all weekend to get the decorating stuff out of the way. Then she could start bright and early Monday with figuring out the client aspect. Aaron wanted her to deal with new clients' preliminary meetings to get a baseline for what services they required. From there, either Aaron or Cameron would take the client.

Though I guess Cameron will be taking them all until Aaron is back in the office.

One problem at a time.

She dropped into her desk chair and pulled a dusty notebook out from the second drawer. A list would keep her on track. Trish gave the room one last look and sighed. Her shoulders dropped a fraction of an inch before she caught herself and forcibly straightened them. *None of that, Trish. Think positive.*

Working as a glorified secretary for her brother's company might not be part of her bright plans for the future, but that didn't change anything. She gave 100 percent. It was what she did—who she was. This job would be no different.

She'd be the best damn glorified secretary Aaron and Cameron had ever had.

Cameron finished the last bit of code for his current client's site and sat back. There were still tests to run and scenarios to play out to ensure he'd filled every nook and cranny with the proper protections and hadn't left any back doors accidentally open, but they could wait until tomorrow. He rubbed a hand over his head and then stretched. He was past overdue for a massage—he usually kept regular appointments to prevent the kinks in his back from getting too bad—but Aaron's pending fatherhood had kept his partner out of the office more and more as his woman's pregnancy got further along, and more work had landed on Cameron as a result.

He didn't mind. His friend was happy, and that was enough for Cameron. He liked the work, liked keeping occupied with it. All he had was an empty apartment waiting for him, so it wasn't as if he missed much by spending more time in the office.

As he pushed to his feet and stretched more fully, he frowned. *What's that smell?* Another deep inhale had him checking his watch. It was well after eight in the evening, so who the hell was painting?

Cameron stalked out of his office, already calculating where the vents could be sending the scent from. It was probably the floor below theirs. The woman who ran the consulting business down there liked revamping her office with startling regularity. Saying shit wouldn't accomplish anything, and it *was* after-hours. He was just tired and hungry and overreacting.

He reached the front office and stopped cold. White cloth covered the floor and blue painter's tape marked off both the ceiling and trim. Half the white walls were now a soothing green, but that wasn't what set him back on his heels.

No, that was reserved for the barefoot woman

teetering on the top of a stepladder—*above* the sign set into the step warning not to stand above that point—her curly blond hair tied back in a haphazard knot that looked like a bird's nest. He started forward, belatedly realizing she still wore the outfit she'd had on earlier, a simple black skirt that hugged her hips and ass and a loose pink blouse in the same startling shade as the heels she'd worn.

This is Aaron's little sister. Get your eyes off her ass.

It was a great ass, though. As she went onto her tiptoes, the muscles in her lower half flexed and he had to bite back a groan. At least until she wobbled and overcompensated. Cameron jumped forward and caught her. He was a bastard and a half because he let himself enjoy the feeling of her in his arms for several seconds before he set her back on her feet.

Trish shoved the cloud of curly blond hair that had escaped its knot back and gave him a blindingly bright smile. "Thanks! I thought I could do this without scaffolding, but those nine-foot ceilings are no joke." Her smile wobbled. "Crap, I'm sorry. I got paint on you."

Cameron looked down to the streak of green marking his shoulder and then back at her. "You just took a nosedive off a ladder and you're worried about my shirt?"

"Well...yeah." She shrugged and leaned over to set the paint roller on the tray perched precariously on the ladder. "I fell. You caught me. Thanks again, by the way. But there's no reason to dwell on it."

He stared into those guileless blue eyes. She truly looked more worried about his shirt than any injuries she would have suffered if his timing had been a little off. "What would you have done if I wasn't here and you broke your leg?"

"At that angle, I'm more likely to break an arm." When he just glowered at her, she huffed out a breath. "My phone is right there, within easy reach." She pointed at the ladder. "If I didn't topple the ladder when I fell, and for some reason I wasn't able to stand, I would have kicked it over, retrieved my phone and called for help. Happy?"

Fuck no, he wasn't happy. The woman was obviously crazy, because she didn't seem the least bit concerned with that scenario. Cameron crossed his arms over his chest. "If I leave right now, you're going to climb right back up that ladder and finish painting, aren't you?"

"No?"

He growled. "If you're going to lie, at least try to pretend you're not fishing for the right answer." He gave up his happy thoughts about the pizza place down the block from his apartment. There was no way he could leave this woman unsupervised. He'd spend the rest of the night worried that she'd fallen again and he hadn't been there to catch her, and there would be no rest and a whole lot of indigestion in his future. Cameron stalked around the ladder, testing its stability. *Should be fine as long as no one stands on the top of the damn thing.* He pointed at the untouched brush near the paint can. "You're on edges."

"Actually, I—"

"You're on edges," he repeated, staring her down. "I'll handle this."

Trish opened her mouth, drawing his attention to her pink lipstick. He'd never had a thing for painted lips before, but the bright pigment made the sharp Cupid's bow of her top lip stand out against her skin and… *For fuck's sake, she's got freckles.* She was downright adorable, and that should be enough to banish any thoughts of getting his hands on her perfectly rounded ass or kissing her until she forgot about whatever argument she was obviously debating delivering.

It wasn't.

He wanted her, and hell if that didn't complicate things.

Cameron hadn't bothered to date in longer than

he cared to think about. It was so much goddamn work getting to know another person. Most of them ended up storming off before the second date because he said something wrong. Or he didn't talk enough. Or he talked too much about work because, God forbid, that wasn't a safe subject, either. It was exhausting just thinking about it, and he hadn't met anyone tempting enough to make him want to run that particular gauntlet. Easy enough to scratch the itch in loud bars where talking was the last thing on either his or his prospective partner's mind, but even that had gotten tiresome recently.

If he'd run into Trish on the street, he might have asked her out. Might have let her obvious enthusiasm and sunny attitude wash over him.

But she worked for him. What was more, her big brother was one of the few people in this world who not only put up with Cameron's bullshit without expecting him to change but also was a genuine friend.

He might want Trish, but she was the one woman he couldn't touch.

CHAPTER TWO

TRISH DIDN'T KNOW what to think of Cameron, but after looking like he wanted to give her a blistering lecture, he just picked up the paint roller, glared at her and got to work. She watched him climb the ladder and gave herself a shake. Staring at her boss's shoulders was *not* going to get this room painted before midnight. He obviously wasn't willing to listen to reason or let her do the job she was hired for, so she might as well take advantage of the extra set of hands.

Unsurprisingly, Cameron wasn't much of a chatterbox and every time she tried to talk to him, she only got grunts or one-word answers in response.

She gave up. Not forever. But it was kind of nice to just paint and not have to worry about being chipper. There was no relaxing, though—not with Cameron taking up too much space in the front office. Every time she moved, she caught a glimpse of him out of the corner of her eye. He moved with perfect precision, each roll of the paint even and uniform.

It took two hours to finish up, and part of Trish was almost sad to end the companionable silence. She stood back and pushed her hair away from her face with her forearm. "Oh yeah, this is the right color."

Cameron surveyed it as if he were a color expert. Hell, maybe he was. His brows furrowed. "It's strangely pleasing."

"That's the point." She placed her brush in the paint tray and started gathering up the various supplies scattered around the room. The tape would come off in the morning and then she'd touch up as needed, but she had a feeling there would be little of that necessary. Cameron was too much of a perfectionist to leave drips anywhere, which served her just fine.

She straightened and realized he was still watching her. His dark eyes studied her face as if he could divine her thoughts. Cameron frowned harder. "What are your plans for the front office?"

So now we have questions?

She bit back the sarcastic response and smiled. "This is the first impression clients get when they walk through the doors, so I want it to be welcoming and designed to set them at ease." Trish's main degree was in sales, but she'd gotten a minor in design. Her dream might be to eventually work in corporate fashion, but she knew how to use that skill set to set the tone of a room—and help people choose clothing that would make them happy. Not that she got to use the latter at all these days.

"We usually meet clients off-site."

"Yes, I'm aware. But that wastes time in transit and Aaron mentioned that there's a boardroom perfectly suitable for conducting meetings." Though, considering the state of the front office, she hadn't had the heart to check out that room yet to see what *perfectly suitable* meant. There would no doubt be more painting in her future, but hopefully it at least had furniture that was acceptable.

Cameron seemed to consider that and looked around the room again. "Tell me your plans." A tiny hesitation. "Please."

He's trying. Throw him a bone. Aaron had warned her that Cameron didn't bother with the social niceties, which set most people on edge, but his abruptness had still caught her off guard. If he was going to make an effort, though, she could do the same.

Trish walked over to stand in front of the door to the elevator. "Come here."

He gave her a look like he thought she was trying to put one over on him but joined her in facing the room. His shoulder brushed hers, sending shivers through her body that she couldn't quite control. He was just so *big*. Big and overwhelming and he smelled really good. *He's your boss, Trish. Slow your roll.*

"Okay." She cleared her throat. "Imagine this. You walk in and are instantly put at ease by the soothing green. I can make the desk work, but there will be a grouping of new chairs there." She pointed to one side of the office. "And a smaller one there." On the opposite side. "The window facing the street brings in enough light to justify some kind of plant, but I haven't decided what will be the best fit. Probably one on each side of the window to create balance. A small water fixture on the other side in the corner. Some kind of art on the wall behind my desk, and maybe on another wall or two, though I haven't decided yet."

"Lots of changes."

He sounded neutral enough, but she couldn't help straightening her spine and lifting her chin. "Yes, but that's what I was hired to do—create the best client-facing aspect of this business as possible. That starts with first impressions. You and Aaron have a company that's one of the best in the business, and as silly as it might seem, presentation matters. Meeting in secondary locations is fine, but this is better."

"One condition." He kept going before she had a chance to protest. "No more painting alone."

"Of all the—"

Cameron turned to face her, his chest nearly touching hers with each inhale. The proximity stalled her breath in her lungs and choked off whatever she'd been about to say. Trish swallowed hard, caught between wanting him to kiss her and wanting him to back the hell up and let some of the air back into the room. He didn't touch her, though. Didn't lean down. Didn't cup her jaw or press her back against the wall and ravage her mouth.

Get yourself together.

His voice disturbed the air between them. "No. Painting. Alone." Cameron's dark gaze dropped to her mouth for the briefest of seconds before it snapped back to her eyes. "Do we understand each other, Trish?"

The sound of her name on his lips turned her knees to Jell-O. She swayed toward him, toward the command in his voice, but caught herself at the last moment. *Do not kiss your boss.* Trish took a step back, and then another. She looked at the floor and swallowed hard. "Yeah, we understand each other."

He helped her finish cleaning up in silence, though she stewed a bit when Cameron made a point of taking the ladder and stowing it in the closet without letting her touch it. He walked back into the front office as she slipped on her shoes. "You're staying with Aaron?"

She could have let him believe that, but Trish had already misstepped enough on her first day without adding lying to the list, too. "I was, but I got my own place." Her brother had fronted her the money for the first month's rent, but she didn't think he wanted her underfoot any more than she wanted to *be* underfoot while he and Becka got used to the whole new baby thing.

Cameron gave her another of those dark looks like he wasn't sure what he thought of that. Good Lord, but the man was cranky. He finally sighed. "I'll call you a cab."

It didn't take much to read between the lines. He'd been on his way out of here when he caught her unfortunate fall. She was keeping him from plans of some sort, but his weirdly stubborn chivalrous streak wouldn't let him abandon her. *Chivalry? More like control freakishness.* Either way, he'd helped her out with painting even though he didn't have to, and she wasn't about to impose on him further.

Trish smiled and grabbed her purse. "Actually, I'm walking. It's only a few blocks from here."

"Then I'll walk you." If anything, he sounded *more* grumpy now than he had before.

"Oh, that's totally not necessary. The neighborhood is just fine and it's not particularly late." She gave Cameron an absent smile and headed for the elevator. "Thanks, though." It was edging toward eleven, but that didn't mean anything. She'd checked the street out last week with Becka—apparently walking could induce labor and Becka had been *determined* to make it happen—and there were several bars that would still be open around now, which meant pedestrian traffic. It was one of the pluses of the area when she was picking a place to live—that and the apartment came furnished and was within walking distance to the office. The rent was still astronomical, but Aaron was paying her an astronomical salary.

He'd promised it wasn't a pity job, that he really needed her specifically to do this, but it *felt* like a pity job.

Stop it. Chin up. You're going to help out your brother, save up some money and explore the city while you figure out your next step. Those are all good things.

She'd been so caught up in her thoughts that she hadn't noticed Cameron walking beside her until Trish stepped out onto the street and was hit full in the face with icy wind. She shivered and barely had time to wish that she'd packed a warmer coat before a heavy weight settled on her shoulders.

She blinked and touched the coat Cameron had just draped over her. "You'll freeze."

"I'm fine."

He shoved his hands into his pockets. "Which way?"

She could keep arguing and let them both stand out in the cold or she could just give in and spend next week establishing that she didn't want Cameron looking after her. She had an older brother. She didn't need two.

You don't see this man in a brotherly light and you know it.

Shut up.

And he wouldn't have stared at your mouth like that if he saw you *like a sister.*

Seriously. Shut. Up.

She picked up her pace and Cameron easily fell into step next to her. Even as she told herself to keep her smile in place and just accept his chaperoning, she couldn't keep her mouth shut. "You realize I'm an adult, right? I can walk three blocks without having you shadow my steps and glower at anyone who looks at me sideways." When he didn't respond, her irritation flared hotter. "I have an older brother. I don't need another one." She jerked her thumb toward the door they'd stopped in front of. "This is me."

"Trish."

God, the things that man could do with a single syllable. She froze, her feet rooted to the ground as he stepped closer, his big body blocking the wind. This time, she couldn't stop herself from swaying toward him, answering the gravitational pull he exuded. He didn't move, but he didn't have to. Trish went up onto her tiptoes and her mouth found his as if there had never been another destination for her.

The contact shocked her right down her to bones. His lips moved against hers, cautious and then commanding, taking everything she gave and then demanding more. Her knees actually buckled at the slow slide of his tongue against hers, and Cameron caught her easily around the hips.

He lifted his head, breaking the contact between them. All she could do was stare as he took his jacket from around her shoulders and shrugged it on. He nudged her to her door and waited for her to key in the code to get through. Then Cameron stood there until she shut the door firmly behind her.

Trish watched him stalk away. *Did that just happen?*

She'd just kissed her boss.

On her first day.

She pressed her shaking fingers to her lips. "I am in so much trouble."

CHAPTER THREE

CAMERON SPENT ALL weekend cursing himself for kissing Trish back. He should have stepped away and clarified that they had a professional relationship only. Reminded her that she was his best friend's little sister. Done literally anything except coax her mouth open with his tongue.

Now he knew what she tasted like. And that she'd melted so sweetly against him at the first contact. Not to mention the delicious way she'd shivered when he'd grabbed her hips.

Fuck me.

When Monday morning rolled around, he almost decided to work remotely. That was the path of a coward. Better to rip the Band-Aid off now and deal with her hurt feelings and move on. It might make the workplace awkward, but if Aaron's glowing praise of his baby sister was any indication, it wouldn't get her down for long.

It was only a kiss, after all.

The elevator seemed to take twice as long as normal, and he had to concentrate to keep from fidgeting. Cameron had arrived thirty minutes early on purpose. If he was safely camped out in his office, hopefully they could just pretend that misstep on Friday never happened.

The elevator doors opened and he barely made it a single step. If not for the walls being painted the same green he'd been elbow deep in a few days ago, he'd have thought he was in the wrong place. Comfortable-looking chairs—a warm sand color with a stripe of burnt red—were arranged on either side of the room. A leafy tree gracefully rose on either side of the window.

A window that had new curtains to match the chairs.

On the other side of the room, a water feature was arranged in the corner, a geometrical design with round stones and dark wood borders.

There was even fucking art on the walls.

When the hell did she find time to do this? She had to have put in long-ass days to find the pieces and haul them up here. He could comfort himself that they'd been delivered, but from what little he knew about Trish Livingston, he had no doubt that she'd physically carried every single piece up here herself.

Without asking for help.

Without once *considering* that she *should* ask for help.

Irritation flickered closer to true anger. He eyed her desk as he passed, taking in the cheery flower arrangement, the stack of bright Post-it notes and the overflowing mug of equally bright pens.

He clenched his jaw and headed down the hallway, but Cameron only made it three steps when the door to their mostly unused conference room opened and Trish herself appeared. She had a handful of paint color swatches in front of her face, and her brow was furrowed and her lips— red, today—were pursed. She hummed to herself. "This blue is too cold. No red. No yellow. I need a power color that's not in-your-face."

He planted his feet, irritation derailed by sheer curiosity. And the woman, damn her, didn't even notice him standing there. She ran right into him and bounced off his chest, and it was only his cupping her elbows that kept her from landing on her ass.

"Damn!" Trish laughed. "Mom always said to keep my head on the here and now. Guess I should have listened, huh?"

Cameron just stared. They were so fucking

close, if she leaned a little farther in, he would be able to see directly down her flowy purple top. He averted his eyes and released her. "You're here early."

"Lots of work to be done."

It was too fucking early for her to be this chipper. He shot her a look. "How much coffee have you had?"

"Coffee?" She frowned. "I don't drink coffee. It gives me the shakes and that's just not my idea of fun. I stick with chamomile tea when I want something warm and cozy in my hands." Trish's blond hair was in a cloud around her shoulders today, her curls giving her an angelic look that was completely at odds with her fitted skirt.

For fuck's sake, Cameron, stop looking at her. She's being professional. You're being inappropriate.

He cleared his throat and took another step back. "The conference room is fine. You don't need to kill yourself for this job. The front office didn't need to be finished so quickly."

She wilted a little, but then her smile brightened until it was damn near blinding. "I like the work." Trish charged forward, and he had to scramble back to avoid making contact with her again. She glanced at him as if he was being ridiculous. "And, no, the conference room is not fine. You can't expect clients to take your presentations seriously when there are spiderwebs in the corners and all the chair cushions are moth-eaten. I'll take care of it."

That was what he was afraid of.

"Trish."

She stopped in her tracks, and her smile dimmed to something closer to a genuine expression. "I was hoping we didn't have to do this, but obviously you've been chewing on it all weekend." Trish sighed and turned to face him fully. "Look, I'm sorry. I was out of line when I kissed you. I could give half a dozen reasons why it happened, but the truth is that it was inappropriate and I put you in a bad spot. So I'm sorry. Let's pretend it never happened?"

Cameron wanted to know what those half a dozen reasons were, but he couldn't ask. Not when she was so determined to put them back into their respective boxes of employee and employer. There was one thing he couldn't let stand. "If you remember, I kissed you back."

Her blue eyes flared with heat, quickly banked. "I remember." Just like that, she was chipper Trish again, so sweet she made his teeth ache. "Don't let me keep you from your work. I was hoping we could sit down later today and go over your current clients and their needs, but other than that I can get the conference room whipped into shape pretty quickly."

"I have some time this afternoon." Which would hopefully give him the opportunity to put a little distance between whatever the hell was going on between them.

"Perfect. If anything pops up between then and now, I'll let you know."

He shifted, realized he was backing away from her like someone trying to avoid being mauled by a wild animal and forced himself to turn away. "Do that." He could have sworn she laughed a little as he strode away from her, but a quick glance over his shoulder showed her sunny expression firmly in place.

Must have been my imagination.

Trish walked to her desk on shaking legs. She'd had a plan. It was a very good plan. The best plan, considering her insane impulse to kiss Cameron a few short days ago. She'd come into the office and pretend like nothing had changed, like she was a professional who'd made a mistake, like she hadn't used that brief kiss with him to bring herself to orgasm no less than seven times over the weekend.

It wasn't her fault. She'd wanted to get the front

office set up for Monday, but everywhere she looked, she saw evidence of Cameron. That was the spot he'd caught her when she'd fallen off the ladder. Over there in the corner was where she'd spent a solid sixty seconds staring at the line of his back muscles pressing against his shirt every time he'd reached over his head to paint. Right here was where they'd stood shoulder to shoulder as she'd told him her vision for the room.

A man shouldn't be able to imprint himself on her inside of two hours with only a handful of words exchanged, and Trish had managed to convince herself that it was all in her head.

Until she'd collided with him in the hallway. They'd been so close, his big hands clasping her elbows in a way that should most definitely not be erotic, his chest rising and falling in the most tempting way possible.

She'd almost kissed him again.

Trish dropped into her chair and bumped her head against her desk a couple times. Sadly, the contact did nothing to clear the desire from her brain—or her body. *I want my boss. I want to kiss him and do the horizontal tango and a few things that are illegal in half a dozen states.*

What a mess.

A footstep had her opening her eyes, and she turned her head to press her cheek to her desk.

Cameron stood in the middle of the hallway, his body tense and expression unreadable.

Because of course.

She couldn't just have that brilliant little scene where she played it cool and professional and totally unaffected. No, he'd had to come back out here and see her for the mess she really was. *Too late to salvage this. Might as well ride with it.* "Can I help you with something?" She kept her tone even despite the fact she had her head on her desk and was obviously in the middle of a lust-driven breakdown.

Cameron looked like he wanted nothing more than to retreat and pretend this interaction had never happened. *You and me both, man.* He finally cleared his throat. "Is everything okay?"

"Sure. Fine and dandy." Since he obviously had something to say, she sighed and straightened. "You don't have to worry about me."

"Somehow I find that hard to believe." He shook his head and held up a thin file. "I have a web meeting to finish up a contract with an existing client in an hour. Would you like to sit in on it?"

She cautiously took the file and flipped through it. She didn't necessarily need hand-holding, but it would be really useful to see how Cameron conducted business—both to see what he'd expect from her and to verify if it was as bad as Aaron seemed to think. But that also meant being in the same room as Cameron, and in close quarters.

It had to happen at some point.

I'm not ready.

You're never going to be ready.

Wasn't that the damn truth?

She took a careful breath and smiled brightly. "That would be great. I'll go over this so I'm up-to-date." She motioned to the file.

"Great." He turned and walked away without another word.

Great.

She spent the next forty minutes going over the file to familiarize herself with the account and what Tandem Security did for the client. It was all pretty basic. They'd beefed up the client's on-line security and added in a secondary package that was biannual upkeep for any major changes the client wanted. *Smart. Keep a long-standing relationship so they come back here if they need more done.*

By the time she walked into Cameron's office, she'd managed to get herself under control. At least until she sank gingerly into the chair next to his in front of the monitor. He'd brought it over so she could be in the camera frame once the video call started, and the positioning put them within easy touching distance. It shouldn't matter. It *couldn't* matter.

To distract herself, she focused on his computer setup. It was more advanced than she'd ever had to deal with, dual monitors showing a variety of programs running that might as well have been Greek for all Trish understood them. She was more than decent with technology, but she'd never come close to what Aaron and Cameron did for a living. It blew her mind a little bit. "Fancy."

"It does the job." He hesitated and then tilted the screen so it faced her a little more directly. "This damn client is always late. Every single fucking time."

Before she thought better of it, she laid her hand on his biceps. "You're almost finished with this account. Just keep that in mind during the meeting and everything will go swimmingly."

Cameron's eyes dropped to where she touched him, and his arm flexed slightly beneath her palm. Slowly, oh so slowly, his gaze dragged up to her mouth, hesitated and then settled on her eyes. "You take positivity to a new level."

A simple sentence, but the way he watched her didn't *feel* simple. It made her stomach twist and ignited the desire she was working so damn hard to keep under wraps. It would be the simplest thing in the world to lean in a little bit, to give him a clear signal that she wanted a repeat of the other night—and more.

He'd kiss her until she forgot her own name, until she wasn't worried about the future beyond where he'd touch her next. Until she felt the ground steady beneath her feet even as he made her fly. She'd hitch up her skirt and climb into his lap and...

"Trish?"

She blinked, her heart beating too hard. "Sorry, I didn't hear what you said."

Cameron reached up to touch the side of her face, gently guiding her to look at the monitor instead of him. "Client just logged on. I'm going to start the meeting."

The meeting. Right. She swallowed hard. "Great."

But he didn't move back. His breath brushed the shell of her ear, drawing a shiver from her. "After the meeting, we'll...talk."

Talk? Or *talk*?

She stared blindly at the monitor, reality sinking its claws into her and digging deep. The attraction she felt for Cameron wasn't going away—if anything, it was getting worse. Stronger. And if he meant what she thought—hoped, dreaded—he meant about *talking*, he was getting swept away alongside her.

Oh God, my brother is going to kill me.

Too bad she couldn't bring herself to care. She'd played it safe for so long and she'd missed her dreams by a mile.

Maybe it was time to throw caution to the wind. *What could possibly go wrong?*

CHAPTER FOUR

CAMERON MANAGED TO get through the final meeting without letting his disdain for the outgoing client show—because he was so damn distracted by Trish's flowery perfume. No, not perfume. It was too subtle. It was probably lotion or shampoo or something, and the faint scent rose every time she shifted. Her hair brushed his shoulders, and his hands clenched against the need to dig into the thick curls and tilt her head back so he could claim her mouth again.

Focus.

He signed off the meeting and sat back, careful to angle his body away from hers. It didn't help. Cameron had always considered his office obscenely large compared to the amount of space he actually needed to do his job. That was before Trish took up residence in it, filling every inch with her sunny presence. He didn't know how to deal with it, and commanding her to get the hell out wouldn't solve anything—and would only make him look like an asshole in the process.

Rightly so.

Cameron cleared his throat. "Did you decide on a color for the boardroom?"

Trish blinked those big blue eyes at him. "That's what you wanted to talk about?"

No, what he wanted to talk about was how she felt about being spread out on his desk so he could kiss her until she was dizzy. Then he'd inch up that tease of a skirt and taste her there, too. Right here. In his office. While they were both on the clock, so to speak.

He was so out of line, it wasn't fucking funny.

Focusing on work when she was so close he could run his thumb over her full bottom lip was a herculean task, but Cameron didn't have any other option. He nodded, his voice gruffer than it had right to be. "The ceilings are just as high in there as in the front office, and you've already proven you can't be trusted to follow the instructions on stepladders. Since I doubt you're going to hire someone to do it, I'll help you." There. That was reasonable.

Except her eyes had gone wide and her jaw dropped. "That is the most ridiculous, back-handed compliment I've ever heard. I'm not even sure there's a compliment in there. I am more than capable of doing my job."

"I never said you weren't."

"Actually, you did. Thirty seconds ago." She shoved to her feet, which put her breasts directly in his line of sight. Cameron jerked his gaze back to her face, but it wasn't any better for his control. She was gorgeous when she was pissed and trying not to be, her hair moving around like a live thing and her body practically vibrating with repressed fury. She pointed a finger at him, seemed to realize she might be crossing a line and let her hand drop. "Aaron hired me to do this job because he knows I'm capable of handling it. That *includes* managing painting." She stalked out the door without another word.

Cameron stared hard at the doorway, walking back through the conversation to figure out where it went wrong. Choosing not to kiss her again was the right call. *That*, he was sure of. Asking about the boardroom was a reasonable thing to do. Maybe he'd spoken a little harsher than he intended, driven by the need to keep the lust from his tone, but he hadn't yelled at her. Telling her to accept his help was only reasonable because she'd about broken her damn neck when she'd tried to do the front room herself. It was possible he could have worded it more carefully, but he'd hardly called her inept. He'd been more abrupt in other conversations and she hadn't reacted so intensely.

Another replay of the conversation and he thought he had the answer. *I am more than capable of doing my job.* Well, of course she was. Aaron wouldn't have hired her if she wasn't, sister or no. Cameron certainly wouldn't have signed off on it unless she was qualified. She might not be well-balanced when standing on a stepladder, and her college degrees weren't an exact fit, but she obviously had an eye for creating a welcoming environment, and how she'd handled herself in the meeting just now had only reinforced that hiring her was the right call. She was fucking perfect for the job.

He'd told her that...

Cameron frowned. Shit, he hadn't told her that, had he? He'd been so focused on the thought that she might pull another stunt like working after hours to finish the front office—and get hurt in the process—that he'd barked at her over it. He frowned harder. He wasn't wrong about telling her not to paint without him. He *knew* he wasn't.

But...maybe he could have approached it differently?

"Fuck," he breathed. He wasn't equipped to tiptoe around another person's feelings. If he was, he'd have been better at the client-facing part of this business. Trish wasn't a client, though. He couldn't just end a meeting and cease having to deal with her. She'd be in this office, day in and day out.

He had to apologize.

Cameron played through his options a couple times, but there was really only one reality. If she was pissed, it would make the office unlivable. What was more, it made her a whole lot more likely to go ahead and paint the damn boardroom—and potentially hurt herself—when he wasn't around. Since he wasn't a fan of either option, he pushed slowly to his feet and went in search of her.

Unsurprisingly, he found her in said boardroom. The chairs around the old table had disappeared somewhere, and she stood on the table, in the process of changing out the overhead light fixture. Cameron froze, not sure if he should rush over to catch her in the event that she fell or that damn light fixture came undone and crashed down on her head.

Trish glanced over and gave him a brilliant smile. "This thing is so coated with some gross combination of dust and time that I'm calling it a wash and tossing it."

"Okay," he said slowly. A smiling Trish was not

what he expected. Was this a trap? "You seem... not mad."

"Why would I be mad, Cameron?" Her tone was as sweet as honey, but her use of his name might as well have been a hook in the gut.

This was most definitely a trap. He cleared his throat. "Earlier, I didn't mean to—"

"To question my competence? To treat me like I'm a child in need of tending?" Every single word was that blend of sweet and sharp, until it was a wonder he didn't bleed out on the floor at her feet. She turned to face him, the light fixture in her hands, as regal as a queen despite the streak of dust over the shoulder of her shirt and what appeared to be a cobweb clinging to her curls near her face. Trish looked down her nose at him. "If you have a problem with the way I do my job, that's fine. You're my boss. You're more than entitled to correct and/or punish me as you see fit."

He got hung up on the word *punish* and had to force himself back to task.

She wasn't done, though. "That said, if you ever talk to me like that again, I'm out. I took this job as a favor to Aaron and, yeah, I kind of need it, but I don't need it badly enough to put up with that level of disrespect. I get that you don't handle people well, but at some point you're just making excuses for bad behavior that's inexcusable..." She trailed off, her breath coming too fast, and seemed to realize she was yelling at him. Trish clutched the light fixture closer to her chest. "So…there."

God, she was something else. Fired up and willing to put him in his place, though she had to be truly pissed to have let the peppy sunbeam mask slip. Cameron leaned against the doorjamb. "I'm sorry."

"Why, you—" Trish blinked. "What?"

"You're right. I was out of line. I'm sorry." He stepped farther into the room and held out a hand.

Looking dazed, she took it and allowed him to guide her off the table. He finally managed to relax a little once her feet were both firmly on the floor. Trish gave him a suspicious look. "Why are you being so agreeable?"

"Contrary to what your brother thinks, I can see reason on occasion. I was worried about you falling again, and so I overreacted. But you're right, I'm your boss." He almost choked over the words—the reminder—but powered through. "Talking to an employee like that isn't okay."

"Exactly." She still didn't look convinced this wasn't some kind of trick.

That made two of them.

Cameron…didn't do this. He didn't do interpersonal relationships. *Too damn bad. Going to have to figure it out as you go, and it's one hell of a learning curve.* He didn't move from his spot. "I respectfully request that you either hire out for the painting or wait until after hours when I can help you."

Trish opened her mouth like she was going to snap back but seemed to consider. "It's an unnecessary expense to hire such a small job out when I'm more than capable of handling it. For that matter, there's no reason for you to take time away from your...whatever it is you do for leisure...to help me. I have it covered."

She had it covered all the way to an ER visit with a broken arm. Or worse.

He met her gaze steadily. "When are you buying the paint?"

Cameron could almost see the gears whirling in her head as she tried to find a way out of this. He could have told her there was no way out. He wouldn't let her paint this room by herself, and her little stunt this weekend had shown her hand—if she thought she could get away with it, she'd do it behind his back to avoid dealing with him.

If she was anyone else, he would have found her independence a relief. It meant he could focus on his job and let her do hers. But Trish wasn't anyone else—she was Trish. He needed to keep her safe, even if that meant keeping her safe from working herself to the bone.

Finally, she sighed. "I'm going to pick it up after work."

"Pick it up tomorrow." He didn't bother to keep the command out of his voice. If she went and got it after hours, she'd be right back here the second he wasn't looking.

She's not a wayward puppy, asshole. She's a person.

Yes, she was. A person who had excellent work ethic and showed every evidence of being just as stubborn as her older brother—the same older brother Cameron would have to answer to if something happened to her. That was all. It was simple, really. Not in the least bit complicated. He certainly didn't have any ulterior motives.

Trish narrowed her eyes. "You can't tell me what to do after hours."

"It concerns this job, so I sure as hell can. We'll take a long lunch tomorrow and paint the damn boardroom. You can pick up the paint late morning beforehand."

For a moment, it seemed like she'd keep arguing, but then she gave him a brilliant smile. "Sure thing, Mr. O'Clery." Trish turned on her heel and marched out of the room.

Okay, that was definitely a trap.

CHAPTER FIVE

TRISH ALMOST SAID to hell with it and bought the paint anyway. She got so far as to leave her apartment and start in the direction of the store… But common sense reared its ugly head. Cameron might have been kind of an ass with his command for her to wait, but he'd also apologized and he wasn't being *completely* unreasonable with wanting to help. It might even be kind of nice for the job to go faster.

Honesty, Trish.

She huffed out a breath and turned in the opposite direction. "The honest truth is that I'm pissed that when he said we'd talk, he meant he'd treat me like a child instead of kissing me again." She shot a look around her, half expecting Cameron to melt out of a nearby shadow and call her on her idiocy. There was only the normal foot traffic at this time in the early evening, and they were obviously all NYC natives, because they didn't so much as blink at her talking to herself like a crazy person.

She grabbed dinner from the little Chinese place a few blocks down and carted it back to her apartment. Behind locked doors, she finally sighed. *Okay, my pride was hurt. I let it get the best of me. We both agreed that the first kiss was a mistake that shouldn't be repeated...but that doesn't stop me from wanting a repeat.*

The trilling of her phone drew her out of her thoughts. When Trish saw it was her mother, she almost deliberately missed the call. It had been a long day and she didn't have the energy to reassure her mother—and through her mother, her father—that she was doing just fine in the big, scary city. She knew for a fact that Aaron hadn't been subjected to these worried phone calls when he moved here.

She took a deep breath and put as much smile into her voice as she was capable of. "Hey, Mom."

"Trish, there you are! I was worried when you didn't pick up."

That was her mother. The eternal worrier. She'd been born and raised in Lake Placid and had always harbored a hope that her daughters would do the same. Trish's older sister, Mary, had followed that path. She'd married her high school sweetheart and settled in after college to become an elementary school teacher. *Mary* was practically perfect in every way. She didn't keep her mother up at night, worrying herself to death.

No, that role had always fallen to Trish.

She kicked her cheerfulness up a notch—the only way to combat her mother's concern when she got like that. "I was just about to sit down to dinner."

"Dinner? Trish, it's after seven. You haven't been working this whole time! Aaron said that partner of his was a good boss, but if he's got you working twelve-hour days, that's abuse!" Her voice took on strident tones.

Trish repressed a sigh. "Mom, you're getting worked up for no reason. I'm eating late because I stopped by Aaron's to see my new niece and got distracted with her adorableness." *There's no need to lead an army down here to haul me back home.* An army of three—her mom, her dad and Mary— but no less fearsome for its numbers. Though her mom hadn't been *happy* about her needing to move back home after college, she hadn't exactly shed a tear to have her youngest daughter under their roof again. Now she was treating this move like Trish had left for college all over again.

And was just as helpless and out of her element as she'd been at eighteen.

"I worry about you. That city—"

"Mom." If she didn't do something drastic, her mother would end up on an hour-long spiel about all the ways she could get mugged or worse in New York. It didn't matter that Trish had found an apartment crazy close to where she worked or that she'd pulled it from a list that Aaron himself had put together. New York City terrified their mother and she would spill that feeling over at every opportunity, whether she meant to or not.

Unless Trish distracted her, she'd be up all night running scenarios—each more terrifying than the last—and her mother would call tomorrow and be a total mess. She cast a longing look at her cooling Chinese food and resigned herself to a reheated meal. "Did Aaron send you the pictures he took of Summer? She was especially cute today. He says she can't really smile yet, but I swear to God she was smiling at me."

The distraction worked. Her mother went on to gush about how Aaron did a video call with her and the baby, and wasn't his fiancée the sweetest thing, though goodness, they should be married by now if they're having babies. Through it all, Trish's mind wandered…right back to Cameron.

She wanted him to kiss her again.

Or, rather, *she* wanted to kiss *him* again. To do more than kiss. To break half a dozen rules and regulations that she wasn't even sure Tandem Security had in place.

Not to mention that Aaron might lose his damn mind if he finds out I'm lusting after his business partner.

She blinked, realizing that her mother had been silent for a beat too long. Trish faked a yawn. "Mom, I have to go. I have a big day tomorrow, and I want a full night's rest."

The silence extended for a beat. Another. Then her mother sniffled. "I just wish you were here."

Oh good Lord. She was going to devolve to sobbing next, and Trish was too tired to be sure she wouldn't snap in response. She was twenty-fucking-four years old. She couldn't live at home forever. She understood that her mother's empty-nest syndrome was in full force, but Trish couldn't form her entire freaking life around making her mother feel fulfilled. Not that her mom wanted her to. Not exactly. She was just emotional and weepy and Trish wasn't capable of stepping back and cutting the cord fully. It would hurt her mom and she didn't deal out pain—only good things.

So she cleared her throat and smiled so hard that her cheeks hurt. "Mom, how am I supposed to find a man to make an honest woman of me and have a bunch of babies for you to spoil if I'm living in the same room I've had since birth? Aaron needs me right now. I can't leave him hanging."

Leveraging Aaron's name got her mom back under control. She gave another sniffle, but the wavering quality of her voice evened out. "You're right. Of course you're right. It's just so hard not seeing you."

"I know, Mom." She touched the side of her Chinese food container and sighed. *Cold.* "I'll talk to you later."

It took another five minutes to actually end the call, and by the time she did, it was all she could do to sink onto her couch. Trish stared at her cold dinner and fought against the burning in her throat. She wasn't overwhelmed. She was capable and positive and could handle anything the world threw at her.

But, God, she was so tired.

"I should eat." Her words barely diminished the growing silence in her apartment. She should turn on the television or do something to get some ambient noise going so she didn't feel quite so alone, but Trish just couldn't work up the energy to reach for the remote.

She closed her eyes. *I'll just rest here for a minute...*

Cameron checked his watch for the sixth time in the last thirty seconds. There was no denying it—

Trish was late. He stalked to the boardroom, half expecting to find her passed out under the table after a long night of ignoring his order, but it was just as drab and empty as it had been yesterday.

She didn't live that far away. How the hell was she late on her third day here?

He paced across the front office and back again and shot a glare at the elevators. Another look at his phone confirmed she hadn't answered his texts or responded to his missed calls. She was too damn excited about painting to have gone out drinking last night…wasn't she?

When it came down to it, he didn't know much about Trish at all. She was Aaron's sister. She was good at her job. She was far too peppy for his comfort. That about summed up his knowledge.

And she doesn't follow safety instructions particularly well.

Cameron stopped short. She was hurt. That had to be it. She wouldn't be late for anything other than a catastrophic reason, and if it involved Aaron and his family, Cameron would have heard about it. Which meant it had happened either in her apartment or somewhere in transit.

She could be injured right now, and he'd wasted time when he could have been helping her.

Not willing to wait for the elevator, he charged down the stairs. Seconds later, he was on the street, nearly running for her place. *Thank God she only lives a few blocks away.* Cameron made it there in record time. He keyed in the code Aaron had given him for safety reasons and then stopped short. He didn't know which apartment was hers.

Cursing under his breath, he yanked his phone out of his pocket and called Aaron. Cameron barely waited for his partner to answer before he cut in. "What's Trish's apartment number?"

Just like that, the sleepiness was gone from his friend's voice. "It's 3b. Why?"

"Call you in a few." He hung up and took the stairs again, nearly sprinting. He had no idea how he'd get into her apartment if she wasn't able to answer the door. *Should have thought that through.* Since he was already there, he pounded on the door and listened closely in case she cried for help.

Instead, footsteps padded on the other side of the door and a sleepy-looking Trish opened it. She yawned and then froze at the sight of him. Her blue eyes went wide. "Uh… What time is it?"

Cameron was too busy casting a worried eye over her to answer. She didn't *look* injured. No blood or protruding bones. Maybe she fell and hit her head? He stepped into the apartment and slipped his fingers through her tangled blond curls, gingerly feeling for a goose egg that might indicate a concussion.

Trish frowned. "What's going on?" She swatted at his hands. "What are you doing?"

"What did you fall from this time?"

She blinked and then backed up a few steps. "What are you talking about?"

She was definitely concussed if she didn't realize what the hell was going on. Cameron pointed at his watch. "It's nine."

Horror dawned across her face. "Oh God, I'm late." She looked down at herself and then at him, which was right around the time he noticed that she wore flannel pajamas with little cats frolicking across the bright blue background. It should have made her look childish, but Trish in pajamas led to thoughts of Trish in bed and Cameron turned to survey the apartment before he could follow *that* to its inevitable conclusion.

Small place, which was to be expected. A little studio apartment with a door on the other side of the room that must lead to the bathroom. Her bed was made—the comforter printed with brightly colored flowers—and she'd managed to imprint herself on the space in a limited amount of time. Flowerpots perched on either side of the kitchen sink, soaking up what little sunlight they could get this time of year. She'd even managed to find time to hang art on the walls—more florals, though they were strangely moody in black-and-white photography instead of bright oil like he would have expected. The only thing out of place was a container of what appeared to be Chinese takeout sitting on the coffee table.

Trish cleared her throat. "Cameron. You're in my apartment."

"You were late." He spoke almost absently, his gaze going back to the paintings. Black-and-white with the faintest hint of color in each. Compelling, though something about the close-ups of the different kinds of flower petals made him a little sad. Or maybe melancholy. One of those less than happy emotions that he wouldn't have thought to associate with the peppy woman in front of him.

Cameron wouldn't have said he was without layers—he was human and humans had layers of personality—but he tended to set aside the bullshit and call things like he saw them. It didn't always work out in his favor, but at least there wasn't room for misinterpretation or confusion.

The more time he spent around Trish, the more he realized this woman was nothing *but* layers. The bright woman who smiled her way through every situation. The flares of irritation and anger on occasion. The pride. And now this new revelation that he couldn't quite place within the puzzle that was Trish Livingston.

He cleared his throat. "I thought you'd fallen off something and hurt yourself."

"Cameron." Her exasperation drew his attention back to her. Trish crossed her arms over her chest. "You know I don't actually fall off things often, right? I'm not particularly injury-prone and just because I took a tumble off a ladder and you caught me like some kind of romance hero doesn't mean you need to get all anxious about my health."

She sounded perfectly reasonable, but perfectly reasonable people read the instructions on ladders and didn't step on the top step and lean precariously while painting. He mirrored her pose. "You're an hour late. What else was I supposed to think?"

"Oh, I don't know." She rolled her eyes. "That I fell asleep on my couch and forgot to set my alarm and overslept. That's a very *normal* thing to do." She made a face. "Wait, I take that back. I don't make a habit of being late, and I'm sorry I am, but you're acting like I'm an accident waiting to happen."

He started to argue, but the bottom line was that she was right. He shouldn't be here any more than he should have done half the shit he'd pulled with Trish up to this point. If he was smart, he'd make some excuse to leave and put this whole awkward encounter behind him.

At least until she showed up at the office to work.

Instead, Cameron stalked around her couch and used a single finger to pry open the Chinese-food container. *Full. Not even a bite missing.* "You skipped dinner."

"Not on purpose."

He glanced over, but she'd set her mouth in a firm line that told him no more information would be forthcoming. All evidence pointed to her sitting down to eat dinner and then falling asleep on the couch. Missing dinner. Missing breakfast. If he turned around and left now, no doubt she'd get ready and rush straight to the office and not eat until lunch, which put a full twenty-four hours between meals.

Unacceptable.

He sat on the couch and pointed at the bathroom. "Get ready. We're going to have a late breakfast before we go back to the office." Since there were no paint cans in evidence, she'd actually listened to his order, which was something at least. "We'll get the paint you want on the way. After you eat."

Trish's eyes sparked, but she got it under control almost immediately. She gave him a sweet smile that did nothing to mask the anger written in every line of her body. "Sure thing. I'll do my best not to slip on a bar of soap and bash my head against the tile. You know, because I'm *so* klutzy." She stalked to the bathroom and shut the door with a resounding snick.

Only then did Cameron relax back into the couch. They'd gone past the point of *should* this morning. He'd crossed the line coming here, but he wasn't sorry. Trish was okay, and that was all that mattered. She wouldn't be late again, and even if she wouldn't tell him what really happened last night, he had to be satisfied with that.

In the bathroom, the water turned on and Cameron groaned. Maybe leaving Trish to her own devices was the smarter option. Because, right now, all he could do was imagine her stepping beneath the spray, to mentally follow the cascade of water down her shoulders, her breasts, to her stomach and then lower yet. He wanted to follow that path with his mouth, to taste her and tease her and bring her to the edge over and over again until he finally tipped her into oblivion.

He just flat-out *wanted* her.

CHAPTER SIX

TRISH REALIZED HER mistake the second she stepped out of the shower. In her huff to get out of the room before she said something *truly* unkind to Cameron, she hadn't grabbed clothes. She wrapped a towel around herself and considered her options. Screaming at Cameron to close his eyes was tempting, but her stubborn streak kicked in and wouldn't let her.

He'd decided to burst into her apartment and then command her to have breakfast with him. Oh, she knew he'd only shown up because he was worried, and he'd decided on breakfast for the same reason. It didn't matter. The man didn't have a subtle bone in his body, but he should damn well try to talk to her like she had a brain in her head.

Or, rather, like she wasn't about to trip over some piece of furniture like she was starring in some old-school slapstick comedy.

Trish wiped down the foggy mirror and stared at her reflection. *You know why you're pissed, and it's not because Cameron was worried about you.* It might even have been kind of nice to bask in his concern if it wasn't attached to so many conflicting emotions.

Cameron saw her as Aaron's little sister. Emphasis on *little*.

He wanted her—she hadn't missed those signals—but he'd just as obviously written her off as untouchable. That should be a good thing. He was her boss, as she had to keep reminding herself. He *was* off-limits.

That didn't stop her from wanting to force him to acknowledge that he wanted her.

You're acting like a crazy person. Get ready in here. Walk to your closet like you totally aren't bothered by a really sexy man sitting on your couch and watching you do it. Retrieve clothes. Retreat to bathroom and get dressed.

It really was that simple.

Trish took a deep breath. She could do this. She'd faked her way out of awkward situations before, and she'd fake it out of this one, too. That settled, she quickly did her makeup and worked some product into her curls. Then there was nothing to do but open the door.

She paused to ensure her towel was wrapped

firmly around her body and straightened her spine. *I can do this. It's ten feet. It'll be fine.*

She opened the door and nearly ran into Cameron. Trish brought herself up short a bare inch from his chest and let loose a squeak of surprise. "Cameron!" Just as quickly, surprise morphed into frustration. She glared at his deep gray tie. "Damn it, Cameron. I didn't fall in the shower. That was a joke. You don't have to kick down the door and rescue me from some magical injury. You really need to relax, you know that? Have a beer, smoke a joint, meditate, do *something* because you jumping up my ass every time I turn around is going to get old fast."

Oh shit, I just said that. Out loud.

Still he didn't respond. She stared harder at his tie, sure that if she looked at his face, she'd see pure fury and then they'd really be fighting. *Think, Trish. Defuse the situation. Do something to distract him from the fact that you're yelling at him in a completely irrational way.* Her mind went blank and she panicked.

Trish dropped the towel.

Cameron's only response was a sharp intake of breath. She'd already gone too far to take it back now, so she lifted her chin and glared at him. Mortification threatened to take hold and drive her back to the bathroom. What was she doing? He had her so twisted up, she was parading naked in front of him, and she wasn't even doing it in a sad seduction attempt. No, this fell firmly into the Panic and Make Poor Choices column. "Don't you dare say anything."

"Freckles."

Her whole body clenched at the way he growled the inconspicuous word. She licked her lips. "What?"

"Freckles," Cameron repeated. He lifted a big hand and hovered a single finger over the center of her chest. "You have freckles everywhere." He traced a pattern over her breasts, connecting them without touching her.

The air disappeared from the room. Hell, the room itself disappeared. There was only Trish and Cameron and that single inch of space that kept him from touching her. Her body warmed beneath his attention, and he just kept tracing freckles, a look of utter concentration in his dark eyes. As if he had nowhere else to be, nothing else to be doing, and he wouldn't stop until he'd connected every single freckle on her body.

This could take hours.

Her nipples went tight at the thought. She actually started to lean forward before she caught herself.

It was already too late.

Cameron took a careful step back, and then another, though his gaze never left her body. Each movement was jerky and filled with barely controlled lust. He wanted her. *That* couldn't have been clearer. It was equally as clear that he had no intention of touching her again. He bumped into the couch and swung around to face the front door. "You should get dressed."

Right. Dressed. Because this thing between them couldn't happen.

Despite the fact he pointedly wasn't watching her, Trish kept her head up and her shoulders squared as she grabbed the first things she got her hands on—a red flare skirt and a white blouse—and retreated into the bathroom to get dressed. She stared at herself in the mirror for the space of a breath. *Yeah, definitely don't need blush if I'm going to be spending time around Cameron. I keep acting like an idiot, so I'm going to walk around with permanently pink cheeks. Wonderful.*

Her life would be so much easier if she could just find another job—preferably in a company run by women so she wouldn't have to deal with falling into lust with her boss.

This isn't just to help Aaron and you know it. You need experience to be able to get in for the jobs you really want instead of an unpaid internship or something entrance level. Because, let's be honest, you couldn't even get one of those *jobs after you graduated. You can't afford to quit.*

She really sucked at pep talks.

Trish found Cameron exactly where she'd left him and she gave a silent sigh. They could be in bed right now, doing fun, filthy things instead of about to have yet another conversation about why he couldn't want her. She got it. She *so* got it.

There was nothing for it. If she didn't do something drastic, he'd sit her down and gruffly reject her over and over again with his words. She'd had quite enough of that for today.

For always, really.

She straightened her shoulders and grabbed her purse from the table. "Shall we?"

"Trish."

Oh no. It wasn't a gruff talk she was going to get—it was a gentle one. *So much worse.* She blasted him with a bright smile. "We've already wasted enough time, don't you think?" She marched out the door and barely waited for him to step into the hall to lock it behind them. Then she was off, charging for the elevator, Cameron's muttered curse in her ears.

It wasn't until the elevators closed—shutting them in—that she realized her tactical mistake.

He shifted to face her, not quite blocking the doors, but ensuring she'd have to slide past him to bolt. Cameron slipped his hands into his pockets. "I'm not rejecting you."

Trish stared hard at the numbers ticking down and silently spit out a few curses of her own. Correct choice or not, it sure felt like rejection. She made a blatant—if panicked—offer. He turned away. End of story.

Except it wasn't the end of the story, because he was still taking up too much space in the previously spacious elevator. Since she couldn't will the machine to move any faster, she smiled at him. "It's irrelevant. Message sent and received. It won't be a problem." She made a face. "Well, it won't be a problem again. I guess I should apologize—again."

"Knock that shit off."

She forced her smile brighter and tried not to hunch her shoulders. "What are you talking about? I'm being professional." *For once, when it comes to Cameron.*

He didn't step back as the doors opened. He just frowned at her like she was a puzzle he didn't have all the pieces necessary to put together. "You don't have to wear the mask with me, Trish."

If Cameron had reached out and slapped her, he couldn't have surprised her more. She jerked back. "Actually, Cameron, I can do whatever I damn well please when it comes to how I arrange my face around you. I am being pleasant and professional and I don't know you well enough to expose an emotional vulnerability just to give you the satisfaction."

"You know me well enough to strip naked."

No way he just went there.

Except he most definitely just went there.

She shouldered past him and into the hall leading to the entrance of her apartment building. Though she could tell herself all sorts of true facts to try to calm down, she didn't much feel like calming down at this point. Cameron might take being blunt to a whole new level, but he was just being a flat-out dick with that statement and she wasn't in the mood to give him the benefit of the doubt.

No, she was more likely to give him a literal kick in the ass.

Into slow-moving traffic.

"Trish," he said as she exited the building.

She ignored him and swung around a group of three guys to head in the direction of Home Depot. It was too far to walk, especially on her way back with paint cans in tow, but if she hailed a cab, either Cameron would climb in with her—which would just piss her off further—or it would be a childish fleeing of the conversation he obviously wanted to have. It didn't seem to matter that she *didn't* want to.

Clear the air. If you don't, it'll fester.

Trish spun on her heel and got a little perverse pleasure at the fact Cameron had to skid to a stop to avoid running into her. She glared pointedly at the distance between them until he backed up a step. They had an audience in the form of people passing by, but she didn't care. "I don't care if you are half owner of Tandem Security or my brother's best friend or richer than sin or anything else. You do *not* get to talk to me like that. Even if we were fucking six ways from Sunday, you still don't get to talk to me like that. You're a cranky asshole. I get it. Everyone gets it. That is no excuse to be a jackass and throw the rejection that's supposedly not a rejection in my face. A good guy would never speak of it again, but I suppose it's too much to hope that you'd know that without me telling you." She pointed at herself. "This is me telling you— do not bring it up again. Do you understand me?"

Cameron narrowed his eyes but seemed to realize that there was only one right answer in that moment. "I understand."

"Good. In that case, I will see you back at the office." She turned and flagged down a cab, sending a silent thank-you to the universe that she didn't have to stand there like an idiot during her dramatic exit.

Even though she knew better, she turned to look

out the back window as the cab pulled away from the curb. Cameron stood there, watching her with an unreadable expression on his gorgeous face. She should have felt, if not peaceful, then at least sure that this was the end of things between them outside of the safe roles of boss and employee. Of Aaron's little sister and Aaron's best friend.

Too bad she couldn't shake the niggling feeling that nothing had been resolved.

That things between them were just beginning.

CHAPTER SEVEN

"No. ABSOLUTELY FUCKING NOT." Cameron shoved out of his chair and nearly threw his phone across the room. It wouldn't help anything and finding a new phone was a pain in the ass, but that didn't kill the impulse to banish Aaron's voice from his ear.

His partner was, naturally, totally unsympathetic. "I already had Trish book the flights. Concord Inc. is a huge company and if we can impress them, they'll keep us on retainer going forward. That's not the kind of account we can afford to turn away just because you're an asshole who hates people—or because you have a history with the COO."

"I don't hate people." He didn't sound convincing, which was just as well because he and Aaron had had this conversation more times than he could count. "They just waste my time." He growled. "And it's hardly a history."

"For the potential price tag attached to this account, it's the opposite of wasting your precious time. Hell, *I* took time out of paternity leave to talk to Nikki Lancaster. They're not going to wait on this."

Cameron paced another circle around his office but slowed as everything Aaron said finally penetrated his irritation over being commanded to leave the city. "You said 'flights.' Plural."

"Yes. I did. Because Trish is going with you. It's a huge-ass leap to toss her into shark-infested waters by doing this, so you're going to have to buck up and try not to make her job harder than it's already going to be."

"She can't go." The sentence burst out before he could stop it.

For the first time since Aaron called, he paused. A second. Two. Three. "Why can't she go?"

Because I have the picture of her naked imprinted on my brain and I've jacked myself off to the thought of tracing her freckles with my tongue every night since. A truth he would cut out said tongue before admitting aloud. Cameron scrubbed a hand over his face. "She's too new. Nikki Lancaster will eat her alive." Nikki had taken over as COO of Concord Inc. when it was a struggling corporate business and had almost single-handedly turned it into a Fortune 500 company over the last five years. Aaron was right—securing that account would not only be a shit ton of money in the bank, but it would open further doors.

Tandem Security wasn't hurting for cash. They accepted the contracts they wanted, when they wanted, and without having to travel to do it.

"Trish can handle it," Aaron said carefully, as if feeling his way.

"It makes more sense for her to stay here and handle the office while I go and deal with Nikki." There. That was a nice logical solution.

That Aaron shot down without hesitation. "She's too new to be left alone, and having on-site experience negotiating with a new client is an asset." He paused.

"Unless there's some problem neither of you have told me about?"

"No problem." No way to get out of this without setting off Aaron's internal alarms, either. He had no choice but to go forward with this trip. Cameron sat on the edge of his desk and stared hard at his closed door. "We have this covered." He might not like the idea of being in close quarters with her—closer quarters, technically, since they'd been working together for over a week since the morning she overslept. It didn't matter if they were going over notes before a client meeting or painting the boardroom. Trish kept a painfully bright barrier between them and deflected anything that might resemble flirting with a beaming smile and blatant change of subject. There was no sign of the temper she'd flashed before she took off in that cab, and the lack bothered him almost as much as having her tear him a new one had.

"Cameron?"

Shit, he needed to keep his head in the game. "Sorry. I missed that."

"I can tell." If anything, Aaron sounded more concerned. "Do you want me to come in and go over the details with you before you go?"

He clenched his jaw to keep his first response inside. Recent years hadn't been kind to his track record when it came to dealing with clients, so Aaron's offer wasn't completely out of line. Aaron knew him better than anyone. Cameron's patience wore thin with increasing regularity, and he found himself snapping at them before he had a chance to dial it back. So he stopped bothering to dial it back at all.

He and Aaron had met in college, and he knew his friend always assumed there was a deeper backstory to his being a dick. Some tragic past he never talked about. Some defining event that made him wash his hands of all the social niceties.

There wasn't.

Cameron's parents were good people. Nothing outstandingly bad had happened to him growing up, and if being a black man in this country came with its own set of bullshit and headaches, it wasn't exactly a surprise. There were always others who had it worse.

No, the truth was that he preferred machines to dealing with actual humans because machines made sense. There was always a concrete answer, one that wasn't open to interpretation. Every aspect of a computer was clearly defined and had its own set of rules to work around—but those rules were clearly stated from the beginning.

People were nuanced and managed to be multiple things, often at the same time. They said things they didn't mean, and then got pissed when he took those things as truth and acted accordingly. They had masks within masks and motivations they rarely put out in the open. Cameron didn't *get* people, and maneuvering through their needs and emotions, even for surface-level interactions, left him exhausted and feeling like an asshole.

Because he fucked it up. Every single time.

Just like you did with Trish.

I couldn't take what she was offering. It would backfire and she'd have been hurt in the process.

There is no good exit route once we step past the point of no return.

Could have handled it better, though.

Yeah, no shit.

"Cameron, you're not even listening to me."

He scrubbed a hand over his head and mentally made a note to shave his head again soon—before they went to London, for sure. Cameron might not handle people well, but he knew Aaron as well as he knew himself. The man didn't want to come back to work yet. He just needed Cameron to say the right thing to assuage his guilt and let him take the break he'd more than earned.

He cleared his throat. "I have this covered. Go back to doting on your fiancée and baby and stop worrying about us."

Another hesitation, but shorter this time. Aaron loved Tandem Security as much as Cameron did, but he loved his new family more. Which was how it should be. Aaron's relationship with Becka had started unconventionally enough, but they'd found a good balance and their love for their new daughter filled up a room in a way that made even Cameron smile. It didn't hurt that Summer was cute as hell and seemed to like *him* just fine. Babies were simple—simple needs, simple desires. If she cried, it was because she wasn't having some need met, and *that* he understood.

Too bad adults weren't that easy to figure out.

He didn't begrudge his best friend his happiness. He just wished Aaron would stop worrying about the company. He was only gone for a couple months. Cameron could manage to apply a filter to himself for a couple months until his friend was back in the office. He wasn't *that* much of a lost cause.

His partner got a dreamy tone. "Summer smiled at me today. The book says it's probably just gas, but I don't give a fuck. It's the cutest thing I've ever seen."

That, he believed. She was adorable. Cameron managed a smile. "I'm glad you're happy." If anyone deserved that happiness, Aaron did. He was a good guy, and he'd spent too many years putting up with Cameron's shit *not* to have earned a good turn or two.

"Thanks. That means a lot."

Cameron checked his watch. "I'll check in once I have things lined up."

"Talk to you then."

He hung up and checked his email. Sure enough, confirmation for a flight to London had appeared. Since there was one for Trish as well, he assumed she had her passport updated. *You're focusing on minor details to avoid focusing on the fact that you're going to be traveling with her.*

Easier to remember why she was off-limits when in this office. There was no escaping the constant knowing that it was inappropriate to follow through on the look he sometimes saw lingering in her blue eyes, or to submit to the gravitational pull between them that seemed to grow stronger with every day he didn't give in.

Put them in a different country, in a hotel together...

Getting ahead of yourself. Trish might have been interested before, but she's made it pretty fucking clear she's not now.

That was a good point.

Cameron sighed and rounded his desk to sink into his chair. Whether Trish did or didn't want to start something still was irrelevant. They had business to conduct and they'd more than proven they could work together when required. He just had to keep his head in the game and not be the one to fuck it up.

Easy enough. Work comes first—end of story.

He had absolutely nothing to worry about.

Trish paced from one wall to the other and back again. "I can't do this. It's going to blow up in my face."

"It might be helpful if you explain exactly *what* you're not doing."

She glanced at her almost-sister-in-law, Becka Baudin. She sat on the couch with Summer propped carefully on a pillow, nursing away. When Trish pictured her big brother with someone, it was some straitlaced woman who probably thought doing taxes was fun and drank expensive red wine and vacationed to exotic places with topless beaches.

On second thought, Becka probably fits the last one.

She didn't fit much else when it came to expectations. She was a blue-haired beauty who was both a personal trainer and led a bunch of hardcore fitness classes—at least before her pregnancy got too far along. She was also hilarious and nice and loved Aaron to distraction. In short, she was perfect.

Trish wasn't here for perfection, though. She needed advice. "I'm traveling with Cameron. To London. Alone. For as long as it takes to secure this account."

"I know it's not super normal for the guys to travel but…" Becka trailed off and her blue eyes went wide. "Oh. *Oh.* You and Cameron?" She leaned forward and winced. "Sorry, Summer." A quick adjustment and the baby was nursing happily again. Becka frowned. "Why didn't I know about this?"

"Because there's nothing to know about." Nothing except she kept throwing herself at him and he kept setting her gently back and trying to explain why he would never touch her. Nothing except her pride being bruised beyond all repair because of her impulsiveness.

It was the height of insanity to still want him after he'd turned her down—more than once— but apparently her self-control had taken a vacation somewhere along the way. She couldn't be in the same room with Cameron without ogling him, and it didn't help that he kept wearing those fitted faded T-shirts that clung to his body like Trish wanted to.

Oh my God, I'm jealous of a piece of clothing.

"That tone of voice says there's definitely something to know about, but okay. Nothing to know about." Becka shook her head. "If you're worried about doing something to screw up the account, neither Aaron nor Cameron would send you if they thought you weren't capable. So they obviously think you can handle it."

"I've been working there like two weeks. I heard Aaron say that Concord Inc. can boost Tandem Security up to the next level. If I botch this, they won't get to that next level." She'd already failed so many freaking times. There was absolutely nothing in her track record that should cause everyone around her to give her yet another vote of confidence.

Not everyone.

She'd bit the bullet and told her parents last night that she'd be out of the country for a while on work and they'd reacted about as well as she would have expected. Oh, her dad was supportive, if worried about his little girl out in the big world without someone to protect her. She didn't hold it against him—he treated both his daughters like that. Her sister just never gave him cause for worry. It seemed like all Trish did was worry him, even when she tried not to.

And her mom…

She sighed. "My mother had some choice words on the subject." Choice words that ended in tears, and demands to know what she'd done as a mother to drive Trish to cross an ocean to get away from her. It had taken two hours and a promise to visit over the weekend once she got home to calm her mother down and get her back to some semblance of normality.

"Oh." Becka made a face. "Look, I'm hardly the authority on healthy parent-child relationships, and your mom is a nice lady, but she really needs to get a hobby that has nothing to do with her adult children. Knitting. Charity. Pole dancing classes.

Doesn't matter, but it might distract her from the whole empty nester thing she's got going on."

Trish stared. "You did not just list pole dancing classes alongside charity and knitting as activities my mom should try."

"Why not?" Becka gave a wicked grin. "It's great core work."

"I'm going to tell Aaron you said that."

"It's been a couple days since I shocked him, so I'm about due for another one."

Trish burst out laughing, and the sound drained out the anxiety that had been building since Aaron called her with instructions for the trip. She sank onto the chair across from the couch and shook her head. "Thanks. I needed that."

"I know." Becka shifted Summer to the other side and adjusted her clothing. "Here's the deal— you're not going to fuck up. Thinking you might is just going to undermine your confidence and ensure you *do* screw up. So do that brilliant shining thing you do and just power through it—fake it until you make it. They'll be so relieved not to have to deal directly with Cameron, they'll fall all over themselves to give you whatever you ask for. Aaron already negotiated a preliminary contract, so it's just a matter of ensuring the actual contract is laid out to his specifications."

She made it sound so easy when she put it like

that. Nice and simple. Trish ran her hand over the smooth fabric of the chair. "Why is everyone so down on Cameron? He's kind of gruff, but he's not a total asshole like everyone says."

Becka shrugged. "Cameron is a difficult personality. I know because it takes one to know one, though we're different flavors." She shifted back and sighed. "I think the real question is, why are you trying so hard not to jump to his defense?"

She shouldn't talk about it. Positivity was Trish's gig, and there was nothing positive about the shame she'd been carrying around since that first kiss. Maybe she could have recovered if she hadn't dropped the towel and had him turn away in response. Maybe. Either way, it wasn't fair to dump her issues on her brother's baby mama and fiancée.

But under those sympathetic eyes, she found herself speaking. Trish shifted her gaze to the pattern on the rug because it was easier to spill her secrets there than to the woman across from her. "I kissed him. And after he politely—for him—told me that it wasn't going to happen, I faked my way through being totally professional and okay with it. Right up until I forgot to set my alarm, slept in and had him show up on my doorstep. I, uh, panicked and it ended up with me naked and him once again explaining that it most definitely wasn't going to happen."

A muffled snort brought her head up. Trish glared. "Are you laughing at me? I've been rejected twice and even if he's right about it being a bad idea to bang like bunnies, it still stings. And if he'd stop *looking* at me like he does, it would make it a whole lot easier to bear." Sometimes she would turn and catch such heat in Cameron's gaze that it was a wonder she didn't turn into a pillar of lustful flames right there in the office. But he turned away.

Every. Single. Time.

"Oh God, you poor thing." Becka let loose a peal of laughter that filled the room to the brim. "Like running headfirst into a brick wall, isn't it?"

"That's not…inaccurate."

Becka grinned. "I'm familiar with the feeling. You've got freckles all over, right?"

The change in subject made her frown. "Sure. Why?"

"Tell me one thing—actually, tell me two things. How long did it take him to turn away when you dropped the towel?"

"Um…" Trish's skin went hot at the memory. "It wasn't instant, if that's what you mean."

"Mmm-hmm. And when he *looks* at you… Is it

possible he's retracing your freckles all over mentally?"

Now that she mentioned it, his gaze did tend to take a specific path when he thought she wasn't looking. A very similar path to the one he'd traced in the air above her skin that day. She cleared her throat. "It's possible."

"That's what I thought." Another laugh. Becka's smile promised all sorts of wicked things. "Have fun on your work trip, Trish. I sure as hell would in your position."

CHAPTER EIGHT

THE FLIGHT TO London was both heaven and hell. Cameron had never had a problem feeling cramped or caged in when he flew first class. The seats there hadn't fallen victim to the desire to cram more paying passengers into the same amount of space that the rest of the plane had. He usually didn't have to worry about his broad shoulders crowding out the person next to him and could relax and work through however long the flight was.

That was before he sat next to Trish.

Even with the space between them, he couldn't shake his awareness of her. Every shift where she crossed and recrossed her legs. Every time her mass of curly hair brushed his shoulder. Every breath. She fell asleep halfway through the flight and ended up slumped against him, her little body curled in the seat and her head halfway in his lap.

He loved every agonizing second of it.

Though he managed to keep from touching her more than strictly necessary, it was all too easy to imagine they were traveling *together*, jetting off to some exotic island or snowy peak to spend a week tangled up in each other and blind to the rest of the world.

Instead, he went over the preliminary contract for the tenth time since Aaron had sent it over. It didn't matter that the terms were standard with a few small exceptions. They'd handled overseas clients before, but Concord Inc. was unique in the way that they had an independent server for all their internal workings. Something like that wouldn't normally need Tandem Security's expertise—impossible to hack what someone couldn't get to in the first place—but Concord Inc. did need access to public servers for outside communications.

And *that* could be breached.

Cameron kept himself busy mulling over the possible options as the plane finally landed. Trish managed to sleep through the entire thing, so he gently squeezed her shoulder. "We're here."

She opened those big blue eyes and blinked at him a few times as if she couldn't quite place where they were or who he was. Awareness rushed over her expression between one breath and the next and she licked her pretty pink lips.

He went rock-hard, and then silently cursed himself for reacting at all. He couldn't seem to stay in line when it came to this woman, but that wasn't her fault. No, the blame lay squarely on his shoulders, and after his dickhead comment that day at her apartment, he'd been careful navigating the minefield that every conversation between them had become.

His fault.

Trish sat up and pushed her hair back from her face. "Sorry. I didn't mean to take over your space."

Since what he wanted most in that moment was for her to take over his space—and his cock—fully, he gritted out, "No problem."

He managed to get control of himself by the time they deplaned, got through the custom's process and grabbed their luggage. It was still relatively early in local time, but they wouldn't meet with Nikki Lancaster until the next day. "Food?"

"Please." She looked a little...wilted...after all the traveling. Trish's hair was fluffier than he'd ever seen it, and she huddled within her large coat, her eyes seeming larger than normal. It was obvious that, despite her nap, what she needed was food and rest and some time to adjust to their new location.

Cameron got them to their hotel—a little boutique place strategically placed a few short blocks from Concord Inc. They'd ended up with a two-bedroom suite, which was what he and Aaron usually booked when their work required travel, but it took on a new significance with Trish.

They were staying behind the same locked door in this place.

For fuck's sake, get ahold of yourself. This is business. This has only ever been business.

Except nothing when it came to Trish felt like business.

He held the door open for her, angling his body away to avoid her accidentally brushing against him. "Take whatever room you want."

"Generous." Trish shot him an arch look over her shoulder, as if she knew exactly why he was being so generous. She didn't say anything else, though. She just dropped her bag in the middle of the small living space and went investigating.

Cameron forced himself not to follow her, but instead walked to the tiny dining room table and started setting up his computer. "If you want a shower, I can run down and grab us some food."

She poked her head out the first bedroom door. "My kingdom for some genuine fish and chips."

"I'll keep that in mind." He left before he could think too hard about what Trish in the shower would be like. Her showering had almost been their downfall before, and Cameron knew himself well enough to know his self-control wouldn't last through a third time of backing away from her. Better to avoid the temptation altogether by removing himself from the building.

He had no idea how they were supposed to get through the next few days without stepping all over each other. Challenging enough to be closeted in an office with her when they were able to retreat to their respective homes after hours. But being together 24-7 in the same workplace, the same hotel suite?

The odds of keeping his hands off her were not in his favor.

Cameron took his time walking down to the lobby and waylaid the bellhop to get recommendations for places with good fish and chips. The nearest one the guy recommended was more than a few blocks, but after being cramped in the plane for so long, he welcomed the chance to stretch his legs.

And it would ensure Trish had plenty of time to shower and get dressed again before he returned.

Satisfied he'd made the right call, he lengthened

his stride and put some distance between himself and the siren call Trish Livingston represented.

Trish took her time in the shower, washing away the grit of traveling. She'd chosen the room with the smallest bed—Cameron needed more space than she did, after all—and it had the added bonus of the better bathroom. There was a claw-foot tub big enough to hold a party in and the shower wasn't exactly orgy-sized, but it was generous for the square footage.

She shut off the water and wrapped a towel around herself. The fluffy fabric slid luxuriously against her skin, drawing out a shiver. Sitting next to Cameron on the plane had her all pent-up and needy. Even after the shower, she was sure she could smell the evergreen soap he used. Her body responded accordingly, skin going tight, nipples pebbling, the spot between her thighs increasingly achy.

God, she wanted him.

Trish padded to the door to her room and peeked out. The suite was silent and empty. She had no idea how long Cameron had been gone— or when he'd be back. A thrill went through her at the thought. *I shouldn't risk it.* But on the heels of that, her innate stubbornness kicked in. *That only makes it hotter.*

She shut her door and tossed the towel over the low-backed chair situated by the window. Naked, she slipped between the sheets and stretched out. It wouldn't take long. She'd been halfway there since she woke up surrounded by him. It didn't matter that they'd been in separate seats and he'd barely touched her. Trish was so damn primed, all it would take was his breathing on her clit and she'd come screaming.

Her toes curled as she cupped her breasts, pretending it was *his* hands there. Not rough. Certainly not gentle. A firm touch. A freaking perfect touch.

It's not perfect because it's not the real thing.

She didn't care. She'd come too far to go back now.

Trish rolled one nipple between her thumb and forefinger and ran her other hand down her stomach to stroke her clit. A moan slipped free as she pushed a single finger into herself. She arched her back, letting the sheets slide down to reveal her breasts. It didn't matter that no one could see her. She *felt* watched, and that was enough to send her skirting along the edge of a truly great orgasm.

Imagining it was *Cameron's* eyes on her?

She circled her clit once, twice, a third time, and as she came, she moaned his name aloud. "Oh my God, *Cameron*." Her orgasm rolled over her, bowing her back and she could have sworn she heard him murmuring her name. Pleasure-induced hallucination, for sure.

Except when Trish opened her eyes, she wasn't alone in her room.

Cameron stood in the doorway, his hand still raised as it must have been when he knocked. The door hadn't even swung open all the way, but there was no way he'd missed the tail end of that self-love session. Especially not the part where she'd moaned his name as she came.

Shit.

She sat up, thought about clutching the sheet to her chest and gave it up as a lost cause. He'd already seen the goods—more than once at this point. The only person who'd seen her naked so many times without there actually being sex involved was her freaking doctor. And Trish didn't want to sleep with her doctor.

Cameron didn't say anything. Didn't move. Didn't seem to so much as breathe.

There was no brazening her way out of this situation. She didn't know who'd cursed her that she seemed to be destined to perpetually humiliate herself in front of Cameron, but it was time to face the music.

She met his gaze directly. "I don't suppose you missed any of that?"

"You said my name when you came." His voice was deeper than normal, and each word rumbled in the pit of her stomach. Lower. "I've tried to stay away from you, Trish."

"I know."

"You're making it fucking impossible."

Was this… Could this actually be happening?

She couldn't go to him. She'd already thrown herself at him too many times for her pride to survive yet another rejection. Trish licked her lips, half-convinced she could taste him there despite weeks passing since their last kiss. "Maybe it's time to try something new, then." *Try me. Touch me. Fuck me.*

He stepped into her room. He moved slowly, seeming to weigh her every breath as if testing her resolve. Little did he know it took everything she had to keep perfectly still and wait for him to approach the bed instead of flinging herself at him.

"Cameron," she whispered.

"Yeah." He matched her tone.

Her next words would either push them over the edge or yank them back to safety. She knew what the smart choice would be, but Trish had been making the *smart* choice for her entire life and look where it got her—nowhere near the path she'd always thought she'd walk. It was time to try something new. She drew in a shallow breath. "Touch me."

He reached down and grabbed a fistful of the blankets covering the bed. "That's not a good idea."

"I know." No point in arguing. It was the truth. "Do it anyway."

He lifted his gaze to meet hers. "You're sure."

Not a question, but she wanted no chance of miscommunication. If they were sprinting past the point of no return, they would do it together with eyes wide-open. "I'm sure."

He drew the blankets from the bed in an agonizingly slow movement. The sensation of sheets sliding down her body had her biting her bottom lip, but the forbidding look in his dark eyes kept her still and silent, unwilling to do anything to break the spell.

"Show me."

Trish stopped breathing. "What?"

"You were imagining me. Us. Tell me what you pictured." He didn't move from his spot at the end of the bed, just out of reach. "Show me how you touched yourself."

She should be embarrassed. Humiliated. But being on display for him set her aflame. She was so close to having what she wanted…

This is exactly what I wanted.

Cameron's eyes on me.

She shifted until she was on her back and resumed the position she'd been in when this all started. With him watching, she cupped her breasts. "You touched me here. Made my toes curl."

"Mmm." His appreciative growl vibrated through her entire body.

She started to slide one hand down her stomach, but he made a negative sound. "Slow, Trish. I've been thinking about tracing your freckles with my tongue since I saw them. I sure as fuck wouldn't rush this."

The heat beneath her skin flared hotter. She licked her lips. "I can't do that myself."

"I know."

Slowly, oh so slowly that she didn't dare breathe, she spread her thighs, revealing everything to him. "Touch me, Cameron. Please."

The bed dipped beneath his weight and then he was there, covering her with his body. His clothes scraped lightly against her skin, a barrier she wanted gone, but Trish couldn't focus with his weight settling over her like the best kind of promise. This was happening. They were doing this.

She grabbed his hand and pressed it to the center of her chest, directly over the spot he'd almost touched her that day back in her apartment. "Touch me," she repeated. "Make it better than I imagined."

He spread his fingers, nearly covering her chest completely from collarbone to collarbone. Cameron shifted his hand up, dragging his thumb along the front of her throat as he cupped the back of her neck and tilted her face up to meet his. He kissed her slowly, beginning with the softest brushing of his lips against hers and then teasing her mouth open with his tongue. The soft kiss was directly at odds with the way he spread her thighs with his own and ground against her clit, his cock a hard ridge in his pants. "This is what you want."

It wasn't a question, but she refused to allow the slightest hint of blurred lines between them. Trish kissed his neck, his jaw, and finally reclaimed his mouth. "This is what I want, Cameron. Don't stop touching me."

CHAPTER NINE

CAMERON HAD SPENT himself more times than he wanted to count with fantasies of having Trish naked beneath him. It was almost enough for him to believe this was a fever dream caused by jacking himself one time too many to the map of the freckles on her body. But as he stroked her tongue with his, there was no denying that this was happening. He kissed along her jaw and down her neck. "I've wanted to do this since that day in your apartment."

He started with the freckle directly over her left breast. Cameron had always had a damn good memory, and he put it to use now, marking a path from freckle to freckle with his mouth. He lingered on the curves of her small breasts, on her pretty pink nipples, on the soft lines of her stomach, before finally settling between her thighs.

Trish gasped out a breath she'd been holding. "Wow."

"That was only one path. I'll revisit…later." He ran his cheek along one thigh and then the other, enjoying the way her entire body flushed at the contact. He spread her thighs wider. As much as he wanted to drive into her, knowing her orgasm had already primed her, he wanted a taste more. Cameron had pictured doing this so many times. He wouldn't let anyone rush him—not even himself.

He dragged his tongue up the center of her pussy and growled at the way she jumped. As if he'd attached a live wire to his tongue. "Relax, Trish. Enjoy this."

"Relax, Trish," she mimicked breathlessly. "You're asking the impossible."

Despite himself, he grinned against her heated flesh. Cameron pinned her squirming hips and gave himself over to the taste of her on his tongue and the way she cried out every time he circled her clit. She was close. Her hips tried to rise to meet his mouth, but he kept her in place, determined to drive her ruthlessly over the edge, to feel her come on his tongue. He needed it like he'd never needed anything before, and like hell would she deny him.

"Cameron." Trish's back bowed as she orgasmed.

He'd barely managed to lift his head when she

grabbed his arms and yanked. Cameron crawled up her body, but stopped while still on his hands and knees. "Fuck. Condoms."

"Oh yeah, that." She rolled from beneath him and teetered over to her suitcase, and he took the opportunity to strip. He glanced over as she returned with a giant box of condoms. Trish caught his incredulous look and gave a sheepish smile. "Hope springs eternal." She yanked out a condom and tore open the foil packet. One well-placed nudge and he was on his back with her straddling him.

The desire in her blue eyes hadn't abated, but there was mischief there now, too. She smiled as she slowly rolled the condom onto his cock and gave him a stroke. "Oh yeah. This is happening."

He barked out a laugh. "Your dirty talk is superb."

"I don't need dirty talk." She shifted up and notched his cock in her entrance. Before he had a chance to brace, she sank down until he was sheathed to the hilt. Trish hissed out a breath. "Lordy, you're big."

He cupped her hips, trying to keep her still while her body accustomed itself to him, but she was already moving, rolling her hips a little. With the faint light from the window behind her, she looked like an angel, blond curls in a halo around her head and the soft lines of her body shifting sensuously as she rode his cock. Trish planted her hands on his chest and picked up her pace, sliding almost completely off him and then slamming back down. "God, Cameron, you feel good. Better than good. There aren't proper filthy words to describe how good."

"You're doing a damn good job of describing it." He arched off the bed and caught her mouth, needing to taste her even as she rode him. She followed him back to the bed, her fucking him turning into something slower, deeper, her breasts sliding against his chest with every stroke. *Yes. This.* He squeezed her ass, using the leverage to grind her clit against his pelvis as he thrust up.

"Yes." She gasped. "Do that again. Keep doing that."

He obeyed. He couldn't have stopped if he wanted to. Pleasure danced down his spine, taking up residence in his balls and the base of his cock, but Cameron ruthlessly held it at bay. He wanted to feel her come again, *needed* it. He thrust again and again and again.

Trish came with a cry loud enough to make the windows rattle. She slumped against his chest and he rolled them so he could settle between her thighs. The look of sated pleasure on her face was almost enough to make him blow right then and there, but he gritted his teeth and wrestled himself back under control.

Then, and only then, did he kiss her. Slow and deep and exploring as if he hadn't had his mouth all over her body not too long ago. He kissed her until she seemed to come back to herself, until she wrapped her legs around his waist and writhed beneath him where he had her pinned to the bed.

He pulled out and flipped her onto her stomach. Cameron smoothed a hand down her spine, enjoying the way her muscles flexed beneath his touch and her ass rose in offering. She had freckles smattering her back and the curves of her ass, too, and he reached between her thighs to stroke her pussy as he mentally traced the path he planned on taking. He had the fanciful thought that one day he'd like to paint constellations on her skin.

"Oh God, I don't know if I can go again." She moaned against her pillow. But her hips moved to meet his hand again and again.

Cameron leaned down and set his teeth against the back of her neck. "I'm not through with you, Trish."

"Oh, well, then… Carry on." She laughed helplessly, the sound turning into a moan as he pushed two fingers into her.

"Ride my hand, Trish. Take what you need." He kissed down her spine, straying to one side or the other to trace her freckles with his tongue. Her hips bucked against his hand, but he held steady, needed to feel her come apart again.

She went still with a shudder. "It's not enough. I need your cock."

The words made him harder than he'd ever been. He forced himself to give the small of her back the same care and attention he'd spent on the rest of her body, but he was more than ready to meet her need as he nudged her knees farther apart and notched his cock in her entrance. He fed her inch after inch, keeping her still with a hand on her hip until he was sheathed to the hilt. He closed his eyes, but the sight of her was too much to resist.

This time, there would be no holding back. He needed this—her—too much.

Cameron gripped her hips and brought her back as he thrust forward. She cried out, and he almost stopped, but Trish reached back and bracketed his wrist with a hand. "Harder, Cameron. I need more."

"I need it, too." He gave himself over to the feel of fucking her, her pussy clamping tight on him with every stroke, her cries and the sound of flesh meeting flesh filling the room. She came with his name on her lips, and he followed her willingly over the edge with a curse of his own.

As Cameron slumped onto the mattress next

to her, he was struck by the thought that he might follow this woman anywhere.

Trish stared at the ceiling and wondered when the hell her life had taken a hard turn into crazy town. Was it when she moved back in with her parents after college? When she'd agreed to take the job working for Aaron? The second she set eyes on Cameron O'Clery?

Wherever the tipping point was, the end result had her naked and breathing hard with the taste of Cameron lingering on her lips.

She'd loved every second of it.

"Aaron can't know."

She closed her eyes and counted silently to five—and then to ten. "Did you think I was going to run straight from being in bed with you to call my brother and tell him we just had sex?"

A pause and, despite not looking at him, she could almost see the gears turning in Cameron's head as he mentally replayed what he'd just said. He cleared his throat. "That wasn't tactful."

"You think?"

His big hand settled on her stomach. "Trish, look at me."

She didn't want to. Opening her eyes meant having to fight to reclaim the mask, and she didn't have the energy right now. Being bright and positive had been her go-to thing for so long, she didn't always notice she was doing it. It barely took effort anymore to smile and make people's days better.

It took effort with Cameron. So much freaking effort. Mostly because he insisted on demanding the truth from her over and over again.

He skated his hand up the center of her chest to cup her jaw. "Trish."

She sighed and opened her eyes. If Cameron O'Clery was devastating in the office while wearing clothes, he was downright heartbreaking naked in bed with her. Something about his expression looked softer here, as if some artist had painted him in gentle golden tones. His dark skin stretched over an impossibly broad chest, drawing her eyes south, ever south, to where the sheets hid the lower half of his body from her view. "You're beautiful."

"Thanks." He huffed out a laugh. He stroked her bottom lip with his thumb. "I've never done anything like this before. It has me all fucked in the head, and I'm even less tactful than normal."

"I didn't think that was possible."

Another of those soft laughs. "That makes two of us." His smile dimmed. "But since we're in an uncomfortable position on two fronts, we have to talk about this."

She knew that. Really, she did. She had just hoped to get to enjoy the afterglow from the glorious sex for a few minutes before they jumped right into talking about the nitty-gritty details. Trish forced herself to smile. "Sure. We can't tell Aaron. I'm aware of that." Her brother didn't usually fall into overprotective jerk mode, but there was a first time for everything. Beyond that, he already had enough to worry about with his new baby and a wedding to plan.

Cameron seemed to weigh his next words. "Our relationship while on the clock can't change. We're already blurring the lines too much as it is. If we let it bleed over into Tandem Security..."

"We won't. It's as simple as that." She glanced at the clock. "What are the odds our food is still warm?"

His laugh rumbled through her body in the most delicious way possible. "Even I can take that hint." Cameron pressed a light kiss to her temple that she felt all the way to her toes. "Let's feed you and then we can go over the next steps."

For a second, she thought he meant they were going to detail the rules and boundaries for sex versus no sex, but as he pulled on his pants and headed for the door, Trish realized he'd already made the jump back to business. She stared after him. *What the hell did I get myself into?*

You know exactly what. This is what you wanted.

It was. She just had to remember that, as she

navigated a new existence where she knew what it felt like to come on Cameron's cock.

Trish touched her hair, but it was a lost cause. She'd need another shower to have any hope of taming it, but since their first meeting was tomorrow, it'd have to do for now. A quick rummage through her suitcase for something comfortable to wear, and she walked out to find Cameron setting out the food on the table.

He glanced at her and went still. "What is that?"

She froze. "What?"

"What are you wearing?"

Oh. That. She glanced down at the oversize shirt she'd bought on a whim. It had Minnie Mouse on it and, now that she thought about it, it was probably something a child would wear. "You have a problem with Minnie?"

"I have a problem with the fact that you need to eat, and I see you in that and all I want to do is toss the food and have *you* on the table instead."

"Oh." Trish blinked. *"Oh."*

Cameron shook his head. "Sit down and eat something."

For the first time in well over a week, she found herself enjoying his abruptness. Trish sank into her seat and grinned. "Is it that the shirt is large enough to fit three of me that gets you going? Or is it a secret Minnie Mouse fetish?"

He set her fish and chips in front of her and dropped into the seat opposite. "You could wear a paper bag and I'd still want to tear the damn thing off you." He picked up a french fry. "It'd be easier to get into than most clothes, so there's something to be said for that."

"You just made a joke."

"I do that on occasion."

"Huh." Trish took a few bites. That seemed to satisfy him that she was going to eat instead of waste away before his eyes, because Cameron set to his food with a single-minded focus she'd only ever seen in athletes and big dudes. When she'd eaten as much as her stomach could handle for the time being, she sat back and found him watching her. "What?"

"I don't get it."

"There's a legion of things you don't get."

He frowned at her, completely undeterred by her attempt at humor. "Aaron is good at making people around him happy, but he's not a people pleaser in the strictest sense of the word. He has no problem telling me to fuck off when the situation calls for it, and he's ended more than a few client relationships when things went south. It didn't tear him up to make that call."

She saw where this train of thought was going, and almost derailed it. Cameron had made abundantly clear that he wanted sex-them and work-them separate, but here in this suite with her body still aching from the wonderful things he'd done to it, the line had already blurred. She took a sip of bottled water. "There wasn't a question in there."

"I'm getting to it." He sat back, the muscles in his chest rippling in a way that made her clench her hands to keep from reaching for him. Cameron gave her another of those searching looks where it almost seemed like he could read her mind. "I've met your parents. They're decent people, and your older sister runs more traditional than either you or Aaron, but she's not a basket case."

"Did you just call me a basket case?"

"So where does the nervous shit come from?" He continued without bothering to answer her question. "You...flicker. I thought you were really sunshine personified, but that's the shield—or the sword, depending on the situation. What happened that you need walls that strong?"

Good Lord, he wasn't just making idle conversation. He'd gone straight past polite small talk and right to her heart of hearts. Trish forced herself not to fidget and met his gaze directly. "Why do you want to know?"

That set him back. "What?"

"It's a pretty simple question."

Cameron seemed to mull that over with the

same intensity he gave everything in life. "I want to know more about you. I don't understand you."

It was both an encouraging reason and one that cut her knees right out from beneath her. Curiosity. He was curious about her, like she was a bug he couldn't quite identify and it would annoy the hell out of him until he had her properly categorized and filed away. Then he'd move on and forget all about her as anything other than a vaguely fond memory.

Isn't that what you want? This was never supposed to be forever.

That was fine. It was even fair.

But it didn't mean she had to rip herself open for the sake of his curiosity.

Trish pushed her food away. "If you want to know more about me, you start simple. It's only the proper way to do things."

"Simple." He said the word as if tasting it. "All right. What do you do when you're not overworking yourself on unpaid time?"

The way he asked the question had her making a mental note to check her direct deposit on payday. She should have known Cameron would be keeping an account of all the time she spent in the office during nonworking hours. Silly of her to think he'd missed it.

Trish almost told him there was nothing simple

about that question, but "What do you do for fun?" was about as baseline as first date questions went. *This isn't a first date. This is a first...*

I don't know what this is.

She took another sip of her water. "I watch horror movies and I crochet."

Cameron sat back and draped his arm over his chair. "The crocheting fits. You have this retro thing going on that is too quirky to be anything but genuine. Explain the horror movies. Why that genre?"

The fact he'd studied her enough to decide that her *retro thing* was genuine and not another mask... Trish pulled at the bottom of her shirt, not sure if she was flattered or flayed wide-open. Maybe this wasn't such a simple question, after all. "I like horror. There are rules and while you get more than your fair share of stupid people doing stupid things, it's usually some offbeat heroine who ends up as the last one standing in the face of whatever evil is killing off nubile teenagers. It's really satisfying to know that, no matter how many sequels you're going to get, good always triumphs over evil—and rarely looks pretty while doing it." She hadn't meant to say that last aloud.

He drummed his fingers on the table. "You'd argue that horror movies are feminist."

She blinked. "Uh, I'm not arguing that one way or another. I enjoy them."

He still had that look on his face, the one like he didn't know what to think of her. "Which are your favorites? Slashers, paranormal or sci-fi?"

"All of the above, though if I have to pick one, it's slashers all the way. They're so...predictable. Usually a dude in a mask with a big pointy object and some sneaky ways."

"Helps if the helpless victim trips a dozen times in the effort to cross her front yard."

Trish laughed. She couldn't help it. "You're not a fan, I take it?"

"It's not that." Cameron's frown cleared and he shrugged. "I don't get them. There seems to be a total lack of common sense required to keep all the victims in one place long enough for the killer to find them and pick them off one by one. Why don't they ever just leave?"

"Because then there wouldn't be a story." She laughed again. Whether on purpose or not, he'd effectively moved them away from the emotional minefield and into something much more mundane. Trish relaxed and crossed her legs. "Though there are a couple movies that actually have a vein of logic through them that might appeal to you. I'll lend them to you sometime, if you're interested."

He met her gaze. "When we get back to New

York, why don't you bring them over yourself and explain to me while we watch?"

Oh shit. He just went there. If she had any doubt about Cameron's intentions—at least outside of work and her brother—he'd just cleared them right up. That was an opening that gave her plenty of room to maneuver without either of them over-reaching. She says no, they both retreat once again and go back to the sexual tension–filled days and lonely nights.

Or maybe Trish was the only one spending lonely nights with her favorite buzzy toy and thinking about the one guy she couldn't have. She had no idea how Cameron spent his time outside of the office. It wasn't her business. Yes, they'd had sex, but that didn't mean...

Fuck it.

She set her bottle of water down. "I'd like that. On one condition."

The light tensing of his shoulders was the only indication of his mood. "I'm listening."

"This might be off the books, but until it runs its course, I would like it to be exclusive."

"Done."

She frowned. "You agreed to that awfully easy."

"You brought it up before I had a chance to." He held out a hand, and she dazedly rounded the table to take it. Cameron tugged her forward to straddle him and ran his hands up the backs of her thighs. "I'm a selfish bastard, Trish. I don't share what's mine, even if it's only mine in part."

"That's very archaic of you." She shivered as his knuckles brushed the curve of her ass. "I'm a person, not a possession."

"Agreed," he said easily. Cameron skated his hands to her hips, taking her shirt with him and baring her from the waist down. His thumb brushed her hip bones. "But that doesn't change the fact that you bring out strong...impulses...in me. You make me crazy." His hands reached her breasts and he leaned down to press a kiss to her stomach. "All I can think about is you, when I should be thinking about work. I've never had a problem with distractions before. I don't know how to deal with it."

"Now I'm a problem *and* a distraction." She lifted her arms over her head and let him drag her shirt off, leaving her naked. "You sweet talker, you."

"If I was better with words, we wouldn't be in this position to begin with."

Trish made a show of looking at where his hands were. "I think I like this position."

That earned her a brief smile. "I'm never going to say the right thing."

"This isn't about saying anything at all." She

leaned down and kissed his shoulder as she un-buttoned his pants. A crinkle had her laughing against his skin. "Is that a condom in your pocket or are you just happy to see me?"

"It would be a shame to put that truly ambitious box to waste, don't you think?"

She sent out a silent thank-you to Becka for giving her the idea in the first place, though Trish would never say as much aloud. She stroked his cock. "I couldn't agree more."

CHAPTER TEN

CAMERON WOULD HAVE spent the entirety of their trip to London without leaving the suite, but the next day dawned with a full schedule. He went over it with Trish while they ate breakfast. "Nikki Lancaster makes me look like I should be winning Miss Congeniality contests."

"You mentioned that. Twice." Trish studied him over the rim of her coffee. "Why are you so nervous?"

"I'm not nervous." Nervous was a strange, prickly sensation, and Cameron had stinging bees swarming in his stomach.

"You're the very definition of *nervous*. If you think I'm not capable—"

"It's not that." He couldn't just leave it at that, no matter how little he wanted to deal with this entire thing. *Damn you, Aaron.* "Nikki and I...

had a short fling a couple years ago. It went sideways pretty fast, and while it shouldn't matter in
the grand scheme of things, I can't guarantee that
it won't affect how she treats this meeting."

Trish sighed. "That would have been good information to have before we started this whole
process. I suppose you said something that pissed
her off and she dumped you?"

He couldn't even bristle because it was exactly
what had happened, but the exasperation in Trish's
tone said she wasn't surprised in the least by this
turn of events. "We never got far enough for someone to be dumped. There was a first date and the
next morning, one minute we were having a conversation that skirted into work, and the next she
was kicking me out in only my underwear."

"Mmm-hmm." She was all false sympathy and
smiles. "You didn't happen to tell her that her company's cybersecurity is inferior or something along
those lines?"

That was exactly what he'd told her. Cameron
poked at his food. "She asked a question and I
gave an answer."

"Oh, you poor thing." Trish's laughter pealed
through the room. "You wouldn't know tact if it
clobbered you over the head in a dark alley. How
long ago was this?"

"A couple years. Three...no, four? I think four."

Shit, he couldn't remember. It had been just another failed dating experience and he'd moved on with his life, assuming that Nikki would do the same. He still wasn't sure that she *hadn't* moved on with her life.

Trish gave him wide eyes. "You don't even know. God, what was Aaron thinking, sending you over here? I'm assuming he knows."

"He knows." They hadn't hashed out details, but considering the power Concord Inc. wielded, it wasn't something he could keep to himself.

"That's something at least." She shook her head. "Let me deal with Nikki. You keep your mighty opinions to yourself for the duration of this, unless there's a need for you to offer specific technical information."

Though Cameron wasn't much a fan of being handled, he could admit that he liked the way Trish assumed power without thought. It wasn't until she ordered him about that he realized she'd been... muted. No, not muted, exactly, but she held herself back normally. Toned herself down. He'd recognized that the sunny disposition was a mask, but he hadn't realized the depth of the deception she offered the world.

Did she even know herself?

Not my problem.

You made it your problem the second you laid eyes on her.

"I *can* have a conversation without pissing off everyone in the room."

"Prove it," she fired back. "This account is important, and it would reflect badly on both of us if we botch it. You know as well as I do that the second Aaron heard the bad news, he'd be on a flight over here to rectify the situation, and that would upset both him and Becka. We can handle it—we just need to *handle it*. That starts with you learning when to keep your opinion to yourself."

"You're handling me."

"Damn right I am." Trish pushed to her feet. She wore a simple black pencil skirt with a deep blue blouse that made her eyes almost glow. It was toned down for her, but he could barely look at her without wanting to slip his hand under her skirt and give her a distraction they both needed.

She pointed at him. "Cease and desist this second."

"I don't know what you're talking about." He stood as well and rounded the table to capture her hips. The height of her heels put her mouth kissably close to his and he found he liked being able to look into her eyes without making the muscles in his neck twinge. Cameron skated his hands over her hips to cup her ass and bring her hips flush against his. "You look devastatingly beautiful today, Trish."

"I… What?" Her perfectly painted pink lips parted. "You can't just go and say something like that! I'm in work mode, and you're flustering me with your pheromones."

"We haven't left the suite yet." He pressed a slow kiss to the pulse fluttering in the hollow of her throat. "Ten minutes won't make much difference."

"Oh no you don't." She smacked his hands and ducked out of his grip. "Focus, Cameron. This is important and you wouldn't be making eyes at me if you were thinking with the right head. *Focus.*"

He huffed out a breath and tried to think past the blood rushing to his cock. She was right. He was better than this. The sex might be outstanding, but it was just sex. It had to be. If he couldn't compartmentalize, he had no business climbing into her bed to begin with.

"Sorry." He gave himself a shake. "Give me a minute."

"Take it. I have to get my purse." She ducked into her bedroom, leaving him wrestling for control of his reaction to her.

Cameron never lost control. He sure as fuck never lost sight of a work goal to pursue his own pleasure or interests. This morning, he'd done both. Hell, last night he'd done both, too. He'd crossed lines, and there was no way to take those actions back.

He was a selfish bastard because he didn't *want* to take it back.

Last night had been the first time in as long as he could remember where his brain had shut off entirely and he'd been functioning on feel alone. It felt good to be with Trish. The sex, yes, but he'd had almost as good a time teasing her about her apparent love for horror movies as he had coaxing her orgasms.

She was a joy.

And he couldn't have her. Not in any permanent sense.

If he was smart, he'd cut this thing off before it went further. It would hurt her feelings and he'd be walking around pissy as hell about it for a while, but better a little hurt now than to have the situation blow up in both their faces later on. She might not be happy with him—that reaction was all but guaranteed—but she'd understand.

He stood there and made himself imagine how that conversation would go. The hurt flaring over her face, pooling in her deep blue eyes, the way her bottom lip would quiver for the breath of a second before she got control of herself. The sunny smile she'd give him to cover up…

No.

Fuck no.

He might not have her for keeping, but he had

her for the time being. And she had him. Cameron wasn't going to give up a single second with Trish until he had to. If it meant she dealt a blow unlike he'd ever felt when she left…

So be it.

After Cameron's cryptic words about Nikki Lancaster, Trish hadn't known what to expect. A fire-breathing dragon, maybe. The woman that approached them as they walked through the doors of Concord Inc. didn't fit any of her preconceived notions.

Nikki looked like a warrior goddess. She had her black hair pulled back into a businesslike coif thing and her pantsuit showed off curves for days. It was the glint in her dark eyes that gave Trish the most pause. A fighter scoping out an adversary.

She turned an identical look at Cameron, before she gave him a tight smile. "O'Clery."

"Nikki." He touched the small of Trish's back, urging her a step closer. "This is Trish Livingston, our newest addition."

Nikki took her in with those witchy dark eyes and Trish couldn't shake the feeling that she'd already had judgment passed on her. Whether it was good or bad was anyone's guess at this point. The woman extended her hand. "Aaron said he'd be sending a keeper for you, O'Clery, but he didn't

mention the fact that it would be his little sister."
No mistaking the emphasis on *little*.

Cameron's hand at the small of her back flexed,
but Trish was already moving to defuse the situation. Whatever the situation was. She couldn't get
a true read on Nikki. This could all be posturing
for the sake of posturing, or it could be exactly
what Cameron had feared. Trish smiled sweetly.
"I think you'll find I'm more than qualified to get
the job done." She glanced at her watch. "Shall we
take this to wherever the meeting is being held? I
would hate to be late."

Without another word, Nikki turned on her designer heels and led the way to a bank of elevators
that took them to the executive floor.

Trish didn't dare exhale the breath she'd been
holding on to. They'd managed to get through the
first interaction without someone calling the whole
thing off or yelling, but they still had the deal to
hammer out. Even with Aaron taking care of the
preliminary stuff, this whole thing was hardly
guaranteed. She very carefully didn't look at Cameron as the elevators opened and they stepped out
into a long hallway lined with doors.

Everything about the building was designed to
create a modern minimalist look. Though Trish
could appreciate the cool gray walls, white tiles
marbled with black and stainless steel everything,

the whole thing left her cold and edgy. As they headed into a small boardroom where three other people were assembled, she found herself longing for the cozy front office she'd created back in New York.

That's not your place any more than this one is. Forgetting that would be a mistake.

Nikki introduced the CEO of the company and their respective assistants. Once everyone had coffee, they got down to work outlining what they needed from Tandem Security. Cameron answered the questions directed at him, but there was a wariness she'd never seen in him before. Trish couldn't tell if it was brought on by dealing with his ex or dealing with people in general, and it wasn't like she could ask.

Not at the moment, anyway.

Through it all, she couldn't help watching the other woman. *This* was Cameron's type? She couldn't be more different from Trish. She was confident and bold and seemed perfectly at home in her skin. Not to mention that Nikki had almost single-handedly made Concord Inc. what it was today. She'd come in as COO, looked around and seen the potential of the company. And then she made it happen.

To say it was impressive and more than a little intimidating was a vast understatement.

They broke for a quick lunch and Trish found herself alone in the room with Nikki. She moved to make a quick exit, but the other woman stalled her. "Sit, sit. You're exhausting me with all your nervous energy."

Trish hesitantly sank back into the chair she'd just tried to abandon. "Something I can help you with?"

Nikki raised a perfect black brow. "How long have you been sleeping with O'Clery?"

Her jaw dropped. "I don't... What... I'm not—"

"You are, and I'd wager that Aaron doesn't know. He loves O'Clery like a brother, but he's not blind to the man's faults." She laughed. "Get that look off your face, honey. I'm not going to go for your throat over some guy I hooked up with half a million years ago."

It sounded totally reasonable, but Trish couldn't make herself relax. She stilled her hands in her lap, doing her best not to give herself away with any nervous movement. "You have a reason for bringing it up."

"I do." Nikki sat back. "I've known O'Clery and Livingston for nearly a decade in one capacity or another, and I've never seen him like this before. He's a grumpy asshole, but he's got a shitty poker face. Every time he looks at you, he goes all soft and gooey."

Yeah, right. This had to be some sort of weird mind game, though she couldn't figure out what the point was. "If you'll forgive me for being blunt, I don't see what my theoretical relationship with Cameron has to do with this deal."

"Nothing at all." Nikki's red lips curved, just a little. "It's a purely selfish curiosity to get a better look at the kind of woman who could manage to have *him* tripping all over his feet like an eager puppy. I'll admit that I don't see it. You're beautiful, of course, but the peppy cheerleader thing doesn't seem like it's a solid match for O'Clery." She lifted a single shoulder. "Then again, what do I know? Good for him. And good for you, too. He's got a heart of gold if you can get past the dumbass shit he says and the pissy attitude."

She still couldn't get a read on Nikki, couldn't tell if this conversation was exactly what it presented to be on the surface or if the woman was trying to undermine something. She couldn't help comparing herself to the other woman. They weren't even on the same planet, and she couldn't be more opposite if Cameron had intentionally picked her for that reason. Rationally, she *knew* it didn't matter. He and Nikki were ancient history—and a brief one at that—but Trish looked at her and saw everything Trish would never be.

Someone completely at ease in their skin and

confident enough to handle any and every situation life threw at them without breaking her powerful stride. Someone who'd perfectly executed their plan for life, despite any hurdles thrown in their way.

No, Trish was just Trish. She let her smile drop. "Frankly, I don't see how that's any of your business."

"So you do have some backbone. Good."

The door opened and the men filed back in. She couldn't shake the suspicion that they'd been hiding out in the hallway while this conversation went down and, as happy as she was that Cameron had managed to keep his temper through the first half of the day, she still wanted to kick him under the table for abandoning her with Nikki.

It shouldn't have mattered anyway. Nikki had never been a girlfriend, and Trish certainly wasn't. They were both flavors of the week... *Maybe we should get T-shirts or something.* Her joke fell flat, even in her own head, and she tried to set the whole uncomfortable feeling aside. It shouldn't matter what Cameron and Nikki's past was, because the woman obviously had no intention of letting said past get in the way of this business deal.

Would he expect the same from Trish when this was all over?

The rest of the meeting passed without incident.

Concord Inc. signed the contract, which extended the trip to London since Cameron had to be on-site to set up the security requirements.

And Trish would go home.

Guess things are ending quicker than I could have anticipated.

CHAPTER ELEVEN

CAMERON MIGHT NOT be entirely in tune with other people's emotions, but he would have had to be particularly dense not to notice something was wrong with Trish. After their lunch break, she'd been subdued, her light dimmed. He'd tried to catch her eye a few times, but she resolutely refused to look his way. He could explain it away as her focusing on the deal…

Right up until she tried that same shit as they walked back to the suite.

He noticed a sign for a pub and hooked her waist. "Dinner."

"I'm not hungry."

Oh yeah, Trish was pissed. Cameron ignored her protest and guided her into the low light of the pub. He took a quick look around and headed for a table far enough into the room that she wouldn't get a chill when the door was opened to let a draft in. He held out a chair for her, his irritation battling with amusement as she huffed and dropped into it.

Once he was settled on the other side, he leaned forward and lowered his voice. "Now you're going to tell me what crawled up your ass back there. I played the good boy and kept my mouth shut, and the deal went off without a hitch. Which means something else happened to make you mad. Tell me."

Trish shrugged out of her coat and let it drape over her chair. Then she started shredding the paper napkin in front of her. Her anger disappeared, replaced by…embarrassment? She finally sighed. "I'll book my return ticket to New York as soon as we get back to our rooms."

He sat back. "I know you're pissed, but running back to the city seems a little dramatic, don't you think?"

"Dramatic?" Her light brows slammed together. "Are you kidding me? I'm not being dramatic. I'm being reasonable. You don't get to call me dramatic."

He knew better than to point out that her tirade was nothing if not dramatic. "Something upset you. If you need to yell at me to get around to telling me what it was, fine. But you *will* tell me."

She drew a breath for what seemed like a solid

dressing-down, but deflated on the exhale. "This is going to end."

Cameron went still. "If you want—"

"No, no, it has nothing to do with want. It has to do with reality. And the reality is that this is going to end." She gave a sad smile. "Every relationship either ends or results in marriage. Even this one." Before he had a chance to process *that*, she was off to the races again. "I mean, it's whatever. We knew this was coming. It's just showing up a little earlier than I thought and it surprised me and sometimes I react poorly to surprises. I know it's not your fault. Of course it's not your fault. It's just the way things are."

He caught the bartender's eye. "Two shots of whiskey, please."

If anything, Trish frowned harder. "I don't see how whiskey is going to help anything."

"A little bit of whiskey helps everything." When she stared, he shrugged. "It's when you tip into too much whiskey that the trouble starts. This conversation calls for a single shot."

When said shot was delivered to their table, he slid one over to rest in front of her. Cameron raised his glass and waited. With a put-upon sigh, Trish did the same. They took them smoothly and the soft clink of glass hitting the wood table was soothing in its own way. He leaned forward again. "Now, down to business."

"If you're going to—"

"Why the fuck do you think this is ending?"

She stopped. Stared. "What?"

Cameron spoke softly and clearly. "Do you want this thing between us to end?"

"It doesn't matter what I want."

"If it didn't matter, then I wouldn't ask you. But I am asking, Trish—do you want this to end?"

She narrowed her eyes. "No. Of course not. I'm enjoying being with you."

Damning him with faint praise, wasn't she? It didn't matter. He'd take it if it meant she didn't call the whole thing off. He hadn't put much thought into the *after* that would come when reality intruded on their little oasis of pleasure. That was Cameron's mistake, because Trish sure as fuck had been thinking about long-term implications. He reached out and took her hands in his. "I'm not ready to let you go."

He wasn't sure he'd *ever* be ready to let her go, but now was hardly the time to broach the subject, with her on the verge of panicking. Cameron had to find a way to ease her into the idea. First, though, they had to navigate through the current issue.

Her pink lips moved but no sound came out. Finally Trish shook her head. "I don't get it. I don't get *you*. A fling is one thing, but a long-distance fling is more than a little ridiculous…"

What was she talking about? "What's long-distance?"

Her hands tensed beneath his. "The contract is finalized. That's all I was here for."

Realization dawned, and he almost laughed in relief. This, at least, had a simple fix. "Woman, you aren't going back to New York without me. You're staying until we get their preliminary security set up."

"What are you talking about? Why would I stay?"

"If Aaron was in the office, it would be a different story, but for the time being, *I* am Tandem Security. That means I need you with me to do your job wherever I am. Most of the time that's in the office, but I can work remotely as required, which is what's going to happen while I'm needed here for Concord Inc. That means you're here, too."

That means we don't have to have a conversation about this ending yet.

"You're serious."

"Yes." He met her gaze steadily. "Unless you want to leave. Aside from client meetings—which we won't be having until I'm back in the States, there technically isn't anything that requires your physical presence. It will make things more challenging, but it's doable."

Trish tilted her head to the side. "Do you want me to leave?"

Now was the time to retreat, to allow her to make the choice for herself without him appearing to pressure her. But... Cameron only had one answer to that question and he was incapable of lying. Not to her. Not when it would endanger what little chance they had. "No." He said the word on an exhale, but once it broke the stillness emerging between them, it was easier to let the honesty flow. "I don't want you to leave. I don't want this to end."

She gave him a look like she wasn't sure if he meant their trip or *them*, but Cameron left her to draw her own conclusions. He never would have pegged Trish as skittish—not when she was a one-woman wrecking ball—but there were definite nerves showing around her too-wide eyes.

The bartender saved them when he tossed two menus onto the table. "You going to eat?"

"Fish and chips?" When Trish nodded, Cameron looked at the bartender. "Fish and chips for both of us."

"All right, then." He snatched up the menus and walked off as quickly as he'd approached.

Trish cleared her throat. "So, this is getting super awkward super fast and I don't know how to deal with it, and I don't know how I want to deal with it, so I'm just going to ignore it for the time being."

Her penchant for talking in run-on sentences when she was nervous shouldn't be endearing, but Cameron had given up trying to reason away his attraction to the woman. Even when she was driving him up the wall, he still found himself drawn to her.

But he could give her a reprieve for the time being. She obviously wasn't ready to make a decision about staying or going—both on a plane and in his bed—so Cameron scooted his chair back the slightest bit to give her space. "How do you feel about ghosts?"

Trish blinked. "Ghosts?"

"Yeah, you know…ghosts. Whether you believe they're energy or memories or literal souls doesn't matter."

Another slow blink. "I think I'm hallucinating because nothing coming out of your mouth makes a lick of sense."

"We're in London. There's half a dozen haunted tours within easy walking distance. There's one starting in an hour or so. It's entertaining, to say the least."

"But…ghosts. That doesn't seem like something you'd be into."

It wasn't, but she'd confessed her love of scary movies, so he'd looked it up this morning while she was in the shower. Logic said that sort of thing would go hand in hand, and as much as Cameron wanted to toss her over his shoulder and haul her back to bed until they were required somewhere, Trish had never been to London before. It was entirely possible she'd like to explore a bit.

He shifted, not sure how to deal with how closely she watched him. "I thought you might be interested in it."

Trish must have hit her head. It was the only explanation that made sense. She studied her water, trying to reconcile the man sitting across from her, shifting like a schoolboy who'd done something wrong and didn't want to admit it, with the confident boss she'd come to expect. "You want to go on a haunted tour," she said again, as if repeating it enough times would transfer the meaning of the words.

"We don't have to." There it was again— Cameron's almost-guilt.

Because he doesn't care about ghost tours. He looked up the schedule because you *do.*

She took a hasty sip of her water and set the glass back on the table. "I would love to do a haunted tour." She noted the almost imperceptible relaxing of his

shoulders. It wasn't guilt she read from Cameron—
it was nerves.

The realization almost made her laugh. She'd
spent so much time tripping over her own feet in
front of him, it had never occurred to her that he
might be in over his head, too. The ground centered a bit below her feet, her perverse nature liking that he didn't have a playbook he was pulling
from. Not that she'd believed that, exactly. Cameron was many things, but a playboy didn't make
the list. That said, he obviously wasn't the settling-
down type or he would have done it by now.

*Unless he hasn't found the right person to set-
tle down with...*

Stop that.

*You don't even know where you're going to land
yet. You can't make choices one way or another
when it comes to being with another person. Even
without all the stuff stacked against you, it would
never work.*

She didn't want to think about that right now.
Reality seemed very far away with them sitting in
a darkened pub in the middle of freaking London.
Trish cautiously reached out and touched his forearm. "Could we..." She swallowed hard, gathering her courage around her. "Could we table any
conversations about the future for now? At least
until we get back?"

"We're only going to be here about a week."

Such a short time and yet longer than she would have dared when she let herself imagine what it would be like if Cameron gave in to the pull between them. *It will have to be enough.* "The question stands."

His dark eyes searched her face. "That's what you want? Not to talk about anything too scary for the time we're here."

"Well, any haunted tour worth its salt is a little bit scary." Her joke fell flat as the bartender appeared and set food on the table in front of them. Her mouth watered as she took in the crispy fish and chips. *Oh yeah, I love London.*

"Trish."

She reluctantly dragged her gaze away from her food and back to his face. "Yeah?"

"You can have this week. After that, we're having a conversation."

A conversation destined to be the death knell of their fling. The writing couldn't have been clearer on *that* particular wall. All she had to do was open her mouth and tell him she wanted to call the whole thing off—that it was wiser for her to leave things as they were and get the hell out of the UK and back to New York, where she could at least pretend she had her head on straight. They'd had sex a few times, but easy enough to chalk it up to temporary insanity and hope a week apart would be enough to cool their chemistry.

Leaving was the *smart* thing to do, and Trish always did the smart thing.

But she found herself smiling at Cameron. "Tell me about this haunted tour."

CHAPTER TWELVE

"THAT WAS THE biggest load of shit."

Trish laughed and slipped her hand into the crook of Cameron's arm. The wind had kicked up during the last half hour, and it cut through her thin jacket as if it wasn't there. She was self-aware enough to admit that craving warmth wasn't the only reason she wanted to touch him. He might be a human-shaped furnace, but being this close to him just felt *good* in general.

He absently rearranged her, tucking her against his body and wrapping an arm around her shoulders as he turned so his big body took the brunt of the wind chill. Cameron shook his head. "He wooed at one point." His voice kicked up a register as he mimicked their hapless guide. *"Wooooooo."*

"Oh stop." She playfully smacked his chest. "He knew his history. It was very educational." Her heart felt like it was two sizes too big after seeing places she'd only read about. The extra flavor from having a haunted tour only made the whole experience that much better.

That, and being with Cameron.

"The information was good. The delivery was off." He turned and guided them in the direction of their rooms, still grumbling about the guide. He cut himself off and shot her a look. "I had fun."

"I can tell."

"No, I'm serious. It was nice spending time with you."

Warmth blossomed in her chest, and no amount of reasoning could dispel it. She'd had fun with Cameron this evening, too. And last night. And this morning. Reminding herself that it was going to end—and probably end poorly—didn't make a difference. This runaway train was out of her control and it would keep going until they ran out of tracks. It didn't matter that she wouldn't be staying with Tandem indefinitely, or that Aaron would be furious when he found out how they'd crossed the line. Nothing mattered but how much she enjoyed being with Cameron. "What's your story?"

"What do you mean?"

She shot him a look. "Well, you didn't just pop into existence in your current form. I'm assuming you were a child at some point, probably had a parent or two in one form or another. Siblings? I mean, let's just start with the basics."

"I think I can do that." He squeezed her shoulders and nudged her to turn right at the street corner. "My parents live in California. My mother is a teacher, and my dad is military—retired now. No siblings to speak of. Apparently I was a difficult child, and—"

"Imagine that."

He continued without missing a beat. "They decided I was enough and didn't have any more kids. We weren't in one place for more than a few years, but they were a solid foundation while I was growing up. They're good people."

Trish had been born and raised in the same place as a long line of Livingstons had. Their roots went core deep in town, and she'd grown up knowing exactly what her place was, whether she wanted it or not. She couldn't imagine switching schools every few years and having to face dealing with figuring out her place in the pecking order... *Makes a lot more sense why he can be so damn standoffish. Easier not to play the game or get close to people when he'd just inevitably move on.* "You met my brother in college."

"More like he adopted me as his pet project in college," Cameron grumbled. "We were lab partners and he decided I just needed a little more structure in my life. Look where that got him."

"Mmm, yeah, terrible life you're both living." She laughed. "You're rich as sin and running a successful company together, and for all of both of your bitching, you never actually fight. Must be terrible." In truth, she envied them their friendship a bit. Trish had friends, but when it became clear she wasn't going to follow the ascending path to her dream career within the corporate fashion industry like she'd always planned, she withdrew more and more. One friend had scored an internship with her dream clothing designer, a position destined to shoot her into greatness if she survived it. Another had secured a junior position in a prestigious law firm.

Trish?

Trish had failed to find even an entrance-level job in her field of choice, and mounting student loan bills had forced her to move back into her parents' place to try to stem the hemorrhaging of her minuscule bank account. It turned out that her chosen field didn't have much in the way of entrance-level jobs, and securing one in their competitive industry had turned into an impossible task.

"Where are you headed?"

She started, belatedly realizing she had dropped her sunny persona and he'd picked up on it. Damn it, she kept doing that more and more as time went on. She wished she could blame it on Cameron's grumpiness rubbing off on her, but it wasn't the truth. Life weighed her down. Or, rather, the truth about life weighed her down.

Not everyone got a happy ending, no matter how many stars they wished on.

Some people had to settle on the mediocre instead of aspiring for greatness.

She just never thought she'd be part of either group.

With a sigh, she tried to focus on Cameron. "I'm sorry, I missed that last bit."

"In life." They turned another corner, and she started to recognize shops from the next street up from their hotel. "I had reservations when Aaron decided to bring you in, but you're good at handling people and situations."

"Yeah, I'm a great glorified secretary." Managing her mother's moods had given her plenty of people skills, though they mostly meant she gave excellent customer service no matter what her personal level of frustration was.

"Trish."

Oh no. She knew that tone of voice. It meant nothing good for the conversation. Cameron obviously wasn't pleased with her blasé comment, and he just as obviously intended to sit her down and…

Well, she didn't know what. A come-to-Jesus talk about knowing her worth? Or maybe one where he pointed out that she wasn't a glorified *anything*—she was literally their secretary.

No matter which way he was headed, she wanted no part of it. They would have their talk when they got back to New York. It could sure as hell wait until then. If this was an escape, she wanted to get her money's worth, so to speak.

Trish turned into him, grabbing the front of his jacket and leveraging herself up to take his mouth. His surprise only lasted a second, and then his hands were on her hips and he guided her several steps until her back hit the wall. Cameron dug his big hands into her hair and tilted her head back to get a better angle. He moved away long enough to say, "I know you're trying to distract me."

Of course he did. He wasn't stupid. She forced an impish grin. "Are you complaining?"

"Not especially." He reclaimed her mouth, but this time the pace slowed down. Cameron teased her with soft, barely there kisses until she growled in frustration, and only then did he set his teeth against her bottom lip and slip his tongue into her mouth.

The man kissed like a dream.

A really naughty one.

Give and take, advance and retreat. Over and

over and over again, until she lost all comprehension of the other people on the street or the fact that they were most definitely in a public place with an audience.

Trish had only meant to keep him from his questions, from pulling her apart at the seams to satisfy his curiosity, from creating a foundation of trust that neither of them could follow through on.

It didn't matter what she'd intended, only the end result.

And the result was that she wanted his hands all over her body, wanted him to stroke her just so, to send her hurtling over the edge. She wanted to take him into her body and ride him until they stopped worrying about the future, because the future was just a distant dream and they were *here* and *now*. That was the only thing that mattered.

He tore his mouth from hers. "Upstairs. Now."

Incapable of words, she nodded. Cameron gave her a look like he wanted to throw her over his shoulder because she wouldn't move fast enough on her own, but he settled with grabbing her hand and towing her behind him. The half a block back to the hotel passed in a blur, and she caught sight of the startled face of the front desk lady before the elevator doors closed between them and the lobby.

Cameron turned to her, but she was already moving. She hopped and he caught her just like she'd known he would. Her legs went around his waist and her back hit the wall as he took her mouth again.

Yes, this.

Yes, more.

He didn't let her down as the elevator doors rattled open. Instead, Cameron walked them down the hallway. His dark eyes looked just as wild as she felt, as if he might take her right there in the hallway if they didn't get through the door fast enough. Trying to anticipate, she dug into her purse for the hotel room key, barely getting it out before they reached the door. "Got it!"

He grabbed it out of her hand and then they were in the room. Cameron strode into the bedroom. "I need you."

"Yes. Now. Hurry." Making out on the street like a couple of teenagers had her so primed, she practically vibrated with it. He kept her pinned in place as she reached between them. Cameron used one hand to grab a condom and undid his pants. It didn't take much to work them down his hips to free his cock, but even the two-second delay was too long without him inside her. "Hurry, hurry, hurry."

He knocked her hand aside so he could roll on the condom and then he thrust, filling her completely, assuaging her empty ache. They froze, both breathing hard. Cameron leaned back enough to check her expression. "You good?"

As if she hadn't been right there with him this whole time. Trish rolled her hips, taking him deeper yet. "Don't stop."

His grin made something in her chest twinge in a way that would have terrified her if not for the pleasure building with every beat of her heart. A tempo that reduced itself to one word. *Yes, yes, yes, yes, yes.*

Cameron lowered her to the bed and shoved her shirt up to bare her breasts. "I like you like this, Trish. It's fucking indecent and I'm never going to be able to look at you in a pencil skirt without thinking about that skirt around your hips and my cock buried deep inside you."

"Good," she gasped. Something to remember her by, even after it was over.

The wildness trying to escape her seemed to translate to him, because there was no teasing, no driving her to distraction before taking what he wanted. No, there was just Cameron moving over her, driving into her again and again in the most delicious way possible. Every stroke hit the end of her, the pleasure-pain building to a desperation unlike anything she'd ever known.

She ran her hands down his strong back and

grabbed his ass, pulling him closer yet. Deeper. Harder. "I never want this to end."

His words were slightly muffled against her temple, but she could have sworn he said, "It doesn't have to."

Trish came between the space of one breath and the next. She could feel Cameron trying to pull back, to get enough distance to keep his own orgasm at bay, but she was having none of it. "Come with me, Cam. Come for me."

He cursed and she knew she'd won. His strokes became rougher yet, driving them both up the bed until his entire body went tense and he clutched her to him as he came. He had the presence of mind to roll to the side, but he didn't release her, so she ended up with one leg sprawled over his hip and his cock still buried inside her. Trish kissed the center of his chest and allowed herself to enjoy the feel of him holding her close.

So good...

So better than good...

She instinctively went tense, sure that he'd say something or she'd let her fear get away from her. But nothing happened. He just stroked a hand over her hair again and again until she finally relaxed. "What kind of movies do you like, Cam?"

"I'm more of a reader."

She smiled sleepily against his chest. "Let me guess—John Grisham?"

"Occasionally, but I'm more of a fantasy fan."

That got her attention. "Really? Like the farm boy is really the chosen one who has to save the universe and he's probably really a king but he doesn't know it… That sort of thing?"

His laugh rumbled through her. "Sometimes. Though there are a lot more stories within the genre than just that type."

"Oh yeah?" She snuggled closer. "Tell me about them." And she listened as he spun out teasers for tales that she'd never heard of. Cameron had a natural storytelling gift, yet she never would have guessed it before now. His low voice soothed the last of her fear away.

It would be okay.

They could have this week, and she could keep her issues at bay long enough to enjoy her time with him to its fullest. The only person standing in the way of that was Trish herself, and she didn't want to do it anymore.

It helped that, for the first time in a very long time, she was well and truly happy and willing to take things one day at a time instead of looking years ahead and seeing only failure.

CHAPTER THIRTEEN

THE NEXT DAY couldn't go fast enough. Cameron had never resented his work before, but it had never kept him from something he wanted before. Some*one*. Trish had set up shop back in their suite, while he was left to make the trek to Concord Inc. on his own. It had seemed reasonable at the time, but he swore he could actually feel the distance between them growing.

Not to mention the seconds ticking away from their time left together.

He didn't know how to fix that. She'd been ready to call the whole thing off before he'd distracted her with an offer for a reprieve. He wasn't delusional to think that more time spent in his presence would endear him to her. His cock? Fuck yeah. But it had been too long since he'd tried to tiptoe around someone else's emotions.

Just from the law of averages alone, he would say something to piss her off and screw things up before the week ran out.

Unless we just keep having sex until we're too tired to talk.

As appealing as that option was, he wanted more. The haunted tour last night *had* been goofy, but Trish's excitement had rubbed off on him, and seeing the tour through her eyes meant he enjoyed the hell out of it. He wanted to watch her favorite horror movies to have her prove him wrong about the genre. He wanted to share his favorite books with her. He wanted to know everything about her, where she'd been, where she was headed.

Cameron could count on one hand how many people he'd actually wanted to spend more time with...and still have fingers left over if he wasn't including family. Trish was so refreshing and amazing, and she never seemed to take it personally when he said the wrong thing. Set him straight? Without a doubt. But she didn't huff and walk away from him and leave him wondering where the hell he'd gone wrong.

Over the years, he'd picked up bits and pieces from Aaron about his two sisters, but Cameron had never paid much attention because he never expected to actually meet them.

He didn't give a damn what Aaron had to say about Trish. He wanted to hear her history for himself.

Moving too fast.

Was he, though? He'd dated enough to know that something like this didn't come around often. It didn't come around *at all* for him. He'd be a fool to let her go, no matter how unfathomable he found this new territory.

Besides, it was hard to move too fast when she was already planning her exit strategy.

He forced thoughts of Trish from his head as he got to work on the security system Concord Inc. had commissioned. It was relatively straight-forward as such things went, for all the nondis-closure agreements and secrecy, but setting it up required time. He could put together the appropriate firewalls and systems in his sleep, but Cameron hadn't gotten to where he was by half-assing anything.

No matter how much he wanted to do just that today.

He made himself keep working until five, and then packed up and headed back to the hotel. With each step that brought him closer, excite-ment thrummed in his chest. He'd drag Trish into the shower with him to ease their thirst for each other, and then they'd head out for food and a little more sightseeing.

He barely made it through the door.

Trish appeared as if by magic—as if she'd been waiting—and gave him a quick kiss even as she started unbuttoning his shirt. She wore a different one of his shirts, and she should have looked absurd in the oversize clothing with her bare legs. Instead, she looked downright delicious. "You've been gone all day."

Surprise kept his feet planted and his hands off her as he watched her finish with his shirt. "That was the plan."

"I know. It was a stupid plan." She shoved his shirt and jacket off his shoulders and gave a little hum of satisfaction. "Do you know how many times I ended up in our bed with my hand between my legs, thinking about you while I worked myself into a frenzy?" Trish had his pants undone and shoved them down before he had a chance to speak. She stroked his cock and gave him a sweet little smile. "We can talk in a minute, okay?"

Cameron leaned back against the wall next to the door and sifted his fingers through her curls. "You're crazy if you think I'm going to stop you. I've been thinking about you all day."

She pressed a kiss to his jaw. "Good. I'd hate to suffer alone."

"Perish the thought," he murmured. He forced himself to keep his eyes open, to watch her kiss her way down his chest until she was on her knees. Cameron used his hold on her hair to push it back from her face and ensure an unobstructed view. He didn't want to miss a moment of this.

She stroked him once, twice, and then took him into her mouth. How many times had Cameron jacked himself to the image of her brightly painted lips wrapped around his cock? Pink, red, and on one memorable day, she'd worn purple. Today her lips were a pink bright enough to be seen from space, and the sight of his cock disappearing between them was almost as good as the feel of her mouth sucking him deep. She went after him with the same desperation he had churning up inside him every time he thought about what would happen once they boarded the plane back to New York.

His cock bumped the back of Trish's throat and it was too much. Cameron hauled her up his body. "I need more than your mouth right now."

"No fair." She wrapped her legs around his waist as he walked them toward what had become their bedroom. "You go down on me all the freaking time. I want my turn."

"Later."

"Why do I think later means never?" She laughed as he dropped her onto the mattress and yanked off the shirt. She wore absolutely nothing beneath it. Her laugh was like nothing he'd ever heard before. Joyfully filling up the room until all he could focus on was this woman in this moment.

As if he'd want to be anywhere else.

Cameron bracketed her hips and dragged her to the edge of the mattress. "If later meant never, then I'd say never. Later means later." He pushed a single finger into her and cursed when he found her wet and tight. "Were you fucking yourself with your fingers while I was walking here?"

Her grin turned evil. "Maybe."

"What am I going to do with you, Trish?"

Her laugh turned into a moan as he pushed a second finger into her. "I have a few ideas."

"I'm all ears." He kept slowly fucking her with his fingers, ensuring he hit that spot inside her that made her eyes damn near cross with every stroke. He circled her clit with his thumb. "Hmm?"

"You're unbelievable." She reached up and hooked the back of his neck, towing herself up to kiss him. "You want it spelled out? I want you. Hands. Mouth. Cock. All of it. Every position. Over and over again."

His stomach dropped, and even though Cameron knew better, he still said, "Your list of my attributes leaves a lot to be desired."

Trish rolled her eyes and flopped back onto the

mattress. "What do you want me to say? That I am having fun with you? That I like how much thought you put into the haunted tour and making sure we eat somewhere that has fish and chips because you know I'm a little obsessed? That I really dig your kind of closet nerdy thing with the fantasy novels? Or maybe that I think it's really sexy how smart you are, and your inability to filter yourself has become charming instead of infuriating? That's the lamest dirty talk out there."

"You like me."

"No, really? Of course I like you—sometimes in spite of yourself." Something akin to vulnerability crept into her blue eyes. "If you haven't noticed, I'm not exactly great at this stuff."

She'd just thrown out a revelation he thought he'd never hear. Oh, he knew Trish enjoyed their time together, but there was a vast difference between enjoying how he made her come and enjoying *him*.

Cameron started to reach for the nightstand where they'd stashed the giant box of condoms, but Trish burrowed her hands under the pillows and came up with one. She tore it open. "Pays to be prepared."

"Words after my own heart." He spread her wetness over her clit as she rolled the condom onto his cock. He pushed into her and they both went still at the sheer perfection of how good it felt. Not enough, though. It was never enough, because it always ended. He hooked her thighs and lifted her legs as he thrust forward, bending her in half and allowing him as deep inside her as he'd ever been.

"Oh, *Cam*." She clutched at his shoulders. "God, that's good. Don't stop."

The same thing she said every time they had sex. *Don't stop.* And he answered just as he always did. "I'll never stop, Trish. Not as long as you want it."

Cameron kept his strokes steady and reached down to stroke her clit how he knew she liked it. He'd had Trish at night and in the morning, but late afternoon Trish might be his favorite. The clouds that had lingered all morning finally parted and golden sunlight bathed her skin, making her damn near glow beneath him. Her expression went ecstatic and her pussy clenched around him as she came. He couldn't hold out longer. He didn't want to. With her milking his cock so sweetly, he let go and came hard enough to see stars.

Never want to let you go, Trish.

He managed to keep the words inside, if only barely. It was time to change how he approached this. Trish had admitted she liked him, and it was a small step from liking to falling for him.

He wasn't going to give her up without a fight.

* * *

After a detour into the shower, Trish finally allowed Cameron to haul her out of the hotel for some exploring. Night had long since fallen, but the city hadn't slowed down in the least. It felt different from New York, though. Less frenetic, maybe. Cameron tucked her under his arm and pulled her close as if they'd walked down the street together a thousand times before.

As if they'd walk down a thousand more streets in the future.

Knock it off. You told him you didn't want to talk about that until you're back in New York, and so there's no point in obsessing over it.

No point, but that had never stopped her before.

She was enjoying this far too much to successfully categorize it as a fling. Not that Trish had much experience with that sort of thing, but it just seemed wrong to enjoy her time out of bed with Cameron as much as she enjoyed her time *in* bed.

"Hungry?"

She glanced at him and smiled. "Always."

He led her into a tiny restaurant. "This place comes highly recommended."

They took a little table near the window so they could see the street. It was so…normal. She fiddled with her fork. Talking about work seemed like a cop-out at this point. They were past that.

She *wanted* them to be past that. *Maybe it's time I stop fighting it and admit the truth?* Trish opened her mouth to break all their rules and broach the subject of *them*, but the distracted look on his face had her chickening out. "Have you been to London before?"

"A few times." He refocused on her and nudged over the menu. "How'd the day go?"

Guess we're talking about work, after all. "It was good. The time difference means a slight lag in emails, but nothing too dramatic has hit since we've been gone. I set up two meetings with potential new clients for the week after next. I figured a little cushion time wasn't a bad idea in case complications arose with the current job."

"Trish."

She dragged her gaze up to his. God, he was gorgeous. The square jaw that she'd spent plenty of time dragging her mouth along, and the sensuous lips and deep, dark eyes. She pressed her own lips together, sure she could still taste him there if she concentrated. "Yeah?"

"I didn't ask how work went. I asked how *your* day went. Did you manage to get out and see anything or were you locked up with a computer the entire time I was gone?"

"It's my job to be locked up with a computer during the day." When he just stared, she sighed and relented. "I took an extra-long lunch break and went to see the Tower of London. The weather was kind of dreary, but it just set the tone." She smiled a little.

Cameron leaned forward, a small smile tugging at his lips. "For someone who's the personification of a ray of sunshine, you sure as hell have a lot of obsessions with dark shit."

"I like it. It's good to try and focus on the positive in life, but that doesn't mean you ignore all the stuff that goes bump in the night. It's entirely possible that Richard III had his nephews murdered in that tower. If that's not a horror story for the ages, I don't know what is." She made a face. "Though, to be honest, a lot of the Tudors could have starred in their own horror show. They were pretty freaking terrible." And she loved it. If ever there was a family that acted as a cautionary tale for the corruption of power, it was *that* one.

"It's a shame we don't have time to visit Amsterdam after we're finished here. There's all sorts of macabre museums and things to see there." He picked up his menu. "Maybe next time."

Next time.

The two innocent little words rang through her like a gong. He'd thrown them out so casually, too. As if they were a given, as if they wouldn't rock her right down to her core. "Cameron." She waited for him to set the menu down and give her his full attention. "What are we doing?"

"Trying to get dinner." He frowned. "Ah, I see. You mean what are *we* doing." The slightest of hesitations, so slight she wouldn't have seen it if she wasn't watching him so closely. "I thought you didn't want to talk about that yet."

"I changed my mind." She'd gone too far to backtrack now. *They'd* gone too far. "I like you," she blurted out. "I know that's inconvenient and you were very clear about boundaries and limits, but I've never been all that good about following the rules, and I like you, okay? I can't help it."

"There are more than a few people who'd think you were crazy for that."

She glared. "Can you be serious, please?"

"I am being serious. Are you sure it's not the intimacy of sex that's clouding your judgment?"

For the love of God. She sat back and crossed her arms over her chest. "Are you seriously trying to talk me out of liking you? Who does that?" But she knew who did that—Cameron O'Clery. The man was nothing if not obstinate.

"No. Definitely not." He reached out and grabbed her hand. "I'm saying this wrong... Which shouldn't surprise you. I'm simply trying to understand the change of heart."

It would be so easy to retreat, to agree that,

yeah, she'd let the sex go to her head, and no, she wasn't *really* falling for him. It wouldn't be the truth, though. The truth was that she liked Cameron despite the fact she couldn't see an outcome where this wouldn't blow up in their faces. One way or another, it would end in tears. She wouldn't stay with Tandem forever, and if she pursued the job she'd gotten a degree for, she'd be traveling. Between that kind of work and the number of hours Cameron put into the company, she didn't see how it could possibly work.

If he even wanted it to work.

He still hadn't said anything in response.

Maybe because he still waited for an explanation from *her*.

She cleared her throat. "I have always had a very clear idea of where I want my life to go and what I want it to look like. It hasn't worked out. Not once. This is the first time where the plan falling apart might not be the end of the world. I didn't plan on enjoying spending time with you so much, but I do. I don't know if I can go back to not being with you once we go home."

CHAPTER FOURTEEN

CAMERON WATCHED TRISH try and fail to dredge up her sunny smile. "Why do you do that?"

"Do what?"

"Fake it." She *was* sunny normally, but she also used it to retreat when she felt awkward or exposed. The fact that it was sometimes genuine had confused him at first, but now he had a better read on her. He wouldn't let her take back what she'd just put out there between them. Cameron squeezed her hand and ran his thumb over her knuckles. "You don't have to hide from me."

"You've said something like that to me before."

"It was true then. It's true now." He had to release her when the waitress finally approached, all apologies for the wait. They ordered food and drinks and as soon as the woman headed to plug the order in, Cameron turned back to Trish. "I like you, too." *More than like you.* He knew her well enough to know he couldn't push harder than he already had. "We're in this together."

"How is this even going to work?"

She always had a plan, and her plans didn't always work out. He reclaimed her hand, wanting to touch her as much as he wanted to offer her a physical touchstone to back up his verbal one. "Occasionally, it's okay to play things by ear."

She snorted. "You don't believe that any more than I do."

It wasn't how he normally lived his life—winging it. Cameron liked a plan as much as Trish seemed to. A plan created boundaries and expectations and efficient measuring sticks for progress. Plans worked great for school and co-running his own business.

One area he'd learned plans didn't work for shit? Relationships.

He brought her hand up and pressed a kiss to her knuckles. "I enjoy the time I spend with you."

She frowned. "I enjoy the time I spend with you, too."

"There's no reason to overthink it, then. We keep spending time together. We keep spending our nights together. We handle each new challenge as it develops, real time." He ignored the unease that slithered through his stomach at the thought of no reassurances for a future with Trish. It didn't matter if it made sense—if it was *logical*. He wanted guarantees that she'd be in his life for the long-term.

Demanding that would mean he'd lose her. She was barely considering extending their fling into something longer. Telling her he wanted something serious, something permanent, would spook her.

She pursed pink lips. "That sounds stressful."

"And trying to plan every development of this thing between us down to the smallest detail sounds like a lesson in insanity." He turned her hand in his grip and kissed her wrist.

"You *do* make me crazy." But something in her relaxed a little and she gave him a genuine—if small—smile.

"Tell me about your parents."

Instantly, the smile was gone. "You already know about my parents. You've known Aaron for ages."

"Sure," he agreed easily. "But his relationship with them is different from yours."

"There's nothing more to add. My dad is a good old boy who has lived his entire life know-ing where his place is and being comfortable in it. He loves all of us, but he works a lot, even still. My mom…" She tensed slightly. "My mom is a worrier. I don't know how much Aaron sees it, but she can work herself up into a panic attack over things outside her control. And no one worries her as much as I do."

"Why's that?" From what Aaron had said about his youngest sister, she was never anything that could be termed a problem child, and all evidence supported that reality.

A shrug, this one too tight to be as nonchalant as she pretended. "I didn't have the same sense as my older sister to find a nice boy, get married and start a family close to home. First I went to college out of state, and now I'm working in the big, scary city—both things my mom is sure are choices I made solely to give her a heart attack. I don't think she was *happy* to see me fail to land a job after I graduated, but she definitely liked having me home again while I figured out where I was going to land."

Cameron considered that new information with what he already knew about Trish. The pieces fell into place with a satisfying *click*. "That's how you learned to manage people so well."

"Clients are no big deal when it comes to un-ruffling feathers. Really, compared to my mom, no one is that big of a deal." She made a face. "I'm not being fair. She's a good mom. She loves all of us to distraction, and she was one hell of a support system growing up. Something just…went a little strange when I graduated high school."

Having her youngest leave the nest had to have been challenging, especially considering that her mother's entire identity seemed to be wrapped up in her children. Or at least that was the impression Cameron got from Aaron. "She tried to clip your wings."

"What? No. No way." Trish used her free hand to take a sip of water. "It's more like she didn't exactly cry when I had setbacks that brought me home."

Which was as good as clipping someone's wings. Cameron's parents had shown him nothing but support from the time he could remember. Even when they didn't really understand his fascination with online security systems, they still sacrificed to ensure he could go to the school of his choosing. "I'm sorry."

"Don't be." She set her glass down. "Your parents sound pretty great."

He let her change the subject without pressing the issue. Her feelings about her mother might be conflicting a bit, but it wasn't something that Cameron could solve in a single conversation. He wasn't sure he could solve it at all—or if he should even try. So he gave her a reprieve and more details about his own parents. "They are. They made sure I never went without while growing up, and they sacrificed a whole hell of a lot to ensure I got to attend my first choice college." He'd known exactly the price required to give him that opportunity. They never doubted that he'd succeed, and he'd never doubted himself as a result. "I don't get to see them as much as I'd like, but I fly over there a few weekends a year, and I fly them over here for Christmas and usually at least once more when they have some free time."

"Aaron mentioned a vacation."

He smiled. "Yeah, they won't take money from me, so I take them on some ridiculously fancy vacation every July. My mom is too damn proud to pick the places she really wants to go, so my dad slips me a wish list every few years and I make sure we get there." She had a strange look on her face and he glanced down. "What? Do I have something on my face?"

"No." Trish shook her head. "That's just…really, really sweet that you do that for them."

"Don't get any funny ideas. I'm still an asshole most of the time. I'm just not an ungrateful asshole. Every opportunity I've had in life is because they helped ensure I was in a place to take advantage of it. It's right that I can take care of them now that I'm in a good place." He was still working on his mom about moving them out to the East Coast when she retired, but that was a long argument that would be years before it reached completion. Cameron got his stubbornness from her, and she wasn't going to agree to move their life without him pulling some serious moves. After moving so much when his father was still in the army, his parents had embraced living in one place and weren't eager to uproot again.

Grandkids might help sway her.

He shut down that thought *real* fast. Too much, too soon.

Trish sat back as the waitress appeared with their food. "Cameron O'Clery, you don't fool me. For all your snarling, you're a good man."

I want to be your *man.*

Trish turned the conversation to lighter topics as they ate, but she kept thinking about the look on Cameron's face when he talked about his parents. *Love.* He loved them without reservation, without caveats, without complications. She wished things were that simple with her parents. There was plenty of blame for that to go around, though. They might have held too tightly to her, but she'd been so damn determined to put miles between herself and her childhood home. To be free.

She still wanted that.

The thought soured her stomach and she pushed

her food around on her plate, conscious of the way Cameron watched her. Faking her way out of her melancholy mood wouldn't work with him—he'd more than proven that—and she didn't have any backup plan. A sweet smile and soft tone had always worked as deflection up to this point.

She was stripped bare for this man, and it wasn't comfortable in the least. How could she have barriers in place to keep herself safe when he saw through every defensive measure she took? "Stop that."

"Stop what?"

"Stop looking at me like you want to crawl around inside my brain."

Cameron didn't look away. "Would you like to fight with me over nothing? Or would you rather talk about what's bothering you?"

Lord, even in this, he somehow managed to cut through all the bullshit she'd thrown in his way, right to the heart of her.

Maybe... Maybe it would be a good thing to talk about the soul-crushing realities she carried around with her. If that wasn't enough to scare him off, maybe this could actually work. The thought made her snort.

"Trish?"

"Okay, fine. I was just thinking about how all I

want is freedom—and how it's the one thing that I seem to miss by a mile no matter what I do."

Cameron leaned back, giving her his full attention. "Explain."

"I'd like to pretend I'm free right now. I have my own apartment. I have a job I actually enjoy. I'm in London."

"You're saying you don't feel free."

It was as if his words opened the floodgates. She couldn't hold back the barrage of words that poured from her lips. "Because I'm *not* free. My awesome apartment? My brother paid for me to get into it, because my bank account was dangerously close to red before I got this job. The same job that Aaron set up for me, despite my qualifications being totally not up to par. Am I really any freer now than when I was living in my old bedroom in my parent's house?"

"Yes." Cameron frowned. "Aaron must know you well enough that you've set up some kind of payment plan to repay him for the money he fronted you."

"Well…yeah. He did do that. But—"

Except Cameron wasn't done. "And I'll admit I had my doubts when he suggested you for the position, but you've proven to be *more* qualified than I could have dreamed. You're an asset, Trish.

It strikes me that everyone around you can see it, even if you can't."

He meant it. Sincerity practically radiated from him, and even if it hadn't, Cameron wasn't in a habit of saying things he didn't mean.

She just wished she could believe it, too. Trish had run so far and so fast, but she kept falling back on the safety net her family represented. She hadn't truly stood on her own two feet...ever.

Cameron might not understand that, but *she* did.

Trish took a hasty sip of her water. Better to change the subject than keep trying to convince him she was a continuous disappointment. And, truth be told, it felt kind of nice to have one person look at her like she was this amazingly accomplished woman...even if she hadn't actually accomplished any of her goals.

Focus. Subject change. You can do this. She leaned forward. "If you're so into fantasy, have you thought about traveling to New Zealand and seeing *The Lord of the Rings* stuff they have set up there?"

"You're trying to change the subject."

"Correction, I *am* changing the subject." When a stubborn look settled over his features, she sighed. "Look, I'm feeling raw and angsty, and I would greatly appreciate it if you'd throw me this bone and talk about your geeky love of all things hobbits and wizards and dwarves." She met his gaze. "Please, Cameron."

"Okay." He gave a surprisingly soft smile. "And yeah, I've thought about visiting New Zealand. My mom is a fan of the series, too, so the summer after this one, we're going. I'll probably strong-arm them into a longer vacation for that one so we can visit Australia as well."

When she met Cameron, she never would have guessed he was too good to be true. She still wasn't sure he was—not when his flaws were readily apparent. But the longer she spent with him, the more the brusque attitude and the painfully truthful comments stopped feeling like flaws and just became part of the man as a whole. "That's really sweet."

"I guess." He got a strange look on his face but masked it almost as soon as it had come. "You do much traveling?"

"Only Stateside. A couple of spring breaks down in Florida. One very memorable road trip to see a Green Bay game with a friend who was a huge fan. Nothing fancy." She looked around at the restaurant they sat in. It wasn't fancy, exactly, but it was in *London*. "Thank you. For bringing me here. To London, I mean. This trip has been surreal in the extreme, but in a good way, and I just… Thank you."

"You don't have to thank me. I needed you to ensure I didn't fuck up this contract."

He said that, but she was no longer sure it was the truth. Nikki Lancaster might be standoffish to a criminal degree, but she obviously put her professional goals before any personal slight she might feel after how things fell out with Cameron. And she had the advantage of knowing how he operated, so she would have been prepared to handle him as needed to close the deal. Trish had been mostly ornamental to the whole situation. "You would have done fine."

"No, Trish. You can claim that now that it's all said and done, but it's not the fucking truth." He shook his head sharply. "There were half a dozen times during that meeting when I started to say something and looked at you—and realized I needed to keep my damn mouth shut. I wouldn't have bothered to show restraint if you weren't there. That might not seem like a big deal to you, but it is to me. I value your presence on this trip— and not just because you're in my bed."

"But I *am* in your bed, and that changes things."

"Yes, it does. And we'll negotiate as needed when we're home."

God, she loved him a little in that moment for not pussyfooting around the truth. No matter how long she stayed on in her current job, there *would* be an adjustment to how they handled themselves in the office, and if he were anyone else, he would have glossed right over that truth. "Okay."

He eyed her mostly full plate. "You're not going to eat, are you?"

"I'm not really hungry," she admitted.

"We'll get something on the way back so you can snack as needed." He twisted and motioned the waitress to bring their check. "Are you tired?"

She blinked. "Not especially."

"Good. There's something I want to show you. I think you'll like it." He made a face. "Though it has nothing to do with untimely death, so maybe we should just go back to the hotel."

"Cameron O'Clery, was that an actual joke?" She playfully smacked his forearm. "I don't just like untimely death, you know. I like flowers and bright colors and telling other people what to do. I'm a well-rounded woman."

"I'm aware." His gaze dropped to her breasts where they pressed against her T-shirt.

She gave a mock gasp. "You're terrible."

"You like it."

She'd had so many different emotions with him—frustration and irritation and lust and en-joyment. Playing fun only made her like him more. She was up to her neck and sinking fast, and she couldn't bring herself to care. "I do. Now, let's go so you can show me your surprise."

CHAPTER FIFTEEN

CAMERON ALMOST CHANGED his mind half a dozen times on the drive. His idea had felt like the right call when he'd first come up with it, but the closer they got to the waterfront, the more he felt like he'd made the wrong call.

Right up until the point Trish leaned against the door of the taxi and gasped. "The London Eye?"

"It's rather touristy but—"

"No, I love it." She barely waited for the taxi to pull to a stop before she opened the door and climbed out. Cameron paid the fare and followed her onto the street. Her captivated expression made her look even younger, and much less world-weary than she'd been since he'd met her. She spun to grab his arm and tugged him toward the giant Ferris wheel. "How did you know? I've wanted to ride this since I was a kid. It seemed like the most magical thing in the world to be able to see a nighttime London from so far up."

"Aaron may have mentioned that you enjoy Ferris wheels." He allowed himself to be towed along like some well-loved toy. It was only after the words escaped that he realized she might find them creepy.

"It gives you a different perspective of the world, and if that isn't magic, I don't know what qualifies." She shot him a look. "I'd say I'm surprised you remembered what had to have been a passing comment, but I'm not."

With her setting the pace, they reached their destination in short order. Cameron gave his information and they were directed to the priority boarding. As they stepped into their capsule, Trish gasped. *"Cameron."* She took in the champagne and chocolates and turned to him, her eyes wide. "When you pull out all the stops, you pull out all the stops."

He started to tell her that it was a normal package offered and nothing fancy, but he managed to filter himself at the last moment. This was important to her, and he *had* done what he could to make it special. "I'm glad you like it."

"Like doesn't even begin to cover it." She explored the capsule, taking in the seats and the clear walls that would give a full 360-degree view of

London once they got moving again. The package was for thirty minutes of uninterrupted time, but Cameron wished he'd booked more, considering Trish's enthusiasm.

"This is amazing." She gripped the railing and leaned out as far as the domed glass would allow. "I can't wait to see it from the top."

He made himself join her close to the edge, wrapped his arms around her and pressed himself against her back, letting the floral scent of her shampoo center him. Even though he'd braced for the movement, his stomach still took a dizzying dip when the wheel started up again. By the time they hit the top point of the Ferris wheel on the first rotation, his palms were sweating and he had to close his eyes in an effort to maintain control.

She turned in his arms. "You're afraid of heights."

"Not afraid. I just don't like them."

"Right. Not afraid at all." She nudged him away from the railing and walked them to the chairs with the champagne. "I don't think the bubbles will do well with your stomach, but maybe it's worth a shot?"

"Sure." With a little distance between him and the sheer drop to inevitable death, he managed to pull in half a breath. "Don't let me ruin the experience."

"You aren't." She poured them both a glass and

passed his over. Trish gave him a surprisingly sweet smile. "You booked yourself a ride on one of the tallest Ferris wheels in the world for me—even though you're not a fan of heights."

"I didn't want you to miss this opportunity." Though he'd bring her back to London sometime in the future when they didn't have work taking up so much time. She had such a unique view on so many things, and Cameron wanted to explore the city and see it through her perspective.

Preferably on the ground level.

She leaned in and pressed a soft kiss to his mouth. "Thank you."

He almost reached for her then and there, to hell with any potential audience, but Cameron didn't want her to miss a second of this ride. He nudged her back toward the railing. "You're going to miss the magic."

"There's absolutely no chance of that." She kissed him again, longer this time, but finally rose and went to lean against the railing.

He watched her watch the city, and something irreversible shifted in his chest. This woman was nothing like he'd pictured for himself in the rare times when he imagined a future where work wasn't his one true love. She was fanciful and stubborn and sunny despite her shadows.

Trish was magic.

Fuck me, I love her.

His world rose and fell with that realization, turning to ash at his feet and rearranging itself into something entirely new. Oblivious to the turmoil going on inside Cameron, Trish took a sip of her champagne and hummed in what could only be described as pure happiness.

He wanted her to look at him the way she looked at London. To feel about him the way she felt about fucking Ferris wheels. He wanted to be her magic.

Cameron couldn't tell her.

Every time they talked about the future, she got a little wild around the eyes. It couldn't be clearer, despite her saying she was willing to give them a shot, that she had no intention of landing with him permanently.

He didn't know how to fix that. People weren't computers. Problems didn't have a guaranteed solution if he just looked hard enough. Trish felt that every plan of hers ended badly. It stood to reason that, no matter how much she enjoyed him, how much she *liked* him, she would view being with him as settling because he had never been part of her plan.

There was a solution here. There had to be. Cameron wasn't romantic enough to believe in soul mates or destiny, but he and Trish *fit*. That sort of thing didn't happen often enough in life to throw it away just because it wasn't part of the plan.

He just needed her to see that, too.

The lights of the city played across her body as the Ferris wheel went round, a slow slide that he ached to re-create with his mouth. If he couldn't tell her how he felt, he'd damn well show her. There was plenty they did right. He just needed her to admit that it *was* right and wasn't yet another of what she considered her life's failures.

Cameron had never had to be convincing before. He usually just powered through any obstacles that life threw in his path.

But for Trish, he'd do whatever it took.

Trish could barely keep from bouncing as they made their way through the hotel lobby and up to their room. "That was amazing, Cameron. Seriously. Beyond amazing."

"It was enchanting," he said as he unlocked their door and stepped aside to let her through.

"I know you're making fun of me, but it *was*." She shrugged out of her jacket and tossed it onto the couch, still riding high.

No one understood her love of Ferris wheels, though Aaron indulged her as only older brothers were able to do. Her sister and their parents mostly rolled their eyes every time she demanded another ride or announced she was going to the fair. It was just another way Trish was a little peculiar, a little too square for the round-shaped hole they expected her to fit into.

Cameron had done more than indulge her. He'd planned a special event solely to give her a private Ferris wheel ride, despite the fact that he was *clearly* afraid of heights.

No one had ever done anything like that for her before. Not at the expense of their own comfort.

She turned to thank him for the hundredth time, and nearly ran into his chest. Trish looked up, her breath stalling in her lungs at the intensity of his dark eyes. "Uh, hi."

"Hey." He slipped his hands over her shoulders and up to cup her jaw, pausing there as if he meant to say something. She found herself holding her breath, waiting for… She wasn't sure what.

But the moment passed. Cameron sifted his fingers through her curls and tilted her head back farther so he could kiss the sensitive spot beneath her ear. "What am I going to do with you, Trish?"

She cleared her suddenly dry throat. "I can think of a few ideas."

"I imagine you can." His dark chuckle curled her toes in her boots. "I'm going to start by taking you to bed."

That sounded like the best kind of plan to her.

She nodded, but he was already moving, scooping her into his arms and heading for their bedroom. Trish couldn't help her breathless laugh. "I can walk, you know."

"I know." He kicked the bedroom door shut. "But why walk when I enjoy carrying you so much?"

Since she didn't have a witty response to that, she kissed him. Cameron let her slide down his body without losing contact with her mouth. He teased her lips open and delved inside, kissing her as if *this* was the main event and he'd be happy kissing her forever.

It wasn't enough.

Unwilling to break the kiss, she undid his pants and shoved them down. Cameron kicked out of his shoes and the pants and walked her back to the bed, working on getting her jeans off in the process. It wasn't smooth or suave, and she ended up giggling as he wrestled the offending denim off, but they finished stripping quickly, until they stood before each other naked.

She stepped closer and pressed her hand over his heart. "This might sound corny, but you're seriously beautiful."

"You're stealing my lines." He pulled her closer, spreading one hand across the small of her back as he fit their hips together. "You know, the first time we had sex, I knew I wanted to someday trace constellations of your freckles."

She'd always liked her freckles—aside from the middle school years where everyone hated everything about themselves—but she'd never considered that someday she'd be with a man who spoke about them like *that*. As if they were as attractive as her breasts or ass. "That sounds unbearably hot." She grinned. "One second."

Trish hurried into the bathroom and dug through her makeup bag. She headed back into the bedroom a few seconds later, wielding her lip liner. "Do it."

If anything, the heat in Cameron's gaze flared hotter. "On the bed."

She scrambled to obey, so turned on she could barely drag in a steady breath. The way he looked at her in that moment would fuel masturbation sessions for the rest of her damn life.

He joined her on the bed and coasted his hand just above her skin, tracing a pattern only he could see. His brows drew together in concentration as he uncapped her bright pink lip liner and carefully connected a series of freckles on her stomach. It tickled, but laughing was the last thing on Trish's mind. "Oh God."

"Mmm." He leaned down and pressed a light kiss to the space in the center of the new constellation. "Hold still."

And so it went. Cameron drew another half-dozen constellations on the front of her body. Her chest. Under her right breast. Just above her pussy. On the inside of her left thigh. The top of each foot.

He knelt between her spread thighs and took in his work. "Fuck."

"Take a picture."

His gaze slammed into her own. "Trish—"

"Do it. I want to remember this always." *Because I won't have it forever. It's something we'll share no matter what happens.* She swallowed past her dry throat. "I trust you."

Another hesitation, longer this time, but he finally nodded and rose to get his phone. Cameron seemed to take the photography as seriously as he took everything in life. He adjusted her position to his satisfaction and snapped a few pictures.

By the time he was finished, her entire body practically vibrated with need. "Touch me."

He rejoined her on the bed and handed her the phone. "Passcode is five-five-six-three."

She realized he'd stuck her photos in a passcode protected folder and typed it in. As Trish swiped through the photos, each sexier than the next, Cameron settled next to her and ran his hand down her stomach—avoiding smudging his work—and cupped her pussy. "You're the beautiful one, Trish." He kissed her neck as he fucked her slowly, thoroughly, with his fingers. He shifted to see the pictures. "That one's my favorite."

In the photo, she had her arms over her head and her legs spread as if she'd just been fucked within an inch of her life. From the angle, she could just make out the slightest glistening of her pussy where she was so wet, she ached for him. The bright pink constellations stood out against her pale skin, turning it from just another sexy-dirty photo into something closer to art.

She lifted her hips to take his fingers deeper. "It's my favorite, too." Driven by the knowledge that this might be one of the few things he kept to remember her by once everything was said and done, she flipped back to the camera and took a picture of where his fingers speared her. *Don't forget me, Cam. Don't forget* this.

"Trish—"

"Not yet." She wasn't even sure what she denied him, only that nothing good came from Cameron saying her name in that rough tone of voice. A tone that spoke of truths she wasn't ready to hear.

She pushed him onto his back and straddled his hips. A few seconds later, she had his cock sheathed in a condom, and Trish wasted no time sinking onto him, taking him as deep as she possibly could, until she wasn't sure where she ended and he began.

She rode him slowly, determined to make this last, to hold out as long as possible. Pleasure built between them, as inexorable as their next heartbeats. The expression on his face was so stark, so possessive, so goddamn *hot*, she had to close her eyes to keep from coming on the spot.

"Don't close your eyes, Trish. Don't shut me out."

Immediately, she opened them again. Cameron pulled her down to claim her mouth as he rolled them and leveraged her legs wider. He lifted her hips a little as he thrust into her, the new angle bowing her back and drawing a cry from her lips. "Oh God, Cameron." She gripped his thighs and wrapped her legs around his waist and he leaned back, and he thrust again, hitting the same spot. Her mind went blank and words sprang from her lips, words she had no control over. *"OhGoddontstoppleasedontstop. IlovethisIlovethisIlovethisIloveyou. Yesyesyesyesyes."* Another stroke and she was lost. Trish came hard enough that she damn near vibrated out of her skin. *"Cameron!"*

CHAPTER SIXTEEN

FOREBODING TOOK UP residence in Cameron's stomach as the plane's wheels touched down in New York. Their week in London had been as idyllic as possible with Trish, but even at its best, he couldn't shake the feeling that a sword hung over his neck.

It didn't help that Trish didn't seem to realize she'd told him she loved him in a fit of passion—or that she hadn't repeated the sentiment since.

He gently shook her awake. "We're here."

"Already?" She pushed her hair away from her face, but it immediately sprang back into place. "I didn't expect to sleep so long."

"You were worn-out." The truth was, *he* was worn-out, too. Cameron needed a solid meal and eight hours of sleep and a couple days' reset before he got his head on straight.

Yeah. Sure. As if that is all it would take.

The ground wouldn't be solid beneath his feet as long as he stood in the shadow of a future without Trish. They'd promised to talk more specifically about what that might look like once they were back in the city, but as much as he wanted a clear conversation, he couldn't bring himself to rush it.

Not when he suspected which way it would go.

So he reached out and laced his fingers through hers. "Let's get dinner."

She glanced at her phone. "It's nine in the morning."

"Breakfast, then. We're not due back in the office until Monday. Come home with me." He formed it as a command rather than a request because he had a feeling if Trish thought too hard about it, she'd try to put some distance between them.

Sure enough, she hesitated. "I don't know... I think my own bed is calling my name."

"If you fall asleep now, you're going to have a wicked case of jet lag and you'll be worthless on Monday."

She made a face. "I know you're right, but a contrary part of me wants to dig in my heels just because of how you phrased it."

"You're too smart to cut off your nose to spite your face." He lifted up their entwined hands and kissed her knuckles. "I have an obscenely large tub. I imagine it would feel wonderful to soak out any kinks."

"Now you're just not playing fair." She gave him a mock frown. "Fine. You've convinced me—on the condition that you don't get weird about me doing laundry at your place."

"Deal."

She smiled a little. "It's weird being back, right? All that time in London felt like a dream, and now it's back to reality."

"Not yet. Not until Monday."

Trish hesitated again, but finally nodded. "I seem to remember my boss—he's kind of a jerk, but he means well—telling me that under no circumstances was I to work on the weekends."

"Sounds like a smart guy." It might be a lost cause to hold on to the dream for a couple more days, but Cameron couldn't bring himself to care. There was no damn reason for his certainty that things would blow up in his face the second they got back into the office. She'd told him she liked him. Fuck, she'd told him she *loved* him, even if it didn't really count because of the timing. Surely that meant more than some plan he wasn't even sure she'd put into motion.

But because he couldn't be certain, he wasn't willing to sacrifice any further time with her. "No work on the weekends—for either of us. No email. No work calls."

"That's a tall order."

He couldn't remember the last time he'd gone more than twenty-four hours in between email checks. It likely hadn't happened since starting up Tandem Security. "A mini vacation."

"I think it's what normal people call weekends?"

He laughed and helped her stand so they could exit the plane. "I don't know these normal people you speak of."

"There it is again—that sneaky sense of humor you have." She looped her arm through his as they walked through the gate and into the airport. "I'll admit—a part of the reason I'm agreeing to this is so I can see your lair."

"Lair? I'm hardly a vampire."

"Well, no, not a vampire." She shot him a look. "Not a werewolf, either. Definitely not a zombie. You're more likely to like the Highlander or one of those other immortals with a quest for vengeance. Loner-ish. Obscenely rich. Doesn't bother with social niceties." She brightened. "Since we're doing a real-life weekend, that means a movie marathon. I'm sure that's in the fine print somewhere."

Her enthusiasm diminished some of the dread eating a hole in his stomach. Maybe Trish wanted this fantasy state to last a little longer, too. "I draw the line at three movies. And there will be breaks in between."

"Breaks for... *Oh*." She grinned. "I think I can handle that. We'll rent a few from my list. I'll make you a horror fan yet—just watch."

"You're welcome to try."

They collected their bags and hailed a cab back to his place. It wasn't until they climbed out onto the sidewalk and headed into his building that he thought about how Trish might react to his suite. He punched the elevator button and turned to her, and sure enough, her blue eyes were wide. "Fancy place."

He tried to see the lobby through her eyes. It was decorated in a modern chic style—whatever the fuck that meant—and was big on stainless steel and minimalism. He'd never put much thought into it before. It was a lobby, and he never spent more than a few seconds crossing it to get to the elevator. It wasn't as if he lingered there. "If you say so."

"Good Lord, you're hilarious. I don't have to say so, because it's the truth." She followed him into the elevator and they took the ride up to the top floor. Trish shot him another look. "You're afraid of heights."

"I don't like heights," he corrected.

"Sure. You don't like heights. And you live in the top-floor penthouse suite?"

"The windows are reinforced," he said stiffly. "And it's not like I spend a lot of time looking out them."

She nodded. "That doesn't make any sense, but I'm going to pretend it does." Trish wandered around his suite and, once again, he tried to see things from her point of view. Cameron hadn't bothered to decorate the place himself. He'd hired a designer to outfit it after he bought it, and the man had done well enough. All the essentials were there—furniture, television, bed, various kitchen tools despite his rarely having time to cook. Everything was nice and neutral but, looking at it through the lens of what he knew of Trish, it seemed...boring.

She propped her hands on her hips. "You didn't pick out a single thing in this place, did you?"

"How do you know that?"

"If you ever sat on that couch, you'd know it was wickedly uncomfortable and it isn't nearly big enough." She peered into the kitchen, hummed under her breath and turned back to him. "The only thing that really feels lived in, aside from the bedroom where you probably spend most of your time when you're home, is the bookshelf." She pointed at the inset bookshelf that he'd filled with first editions over the years. It was one of Cameron's few extravagances, and he forced himself to limit how many he bought a year for the sole purpose of keeping it under control.

Trish drifted closer to the bookshelf. "This case is pretty impressive."

"Some of those books are worth obscene amounts of money." When she raised her eyebrows, he flushed. "I like to see them displayed like this. They make me happy."

"You're such a nerd. I like it." She cupped the side of his face, gave an absent smile and wandered through the door to his bedroom. He followed her into the bathroom and laughed at her expression. "I did say the tub was large."

"It's humongous." Trish fiddled with the faucets until they turned on, sending steaming water cascading out. She sat on the edge of the tub. "You just need a little color in this place, that's all. Nothing too outrageous because it would drive you crazy. Just some soft tones to warm up the place and a few key pieces to bring it all together." She frowned. "Maybe a plant or two. You have someone who cleans?"

"Once a week." He didn't spend enough time at home to truly make a mess, but he liked how fresh the place felt after his cleaning lady had been in.

"Often enough to keep certain plants alive as

long as it's not too fussy." She nodded to herself. "Maybe a fern or something. I'll have to think about it."

Despite his determination to hold on to the promised reprieve, he couldn't help speaking. "Have you ever thought of doing this?"

"We are doing this, Cameron." She waggled her eyebrows at him.

He snorted. "Get your mind out of the gutter. I mean this—the interior designing thing. You've been in here five minutes and already have a better bead on things than the original guy I hired. You totally changed the feel of both the front office and the boardroom in a way I would have said was impossible before I saw it done. With the ability to work both in commercial spaces and private residences, you could make a killing."

Something like interest flared in her blue eyes before she shook her head. "I have degrees in sales and design. That's barely in the same realm."

"Because it's not part of your precious plan." Bitterness soaked into his words, turning them ugly.

Trish crossed her arms over her chest. "There's nothing wrong with having a plan. You wouldn't have gotten to the place you're in now without a plan."

"Plans are nothing if you can't adapt them,

Trish. They're not meant to be set in stone. Life changes things." He could keep going, but every line of her body screamed a resistance to talking about this. "Take your bath. I'm going to order food." He turned on his heel and stalked out of the bathroom.

When he'd realized he loved her, he'd truly thought there was some solution to the way she clung to plans as if they were the word of God. He *still* thought there were options moving forward... but she had to meet him halfway.

Not today.

Nothing would happen today.

He chafed at the restraint, hated the fact that things remained up in the air because of his own doing, but hell if Cameron saw a way around it. *Lose her now, or lose her in a few days.*

I know which one I choose.

The weekend wasn't the relaxing oasis Trish had hoped. Tension strummed between her and Cameron, a cord growing tighter with each passing hour, filled with things neither of them said. The sex remained better than amazing, but after every time, she lay in Cameron's arms, feeling like they were saying goodbye without words.

Worse, she didn't know how to stop it.

He'd thrown out the interior design thing so

casually, as if it was the easiest thing in the world to change her life course. She wasn't flighty. She didn't jump ship just because things got hard and the future didn't look like she thought it would. Just because she was good at colors and getting a feel for a room didn't mean that her dream of being in corporate fashion wasn't valid.

You're talking yourself in circles.

It was all she seemed capable of doing.

To distract herself while Cameron was in the shower, she checked her email on her phone. A small break of their rules for the weekend, but justified. Mostly. She scrolled absently, deleting junk mail to whittle down the number she'd have to handle on Monday, but stopped when she recognized a name. *Mandy?* Trish clicked on the email and nearly dropped her phone.

Hey girl,
So I'm sure you remember my brother, Tom. He's working for Barton Fashion and they're looking for a corporate buyer. I was a total brat and sent your résumé along without mentioning it, but they want an interview! Below is the contact information, so just give them a call and set it up.

Fingers crossed for you!
XOXO, Mandy

Trish read the forwarded email, her heart beating harder with every word. It wasn't just *any* fashion retailer company. It was Barton Fashion. They were in her top three dream companies to work for when she'd first compiled her list back in college. Getting a job there…

Except she was already committed.

Damn it.

She closed her eyes, took several deep breaths and tried to focus. An interview wasn't a job offer. Surely Cameron could do fine without her for a day once they scheduled it. It wouldn't be the end of the world.

What if you get the job?

The thought was almost enough to make her laugh. What if she got the job? Her life plan hadn't worked out once in the two years since she graduated college. There was no reason to think her cursed streak would end *now*, when she was finally starting to come to terms with the fact that maybe her plan wasn't her be-all and end-all. She forwarded the email to Aaron as a courtesy and set her phone back down.

What would happen to her and Cameron if she got the job?

Barton Fashion was based out of San Francisco, which was about as far away from New York as someone could get and still remain in the continental United States. That was part of the attraction when she'd first put the company on her list. She'd wanted distance and enough time to figure out who she was without her family hovering. Without a safety net firmly in place should she fail. If she got the job, it would be a chance to see if she could actually stand on her own two feet without someone there ready to catch her.

Long-distance relationships happened, but she wasn't sure if she and Cameron had a strong enough foundation to pull it off. Yes, she liked him. Yes, she kind of more than liked him. But without the amazing sex cementing them together? With work pulling them both in different directions?

She just didn't know.

Trish picked up her phone again and emailed Barton Fashion to arrange an interview. There was no point in borrowing trouble.

She had enough as it was.

CHAPTER SEVENTEEN

CAMERON STALKED AROUND his office. Something was off, but he couldn't put his finger on the source. It could be all in his head…but he didn't think so. Instead of the weekend bringing them closer together, Trish had become more and more withdrawn as it went on.

He stared hard at his door, but he'd effectively trapped himself in here. He told her he would respect the work boundaries between them, which meant he couldn't haul her in here and demand an explanation. And after the day was done, she'd go back to her apartment and…

And what?

Nothing had changed. There was no reason for the dread curdling his stomach. Tomorrow she would be back in the office, and the next day, and the next. They didn't have to spend every night together, despite the fact that he wasn't keen on the idea of more distance between them.

You hold her too close, and you're going to suffocate her.

Fuck, he didn't know how to do this. Relationships were iceberg-scattered waters under the best of circumstances, and this was hardly that. It didn't help that Trish wouldn't *talk* to him.

Footsteps sounded down the hallway, and Cameron's chest got light. She was coming to talk to him. This weirdness had to bother her as much as it bothered him, and she wasn't too conflicted to put it all out in the open here and now. Trish had never been afraid of anything, so there was no reason to think she'd start now.

Except it doesn't fit in with her plan.

He opened the door and froze. "What the hell are you doing here?"

Aaron raised his eyebrows. "I know I've been gone a few weeks, but last time I checked, I'm still the other owner of Tandem Security."

Suspicion flared. "You're on paternity leave for another month."

"Technically, yes, but with the way things are falling out, I thought it'd be prudent to come back on a part-time basis for the rest of my leave. I'll mostly be working remotely, but I'm officially back."

Nothing short of a catastrophic event would drag Aaron away from his new family earlier than planned. "What happened?"

His friend's smile faltered. "Nothing happened, not yet. But since Trish has an interview for a job in California later this week, things might be moving for her, and I don't want to hold her back. We can find someone else to work the front desk if she needs to quit, but I'm not going to put everything on you while we figure that out. It's really not that big a deal. Becka and I have found a good rhythm, so cutting out a few hours while they nap to work from home is doable."

Cameron picked apart everything Aaron had said and focused on the single most important statement. "Trish has an interview."

"Yeah, she just found out this weekend."

It struck him that his friend had no idea about the change in their relationship. Cameron sure as hell hadn't told him and Trish obviously chose not to as well. They'd more or less agreed on keeping things to themselves, but the knowledge stung unexpectedly. Aaron had no clue that his casual mention of Trish making life plans without Cameron would be an issue at all. And why would he?

She didn't tell me.

If she found out this weekend, she had plenty of opportunity to share that information with him. While they were watching her favorite horror movies. While they were walking down to the restaurants he liked to frequent on the weekends. While they were lying in bed and talking about nothing.

Trish hadn't said a word.

He knew Aaron was looking at him strangely, but he couldn't get his reaction under control. "Excuse me." He shouldered past his friend and stalked down the hall to the front office. Trish looked up as he crossed the threshold and if he hadn't already known that she kept something from him, her guilty look would have made it clear. "Why didn't you tell me?"

"There was nothing to tell."

It shouldn't be possible for five little words to bring his hopes for the future crashing to the ground. "You don't think taking an interview for a position across the country is worth mentioning to me? I was under the impression we were on the same page." Every word got colder and more remote, but his mouth was a runaway train, and Cameron had never been that good at filtering himself to begin with. "It appears I was mistaken."

"It's an *interview*." She pushed to her feet and gave him a pleading look. "We talked about this. Every single thing that's happened to me after graduation has been one step forward and seven steps back. This could be the thing that finally puts my plan back in action. This could be the thing that finally gives me my freedom."

"Your freedom." He clipped out the words. Cameron felt Aaron come up behind him, but they'd gone too far to pretend like everything was all right now. "And your fucking *plan*. You love that damn plan more than you can ever love another person. I understand wanting to get out from beneath your mother's presence, but fuck, Trish. Did this thing between us really mean so little to you that you're not even willing to reconsider that plan you worship so much?"

Her guilt disappeared, replaced by anger. "Easy for you to say. You are living your dream job in your dream city, and you'll eventually succeed in convincing your parents to move out to this side of the country and won't have to compromise on *that*, either. What the hell do you know about constantly reaching for something and being constantly told that you're not good enough?"

"I'm a black man in America, Trish. I think I know a thing or two."

She stopped, pressed her lips together, but charged on. "Point conceded. But the fact remains that working for Barton Fashion is one of my dream jobs and prematurely saying no to an interview with them because of a guy I'm sleeping with is the height of stupidity."

"The guy you're sleeping with," Aaron muttered behind him.

The guy you're sleeping with.

That was all this was to her. He'd known. Damn it, he'd been the one to set the terms to begin with. Stupid of him to think that just because things had changed for him that meant they'd changed for her, too. He couldn't tell her he loved her now. She'd accuse him of trying to keep her from taking the interview—from potentially taking the job—and she'd be right.

He had to let her go.

The realization nearly took him out at the knees. He couldn't ask her to stay. He might love her, but he had no right to ask her to give up her dreams just because those same dreams would take her away from him. Damn it, he had to end it. "You're right."

Trish blinked. "I'm sorry, I thought you just said that I'm right."

"Because I did. You have to take the interview—and the job, if they offer it. It would be idiotic not to." *Even if you made that choice for me.* If she did, she'd spend the rest of their time together resenting him for clipping her wings the same way she felt her mother wanted to, and it would spell the end of them before they had a chance to begin.

Cameron drew himself up, cloaking himself in the coldness he was so often known for. He'd never had to fake it before, though. "Good luck on your interview, Trish. I'll start looking for your replacement this week."

Trish barely saw Cameron the rest of the day, and when she did, he was colder to her than he'd ever been—even when she'd first started working for Tandem Security. She hadn't wanted him to yell at her or to... God, she didn't even know *how* she had wanted him to respond to the news that she had an interview elsewhere.

Not like this, though.

And dealing with Aaron hadn't been any better. When she'd made it clear that her personal life wasn't any of his business, he'd announced he was working from home and abandoned her in the office alone with Cameron.

She went over their fight—if someone could call it that—over and over again as the day wound down. Every single point she made still stood. She was sleeping with Cameron, but that didn't mean she should make life choices based on that fact. She would be worse than an idiot *not* to take the interview because of a relationship, let alone a relationship that had started barely a week previous. That kind of decision-making was the height of madness. If things with her and Cameron exploded or fizzled out, he'd still have his company... and she'd be back to square one. He was his own safety net.

She needed to be her own, too.

But that didn't change the truth. She felt utterly terrible. Her chest was one aching hole of despair and her stomach hadn't stopped twisting itself into knots. Half a dozen times during the day, she rose to walk back to Cameron's office, but she never made that first step. What was there to say? She *had* to take this opportunity. Begging him not to be mad at her wasn't fair to him, not when she'd seen the hurt written on his face before it fell into his distant cold mask. Hurt *she* had caused. Forcing him to rehash it when she knew they'd both come to the same conclusion was just cruel.

Knowing that didn't make her feel the least bit better.

Five o'clock rolled around, and she reluctantly clocked out. Trish turned to the elevator, but she couldn't leave things how they were. She *couldn't.* She walked into Cameron's office. "You would make the same call if our situations were reversed."

"Undoubtedly." He didn't look up from his computer. "I already gave you my blessing, which you already pointed out that you don't need. I'm just some guy you're sleeping with, remember?"

Hurt lodged in her throat, and knowing she was the one who'd caused this mess only made it worse. "I don't see any other option available to me, Cam. I don't know what you want me to do."

He sighed in irritation and turned to face her. "This is the only option available to you. But since you're obviously obsessing over it, let's play this out. You turn down the interview for some guy you're fucking, and two options are available as an outcome. Option one—you end up developing a relationship with him, but you resent him because you turned down what could have been your dream job. Things end badly. Option two— the fling fizzles out as flings are wont to do. You can't deal with working with the guy you were fucking and now aren't, so you quit and end up moving back in with your parents. Things end badly." He recited the potential outcome for them as if reading from some report that had nothing to do with him.

As if he didn't care.

Her throat was too tight, and she tried to swallow past it. "That's not fair."

His composure cracked. "What do you want from me?" Cameron slid his chair back, as if even with the desk between them, he couldn't stand to be that close to her. "Seriously, Trish. What the fuck do you want from me? Do you want me to rail at you and tell you not to go because I love you? Do you really think I'm that selfish? You've spent the entire time we've known each other talking about your plan, and now you have a chance at achieving it. Good for you. I wish you well. But give me the fucking courtesy of not forcing me to rehash this over and over again until you get the job offer because you feel guilty and want me to grant forgiveness or whatever the hell you want. We had fun while it lasted. It's over now. The end."

"You love me?" If anything, the pit in her chest got wider and deeper at the truth he'd spit, a swirling sensation inside her threatening to swallow her whole.

"It. Doesn't. Matter." He stood slowly. "Like I said—it's over now. Get out of my office. Please."

The *please* sent her spinning into motion, hurtling out of his office as if the hounds of hell were on her heels. He loved her and it didn't matter because he'd put his feelings aside so she could accomplish what she'd always wanted to do. She couldn't stay and keep hurting him just because she didn't know what the hell she was feeling. She didn't know what she wanted him to say, but every word had just made it hurt worse.

If they offered her the job, Trish would take it.

Cameron will be okay. He's too strong to let something like a little heartbreak get him down for long. He'd recover and get back to his normal brilliant, cranky self. It would be okay. They would both be okay.

At the end of the day, that was the only thing that mattered.

Not her broken heart. Not her guilt.

Her plan.

She just had to remember that, because it would be the only thing that got her through the coming months.

CHAPTER EIGHTEEN

"ENOUGH IS ENOUGH. Stop moping."

Cameron almost ignored Aaron looming in his doorway, but he'd been avoiding his friend for the week since Trish took the interview—and got the job. Even though he'd suspected she'd nail the interview, he still hadn't come to terms with just how comfortable he'd gotten with her in the office. The new girl was always underfoot and, though she didn't exactly curl up in a ball and cry when he snarled at her, she was no Trish.

That was the problem, though.

After Trish, no one else would do.

Not just for the job. For his fucking life.

"Cameron."

"I'm not moping. I'm working." He closed the window and shut down his computer. He wasn't going to get anything else accomplished today, so there was no point in sticking around.

Especially if Aaron was going to corner him for some kind of misguided intervention. He pushed to his feet, but his friend hadn't moved from his spot blocking the doorway. Cameron stopped short. "We're not having this conversation."

"Wrong. The fact that I've waited this long is only because we're friends and I was waiting for you to pull your head out of your ass and fix things. Since you're showing no signs of doing so, I'm stepping in." Aaron walked into his office and closed the door. He leaned back against it. "When were you going to tell me you're in love with my sister?"

He should have known Aaron would pick up on that. He'd overheard their conversation, after all, and he wasn't an idiot. "I wasn't going to tell you. It's a moot point. She left."

"No shit, she left. She got a job with one of her dream companies. You can't actually have expected her to stay."

Why did people keep speaking the obvious to him? Of course he didn't expect her to stay. Hoping that she would was akin to hoping her dreams would be dashed yet again, and Cameron wasn't monstrous enough to wish for something that would hurt her.

No matter how much her leaving felt like she'd ripped his heart out of his chest and taken it with her.

Since Aaron obviously had more to say, he crossed his arms and leaned against his desk. "I want her to be happy. I wasn't going to hold her back."

Aaron stared at him hard, a flinty look in his blue eyes. He shared similar coloring as Trish, though where she seemed soft and almost innocent in some ways with her curls and freckles, Aaron's looks were carved of ice when he wasn't in the mood to deal with people's bullshit. Much like he seemed to be in that moment. He finally shook his head. "How long have we known each other?"

Was that a trick question? "Going on fifteen years now."

"Yeah. Fourteen years and some change. In all that time, I've never seen you hesitate—not even when you *should* hesitate. If you really love her… Fuck, Cameron, is *now* going to be the moment you decide to break your streak? You're better than this."

"What the fuck do you want from me?" he roared. "I didn't hold her back. I stepped out of the way so she could do what she needed to do without feeling guilty. Why the hell am I being asked for more? I'm not a fucking magician to perform a trick and suddenly make this all okay."

Aaron didn't so much as blink. "This is a problem, and you fix problems."

"I fix problems with computers—*not* with people."

"Figure it the fuck out, Cameron. If you don't, you're going to lose her. The clock started running down the second you let her walk out that door without offering a solution, a compromise, a single goddamn *word*." He pulled an envelope out of his suit jacket and tossed it onto Cameron's desk. "She's miserable, in case you were wondering. This is the happiest she should ever be, and she's so sad, she can barely pull together a fake smile for our parents. She hasn't even bothered trying with me and Becka."

He didn't want to hear that. If he was falling on his sword for her, he wanted her to be happy. More than happy. He wanted her to be walking on air and untouchable. "Why the hell are we doing this if we're both miserable?"

"*That* is the question you should be asking—and answering." Aaron pushed off the door, opened it and walked out without looking back. "Let me know when you have an answer."

Cameron slumped down onto his desk and stared at the plain white envelope. It was smaller than standard, half the width and length of a normal envelope, and the only thing written on it was his name. Even after such a short time together, he recognized the rounded letters of Trish's handwriting.

What else could she possibly have left to say?

He shut and locked his door and sat behind his desk once more to carefully open the letter. It was a torn piece of paper that looked like she'd written on as an afterthought.

Or written on in a flurry before she could second-guess herself about the wisdom of writing in the first place.

He took a second to wish he kept whiskey stashed in a drawer, then began to read.

Cam,
God, I don't even know what to say. You're right. This is what I wanted…except it's not what I wanted. I never expected to fall in love with you. I never wanted it. It hurts, Cam. A lot. I know love is complicated and not as easy as in the movies, but this is just ridiculous. How am I supposed to choose between the career I've spent most of my life wanting and you? It's not fair, and I know that's a child's plea, but I'm feeling suitably dramatic.

You're probably gritting your teeth about now and wondering what the hell my point is.

It goes like this—you hurt me when you didn't try to stop me from leaving. Stupid, right? I know it is, so you don't have to tell me so. I had this moment of surety that if you turned that indomitable will to us, if you loved me, too, then maybe we could figure things out.

You were pretty clear about where you stood, and I'm trying to respect that. I'm sorry if I hurt you at any point, because that really wasn't my intention. But you know what they say about good intentions...

All this is just a long way of saying goodbye. And I'm a selfish ass, because I'm doing it in a letter that you won't have a chance to respond to because I'm afraid if you say a single word, then I won't go. You were right about that, too—I have to go. If I don't, I'll always wonder what my life would have been like, and that's not fair to either one of us.

I hope you end up happy, Cam. I really do. Maybe not right now, or next week, but at some point in the future.

—Trish

He let the letter drift to his desk. "The *fuck* you think you get to have the last word, Trish. God-damn it." She loved him, and she was going to send him a goddamn *letter* instead of giving him a chance to fix this. She was going to *wish him well*, as if that wasn't the height of insanity.

He stared blindly at his blank computer screen. There was a solution to this. Aaron was right on that count, though there'd be no living with him once Cameron admitted it. He just had to figure it out. The old saying about not being able to have your cake and eat it, too, was bullshit. He wanted his fucking cake.

He wanted Trish.

He'd find a way for them to be together.

There was no longer an option where he sat back and let her ride into the sunset without him.

Not when he knew she loved him, too.

Trish clicked Play for the third time in a row and waited for the credits to play out to restart *The Proposal*. She wasn't sure if she'd even liked this movie before this weekend, but it was on demand on the hotel TV and after the first time watching it, she'd cried and cried and started it over from the beginning.

She pulled her comforter tighter around her shoulders. She only had one more day to get this out of her system before she had to show up for work on Monday. Barton Fashion hadn't hired brokenhearted and can't-stop-crying Trish, they'd hired bright and peppy and *sunny* Trish. She didn't know how she was going to pull it off, but she'd figure it out sometime in the next twenty-four hours.

Plenty of time.

Just like the rest of her life, stretching out before her in a uniform without-Cameron road.

She shouldn't have left that letter with Aaron. It was cowardly and stupid, and begging Cameron to fix things after *she* made this choice wasn't fair. Trish used a tissue to wipe at her eyes, wishing the tears would just *stop*. What if Cameron had already read the letter? What if he was... God, she didn't even know, but dread cloaked her in an unrelenting wave with the suspicion that she'd just somehow made everything so much worse.

She dialed her phone before she could talk herself out of it. *It's just to fix things. It's definitely not so I can hear his voice again.* She didn't really expect him to answer. He had to hate her now, which meant he'd let the call go through and she'd leave a stammering voice mail begging him not to read any absurd letter that Aaron gave him, and that would be that. Simple.

Liar.

"Trish?"

Her heart tried to beat its way out of her chest. *Oh God, he answered.* "Cam?"

"Is everything okay?"

How could he sound so calm and put together when she'd cried her way through a jumbo box of tissues and eaten her weight in chocolate chip cookies? *My fault. Not fair to ask him to react the same when I made this call.* She cleared her throat. "I, uh, wanted to apologize." He didn't immediately say anything, so she kept talking, needing to get it out before she lost her last connection to him, however small. "I did a selfish thing and wrote you a letter, and if Aaron hasn't given it to you, I would really appreciate if you burn the damn thing once he does. And if he has—"

"He has."

Oh shit. "Oh. Ah… Okay. Maybe we can pretend it never happened and move on with our lives?" She looked around the hotel room and her gaze settled on the hot mess the mirror reflected at her. Eyes red from crying, hair in a permanent case of bedhead, still wearing the same pajamas she'd changed into when she'd left her training on Friday.

"Is that what you really want?"

She didn't have an answer to that. Not one that had any kind of solution. Did she want to move on with her life without Cameron? Hell no. But she didn't see a way forward for them, no matter how hard she'd tried. "I don't—"

"Honesty, Trish."

She could do this. She could be honest with him. Trish clutched the phone to her ear. "No, I don't want to move on with my life."

"What do you want?"

"I want you."

He exhaled harshly. "Thank fuck for that."

A knock sounded at her hotel door. She froze, half-sure that she was imagining things, but it came again almost immediately. "Just, uh, one second." She climbed off the bed and padded to the door. Maybe it was the maid service? Though it should be too late in the day... Trish opened the door and stared. "Cameron."

"Hey, Trish." His voice echoed in her ear where she still held the phone. She gave herself a shake and ended the call. "I don't... What are you doing here?"

He glanced past her into the hotel room and raised his brows. "Can I come in?"

"Oh. Yeah. Of course." She skittered back and wrapped her arms around herself. He was here. Why was he *here*?

He only moved into the room enough to shut the door. "I read your letter." He pinned her with a look. "What the fuck kind of cowardly shit was that? You wrote me a letter, Trish. A phone call would have been a hell of a lot better, if only because it would have given me a chance to respond."

"I'm sorry," she whispered. Had he come all this way to yell at her about the stupid letter?

"I'm not." Still, he didn't approach her. "I found a solution, though your brother thinks I've lost my damn mind. I don't care. I watched you walk out of my life once, and I'll be damned if I sit back in New York knowing that you love me and I love you. Fuck that. I choose you, Trish."

What was he saying? Hope fluttered cautious wings in her throat. "A long-distance relationship—"

"I split the company. It's past time we had a West Coast base of operations, and Aaron is more than capable of handling anything that pops up in New York by himself with his new assistant. We're going to each build a little at a time and expand Tandem Security accordingly. Right now, I'm working remote until I figure out where we're landing, but that's the deal—I land where you land, Trish." He hesitated, something vulnerable creeping past his customary confidence. "That is, if you still want me to find a solution. If you still want *me*. I know I was a dick before and—"

"Shut up." She threw herself into his arms and kissed him with everything she had. By the time she came up for air, she was shaking. "You're serious. You moved across the country for me."

"I haven't actually moved yet. But the plans are in place." He gave a soft smile. "I wanted to be sure you hadn't changed your mind before I chased you down and branded myself a stalker."

She peppered his jaw with kisses. "Of course I didn't change my mind, you crazy man. How could I? I love you. I love you so much, and I'm sorry I never told you. That stupid letter—"

"I'm framing it."

"What?"

"The letter." He lifted her into his arms and started for the bed. It took Cameron all of three steps to reach it in the small hotel room. "I'm keeping it forever. I'm keeping *you* forever." He tumbled her back onto the bed and settled beside her. His gaze snagged on the television and he frowned. "Sandra Bullock?"

"The movie makes me think of you. She's this cranky boss who overworks her hapless assistant and they end up falling in love." She leaned up and kissed him. "You're cuter than she is, though."

"Thanks." Cameron pushed her curls back from her face. "I'd like to take you to meet my parents next weekend."

"I'd like that." She cupped his jaw. "I bet they'll

be happy to know that you're in the same state as they are."

"Probably." He gave her a wicked grin. "But, mark my words, my mom is going to start in on when we're going to give her grandchildren."

Trish laughed. She couldn't help it. She hadn't dared think there might be a way for her and Cameron to be together, yet here he was, in her bed again and offering her the solution to everything. She snuggled closer to him. "It'll be at least a few years."

"No doubt." He sounded a little choked, as if the thought of kids panicked him, which only made her laugh harder.

She wrapped her leg over his waist and pulled him closer. "But there's no reason we can't practice in the meantime. Lots and lots of practice."

"I love you, woman."

"Say it again."

His lips brushed her ear. "I love you," he whispered. "And I'm never letting you go."

"Good," she breathed. "Now take off your clothes."

* * * * *

MAKE ME YOURS

To Lauren

CHAPTER ONE

"HAVE I MENTIONED how much I loathe weddings?" Becka Baudin grabbed two champagne glasses and handed one to her best friend, Allie.

"Only about half a dozen times—in the last hour."

She drained the glass and waited for her stomach to settle. Only then did she focus on her best friend's amusement. "It's not my fault. They give me hives. Even this one." *Especially this one.*

"Here." Allie passed over the second champagne glass, her expression sympathetic. "You know you're not losing her, right?"

"Of course I know that. I'm not a child." But she still glanced at her big sister gliding across the dance floor with her new husband. They looked like something out of a fairy tale, Lucy in a gorgeous white dress that hugged her lean form. It was overlaid with lace and gave a little sparkle with every move. Her dark hair was twisted in an intricate style that left her neck and shoulders bare except for the truly out-standing necklace Gideon had bought her.

And Gideon.

Lord, the man could wear a tux.

But it wasn't the clothes that made them the most beautiful couple in the room. It was the way they looked at each other.

She sipped her second glass of champagne. "They seem happy."

"Yes, well, that generally happens on someone's wedding day."

Becka rolled her eyes. "Yeah, yeah, I know. I'm being an asshole. It's not *this* wedding I object to—it's the rest of them." Weddings were nothing but false promises of happily-ever-after. They sold a dream most people never actually realized—more than half ended in divorce.

She gave herself a shake and eyed her glass. "I think it might be time to start with the vodka." She'd already done her duties as maid of honor, from the pictures to the people herding to the speech. Now it was just a matter of keeping her head down until it was time to see Lucy and Gideon off to the limo. *Yes, a drink is exactly what I deserve for keeping my happy mask in place.* If she didn't do something to break the tension soon, she was liable to snap at someone and make an ass of herself, and end up on some Maids of Honor Behaving Badly list. She couldn't do that to Lucy. Today was like playing through one of her personal nightmares, but Becka could do better than to act out like a spoiled child as a result. She *was* better than that. She had to be.

Becka turned to the bar and froze.

Blue eyes captured hers, rooting her feet in place even as her body tried to sway forward. Toward *him*. Square jaw, straight strong nose, sensual lips that quirked up as he gave her his own perusal. She straightened, suddenly glad that her sister hadn't followed the shitty tradition of clothing her bridesmaids in the ugliest dresses imaginable. Her purple dress set off the rich blue color she'd settled on for her hair, and it hugged what few curves she had. The stranger wore a tux even better than the groom, his broad shoulders tapering to a lean waist.

She'd never seen a more striking man in her life.

"That's Aaron Livingston." Allie's shoulder brushed hers, effectively grounding her. "He's friends with Roman and sometimes business associates with Gideon, I think. I didn't realize he'd be here."

Aaron. I like it. "I should go say hi, be hospitable…or something."

Allie snorted. "Yeah, sure. That's exactly what you're going to do." She grinned. "Have fun. I'm going to go dance with my man."

"Yeah, yeah, rub it in that you're deliriously domestically happy." The words held no sting. She *was* happy her best friend had found the love of her life in Roman Bassani. Between Allie and Lucy, it was almost enough to convert Becka to a romantic way of thinking.

Almost.

Too bad I'm well acquainted with the downsides of romance. Hard to put on rose-tinted glasses when I've been up close and personal with everything that can go wrong.

God, she was a mess. She needed to do something—fast.

There was nothing quite as distracting as a man. The one currently staring at her as if memorizing every inch of her would fit the bill nicely.

It's just a Band-Aid.

She shoved the knowledge aside and made her way to the bar, never taking her gaze off Aaron. He watched her but didn't move from his spot. Letting her approach. Letting her set the tone. Smart man.

Becka sidled up to the spot next to him and broke eye contact to order a vodka seven. This close, she could smell his cologne—something expensive that made her think of hot and dirty sex in the best way possible. *Down, girl.* If this wedding was for anyone else, she wouldn't hesitate to haul him to a convenient closet or bathroom stall to silence the ugliness inside her, but she wouldn't do that to Lucy. Her sister deserved the best on her wedding day, and damn it, Becka would make sure she had it.

At least until Lucy got into the limo.

Then all bets were off.

"Maid of honor."

God, even his voice was wonderful, low and even with just a hint of growl. She twisted to face him. "Wedding guest." He just raised his eyebrows, and she smirked. "Sorry, I thought we were throwing out labels." She held out her hand. "Becka Baudin."

"Becka being short for Rebecka?"

"Something like that." No one called her Rebecka—not even Lucy. She certainly wasn't going to hand out that name to this guy, no matter how magnetic he was or how he seemed to be so close to what she needed in that moment, it was a wonder she hadn't conjured him into existence.

But then, Becka didn't believe in magic any more than she believed in romance.

"I'm Aaron." He took her hand and pressed a kiss to her knuckles. His five o'clock shadow scraped against her skin, completely at odds with the softness of his lips. It would feel good to have him sliding his mouth along other parts of her. Better than good. Decadent and sinful and absolutely perfect.

Not yet.

She licked her lips. "I know."

"I see you've done your homework."

"More like your reputation precedes you."

"Can't complain about that if it brings a woman like you my way." He let their hands drop but didn't release her. Aaron slid his thumb over the same path his lips had just taken, as if he had every right to seduce her with a single touch. His lips quirked into a smile and, damn it, it made him even more handsome. "Nice wedding."

Come on, Becka, you can do better than this. Stop staring at him like a lust-struck idiot. She cleared her throat and reclaimed her hand just in time for the bartender to deliver her drink. She turned to face the bar fully, needing some distance, even if it was only in her head. No matter what her plans for this man were, she couldn't afford to lose focus until later. *Maybe this is a mistake. Maybe you should find someone less magnetic, less overwhelming, to lose yourself in.* Even as she thought it, she knew she wasn't going to. A few short minutes of conversation and Aaron Livingston had dropped a lure she couldn't have resisted if she tried. Better to just let things unfurl on the path they were both obviously heading down.

It's only one night. Tomorrow I'll go back to my life and it will be nothing but a fond memory.

What had he asked her? Right. The wedding. Of course it was the wedding. That was all anyone had been talking about for months, and they were at the damn event right now.

She downed half her drink. "It's a wedding. They're all flavors of the same thing." Damn it, that sounded bitter. She took a careful breath and pasted a happy smile on her face. "It's what Lucy wanted, and she's happy, so I'm happy." That, at least, was the truth.

"I take it you don't subscribe to the American dream that ends with a white picket fence?"

Becka shot him a look, trying to gauge where he was going with that comment. Even if he shared her views on marriage and weddings, this was hardly the event to start bitching about how cynical they were. "We live in New York. We don't do white picket fences here as a general rule."

"True enough." Aaron's blue eyes took her in, and she couldn't shake the feeling that he saw too much. That if he looked deep enough, he'd be able to trace her aversion to the fictional happily-ever-after right back to her parents' destroyed marriage and...

Enough.

Keeping ahold of her drink, she gave him her full attention. No reason to avoid pulling the trigger on this. If by some miracle she'd misread the situation, she still had plenty of time to bounce back from any rejection he dealt and move on to someone else. "You want to get out of here?" She waved a hand at her sister still on the dance floor. "I mean, after this dog and pony show has reached its natural conclusion."

His grin widened, just a little. "I wouldn't say no to another drink somewhere quieter, where we could have a conversation."

A conversation? *Hard pass.* The conversation, the

drinks, the quiet place… It was all just frills to fancy up the fact that they wanted to bang each other's brains out. Whatever his reasons, he seemed just as onboard with this plan as she was. Except he wanted to talk. If he was anyone else, if the attraction was any more manageable… But he wasn't, and it wasn't. She knew her strengths, and while she didn't believe in love at first sight, what she had with Aaron was definitely *lust* at first sight. Better for both of them to keep things simple and define clear boundaries from the start.

Becka reached up and traced the top button of his dark gray shirt. "Is a conversation really what you're after?"

He opened his mouth and seemed to reconsider. "I'm after you."

The honesty washed over her, a fresh breeze that made the choking environment of this fucking wedding a little more bearable. *I am happy for Lucy. I am. I just can't look at her without seeing our mother, and we both know how* that *turned out. It's not the same and it won't have the same outcome, but that doesn't change anything. Not really.*

Becka managed a smile. "In that case, let's skip the drinks and you can take me back to your place for a nightcap."

If anything, his brows rose higher. "A nightcap."

"Yep." It would be good with Aaron. Exactly what she needed. The lightning nipping at her fingertips from just this small touch told her as much. They could offer each other an enjoyable night, and then she'd get back to her life with only a fond memory to balance out her mixed feelings about her friend and sister leaving her behind.

They weren't *really* leaving her. Rationally, Becka knew that. Most days, she even believed that nothing would really change even though both Lucy and Allie had gone and fallen in love.

Stop that.

Becka finished her drink and set it on the bar. "Another, please."

Aaron covered the glass with his hand. "If you want that nightcap, then you're done for the night." When she opened her mouth to protest, he shifted closer, placing his free hand over hers, his broad shoulders blocking out the rest of the room. "Trust me—you'll want to be sober for this."

His audacity made her laugh. "Yeah, no, you don't get to decide when I'm done." She was buzzed, but she wasn't anywhere near drunk. Another drink or two wouldn't make a difference.

"All the same." He removed his hand, but he didn't move away. "You're more than welcome to drink yourself stupid, but you won't be coming home with me if you do."

Sheer stubbornness almost made her tell him to fuck right off. Becka responded to commands about as well as she did to ultimatums, and Aaron had issued both in the last thirty seconds. The whole point of a night of wild abandon was the *abandon* part, and that only worked if they were equal. Letting him set the pace and lay down the boundaries was *not* part of the plan.

But then the DJ's voice laughed from the speakers. "It's about that time, ladies and gentlemen. All the single ladies on the floor to catch the bouquet!"

Desperation clawed at Becka's throat. She had to go out there and smile and be supportive, and all she wanted to do was crawl under the bar with a bottle of vodka. She glared at Aaron. "Fine. No more drinks." She turned on her heel and stalked toward the group of women gathering in the middle of the dance floor.

He'd better be as good as he thinks he is.

Aaron spent the rest of the reception watching Becka. Taking her home was likely a mistake. He might be on decent terms with her sister, but her newly acquired brother-in-law was a different story altogether. Pissing off Gideon Novak wasn't on his list of things to accomplish, especially with Aaron's business on the verge of expanding. He'd need the headhunter in the future, which was part of the reason he'd accepted the invitation to this wedding.

Becka's laugh drew his attention, the sound just as bold as the rest of her. From her blue hair to the piercing glinting against her red lipstick to her tight little body… Yeah, *bold* summed up Becka Baudin pretty damn well. She couldn't be more different from her straitlaced older sister, and even though he knew better, those differences intrigued him. She was the kind of woman who saw what she wanted and went after it, no holds barred.

Tonight, it appeared that what she wanted was *him*.

He set his empty tumbler on the bar as Becka grabbed a microphone and instructed the guests to head out front to see Lucy and Gideon off. She was the kind of woman born to stand in the spotlight. She held everyone's attention easily as she laughed and made a joke, but still managed to be firm and get everyone moving toward the door. Most of them would be coming back into the reception to keep drinking while the bride and groom went off to do what new couples did on their wedding night.

Aaron had other plans.

Becka's gaze found him across the small sea of people between them, and the barely banked heat in those blue eyes seared him to the bone. He started for the door with the rest of the guests. Despite all the jostling, he never lost sight of her in the crowd. How could he, when everything about her seemed designed to draw attention? Aaron let himself be borne along, but he managed to ensure he ended up close to her once they reached the sidewalk. As more people piled out in front of the venue, he had to step closer until he nearly bumped into her.

She glanced over her shoulder and grinned. "Hey there, handsome. You come here often?"

Before he could answer, Lucy and Gideon walked out the door, hand in hand. A cheer went up from the people around him, and the crowd surged as guests started blowing bubbles at them. The movement sent Becka teetering in her sky-high heels, and Aaron instinctively grabbed her arm and steadied her. It pressed their bodies together, her back to his front. This close, there was no way to avoid noticing the curve of her ass, or the way it lined up so fucking perfectly with his cock.

He gritted his teeth and tried to get his body's reaction under control, but Becka chose that moment to lean back against him and roll her hips, ever so slightly. In case he missed it—not likely—she shifted his hand from her arm to her stomach, tucking them tighter together. Another roll of her hips had him cursing softly. He resisted the temptation to let his hand drop lower to brush the V between her thighs. They were in the middle of a goddamn crowd, and her sister was only a few feet away.

But he wanted to.

Fuck, he wanted to.

Aaron wanted to hook his fingers beneath the hem of her dress and stroke her pussy right here. To bring her to the edge and leave her there, teasing her to see how long she could hold out from making a noise that would give them away.

Holy shit, get ahold of yourself. This isn't you. You don't lose control like this—especially with a woman who's barely more than a stranger.

A few precarious minutes later, the newlyweds were safely tucked into the limo. Before he could decide how he wanted to play this, Becka turned in his arms and laced her hands around his neck. The move pressed her more firmly against his cock, and hell if her lips didn't part and her blue eyes go hazy with need. For *him*. She leaned up until her lips brushed his ear. "You are the sexiest goddamn distraction I've ever seen."

He traced the curve of her ass and lost his battle with control. Aaron dipped his fingertips beneath the hem of her dress. "I'm not the only one." Weddings made people crazy, and he'd always thought he was immune to that particular insanity, but then, he'd never met a woman like this before. The attraction was too strong to resist, and it came on too quickly to do anything but let go and see where it took them.

Becka nipped his earlobe. "Let's get out of here."

"One thing before we go." He walked them back until his shoulders hit the brick wall, away from the people already disappearing through the door into the hotel. It took several long minutes before the sidewalk cleared of the wedding guests. All the while, he studied Becka's face, the dark fringe of her lashes, the curve of her lower lip, the way her breath caught when she met his gaze.

Aaron cupped her jaw and tilted her face up to claim her mouth. She tasted minty, a burst of freshness as intoxicating as the woman herself. Becka went soft in his arms, melting as she opened for him, her tongue eagerly meeting his, stroke for stroke. As if she'd been as impatient for this moment as he'd been.

She'd called him a distraction.

She was the distraction—one he wasn't sure he could afford.

He pressed his forehead to hers, trying to regain control. "Let's go."

"How far is your place?"

A forty-minute cab ride.

Too far.

Inside the building, a burst of laughter trailed down to them. *Perfect.* "About twenty yards."

She laughed. "That works. I don't want to wait anymore." She grabbed his hand and towed him back inside the building. They bypassed the entrance to the ballroom where the reception was being held and headed for the main desk.

Ten minutes later, they stumbled through the door to a room and slammed it behind them. Aaron guided Becka to the bed and laid her on top of it. He kissed her neck, her shoulder, the line of her heart-shaped bodice. She was fire in his arms, arching to meet his mouth, her hands busy on the front of his shirt. She shoved it down his shoulders, and he released her long enough to shrug it off. Aaron tugged her dress up over her head.

Need shot through him, rushing his movements even as part of him wanted to slow down.

To savor every moment.

He stopped short, drinking in the sight of her. She wore nothing but a silk thong in show-stopping pink. Against her pale skin, the neon color practically glowed, just as brilliant as her hair. Aaron traced the rose tattoo nestled on the inside of her left hip, noting the thorns circling the full petals of the flower, and then he smoothed his hand up her taut stomach to her high breasts. She was lean, every muscle defined in a way that spoke of serious time spent in the gym. "Strong little thing, aren't you?"

"Well, I'm a spin and TRX instructor, so that goes with the territory."

He bracketed her ribs with his hands and then cupped her breasts. "Maybe I'll take one of your classes sometime."

Becka laughed even as she twined her hands over her head, offering her body to him. "Honey, you wouldn't last ten minutes."

"Think so?" He lightly pinched her pale pink nipples, gauging her reaction. Her sharp inhale only fanned the flames within him. He needed her. Now.

"I *know* so." She grinned. "But let's be honest—

there's only one kind of exercise we're interested in right now, and it doesn't have a single thing to do with a bike. Now, stop teasing me and take off your pants."

CHAPTER TWO

BECKA COULD BARELY breathe at the look on Aaron's face as he ran his hands over her body. Learning. Reveling. *Worshipping*. It left her feeling off center, as if this was more than some horny wedding sex between two single people who'd never see each other again. She covered her uncertainty the only way she knew how—brazenly charging forward. "You're still wearing pants."

"Don't rush me." He lifted her farther onto the bed and lay next to her, his head propped on his hand. She started to protest, but Aaron cupped her pussy and she forgot whatever she'd been about to say. He stroked her over the silk of her panties, his blue eyes arrested on the spot he touched her. The slick fabric lent an erotic edge to the slide of his fingers. "Spread your legs."

She obeyed instantly. Becka normally preferred to take charge of her sexual encounters. She knew what she liked and had no reservations with demanding exactly that. Most guys found it sexy as hell and—more importantly—it ensured they both had one hell of a good time.

Aaron wasn't going to let her lead this encounter. She'd known it from the second he commanded her not to drink any more that night. And the kiss... God, that kiss had been claiming in a way she wasn't prepared to deal with.

Doesn't matter. I'm a grown-ass woman. I knew what I signed up for. I can handle it.

That didn't stop a shiver from working its way through her body as he traced her opening through her panties and moved up to circle her clit. This wasn't the rushed fucking she'd prepared herself for. He touched her as if she meant something beyond a mutually satisfying night. "Stop that."

Aaron met her gaze, his hand stilling. "Problem?" There was no anger in those blue eyes, just a kind of knowledge that said he already knew what her protesting was about and didn't give a damn.

"Don't make this into something it isn't." He didn't respond other than to slide his hand back down to cup her again. *Possessively.* She swallowed hard, fighting not to rub against him like a wanton thing. *Focus.* "I'm just here for the sex." *For the desperately needed distraction.*

He raised his eyebrows. "You're just here for the sex."

"That is literally what I just said."

"I heard you." His thumb dipped beneath the edge of her thong. "Becka, if you think this night is going to end before I've stroked, tasted and fucked you until we're both damn near comatose…" He shook his head in mock sympathy even as he kept up that teasing stroking beneath her panties, not quite where she so desperately needed him.

"I signed up for *that*." She gritted her teeth in an effort to keep still. "I didn't sign up for *this*."

"Do you want me to stop?" The arrogant tilt of his lips said he already knew the answer. She hated that he was so sure of her, hated even more that he was right.

Becka smacked his hand away from her and shoved his shoulders, well aware that he allowed her to tumble him onto his back. She was strong for her size, but he had a good six inches and fifty pounds on her. She grabbed his wrists and pinned them over his head, and he let her do it. "I don't want you to stop." She shifted, dragging her breasts against his bare chest. *God, he's breathtaking. All I want to do is rub myself all over him like some horny teenager.* She pressed down against his cock and had to bite back a whimper.

"Come here, Becka." The way he said her name was almost a purr, a soft coaxing that was no less a command than all his others tonight. "Give me your mouth."

She kissed him, telling herself she did it because

she wanted to and not because part of her quivered with need at the rough growl in his voice. He tasted like the scotch he'd been drinking at the reception, and it went straight to her head. She forgot she was supposed to be in the dominant position, to be driving this encounter, to be the one calling the shots. Instead, she released his wrists and cupped his jaw on either side, losing herself in the feel of his tongue sliding decadently against hers, his lips hard and unyielding and yet giving her everything she needed.

It was too much.

He kissed her like this meant something.

She didn't want him to be right.

She leaned back, desperate to put some distance between them, to remember the purpose for that night.

Her plans disappeared through her fingers like smoke when his lips curled into a wicked smile. "Let me taste you, Becka."

It took everything Aaron had to leash himself, to hold still as Becka considered him. The first impression he'd gotten of the wild thing on the verge of fleeing was only reinforced by the skittish look in her eyes. *She'll run at the first hint of a cage.* He filed away that information, but the truth was that he didn't want to cage her.

That isn't what tonight is about.

She worried her bottom lip even as she shifted

deliciously against him. "I can't think straight when you say my name like that."

Good. He didn't say it through sheer force of will. "This thing with us has nothing to do with thinking straight." He'd accepted the offer of a nightcap because she was beautiful and interesting, and it had been a long time since he'd let himself indulge in anything resembling a one-night stand. But this bold and slightly brittle woman intrigued him despite himself.

She sat up a little, pressing herself down against his cock. "That's a good point. A brilliant point, even. I'm overthinking things." She wrinkled her nose. "I don't usually bring this much baggage to banging. Sorry. The wedding has me all twisted up for various reasons."

"Becka—"

She charged right over him. "But that's neither here nor there." She gave a brilliant smile. "You wanted a taste."

He kept himself perfectly still as she sat up fully and stretched her arms over her head, showing off her body. And, fuck, what a body. Aaron wanted to pin her down, to lick and kiss every inch of her until she felt the same desperation coursing through his veins. *I do that, she leaves.*

Unacceptable.

Becka moved up until she straddled his face. He could *see* how wet she was against the silk of her panties, and he ran hands up her thighs, urging her to spread a little farther for him. "Perfect."

"Hey now, remember who's in the driver's seat."

He shifted his hands higher so he could hook a thumb into her panties and tug them to the side, exposing her. "Let me know if I miss the mark." He lifted his head, still holding her gaze, and flicked his tongue out to taste her.

She braced her hands on the wall over the headboard and bit her bottom lip. "More of that, please and thank you. Suck my clit, Aaron."

Fuck me.

His control snapped. He obeyed her hoarse command, sucking her clit into his mouth and rolling the sensitive bud against his tongue. Becka let loose a whimper that sent a bolt of lightning to his cock.

Getting her to make that noise again shot to the top of his list of things to do.

He lost himself in her taste, in the way her thighs went tense beneath his hands when he licked her just right. It didn't take long to find the blend of rhythm and pressure that had her rocking against his mouth, her whimpers turning into gasping cries. Higher and higher he took her, driving her ruthlessly into her first orgasm. She let loose a breathless giggle when she came, as if overtaken by sheer delight the same way she'd been overtaken by pleasure.

He fell a little bit in love with her right then and there.

"Safe to say you didn't miss the mark." Becka laughed again and slumped to the side, letting one leg sprawl across his chest as she blinked at him from beneath a curtain of blue hair. "I was right—it *is* good with you."

"Happy to live up to expectations." For the first time in so long, he wasn't thinking about his next business move or the future, beyond the moment when he got inside this woman. *Tonight. Even if it's only tonight, it's worth it for the reprieve she's offered.* Aaron rolled onto his side and smoothed back her hair. "I like the blue."

"I live to please."

He lightly pinched her nipple. "So snarky."

"Hmm, you know it." She stretched from her fingers to her toes, her body perfectly on display for one breathtaking moment before she relaxed and grinned at him. "That was a great appetizer, but I'm more than ready to move on to the main course."

He dug his wallet from his pocket and fished out the condom he'd stashed there earlier that week. Aaron always carried one with him—the better to be prepared for any given situation that arose, so to speak—but he switched it out regularly to avoid any mishaps. He took her hand and pressed it to her palm. "Do the honors."

"The honors." Becka smirked. She ripped the foil packet open. "Someone's got a high opinion of themselves." She took her time rolling the condom on, teasing him, prolonging the moment when this reached the point of no return. As if she wanted this to last as much as he did.

"That's enough." He cupped the back of her neck and towed her up so he could take her mouth. Aaron rolled them without breaking the kiss, loving the way she moved with him as if they'd done this a thousand times. She stroked her hands down his sides and gave his ass a playful squeeze as he settled between her thighs. He chuckled against her mouth. "Cheeky."

"Just call me a saucy little minx." She nipped his chin and pressed an openmouthed kiss against his neck. "I don't want to wait anymore, Aaron. I need you."

"Next time we go slow." He reached between them to position his cock at her entrance. "Ready?"

"Baby, I was born ready." She hooked a leg around his waist and arched up to meet him.

He'd expected the move, so he countered it, letting himself sink into her a single inch and no more. "Slow, minx. I don't want to hurt you."

Her laugh seemed to vibrate her whole body, and her blue eyes shone with true amusement. "That giant cock of yours is impressive, but I can take it." Becka grinned. "Do your worst."

Impossible to resist the playful challenge in every line of her body. He didn't really want to hold back any more than she seemed to want him to. Aaron slammed into her, sheathing himself to the hilt. She jolted, that delicious whimper slipping free again. He ate the sound, kissing even as he began moving. His leash had snapped without his realizing how close he was to losing control. This woman, this wildfire in his arms, she brought out something he'd fought long and hard to tame within himself.

Something savage.

He tried to pull back, tried to regain control.

As if sensing his withdrawal, Becka wrapped both legs around his waist and grabbed his hands, lacing their fingers together. She stretched her arms over her head, guiding him to pin her down. "I'm not breakable, Aaron. You don't have to be careful with me." She squeezed his hands. "I want everything."

He could no more resist her command than he'd been able to turn away from her at the bar. Aaron put his weight onto her hands and pounded into her, each thrust making her breasts bounce and drawing a cry from her lips. He watched her face the entire time, finding only a mirror to the delirious pleasure spiraling through him. Feeling more animal than man, he shifted his grip to her wrists, and her splayed fingers only drove him to fuck her harder.

"Yes, yes, *yes*!" Becka let loose another of those intoxicating giggles, her pussy clenching around him in climax hard enough to pull him over the edge with her. He thrust into her roughly, his grip on her the only thing that kept them from sliding right into the headboard, his orgasm hitting him with the force of a tidal wave.

Aaron dropped his face to the curve of her neck and pressed a careful kiss there. "Fuck, minx, nothing could have prepared me for you."

Becka shouldn't let a comment like the one Aaron just made stand, but she couldn't work up the energy to remind him yet again that this was a one-shot deal. Not with his big body pinning her to the bed, his hands still holding her down in a way that had her squirming despite coming twice in quick order. Aaron made her feel… She didn't know how to put it into words. She wasn't submissive—not really— but being at his mercy while he fucked her within an inch of her life?

Yeah, that moment was going into her hall of fame.

She stroked a cautious hand down his back and shivered as he thrust into her a little. He was still half-hard, which had her glancing at the clock and doing a quick calculation to how much time was really left in this one-night stand. *More than enough. It doesn't really end until the sun rises, right?*

Aaron kissed her neck again and then took her mouth. There was no other way to describe his mouth claiming hers, his way of controlling the kiss that made her head spin. He thrust again, and she clenched her legs tighter around him. "More. I need more. Again."

He set his teeth to her bottom lip, but just when she thought he'd give her exactly what she wanted, he cursed and retreated. "We're going to have to go back to my place for that nightcap. I have exactly one condom on me, and we just used it."

Disappointment threatened to sour her good mood, but she shoved it aside. What would it hurt to catch a cab back to his place and keep this thing going for a few more hours? He'd already more than proven he could give it to her better than ninety percent of the guys she'd hooked up with in the past. Letting a tiny technicality get in the way of more orgasms wasn't her style.

Becka reluctantly uncrossed her ankles so he could move. "I suppose you'll make it worth my while if I suffer through a cab ride."

"You know it." Her heart skipped a beat at his answering grin. His buttoned-up attitude hadn't lasted past their first kiss, but there was such mirth in that expression she couldn't stop herself from grinning in response.

Aaron pressed a quick kiss to her lips. "Let me clean up and we'll get out of here." He slid off her... and froze. "Fuck."

"What?" She scrambled back, her stomach doing a slow flip at the sight of the broken condom. *Fuck, indeed.* "Shit."

"I'm clean."

It was too much on top of everything else that

had happened that day. Becka shook her head and edged around him to get off the bed. "Thanks for the memo." She believed him, even though she had no right to take his word for anything at this point. She reached the edge of the bed and hesitated. *Think, Becka. Don't be a jackass.* "I'm clean, too. I get tested regularly." He deserved to know that, at least.

She pushed her hair back, hating that his face had immediately fallen back into the cold lines he'd worn when she first caught sight of him. *This was never going to work. Get out now before it gets even more awkward.*

"Becka—"

Becka. Not *minx.*

She shook her head. "No, it's fine. I'm on birth control. If you're clean—"

"I am."

"Then there's nothing to worry about." She grabbed her dress from the floor and tugged it on. "This has been fun, but I need to go home now."

He disappeared into the bathroom for a few seconds, and then he was back, unabashedly naked and stalking across the room to her. "We need to talk about this."

"Actually, we don't. Clean." She pointed at him. "Clean." She pointed at herself. "Birth control. End of story. This has been fun, but it's over now." Becka didn't see her panties, but she wasn't about to stick around to search for them. Instead, she grabbed her shoes and ducked under Aaron's arm.

"I'd like to see you again."

She reached the door and paused. It *had* been fun. A lot of fun, right up until that shitty ending. Becka closed her eyes, letting herself picture—just for a moment—what it would be like if she said yes. Maybe he was talking about just sex, and they'd spend a prolonged one-night stand blowing each other's minds until he got tired of her and decided to try to let her down easy, bruising her in the process. Or maybe he'd try to take her out on a date, and they'd end up fucking again, and it would end exactly the same. Even if things *did* work for a while, eventually they would explode in her face, just like every other relationship she'd been in.

Historically, men looked at her appearance and assumed one of two things.

They figured that she was some kind of manic pixie dream girl who would help them find themselves. Or, more often, they assumed that she was a kinky sex fiend who'd be down for everything and anything and not be bothered by days gone by without communication as long as the sex was on point.

Becka wasn't about to play prop to a man, and she might like sex, but she had more respect for herself than to be some guy's one A.M. booty call while he was trying to date other women. As a result, every single time she'd tried to actually *date* someone, it had gone down in flames sooner rather than later.

Like mother, like daughter.

She straightened her spine, but she couldn't look at him. If she met those gray-blue eyes, she was a goner. "It's been fun. Really fun. But let's leave this on a high note. I want to be a fond memory, something that will never get a chance to lose its shine."

His bitter laugh made her stomach drop. "Sounds like you already have the narrative set."

Better me setting the narrative than playing supporting role in someone else's. "I do." She forced her hand to turn the doorknob and open the door, because if she didn't move *right then*, she'd go back to him and let him spin whatever pretty fantasy until she actually believed it. It wasn't the truth. *She* knew that, even if he wasn't willing to admit it. "Have a nice life, Aaron."

Becka walked out the door without looking back.

CHAPTER THREE

Twelve weeks later

"THAT ABOUT SUMS it up. The new account didn't request anything fancy, but we'd be assholes if we left them exposed. Better to just go the extra mile." Aaron slid the file across the table to his business partner, Cameron O'Clery. "You want to handle this one, or should I?" Their security business focused heavily on all things tech related, and this new account was no different. Once they got the initial cybersecurity laid down, they would maintain it for as long as their retainer was paid, but it took time to figure out exactly what the client needed—and often enough, it wasn't what the client *thought* they needed.

Cameron flipped through it. "You usually don't ask me—you just dole out the clients."

Aaron tensed, but it was the truth. He tended to be the client-facing part of the company, and he picked and chose which ones he passed to Cameron because

Cameron…wasn't particularly patient with people he considered too stupid to live. Unfortunately for any prospective business-client relationships, Cameron found ninety percent of the world too stupid to live. Some clients could handle his attitude because he was the best cybersecurity expert in the city, and some couldn't. Part of Aaron's job was figuring that out. "We're partners."

"Never said we weren't." Cameron sat back and laced his fingers behind his head. He was a big fucker, his white T-shirt stretched tight against his dark skin. He narrowed brown eyes at Aaron. "You're off your game—have been for weeks. I didn't ask, but if it's going to affect the job, maybe it's time to."

"It's nothing." Just a blue-haired woman he couldn't seem to scrub from his mind. He hadn't tracked Becka down after she'd left so abruptly because she couldn't have been clearer in wanting nothing to do with him. If he was smart, he would have left what happened between them in that room behind as easily as she had.

But she haunted his dreams.

He kept waking up and reaching for her, only to find himself alone in bed. It didn't make a damn bit of sense. It had been sex—outstanding, earth-shattering sex, but sex. A single fuck shouldn't screw with his mind so effectively.

"Doesn't look like nothing to me." Cameron held

his hands up. "Not my business. Just handle your shit, Aaron. I can take this client."

He thought about the timid man who had signed the contract earlier that day and sat back. "Nah, I got it. This guy needs a softer touch."

"Shit. Take it." Cameron slid the file back to him with a disgusted look on his face. "I've got to tie up a few loose ends with the last one. She came back wanting changes despite the job being done. Nothing I can't handle, but it's a pain in the ass."

"Always is." Aaron grabbed the file and rose. "Let me know if you need an assist."

"I don't." Cameron frowned. "Though I think we might need to expand the team to include someone to handle paperwork and all that shit. It's taking too much time from the jobs themselves, and you know how I feel about paperwork."

"The same way you feel about most things." He hated it.

Cameron nodded. "I'll post a job opening. Figure they can man the phones and the main email account to field and file prospective clients. Frees you up to focus on the jobs and stop handling me."

Considering Aaron didn't know *who* they would hire who was capable of handling Cameron, he just nodded. It was a problem for another day. First, he had to arrange a secondary meeting with the new client and bring them up to date with the prospective client list sitting in his inbox. Throwing a new person into the mix without them being caught up was a recipe for disaster.

That said, it *would* be nice to delegate some of the more tedious tasks. "Sounds like a plan."

He headed out of the room. They owned the entire floor of this building, but they really only utilized their respective offices, a boardroom and a waiting room that was more neglected than anything else.

Their cybersecurity company was small, but both he and Cameron preferred it that way. With the reputation they'd spent years building, they could handpick their clients and charge top dollar for their services. But the demand seemed to be increasing lately, which meant they'd have to hire that secretary—and potentially add a cybersecurity specialist or two to their team—sooner, rather than later.

Aaron stopped in the hallway and tried to picture what the waiting room would look like with someone at the desk livening up the place. He preferred to take his meetings with clients off-site, and Cameron preferred not to take them at all. Aaron shook his head. If the secretary stayed on for more than a week, it'd be a fucking miracle.

His phone started ringing as he strode into his office. He cursed and fished it out of his pocket. An unfamiliar number scrolled across the screen. Aaron took a breath and put his professional persona on. "Aaron Livingston."

"Hey, Aaron."

Three months later, he'd still recognize Becka's voice anywhere. He walked back to his office, shut his door, and moved around his desk to sit down. "I didn't expect to hear from you." He realized how that must sound and grimaced. "But I'm glad you called."

"Yeah, well, I didn't expect to call." Her voice went thick as if she was…holding back tears? "Funny story. Remember when the condom broke? Well, apparently the pill isn't one hundred percent foolproof because, surprise, I'm pregnant."

He waited for the words to rearrange themselves into an order that made sense. They stayed stubbornly in place. "What?"

"Pregnant. With your kid." She cleared her throat. "I, ah, I wasn't going to keep it, but I chickened out at the last second, and it turns out I want this baby. I'm sorry. I swear to God I didn't know this would happen, and I don't expect anything from you. It's not your problem—it's mine. I just… I thought you should know."

A baby.

His baby.

With Becka.

He closed his eyes and tried to focus. She thought he would wash his hands of this. Aaron had questions—a whole hell of a lot of questions—but he didn't honestly believe that Becka had tricked him into getting her pregnant. She sounded upset and scared, and the fact she'd let that slip through what he surmised were impressive shields meant she was exponentially *more* freaked out. *How long have you been sitting on this knowledge, scared and alone?*

He wasn't about to let her shoulder it by herself. That child was half his, and if she was keeping it, he would be in the baby's life. End of story.

That decided, he opened his eyes, plan in place. "Where are you?"

"What? I'm at home."

"Text me the address."

She hesitated, and he could almost see her arguing with herself about having him in her house. Well, too fucking bad. Whether she liked it or not, Aaron was in her life, and he wasn't going anywhere. They had a future in common, one way or another. Finally, Becka sighed. "Okay."

"Good. I'll see you soon." He hung up and stared at his phone.

His life had just taken a hard right turn. He had no fucking idea how he was going to keep it from going off the rails entirely. *One step at a time. Talk to Becka in person. Be calm. Reassure her. Get her to see things your way.*

Shouldn't be too difficult. Right?

Becka nearly paced a hole in her floor waiting for Aaron to show up. She should have realized he was going to demand to see her face-to-face when she called, but part of her had honestly thought he'd be relieved not to be asked to do anything. Isn't that what most guys wanted in a shitty situation like this? To be absolved of all responsibility so they could go on with their lives unscathed while the woman was left to clean up the mess they'd created together?

You were projecting and you damn well know it. She caught herself wringing her hands and cursed. "I can do better than this. It's just a baby."

A baby she hadn't signed up for.

She touched her stomach gingerly. There were none of the symptoms movies had told her to expect—aside from being extra exhausted all the time—but her doctor had confirmed there was, in fact, a baby growing inside her. *A freaking baby.*

She didn't know how to be a mom. Lucy was the nurturer. The planner. The one who took care of everyone around her and was universally loved as a result. Becka had too much of their mother in her. She was too selfish, too bitchy, just too much across the board. Up until she made the call to keep the baby, she'd been sure she didn't want kids at all—better to let the sins of the past lie and not tempt fate. Lucy always told her there was no reason to think they'd end up like their parents, but Becka didn't believe her any more now than she had as a kid.

The buzzer sounded, and she jumped half out of her skin. "Shit." Aaron was here. There was no time to think of a new, better plan. There was nothing left to do but buzz him up.

Thirty seconds later, she opened the door and froze. How had she forgotten how magnetic he was? His broad shoulders took up the space of her narrow door frame, and he wore a suit that probably cost as much as a couple months of her rent. Becka belatedly realized she was blocking the entrance and stepped back, letting him into her apartment.

He looked around, and she could almost see the thoughts rolling through his head. Shabby place. Secondhand furniture. A hole in the drywall from where she'd accidentally kicked it in when she fell out of a headstand a year ago. It was clean, but she was barely there long enough to sleep between teaching classes at Allie's gym, Transcend, and her second job as a personal trainer at an upscale facility downtown. She'd never seen a reason to spiff up the place when that money could be spent in better places.

Now, she kind of wished she'd told Aaron to meet her somewhere else so he wouldn't have seen this.

He turned as she shut the door and gave her an equally thorough examination. His gaze landed on her flat stomach and then rose to her face. "You're not facing this alone."

It was tempting to throw herself at his feet and beg him to hold her until this whole thing went away. Fear ate at the edges of her mind, and there was no easy answer to combat it. Hell, there were no answers at all.

But Becka had spent all her adult life fighting to

stand on her own. She wasn't about to compromise that now for a man who was essentially a stranger. She lifted her chin. "Easy for you to say. I'm the one incubating the kid, and I'm going to be the one solely responsible for its needs."

"In this…apartment." The way he said the last word translated to *hovel*.

She glared. "There's nothing wrong with my apartment."

"You have a hole in your wall." He stalked around her kitchen. "Water damage on the floor." The living room. "The rugs are worn down to nothing." Aaron almost sounded like he was talking to himself instead of her. "If you don't have money to repair this place, you sure as fuck don't have money to give our baby everything he or she needs."

She wanted to tell him she didn't need him at all, that she'd find a way, but the hard reality was that Aaron had money and Becka didn't. She made a comfortable living for herself, but she didn't need much to get by in the grand scheme of things.

A baby changed that.

She turned away and wrapped her arms around herself. *You can compromise. Try it—just this once.* "I'm willing to negotiate some kind of…child support or something. If that's something you're comfortable with." *She* wasn't comfortable with it, but she'd suck up her pride and get over herself if it meant he could help her meet the baby's needs.

"No."

Becka turned back to find Aaron shaking his head and doing another circuit around her apartment. "What?"

"I said, no." He poked the threadbare pillow on the couch. "You can't live like this while you're pregnant. You shouldn't be living like this right now."

"Excuse me?" Anger flared through her, and she welcomed it with open arms. Easier to be angry than to be scared, easier to fight than to admit she was in over her head and didn't know what she was going to do. "There's nothing wrong with my apartment."

"The list of everything wrong with this place is longer than we have time for. Pack your bags. We're leaving."

Her jaw dropped. "You're crazy."

"No, *you're* crazy if you think I'm going to let the mother of my future child live in these conditions when I have a perfectly adequate apartment that will fit both of us and the baby without crowding." He crossed his arms over his chest and frowned. "I have a spare room, if that's what you're worried about. I don't expect you to be in my bed."

The top of her head damn near exploded. "No."

"Wrong answer."

She sputtered. "You can't just decide to move me in with you. That's not how any of this works."

Aaron stalked to the fridge and opened it. He barked out a laugh. "I suspected as much. There isn't even fucking food in your fridge." He turned and glared. "Let me lay it out for you—you have two options."

"I choose the option where you get the hell out of my life."

"That's not on the list." If anything, her anger only made him calmer, icier. He nodded at the door leading into her bedroom. "You can walk in there, pack your shit and come with me to my place. You'll settle in. It will take some adjusting, but it's doable." He shrugged. "Or I can call your sister and brother-in-law—and Roman and Allie, since they have a vested interest in your well-being—and we can all have a sit-down about your current living conditions and how you're rejecting a perfectly reasonable plan out of hand."

Checkmate.

She could actually hear the cage click into place around her. Becka didn't have a chance in hell of winning that argument with all the parties involved. Allie would be sympathetic to her plight, but Lucy would offer a secondary option of moving in with *her.* Both Gideon and Roman would go into protective older brother roles and, no matter which way they fell on the argument, Becka wouldn't come out on top. She didn't stand a chance.

She snarled. "That's blackmail."

"It's called skillful negotiation. You should try it sometime."

I will not punch my baby daddy. I will not just chop him in his stupidly attractive throat.

She counted to ten, but it did nothing to lower her blood pressure. There had to be a way out of this. Aaron was obviously only steamrolling her because he had an honorable streak that apparently demanded he borderline kidnap her. *Okay, maybe not that honorable.* She just needed to buy some time, to get a little distance to figure out what *she* wanted.

It was the one thing Becka couldn't pin down.

She knew she wanted the baby. The rest was terrifyingly hazy.

She gritted her teeth. "I'll consider it."

He stared at her so long, she just *knew* he was weighing his options—including throwing her over his shoulder and hauling her ass back to his place. Finally, Aaron nodded. "You have until tomorrow."

"Tomorrow?"

"At that point, I'm coming back here. Whether I come back alone or with Roman and Gideon in tow is entirely up to you." He strode to the door and paused to look over his shoulder at her. "Don't let stubbornness get in the way of what's best for the baby." He was gone before she could give in to the impulse to throw something at his head.

Becka stumbled over to her ugly green couch and sank onto it. She let her head fall to her hands and spit out every single curse she knew. It didn't make her feel better. She wasn't sure *anything* could make her feel better at this point.

"I am so freaking screwed."

CHAPTER FOUR

"OKAY, LET ME see if I have this straight—you're pregnant."

Becka didn't lift her face from the pillow. Maybe if she concentrated, her couch would swallow her whole and she wouldn't have to deal with this mess anymore. She'd called Allie in desperation, but confessing the truth had taken the last of her energy and now all she wanted was to curl up in a ball and wait for this to blow over. *Fat chance of that happening.*

Allie's footsteps echoed through the apartment. "You're pregnant," she repeated. "Okay, right. Pregnant."

"You said that already. Three times."

"Right. And it's Aaron Livingston's. And Aaron wants you to move in with him for, what, the duration of the pregnancy? Or are you supposed to live there forever?"

She groaned and pressed her face harder into the pillow. "He didn't specify."

"Because you kicked him out after yelling at him that you'd live with him over your dead body."

Becka frowned and lifted her head. Allie stood across the small living room, her hands on her hips. She looked like some kind of plus-size superhero on her day off, her blond hair windblown and her black leggings and fitted sweater comfortable and stylish. But it was the contemplative look on her face that sent alarm bells pealing through Becka's head. "You don't sound angry and self-righteous. Why don't you sound angry and self-righteous? You *should* be angry and self-righteous."

"Unpopular opinion—but Aaron Livingston isn't a total monster."

She rolled onto her back and flung her arm over her eyes. "That lack of monstrosity really commends him to be my baby daddy."

"Becka, I'm serious. He and Roman are good friends. I've hung out with him a few times." She hesitated long enough that Becka lifted her arm and shot her a look. Allie seemed to be silently arguing with herself. Finally, she said, "I think you should do it."

"What?"

"I know you, and if I offer for you to stay with me and Roman, you're going to say—"

"Hell, no." She didn't need her family and friends to swoop in and take care of her. Becka had gotten into this situation on her own—well, technically with

Aaron, but whatever—and she wasn't going to drag anyone else in alongside her. Allie and Lucy finally had things working out for them. They didn't need Becka's mistakes putting a damper on their happily-ever-afters.

Which really only left her one option.

She closed her eyes. "Damn it, I have to do it, don't I?"

"I mean, you could put on your martyr's sash and try to power through it on your own, but that's not going to accomplish anything but to save your pride—and only for a while."

She *would* need help eventually. Whether it was financially or with babysitting or... God, Becka didn't know where to start.

Easy. You start with Aaron and go from there.

"If I change my mind, he's going to have me over a barrel."

"Sounds like your kind of kink."

Becka made a face. "Very funny." The earlier encounter with Aaron had been over so quickly, she could almost tell herself she hadn't noticed how good he looked. Life was complicated enough without her still being attracted to Aaron. *Stop borrowing trouble. You have enough of it as things stand.* She sat up and pulled her knees to her chest. "I'm in over my head. I want this baby, but...there are so many strings attached. I knew there would be, but I really didn't expect him to go full-on caveman on me over this. He was seconds away from knocking me over the head and dragging me out of here by my hair."

Allie circled around the coffee table and crouched next to her. "You have options, you know. No matter how cornered you feel right now, there's always more than one path forward. We just need to sit down and figure it out."

That was the problem, though—she'd been doing *nothing* but thinking about her options going forward. Becka had always been better at acting first and worrying about the consequences later. So much inaction was not only unnatural, it stressed her the fuck out.

Allie nodded as if she'd said something. "You've already decided you're going to do things his way. That's okay. But if you change your mind at any point, that's okay, Becka. You're not trapped, no matter what it feels like right now."

Trapped.

That was a good word. Becka rubbed a hand over her face. Now that she'd actually let herself decide, there was no reason to delay. If she held off too long, she had no doubt Aaron would come charging through her door again and then she'd have to tell him to fuck off out of sheer principle and it would be a case of cutting off her nose to spite her face. That wouldn't actually help anyone.

She grabbed her phone off the coffee table and

typed out a quick text to Aaron. You win this round. Text me your address.

The reply appeared before she had a chance to set the phone back down. I'll pick you up in two hours.

Becka glared. "The man is *insufferable*."

Allie leaned over to read the message. "Insufferable in kind of a sexy way, though. There's something about a guy who takes charge that's really attractive."

"You only say that because you're deeply in love with Roman. Seriously, do alpha males travel in a pack, because between Roman and Gideon and Aaron..." She shuddered. "You would have thought they'd do the lone wolf thing."

"Lone wolves and alpha wolves are two very different things."

"Thanks, *National Geographic*." She glared harder at her phone and stabbed out a response. I will haul my own damn things. Give me your address. Compromise is your friend.

I can compromise. You have three hours.

"God!" She tossed her phone onto the table and shot to her feet, nearly knocking her friend over. She stalked to her bedroom and started throwing clothes onto her bed. She *wasn't* moving in with him, but she would give him the benefit of the doubt—

barely—and stay there for a little while to give the whole thing a trial.

The way things were going, it might be a very short trial.

Allie wisely decided to stand in the doorway and out of range. "What do you need from me?"

She loved her friend so freaking much for not putting any demands on her or trying to tell her how she *should* be reacting or feeling. That was Allie, though. She devoted her life to supporting women who needed it. Allie's gym, Transcend, was linked up with a local women's shelter, so the classes were women only. Becka always enjoyed getting them pumped up. It was a safe space for them to do something for themselves, and Becka was just a small part of that, but she loved it.

Allie might be understanding to the extreme, but Lucy wouldn't be. Her sister had always been her opposite, and for better or worse, Lucy would have something to say about this whole baby situation. It was the logical, collected nature of her older sibling. Becka had to tell her eventually, but she wasn't ready. Lucy would give her that look, the one that always got on her face when Becka screwed up or went too far.

When I act too much like our mother.

She couldn't stand the thought of her sister's disappointment. And there *would* be disappointment. This wasn't an oops baby between Becka and some longtime boyfriend. This was a pregnancy as the result of a one night stand with a man she barely knew.

No, she wasn't ready to tell Lucy about the baby.

She didn't know if she'd ever be ready.

Becka dumped her gym bag next to the growing pile of clothes. "I don't know what I need." She stopped. "I'm a mess, and I don't think that's going to be changing any time soon, but I promise not to be too unbearable."

"Oh honey." Allie crossed the room in a few short steps and pulled Becka into her arms. She hugged her hard. "I know this is scary and you're overwhelmed, but I don't have a single doubt about you being the best mom out there. You have the luckiest little lima bean ever."

"Lima bean."

"Well, yeah. That's about the size the baby is right now? I mean…"

"It's actually closer to a lime." She'd looked it up after the doctor confirmed the pregnancy.

"Oh wow, that's a huge difference." Allie laughed. "That's not a very cute nickname, anyways. I can come up with better."

Becka hugged her back hard. "No, I like it. Lima bean fits." She didn't have the heart to tell Allie that she wasn't sure about being even a good mom, let alone the best one. Becka didn't have much of a role model for that one, but she'd be damned before she made the same mistakes her mother did.

Except for the part where you got knocked up by a near stranger out of wedlock. So far, I'm swinging for the fences with walking in her footsteps.

Aaron half expected Becka not to be home when he arrived. He was pushing her too hard and he damn well knew it, but he couldn't seem to get control of himself. The thought of her living in that run-down little apartment by herself, where the security was lackluster at best and the walls seemed a strong breeze away from coming down around her ears… It made him crazy. He'd never really thought about kids, other than as a vaguely theoretical "someday" in the equally vague future, but now that he had an actual baby on the way, he wasn't about to stand back and let it want for anything.

That included living arrangements.

He clenched his jaw as he walked through Becka's door. The place wasn't any better than the first time he'd been there. If anything, the flaws were only more glaring. He'd missed the water stain on the wall before, where someone overhead had obviously had a leak that had come through to Becka's apartment. Or the crack in her window that wouldn't keep out the cold—or the heat.

She didn't look at him as she reached for the pile of bags at her feet and shouldered her backpack. "This is temporary, Aaron. I'm not prepared to sign my life away to be your kept woman, baby or no. If you pull another high-handed move like you did earlier, I'm out and I'm not coming back."

He clenched his jaw harder. *Do not yell at her contrary ass. Be calm. Be fucking rational.* "You mentioned compromise."

"I'm surprised you know the word."

Aaron scooped up the remaining three bags and shot her a look that dared her to argue with him taking them. "Let's go. I have a car waiting downstairs." He chose to ignore her muttering uncomplimentary things and followed her down the dim hallway to the rickety elevator. Through it all, he kept his damn mouth shut. They were both on a hair trigger, and he didn't need to be the one to set things aflame. Especially not now that they needed to sit down and have a serious discussion.

But he still couldn't stop himself from asking. "When did you know?"

"Four weeks ago." She hitched her bag higher on her shoulder and marched out of the elevator as soon as the doors opened, Aaron on her heels.

"You've known for a month and only called me yesterday."

"That is how math works."

He instinctively held the front door open for her and pointed at the black car idling at the curb. Aaron grabbed her backpack and loaded all the bags into the trunk. He joined Becka in the back seat, his irritation only growing when she pulled out her phone and started playing some puzzle game. "Why didn't you call me as soon as you knew?"

"I didn't know what I wanted to do, so there was no reason to bring you into the conversation until I made my decision."

If she wanted to keep it or not.

He stared straight ahead as his driver merged into traffic. Aaron knew he ultimately had no say in her choice, and he wouldn't have taken that from her even if the thought of her terminating the pregnancy opened a hole in his chest that he didn't know how to process. He'd known he was going to be a father for less than twelve hours. There was absolutely no logical reason for him already to be attached to the idea of this baby, let alone the baby itself. It wasn't even really a baby yet.

None of that seemed to matter.

He looked back at Becka, noting the changes he'd been too distracted to take in earlier. Even without the makeup she'd worn the night he met her, her skin damn near glowed, and her still-blue hair, though now more turquoise than actual blue, seemed glossier. His gaze skated over her black leggings and still-flat stomach to her breasts pressing against her tank top. *Those have definitely changed.*

"Stop ogling me." She spoke without looking up from her phone.

Since there was no question that ogling was *exactly* what he'd been doing, he went on the offensive.

"Have you been eating? You don't look like you've gained any weight."

Becka snorted. "Yes, Mother, I've been eating. It's normal not to gain much in the first trimester, especially since I'm so active and this is my, ah, first pregnancy."

He racked his brain for what little pregnancy knowledge he had and...came up short. Aaron's sisters were both younger than him and hadn't had children yet. His mother wasn't much of a sharer, and even if she was, she wouldn't have gone into detail with her only son when it came to her pregnancies. Besides, he'd never had a reason to ask before.

He had to brush up on his knowledge, maybe read a few books. He'd attend the doctor's appointments with Becka, of course, but Aaron didn't like to walk into any encounter without having a decent idea of how it would play out. He'd rather be armed with all the information and possibilities before the conversation even began.

He shot another look at her to make sure she wasn't paying any attention to him, and then spent several minutes ordering the top-rated pregnancy books available. Aaron hesitated, then put express shipping on the order and plugged in the address to the office. If Cameron bothered to open the box, he might give Aaron shit, but it was better than the alternative: Becka finding them and getting her back up.

Even with traffic, they made it to his penthouse in

good time. He led the way through the lobby and to the elevator. "I'll get you added to the list of people with access to the floor tomorrow. Tonight, we'll get your space set up and talk over dinner."

"I'm not really hungry."

He punched the button for his floor. "You just got done telling me that you eat."

"I *do* eat." She sounded like she was clenching her jaw as hard as he was. "I also only eat when I'm hungry, and right now I'm not hungry."

She was too skinny, surely. Aaron opened his mouth and then reconsidered. Becka might have chosen to be here with him, but it was a tenuous alliance. Even with his threat of involving her sister and friend and their respective men, there was nothing really holding Becka to him. He'd be on the birth certificate—he'd sue for paternity if he had to—but they had at least eighteen years of dealing with each other in front of them.

And he'd essentially gotten them started by blackmailing her.

Way to go, Livingston. You played this all wrong.

The doors opened into a foyer that separated his penthouse from anyone who had access. He keyed in his code and held the door for her. "This way." He slipped past her and led the way through the open living room and kitchen to the short hallway. There were three doors. Aaron pointed at the one on the right. "Bathroom." Center. "My room." Left. "Your room."

"Thanks," she bit out. Becka slid past him and walked into the room. She took it in with a cursory glance and crossed her arms over her chest. "Leave my bags. Please." The last sounded more afterthought than genuine politeness.

Aaron didn't move. "We need to talk, Becka."

"And we will." She looked everywhere but at him. "You got what you wanted, Aaron. I'm here. I know this might sound shocking, but today wore me out. I want to unpack my clothes and maybe take a bath and just decompress a little without having to plan the next six months—the next eighteen years—tonight. That okay with you?" She lifted her chin, her posture telling him she didn't give a fuck if it was okay with him.

He could keep pushing. She was off center and defensive, but maybe she needed to know he was actually all in with this shit.

Then again, Aaron didn't know Becka well enough to anticipate how she'd respond. His threat earlier was a well-placed guess based on her close relationship with both her sister and Allie—and his knowledge of Gideon and Roman. But going forward, he was in the dark in a big way. He needed more information, and he needed it fast.

Until then, there was nothing wrong with letting Becka settle into his home and make herself comfortable. He could use the time for a little reconnaissance to pave the way before the baby books arrived.

"If you change your mind about food, I can order takeout." Aaron hesitated. "Is there anything that's a hard no for you foodwise right now?"

She narrowed her eyes. "So you can keep trying to feed me?"

"No, minx, so I don't order some kind of take-out that triggers your morning sickness and makes you miserable."

Becka's eyes widened. "Oh. Well." She uncrossed her arms and shifted her feet. "No fish. I wasn't sick the first trimester, so no reason to think it will start now, but fish is a hard limit."

He kept his smile under lock and key. "No fish. Got it." He stepped around her and set her bags on the bed. "If you need anything—"

"What I need is space." She bit her bottom lip, worrying the piercing there. "But thanks. I know this wasn't exactly expected news and you're han-dling it a lot better than I thought you would." Becka made a face. "Stop trying to steamroll me, though."

"I make no promises." He almost reached out, almost drew her into his arms and promised that whatever came, they would face it down together...

That wasn't how this story went. The sex might have been outstanding, but the ultimate truth was that Aaron didn't know shit about Becka Baudin. He didn't know her likes and dislikes, her favorite things, her history, what kind of mother she'd be.

Six months didn't seem nearly long enough to figure it out.

One day at a time. First get the information you need, then formulate a plan of attack.

If he wanted to be in Becka's life—in the baby's life—then he needed to convince her that she wanted him there. Right now, his chances didn't look particularly promising, but Aaron had faced down impossible odds before. He would again.

After he regrouped.

But tomorrow was a new day, and he wasn't about to give her enough space to keep building the already impressive wall she had in place between them.

CHAPTER FIVE

BECKA'S ATTITUDE LASTED until she walked into the bathroom. She turned a slow circle, taking in the broody gray walls, the silvery tiles blocking out a walk-in shower, and a jetted tub big enough to fit three people. *Or a pregnant woman who's twice her normal size.*

Worry about that later.

The list of things she would worry about later continued to grow, but she'd add *that* to the list, too. Right now, her entire body hurt, as if she'd done three spin classes in a single day, and she just wanted a hot soak and to not think about anything at all. At least Aaron had backed off and given her space. Despite the nine-foot ceilings and massive square footage, the walls of this penthouse threatened to close in on her.

She wasn't trapped.

She could leave whenever she wanted.

Knowing that was the only thing that kept her from running screaming into the night. She was here by choice. It might be a manipulated choice, but it was still her choice.

Becka got the water going at the right temperature and then went snooping around the room. The cabinet under the sink had the expected cleaning tools, all damn near shining from being so clean themselves. Next were the artfully displayed soaps situated on the little corner table next to the bath. There were essential oils and bath bombs and lady-looking shower gels. Becka picked up a bath bomb and gave a sniff. It was something flowery and feminine and had no place in this supermasculine home.

She shot to her feet and marched out of the bathroom. Following the clacking of keyboard keys, she stalked into the living room and waved the bath bomb at Aaron. "When did you buy this?"

"What?"

"This." She shoved it nearly under his nose. "Were you so damn sure of yourself that you went and bought me bath products? What the hell is even wrong with you?"

His lips quirked. "I didn't buy those."

"They're in *your* bathroom." She realized what she was saying and took a hasty step back. Of course Aaron hadn't bought them. They were clearly a woman's choice, and Aaron was very much not a woman. *Oh God.* Becka pasted a smile on her face, hoping it looked realer than it felt. "I didn't realize you were

seeing someone." He hadn't been three months ago…
She was pretty sure.

*No, I might not know a lot, but Aaron was single
when we were together. He's not that kind of guy.*

But three months was a long time in the grand
scheme of things. She hadn't called him, hadn't given
him any indication that she ever *would* call him. Of
course he hadn't waited for her. She hadn't expected
him to. It certainly wasn't disappointment souring
her stomach at the thought of some mystery woman
in Aaron's bed, using Aaron's ridiculous bathtub,
lounging next to Aaron on his leather couch at the
end of the day.

He set his laptop aside and pushed to his feet in
a smooth move. It left him towering over her, and
he took a step closer, bringing them nearly chest to
chest. "I'm not seeing anyone, minx."

Minx.

She tried not to let the casual endearment warm
her, tried to stand firm and hold on to her anger.
"Then, what is this?"

He studied her, his blue-gray eyes seeing too
much. "You're jealous."

"Not even a little bit." *I am totally jealous.* She
took a quick step back. "There's nothing to be jealous of. I just wanted to know if I'm stepping on some
woman's toes. It is such a man-stupid thing to do to
invite your baby mama to live with you without talking to your girlfriend about it first."

Aaron didn't move, but he seemed closer. "Give me a little credit. Pulling something like that is a piece of shit move, and I'd never do it. Which is all a moot point because I'm not seeing anyone. I haven't since the wedding."

Since they'd had sex.

It probably had no significance. She'd be a fool to think it could possibly mean anything. *The only thing that's a moot point is this playing out in anything less than disaster. I'm having his baby. I don't know him. He doesn't know me. Moving me in with him doesn't change that.* She looked away. "That's not my business."

"Considering you're now living with me, it's at least partially your business." He paused as if debating something with himself and then shifted to bring her attention back to him. Aaron was oh so serious when he said, "I won't bring anyone back here without talking about it with you first. I don't think it's too much to ask that you give me the same courtesy."

Men. He means men.

Maybe she wasn't the only one who was jealous. Aaron hadn't questioned the baby being his, and she hadn't offered up any information. *He put himself out there, a little bit. Would it kill me to do the same?* Becka wrapped her arms around herself and stared at his left collarbone where it pressed against his plain black T-shirt. She had no business noting that he looked good in lounge pants and a shirt. Comfortable. As if in addition to doing whatever his job was—something high-powered and expensive, from the penthouse and the suits—he could also kick back with a beer and some football on the weekends.

She backed away, one careful step at a time. "I left the tub on."

"Becka."

She moved faster but paused in the entrance to the hallway. "I haven't been with anyone since then, either." She wasn't about to examine that fact too closely. In the months leading up to the wedding, she'd been too busy to bother finding someone to scratch that particular itch, and after...

"The bath shit is from my sister." He still watched her too closely. "My youngest sister, Trish, seems to think it's a crime against God for me to own that tub without some equally fancy bath products to go into it."

"She's not wrong." It was all she could handle. The strange mix of emotions curdling her stomach sent her fleeing back into the bathroom and locking the door behind her. Not because she thought Aaron would barge in, but because she didn't trust *herself*. If the sound of the water running hadn't been in the background for their entire conversation, a constant reminder that their time was limited, Becka might have done something unforgivable.

Like kiss Aaron.

She turned off the water—not a moment too

soon—and gave the bath bomb another cautious sniff. When it didn't set off any crazy pregnancy reaction, she unwrapped it and dropped it into the tub. While it fizzed and turned the water blue, Becka stripped. She took baths all the time, though the tub in her apartment was so small, she either had to have her legs halfway up the wall or sit with her entire torso freezing. She'd never once been so aware of the slide of her clothing against her skin before it fell to the floor. Impossible to ignore the fact that Aaron was *right there* on the other side of the door. In the same penthouse. Looking good enough to lick.

She gave herself a shake. *Stupid pregnancy hormones.* Everyone promised morning sickness and strange food cravings and exhaustion that never seemed to end. Becka was more tired than normal, sure, and she'd developed a fondness for peanut butter that bordered on obsession, but the main difference she'd seen was that she was turned on. All. The. Time. She'd been getting herself off twice a day for months, and half the time it barely took the edge off. She wanted, needed, and hadn't been able to take that leap.

The truth was that she hadn't wanted to.

Because the man she pictured every time she slipped her hand between her thighs to stroke her clit was *Aaron*.

The same man only a few rooms away.

"I will not be ruled by my stupid hormones. Hormones are what got me into this situation in the first place." She carefully stepped into the water and sank down until her body below her neck was submerged. A moan slipped free despite her best efforts. "Oh *God.*"

Who needed sex when she had this bathtub?

Becka reached over and flipped the switch to get the jets going. She leaned back and closed her eyes. It would have to be enough. Things were complicated enough without falling back into bed with Aaron. It was one mistake she couldn't afford to make twice.

If she could just convince herself of that, everything would be fine.

Aaron waited for the water to start running before he walked to the kitchen and pulled the book from his briefcase. He and Becka had fallen into something of a pattern over the last week. An agonizing pattern, but one all the same. She left sometime around five each morning to teach one of her classes, pausing barely long enough to grab a cup of coffee and mutter a greeting to him. They both arrived back at his place around six and then shared some kind of dinner. Then she took a shower followed by a bath. In that order.

If the last seven days were anything to go by, she'd emerge from the bathroom in a little over an hour, wrapped in a towel that covered her from chest to knees and dart into her bedroom. He wouldn't see her again until morning.

It was like living with a wild animal that feared contact. Every time he got too close, or moved too purposefully toward her, she fled back into her room and shut the door. If it hadn't been for the first night, for her anger over the idea of him with someone else, he might have thought...

Aaron didn't know what he would have thought. This wasn't proceeding like he'd expected, but then he hadn't had shit for a plan to begin with.

He settled onto the couch and flipped open the baby book. It tracked pregnancy by week with the various changes to both the mother and the baby, as well as overviews of each trimester and what to expect. He was more than a little in awe, but the new knowledge wasn't enough to ignore the fact that he and Becka still hadn't actually talked.

He flipped the page to the next set of FAQs. Aaron paused, the first sentence catching his eye. *Bathing while pregnant.* He read with increasing agitation as the book outlined the recommendation of keeping bath temperatures below ninety-eight degrees, and comparing that information with Becka's pink skin and flushed cheeks every night. "Goddamn it." He shot to his feet and stalked down the hallway to the bathroom door. Aaron banged on it. "Becka! Open the door!"

Cursing sounded, and a second later, she yanked

the door open, a towel clutched at her chest. Her hair was wet, but from the half-filled tub behind her, she'd only gotten through the shower portion of her nightly routine. She glared. "What the hell do you need *right this second*?"

He held up the book and pointed to the section he'd just read. "No more hot baths."

Becka's brows slammed down. "My baths are fine."

"Yes, yes, the baths are fine. I'm talking about the scalding temperatures." He shoved the book at her and headed into the kitchen to find the thermometer Trish had insisted he needed the last time she visited New York. It was technically for meat, but it should work in a pinch. He strode back into the bathroom, finding Becka exactly where he'd left her, reading with a pinched look on her face. Aaron slid past her and stuck the thermometer into the bathwater, impatiently watching the red line climb. It hovered just over one hundred degrees, so he cranked the cold water more fully on. "It's bad for the baby—and you—if it's too hot."

"Aaron."

He waited for the thermometer to read the appropriate temperature before he sat back on his heels and turned to find Becka watching him with a strange look on her face. "What's wrong?"

"You bought a pregnancy book." She looked at

him like she'd never seen him before. "You're *reading* a pregnancy book."

"Well, yeah." He stood and dried off his hand on his shirt. "I said you aren't in this alone, and I meant it. I don't know shit about pregnancy or babies, and until we know our plan, I'm hardly going to call up my mother and ask her for information. Books are the next best thing."

Emotions flickered over her face, too fast for him to decipher. "You'd call your mother and ask her about my pregnancy."

There was something going on here. Something more than just her being surprised he was doing his homework. Aaron approached her slowly, carefully. She just watched him without moving, her hand still fisting the towel just above her breasts. He stopped just within arm's reach. "My family might kick my ass for knocking you up and letting you falter for three months without my being there, but this baby will be my parents' first grandbaby. They're going to care." He made a face. "Honestly, as soon as he or she makes an appearance, I fully expect the entire Livingston clan to descend on this penthouse."

Her lower lip quivered, just a little. "I didn't know you were close to your parents. They're still together?"

The question sounded innocent enough, but there were undertones there. Deep ones. "Thirty-seven years and counting. I'm the oldest, and I have two younger sisters. We're close, though they both live a few hours north of the city so I don't see them as much as everyone would like."

"That's nice." The words were right, but they sounded forced.

He could pick up a clue, so he didn't ask about her parents. He knew enough from Lucy to know that they weren't in the picture—and hadn't been for a while—but Aaron wasn't willing to poke until Becka wanted to tell him. He *wanted* her to want to tell him, but he didn't expect miracles. It wouldn't happen this week. Or this month.

Patience.

His gaze snagged on Becka's mouth, on the perfect curve of her bottom lip. Even after all this time, he could still taste her. *Wanted* to still taste her. He clenched his fists to keep from reaching for her. He was the one with all the power in this scenario. He wouldn't abuse it. He refused to. What were they talking about before?

Right. My family. He cleared his throat. "I think you'll like them."

"Aaron?"

"Yeah?"

"I don't want to talk about your family anymore." She let the book fall to the ground and released the towel. It hit the floor and Aaron found himself holding his breath as he traced her naked body with his gaze. He'd been wrong before—her stomach *had* changed, but it was such a gentle curve, he wouldn't have noticed if he wasn't looking for it. Her rosy nipples had darkened, and they pebbled as he watched, goose bumps raising along her skin in a wave.

He held himself chained in place. "What do you want, minx?"

"I think that's kind of freaking obvious, don't you?"

Yeah, but he wasn't willing to make a single fucking assumption right now and risk damaging this tentative thing between them. "I'm going to need you to say it."

She huffed out a breath and propped her hands on her hips. "You, jerk. I want you. Preferably naked, with your hands and mouth all over me, cumulating with me coming on your cock."

CHAPTER SIX

BECKA WOULDN'T REACH for him. She had little but her pride left at this point and, honestly, she didn't have much of *that*, either. Whether he realized it or not, Aaron threatened to hold all the cards in every single one of their interactions. She couldn't give him even more power by following her very clear invitation up with anything other than waiting.

She'd made her move.

The ball was in his court.

Thank the Lord above, he didn't make her wait long.

He walked to the bath and shut off the water and then he was there, engulfing her with his presence, wrapping his arms around her until her entire world narrowed down to him. As if he meant to shield her from anything life threw at her.

Stop that. He didn't make anything resembling a promise when it comes to me. *I can't afford to get mixed up over him wanting to take care of the baby and him wanting me.*

That didn't keep her from leaning into his strong chest and inhaling deeply. His faint cologne made her toes curl, and she wanted to get beneath his shirt to see if it smelled different on his skin. Things had happened so quickly the first—the only—time, she hadn't had a chance to explore him.

She wanted that chance now.

Becka reached for the hem of his shirt and tugged it up and over his head slowly. She silently marveled at the cut of his muscles. They were even more pronounced now than they had been three months ago. "Someone's been spending time in the gym."

"I had a lot of frustration to work out." He rested his hands on her hips, letting her explore his chest and stomach. She was so busy tracing the line of his pecs that she almost missed his next words. "I still do."

No way to misconstrue *that* statement.

He's talking about me.

"Oh." *Good job, Becka. Excellent witty response.* To cover up her confusion, she went onto her tiptoes and kissed him. The move pressed her breasts against his chest, and she moaned at how good it felt. Everything was more sensitive than normal, as if someone had hooked a live wire up to her and it covered every inch of her skin. "Touch me."

He grabbed the backs of her thighs and lifted so she could wrap her legs around his waist. Aaron turned around and walked them to the bathroom counter and set her carefully on the marble. He ran a hand down the center of her chest, guiding her back to prop herself onto her hands and let him look at her. Though *look* was too mild a term. The man devoured her with his eyes, staring at her like she was an oasis in the middle of a desert and he wasn't sure if she was real or a figment of his imagination. He was so damn buttoned up the rest of the time, but when he got his hands on her, a different part of Aaron came out to play. It made Becka feel just as wild and out of control to know that *she* was the cause of that switch being flipped.

She shoved down his pants just enough to free his cock. Becka stroked him, every muscle in her body shaking in anticipation. A person shouldn't be able to be addicted to a cock after a single sexual encounter, but the sight of Aaron looming with his hands braced on the counter on either side of her hips and his cock in her hand…she couldn't think of another place she'd rather be or another person she'd rather be with.

All she wanted was this moment.

This man.

Becka met his gaze as she guided his cock into her. There was no need for protection, not when that ship had most definitely sailed already, not when neither of them had been with anyone else in the meantime. And, crazy as it might be, she wanted him inside her with no barriers.

They had enough barriers in every other part of their lives to keep them apart. She didn't want one here, too.

A muscle in Aaron's jaw jumped as he sank into her inch by delicious inch, filling her completely. "You make me crazy."

"You're not the only one." She didn't even sound like herself. Her voice was too low, too breathy. Becka didn't care. Not as long as the pleasure kept spiraling through her. "I need more, Aaron."

"I've got more to give you, minx." He hooked an arm around her waist and pulled her to the edge of the counter, until she had to cling to him to keep from toppling off. He used his free hand to cup her jaw, tilting her face up so he could claim her mouth, and then he began to move.

Aaron slammed into her even as his tongue gently teased her lips open. He pounded into her while giving her the sweetest kiss of her life, and her body couldn't make the two dueling sensations match up. There was no fighting it, though, and she wasn't even sure she wanted to. Instead, she clung to him and let him have full control of everything.

He tilted her back, still kissing her slowly, luxuriously. The new angle allowed him deeper, until his cock bumped the end of her with every thrust. It was too much and not enough. Pleasure built in brutal waves, each taking her closer and closer to the edge of no return. She gasped against his mouth, begging without words for completion. He responded by grinding his pelvis against her clit, and the friction sent her hurtling into an orgasm that made her toes curl. Aaron kept moving, drawing out her pleasure until she went limp in his arms. "Damn, that was good."

His chuckle vibrated through her entire body. "We're not done yet."

She belatedly realized he was still hard inside her. Becka shivered. She wanted more. Of course she wanted more. But there was a difference between losing her mind and having a quickie in the bathroom and an entire night's worth of sex.

What was that you were saying about the ship already sailing? If you wanted to keep the lines between you firm, you shouldn't have jumped on his cock the first chance you got.

Shut up.

"Aaron…"

He leaned down to rest his forehead against hers. She closed her eyes and simply breathed in the scent of him—of them. It was easier to talk like this, to open up just a little. "I don't know what we're doing."

"I don't, either." His words brushed her lips. "But I don't want to stop."

She opened her mouth to tell him she did, but it would be a lie. There were so many reasons she should call this whole thing off, but she wanted to pretend, just for a little while, that she wasn't really alone. He made her feel so damn good, and she wasn't a decent enough person to turn away from what he was offering tonight. Becka licked her lips. "I don't… I don't want to stop, either."

Aaron shifted back and ran his hand down the center of her chest. He paused for the beat of a heart, with his hand over her slightly rounded stomach, and lifted her, her legs still wrapped around him, to walk out of the bathroom and down the short hallway to his room. The movement of his steps had his cock shifting inside her, and she squirmed in his grip. He nipped her ear, and she could have sworn he was grinning when he said, "This time, we're going slow."

How could he be so measured when she had just come out of her goddamn skin?

Becka ran her hands up his arms to grip his biceps. "I'm willing to be convinced."

"Mmm." He laid her down in the center of his stupidly large bed. "We're just getting started."

He should have been talking to Becka, not fucking her brains out, but Aaron couldn't convince himself to stop. It felt too good to be inside her again, to have her moving in sync with him as they both chased pleasure. Even if they figured nothing else out, they could figure *this* out.

She wanted control. Hell, he wanted it, too.

It wasn't on the agenda right then.

Aaron pulled out of her and moved down her body, reacquainting himself with her. He palmed her breasts, kissing her nipples gently, and then harder when she laced her fingers through his hair and moaned. She'd been responsive before, not shy about telling him what she wanted, but seemed even more so now. He grinned against her skin. "Sensitive, aren't they?"

"You have no idea." She arched her back, offering her breasts to him again. "Don't stop."

He didn't stop. He lavished her breasts with attention until she was writhing beneath him and cursing and praising his name in equal measures. Then and only then did Aaron move down her body to settle between her thighs. He was too wound up to keep teasing her, and the sight of her wet and wanting overwhelmed him. He fucked her with his tongue, stopping only when he had to hold her hips down, and then he shifted to suck her clit, working her with his lips and tongue. Her cries only spurred him on, making him as crazy as he was determined to make her.

Her breathless little laugh when she came did things to his chest that he didn't know how to deal with.

Becka tugged on his shoulders. "Come here."

He crawled up her body, but she was already turning, going up on her hands and knees. The picture she presented, the muscles lining her spine drawing his gaze down to her biteable ass… "Fuck, minx. The things you do to me." He nudged her legs wider and guided his cock into her. Becka immediately dropped her chest to the mattress, the new angle drawing a curse from his lips. She didn't just feel good. She felt like fucking heaven. He smoothed a hand up her spine and braced it against the mattress next to her head.

And then he started to move.

It had been fast and hard in the bathroom, but Aaron was determined to hold himself in check this time. He noted every catch of her breath, every moan, every time she pushed back to take him deeper. He gave her everything, focusing everything he had on coaxing another of those addicting giggles from her lips.

Lightning shot down his spine, but he fought it back, fought to hold out as long as he could. "Touch yourself. You promised to come around my cock. I want to feel it again."

She snaked a hand under her stomach. He knew the exact moment her fingers made contact with her clit. She gasped and clenched around him, and it was everything he could do not to release then and there. So good. There were so many things wrong with this situation, but *this* wasn't one of them. Every move she made was perfection, her body flowing in direct counterpoint with his, heightening his pleasure until he could barely breathe past it.

He wanted this to last forever.

He was afraid it might kill him if it did.

Aaron clenched her hips tighter and drove into her harder. She met him stroke for stroke, and then her entire body went tight and tense and that god-damn giggle slipped free. *I could spend the rest of my life pursuing that fucking sound.* He'd thought it before, but it never seemed realer than in this moment. His strokes became more frenzied, the need to imprint himself over every part of her taking him to the edge and beyond. Aaron cursed as he came, the pleasure going on and on until he slumped onto the bed next to her.

"Feel better?" Becka rolled to face him. Her hair was tangled on one side, and she had a sleepy smile on her face. The fact she was in *his* bed didn't escape him in the least. *It could be like this if we got out of each other's way long enough to give it a chance.* That was the problem, though. He didn't know if it was possible to create a lasting peace. He didn't know nearly enough about a lot of things when it came to Becka.

Belatedly, he realized she'd asked him a question. He propped his head on his hand. "What?"

Some of the sleepiness disappeared from her eyes. "Did the sex distract you from your worrying long enough to make you feel better?"

Was that all this was? No. He couldn't believe that. He *wouldn't*. Aaron reached out and tucked a strand of her brilliant blue hair behind her ear. "I could think of worse ways to relax."

"Me, too." She closed her eyes, almost seeming to lean into his touch. "God, I would kill for some pancakes right now."

"Pancakes," he repeated. He glanced at the clock. "It's after ten."

"I know. I shouldn't."

This was his chance to extend their connection past a couple of shared orgasms. He forced himself to drop his hand, to not cage her in even that tiny way. "I think I have the stuff to put together some if you're in the mood."

Becka opened her eyes. "Are you serious?"

"As a heart attack." Unable to help himself, he leaned down and pressed a quick kiss to her lips. "I wouldn't tease a pregnant woman about food."

He regretted the words as soon as they were out of his mouth.

She shut down. He could actually see her walls coming back up to keep him out, her posture becoming more guarded, her gaze resting on the sheets instead of on him, her lips pressed together as if she attempted to keep sharp words inside. This was it. She'd tell him to get the fuck away from her, and what little ground he'd gained would be lost.

But Becka finally sighed. "Pancakes really do sound good."

"Say no more." He knew better than to push her now, not after his idiotic misstep. As Aaron climbed out of bed and headed into his closet for a pair of pants, he allowed himself a kernel of hope. Even with everything stacked against them, he now had two avenues to make headway with Becka—food and sex.

He could work with that.

CHAPTER SEVEN

BECKA COULDN'T STOP looking at Aaron. He was shirtless in the kitchen, making pancakes for her, and she'd never seen a more beautiful man. The muscles of his back flexed as he moved, and she clenched her thighs together despite the several outstanding orgasms he'd just delivered. The whole thing was so…domestic.

The only time she'd lived with anyone was roommates back in college. They were always too noisy, too messy and too in evidence everywhere she looked.

Becka didn't mind noise—her spin classes were so loud with their pumping music that some people wore earplugs. Having the bass thrum through her body as she shouted and directed and got everyone moving for the workout of their life was her happy place.

She didn't even mind people. Not really. Being a personal trainer was a different kind of happy, working with people who wanted to get healthy or accomplish some specific goal. She loved watching them put in the work and being their own personal drill sergeant and cheerleader, all wrapped into one. And the look on their face when they realized the moment their hard work had paid off and that they'd accomplished what they'd set out to do? Priceless.

But when she was done with work for the day, she wanted to come home and just...be.

Roommates normally made that impossible.

Aaron as a roommate should have made it doubly so.

She twisted on the bar stool to look over the apartment. It was a study in minimalism—a place for everything and everything in its place. There wasn't a speck of dust on the entertainment center that framed the massive TV, and the leather couch and twin chairs on either side of it didn't have any wear and tear or so much as a scrape on them. The kitchen was equally freakishly clean. If he wasn't cooking in it right this second, she would have suspected that he *didn't* cook by how clean the countertops were. The man obviously didn't believe in clutter.

Which was a relief, but at the same time, Aaron being a control freak was stamped over every inch of this place. This was a man who didn't like messes, and their situation was the very definition of a mess.

As if sensing her thoughts, he flipped the pancakes and turned to lean against the gray marble countertop. "I think it's long past time for us to talk."

She couldn't keep dodging him. It was freaking exhausting, and if Becka actually planned to reduce Aaron's position in the baby's life to sperm donor, she never should have moved in with him in the first place. She wrapped both hands around her orange juice and stared hard at the swirl in the marble that looked like Abraham Lincoln's beard. "You are going to be in the baby's life. I'm living in your penthouse. Don't you think that's enough for now?" Even without looking up, she knew his expression had turned stormy, his eyes leaning more gray than blue. She pushed her juice away. "You keep pushing me, and it's stressing me out. The learning curve on this situation is pretty rough and, this might be shocking, but I'm overwhelmed. You trying to micromanage everything from my bath temperature to…"

"Drink your orange juice."

She gave a half-hearted laugh. "Yeah, like that."

"I'm serious." His big hand appeared in her line of vision and nudged the glass back into her hand. "The calcium and vitamin D are good for you."

She closed her eyes and counted to ten. Twice.

Maybe we should just keep banging it out and stop talking, because obviously we are not *even close to being on the same page.*

"Aaron—" She stopped short at the sound of his sliding a plate to her. Becka opened her eyes to find two perfectly shaped pancakes on the plate. She might have stopped breathing completely when he set both the smooth and the chunky peanut butter next to the plate, each with their respective knives. "How did you know?"

"I'd have to be extremely dense not to notice you walking around with a spoonful of peanut butter in your mouth the few times you've graced me with your presence." He eyed the tubs of peanut butter with narrowed eyes. "They're both depleted from the last time I checked, so I wasn't sure which you'd prefer. Let me know and I'll pick up more next time I get groceries."

Heat spread up her chest and took residence in her cheeks. It shouldn't surprise her so much that he picked up on her eating habits, not when he was obviously watching her *so* closely, but the thoughtfulness of the simple gesture had her throat closing and her eyes burning. "I, ah, use both."

Conscious of his eyes on her, she spread first the chunky onto each pancake, and then took the other knife and covered it with smooth peanut butter. She carefully cut the food into tiny bites instead of rolling it up like a burrito the way she would have if she was alone. "Thank you."

"We can make this work, minx. You just have to trust me."

That was the one thing she couldn't do. She *did* trust that he wasn't a total asshole, and that he showed every evidence of probably being a good father and a decent friend. But if she let herself sink into the ease of being with him, she was in danger of forgetting exactly how devastating her inevitable heartbreak would be. Everything else might have changed, but *that* hadn't.

If anything, her reasons for not tumbling head over heels for Aaron had just multiplied. This wasn't some guy she could avoid after things fell apart.

He was the father of her future child.

She couldn't just keep shutting him out, though. He was right about that. There had to be some kind of compromise that got them through this with the least amount of strife. *That compromise probably doesn't include amazing sex and screaming his name. Way to muddy the waters.* She silenced the snide little voice inside her. There would be plenty of time for self-recrimination on her seventh run to the bathroom in the middle of the night.

She finished her pancakes and sat back. "Did you want kids? I mean, if life played out according to your perfect plan."

"What makes you think I have a perfect plan?"

Becka rolled her eyes. "I pay attention, that's what. I think you're even more type-A than Allie and Lucy—combined. That's saying something."

He made a face. "Guilty as charged. Though I only ever really had a plan for my professional life. I've known I wanted to work in cybersecurity since I was in high school, and it only took my first internship in college to solidify that I wanted to work for myself and own my own business. That goal kept me busy enough that the personal stuff was always being pushed to the back burner. And the last time I agreed to a date, my prospective date ran off with the matchmaker."

His date, her sister.

It hurt to think about, but he and Lucy might have fit. They were both ambitious and driven and more than a little pretty. Lucy and Gideon were perfectly matched, of course, but that didn't change the fact that Gideon had thought *Aaron* was a good match for Lucy when he compiled his list of bachelors. That was back when Lucy had hired the headhunter to find her a husband—a position Gideon ended up filling in the end.

Becka couldn't be more different from her sister if she'd tried. She was driven, sure, but her dreams had never been to make partner in some law firm or to own her own business. All she wanted to do was live her life to the fullest, to do what she loved and make enough money to pay her bills and travel to places she'd never been before.

Hard to travel with a baby.

She took a hasty drink of her orange juice, aware of how closely Aaron watched her. "That's nice."

"Uh-huh. To answer your question—yeah, I want kids. I always have. My sisters might have been aggravating to grow up with, but we're pretty close now, and there's something comforting about the chaos of a home filled with a family."

She wouldn't know anything about that. Becka's parents had divorced early on, and her mother had always been more concerned with *her* agenda than with her daughters. When Becka was bullied, it wasn't her mother she ran to. It was Lucy. Her sister had started filling that parental role from an early age, and she'd never quite stopped.

She still remembered the moment when she realized she was more like her mother than she'd ever be like her sister. Becka was fourteen and had been going on about some drama that she didn't even recall now, years later, and thirty minutes into her bitchfest she'd realized that Lucy was upset—had been upset through the entire conversation while Becka went on and on about her petty problem.

It turned out, Lucy hadn't gotten into the school she'd pinned her hopes and dreams on and was crushed.

And Becka hadn't even noticed.

She'd promised herself right then and there that she wouldn't walk their mother's path. She wouldn't keep being a burden on her sister the same way their mother was. She'd be independent and strong and take care of her own problems.

A promise she'd mostly kept over the years. Sure, Becka developed a wild streak in college that never quite went away, and she knew her sister worried sometimes about her resistance to the idea of settling down, but those were small sins compared to the kind they'd grown up witnessing.

At least... they *had* been small sins.

Until now.

She shook her head, suddenly aware that Aaron was looking at her like he expected some kind of answer. "I'm sorry, I missed what you just said."

"I asked you if *you* had ever wanted kids."

She pushed to her feet. "No. I never wanted kids."

Aaron watched Becka walk away with her shoulders bowed, looking like someone had just kicked her puppy. Things had been going well. Better than well. They'd been going *good*. She'd teased him a little, the sex had been outstanding and they'd managed to share a meal and half a conversation.

It's possible you need to set the bar for "well" a little higher.

He wanted to chase her down, to try to talk her into telling him what put that haunted look on her face. It was more than not wanting children. Even as the words came out of her mouth, she looked conflicted, as if it wasn't quite the full truth. She wanted kids. She wouldn't have gone forward with the pregnancy otherwise.

Which meant there was something holding her back, some reason she thought she *shouldn't* want kids.

He could call Lucy, but that meant letting her in

on the fact that Becka was pregnant, and if Becka didn't want her sister to know yet, it wasn't his place to share that information. He'd threatened to, of course, but what had been said in anger and frustration before would be a betrayal of trust now. No, that wasn't an option.

Not to mention, he wanted Becka to trust him enough to let him in and let them both get to know each other. He couldn't do that if he kept fumbling shit so thoroughly.

Aaron weighed his options against the inherent risks that went with any path forward. It was possible that if he left things alone and maintained the course, she'd come to him again.

He couldn't risk being wrong, though. The stakes were too damn high.

So he did the slightly less risky option and called his baby sister. Aaron had always been closest to Trish, partly because she never allowed him to take himself too seriously and partly because their age difference meant they were never competing quite the same way he and Mary did through their younger years.

That mattered, of course, but the reason he called her now instead of Mary was because at twenty-four she was the closest in age to Becka—and the closest in personality. Though Becka was all thorns and prickly edges and Trish was both softer and sweeter, they both harbored free spirits and avoiding being tied down. It was comfortable to be the older brother to that kind of personality. It was significantly less so to be having a child with someone like that.

The line rang several times before it clicked over. "Hey, Aaron. Is everything okay?"

He glanced at the clock and cursed himself. It was almost midnight—way too late for this to be a casual call. "Yeah, everything is okay. I just need some advice and didn't think to check if it was too late to call."

"My big brother asking me for advice? You're right, that's not remotely serious at all." She laughed softly. "I'm awake, and you have me on the phone, so stop thinking about how you're going to make some excuse and call me tomorrow."

Since he'd been about to do exactly that, he gave a rueful grin. "How are you?"

She sighed. "I'm fine. Just as fine as I was a couple weeks ago when we talked, though I'm about to start chewing through the wall if I don't get out of this house soon. I love Mom and Dad, and they're trying to be supportive and not push me, but it's driving all of us crazy."

Trish had moved back home after college until she could find a job and it…hadn't gone particularly well. He made a sympathetic noise. "Well, I have some news that will get you out of the doghouse as least favorite child."

"That sounds like trouble." She lowered her voice. "Are you sure everything is okay?"

"Yeah. I mean, it's not, but it will be." He had to believe that. He couldn't allow for any other outcome. Aaron had half a second to wonder if this call was a mistake, but he had gone too far to change his mind now. "I don't know what I'm doing, Trish. There's this woman, and we connected, but she won't give me the time of day and…" *She's going to have my child.*

She laughed. "Oh, Aaron. She's got you twisted in knots, hasn't she? You already tried to plan your way out of this and it blew up in your face."

He narrowed his eyes. "How'd you know?"

"Because you're our fearless leader. You attack every single problem the exact way—as if you're going into battle. Which is great, and useful, and the reason that you're as professionally successful as you are now." Another laugh. "But you can't date like that, Aaron. I mean, you *can*, but if you're calling me, that means she's independent and isn't going to respond well to that sort of thing."

Aaron started piling plates in the sink. "Everything I do pisses her off."

"Hmm. Have you tried *listening*?"

"She doesn't want to talk."

"Because you make it into an interrogation when you aren't paying attention. Figure out what she likes. Do that. See if you relaxing doesn't relax her a little bit." A hesitation. "Though if she's fighting you this hard, maybe it's time to write the whole thing off? Some walls aren't worth beating your head against."

"This one is." He forced a smile into his voice. "Thanks, Trish. You should come down to the city to visit soon."

"Sure thing. Just as soon as I figure out the rest of my life. Love you, big brother."

"Love you, too." He hung up the phone and went to work on the dishes. His sister's advice wasn't necessarily groundbreaking, but she had a good point. He'd approached this from the baby standpoint, because the baby was the only thing they appeared to have in common.

Well, the baby and the sex.

Aaron shook his head and scrubbed harder at the pan. If he wanted to pave the way to a future with Becka and the baby, he needed to *know* Becka.

He stopped.

Was that what he wanted? Both of them? Because that was a different scenario than simply being a father. He just had to be able to be cordial with Becka in order to do *that*, and they'd both go on with their separate lives. It was the simplest solution for a child born of a one-night stand.

And yet.

He thought about the vivid woman who'd caught his eye in the first place, the determined one who'd faced him down time and again over the future, and the bowed shoulders she'd worn tonight when she walked back to her room alone. *Complicated* did not begin to cover Becka Baudin.

There was nothing wrong with complicated, though.

Aaron finished the dishes and dried the pan, still thinking. He just needed to figure out what common ground they had and work from there. It was entirely possible that they had *nothing* in common and this was all a lost cause, but he wasn't prepared to believe that. There was *something* there. Aaron just needed to figure out what it was.

CHAPTER EIGHT

AARON WAS GONE by the time Becka crawled out of bed the next morning. She tried to tell herself that it was for the best, that she didn't *really* need to see him every single morning before they both left for their respective jobs, but the truth was that she'd gotten used to their shared silence as they drank their daily cup of coffee in the kitchen. He never seemed to feel like he needed to fill the silence. It was nice.

She opened the fridge and stared. Three plates sat on the shelf at eye level, each with a yellow sticky note attached. *Peanut butter and grape jelly. Peanut butter and strawberry jam. Peanut butter and sliced bananas.* Becka smiled, shook her head and grabbed the peanut butter and banana sandwich. She turned to the coffeemaker and found another sticky note. Still smiling, she read his chicken-scratch handwriting. *Have dinner with me tonight. No baby talk, promise.*

"How can I resist an offer like that?" She checked

the time and typed out a quick text promising to be home by six.

The day flew by. She had spin at nine, TRX at eleven. The first two classes were at Transcend.

After TRX, she got cleaned up and changed then headed to the elite gym where she coached. Half her clients were looking for weight loss, and the other half were hard-core training for various events. All four of her sessions that afternoon were of the extreme variety. She normally liked to switch up her schedule a little more—the intensity could wear on her after a while—but today she welcomed the requirement of extra concentration.

Anything to keep her from watching the clock and counting down the hours until dinner tonight.

She probably shouldn't have agreed to go. It wouldn't end well, and the whole point of this exercise was to create a stable foundation between her and Aaron so that the baby wouldn't suffer. Dates were *not* part of the equation.

Still, she didn't linger at the gym like she usually did after work. Becka took a cab back to Aaron's apartment and, after arguing with herself for a solid five minutes, jumped in the shower and started her beautifying process. She didn't have to pull out all the stops for dinner—it would look weird if she *did*—but that didn't mean she had to go in fitness wear and without makeup.

Compromise. Jeans. Nice shirt. Decent makeup but not over the top. Blow out your hair.

She wasn't overthinking this. She was just being reasonable.

I'm totally overthinking this.

Despite being out of practice, she was nearly ready well before the time Aaron had given her, but she ran into a problem when she pulled on her jeans.

They wouldn't button.

Becka stared down at the offending button and the gap between it. She knew she'd been putting on weight—that happened in a pregnancy—but she'd mostly stuck to leggings and workout pants, so she hadn't put too much thought into what that meant for her wardrobe. "No jeans for me, apparently." She wiggled out of them and considered her options. It was early enough in the fall that New York hadn't gotten totally frigid, so a dress would have to do— preferably something stretchy.

Except she hadn't packed any dresses, because why would she? The only thing she'd needed when she was bullied into agreeing to these living arrangements were her workout clothes and…that was it. She sat on her bed and dropped her head into her hands. *This is* not *something to get emotional about. They're just clothes. You can run back to your apartment and…*

But there wasn't time.

She pressed her lips together. Hard. She was overreacting, turning this into something bigger than it should be. Yes, she wanted to dress nice for whatever this date entailed, but there were workarounds that didn't involve dresses or trying to jury-rig her jeans into place. Becka took a steadying breath and went through her clothes again, more slowly this time. She finally settled on a pair of black leggings and a lightweight tunic-length sweater in her favorite color of pink. It was a little more laid-back than she would have preferred, but it would work.

She'd just pulled the sweater over her head and smoothed it down her hips when the front door opened and Aaron called out. "I'm late, I know, I'm sorry. Give me fifteen minutes and we can go." Footsteps sounded past her door, and a few seconds later his shower started.

It was all too easy to picture Aaron in the shower, tilting his head back beneath the spray, letting the water sluice down his body. Becka mentally traced the path the droplets would take. Down his chest, over his cut abs, to his cock…

Down, girl.

Exactly fifteen minutes later, Aaron walked out of his bedroom in a pair of slacks and a button-down that looked indistinguishable from what he wore to work every day. He took one look at her and frowned. "More low-key date, then."

She didn't really want to admit that she couldn't fit into her pants anymore. It wasn't that she thought

Aaron would be an asshole about it—actually, the opposite—but knowing what little she did about him, he'd do something like drag her out shopping for clothes she couldn't afford. And then insist on paying for said clothes, which was a nice gesture, but she couldn't take a wardrobe in addition to everything else he was providing and... Becka studied her thick gray wool socks. "Ah—"

"Say no more." He walked back into his room and reappeared a few minutes later in a pair of dark jeans that hugged his thighs and a cable-knit sweater. When Aaron caught her looking, he ran his hands over the deep green wool. "My mother is a knitter, so for every Christmas, we all get sweaters." He made a face. "I don't wear mine often, though. Mostly when I go home to visit during the winter months."

His mother loved her children so much, she spent hours upon hours knitting them sweaters. It took Becka two tries to speak. "That's really, really nice." She studied the fit of the sweater—perfect—and how the coloring complemented Aaron's features perfectly. "Green is your favorite color, isn't it?"

"Guilty as charged." He chuckled. "Though she tends to lean more toward grays, since they're staple pieces, according to her."

"She's right." The amount of thought and love that went into that gift blew Becka way. She knew good parents existed. Of course they did. They weren't magical unicorns that subsisted on mere myth. But she'd never had cause to come across them. Growing up, most of her friends' parents were divorced, and there was an aura of benign neglect that everyone just sort of dealt with. No harm, no foul. There were always kids in her groups of friends that *did* have the happy life everyone was told to want, with loving parents who didn't forget birthdays and showed up for every extracurricular activity and always had dinner on the table around the same time every night. It just hurt too much to spend time in those households and have her face rubbed in everything she was missing.

She'd had Lucy, though, and Becka thanked her lucky stars every single damn day for that. Who knew where she would have ended up without her strong older sister plotting their course? Their parents being flakes never seemed to affect Lucy. She just adapted and moved on, never letting their dropping the ball get in the way of her goals and aspirations. It wasn't that she didn't care, she just managed her expectations, and after a while, the disappointment and rejection lost its sting.

Becka had never quite mastered that trick.

"Minx, what's wrong? What did I say?"

She shook her head and swallowed past the burning in her throat. "It's nothing. I'm just really glad the baby will have awesome grandparents like your parents."

He narrowed his eyes but seemed to reconsider

pressing her for more information. Aaron's smile was only the slightest bit strained. "What sounds good for dinner?"

"Taco truck tacos."

Now he was really looking at her like she'd grown a second head. "You know, from what I read, pregnancy is supposed to create strange cravings but peanut butter and taco truck tacos..." He shook his head and offered his arm. "I wouldn't dream of standing between you and your desired food."

"Smart man." She gingerly placed her hand in the crook of his elbow, feeling a little ridiculous, but then they were moving and there was no more time for second-guessing. As they stepped out onto the sidewalk, Becka inhaled the crisp autumn air and sighed. "I love this city."

"Are you originally from here?" Aaron studied the street and turned them left.

"Sort of. We were born down in Pennsylvania, but Lucy and I both grew up here. Not in this part of town, obviously, but in the city." It felt good to stretch her legs, good to walk next to Aaron and talk as if the future wasn't hanging in the balance.

Pretend there isn't a pregnancy. Pretend this is a real first date that might have happened if you hadn't run scared.

It sounded good in theory, but Becka didn't make a habit of dating. Dating led to expectations and demands and compromises—usually involving her.

And that was if she even bothered to get past the lackluster text conversations and unsolicited dick pics to actually *go* on a date in the first place.

No, things were easier when everyone's boundaries were clearly defined, and she avoided anyone who might tempt her into changing her internal rules when it came to romance and love.

Until now.

There was no avoiding this.

They dodged a power-walking man on his phone, and she continued. "I know the American dream is supposed to be to raise your kid in a small town with some random field in the distance and a whole lot in the way of overalls, but I think it's bullshit. This city has a culture and life all its own, and I wouldn't be the person I am today if I hadn't spent my formative years here." It struck her that their child would be raised in the city. She pressed her hand to her stomach, staggered by the thought. "I sound preachy, don't I?"

"I'd say passionate." He smiled. "And small-town living isn't for everyone. I might have grown up in one, but I happen to agree with you when it comes to the city."

They walked for several more blocks while Becka chewed on that. She both wanted to know more about Aaron's past and didn't. *This is dumb. Being jealous that he grew up in an unbroken home is the height of stupidity.* She took a deep breath. "Tell me something no one knows about you."

"I watch poker tournaments on TV."

She shot him a look. "You're joking. That's like saying you watch NASCAR or golf."

"I know." He pressed his free hand to his chest. "It's my deepest, darkest secret. I can't get enough of that shit. Playing the odds and being able to see the entire table's hand at once is addicting. Even while I'm telling myself I should turn it off, I get sucked in and can watch for hours."

Becka could see it. His mind obviously ran analytical, and there were few games more analytical than poker. She frowned. "Why not blackjack?"

"Blackjack, you're playing the odds. Poker, you're playing the rest of the table. It's a combination of playing the odds and reading the people you're playing against that I love."

"Remind me never to play strip poker with you," she muttered.

His slow smile made her stomach flip. "Didn't I tell you? That's what we're doing after dinner."

Aaron meant the words to be a joke. He wanted to get to know Becka better, and though there were certain things playing poker with her would tell him, *strip* poker was sure to short-circuit his brain the same as every time they got naked together. But she licked her lips and flashed a grin and suddenly he was looking at the woman he met three months ago instead of the cagey one who'd been living with him for the last week.

Not wanting her to switch back—which always seemed to happen when she let herself think too hard—he tugged her closer and slipped his arm around her waist. "Okay, you convinced me. Strip poker is on the table."

She laughed. "It was never on the table, though that was an excellent try. Very nice line. You get a B minus."

"B minus!" He turned them around the corner down in the direction of a taco truck he knew of. "My delivery was spot-on."

"Mmm, yes." She leaned into him as the wind kicked up. "But you should have saved it until after dinner, once you had me back at your place and were plying me with drinks."

"Sounds underhanded."

"Only if I wasn't planning on getting naked with you already." She tilted her head back to look at him, her lashes seeming impossibly long against the blue of her eyes. "If I let you ply me with drinks, it's already a done deal."

"I'll keep that in mind." He stomped down on his body's reaction to her words and her nearness. It might be sexy as hell to press her against the nearest wall and go for a repeat of their first kiss, but that wasn't the goal. It *couldn't* be the goal. "What did you want to be when you grew up?"

"Travel agent." She made a face. "Right up until I realized most travel agents don't actually travel that much. There's nothing quite as agonizing as planning someone else's trip over and over again while stuck in a crappy office surrounded by four beige walls."

He was inclined to agree, though the travel bug had never bitten Aaron. "You were just down in the Caribbean not too long ago, right?"

She missed a step and shot him a look. "Right. I forgot. You and Roman are friends." If anything, her expression became more agonized. "Allie's going to want a double date before too long—mark my words. And once she decides on something, no one in their right mind gets in her way."

A double date didn't sound like the hell she seemed to consider it, but he chose to keep that opinion to himself. "She's good for Roman. He's been more relaxed since they started dating than I've ever seen him."

"Regular sex will do that to a man," she muttered.

"And to a woman."

She chose not to comment on that, which was just as well. They reached the taco truck and got in line behind a mother and her two kids. Because they were standing so close, Aaron could feel the tension bleeding back into Becka's body until she stood rigid against him. He studied her, trying to figure out what the issue was. The mother? The woman was in her midtwenties, and though she looked tired, she was handling herself well and both her young children were relatively well behaved. They collected their tacos and disappeared down the street, leaving Becka staring after them.

He bided his time, waiting until they'd ordered, collected their food and eaten it at one of the benches not too far from the truck. Only when she crumpled her paper napkin did he sit back and say, "What was it about her that bothered you so much?"

She gave him the courtesy of not pretending she didn't know what he meant. "I don't know if you guessed it, but my family life was hardly idyllic growing up. Lucy was the bright spot, of course. She still is. But my parents were a hot mess from day one, and they only seemed to get worse over time. My mom never would have done something as simple as that." She waved her hand in the direction the mother had gone. "That's sad, right? I'd more or less made my peace with it, but the whole impending-motherhood thing has the ghosts of my past banging on my closet door again." She shook her head. "Sorry. I'm a mess."

"No apologies necessary." He took her hand and laced his fingers with hers. "Were they…"

"Abusive? No, nothing like that." She stared at the people walking past, but she didn't take her hand from his. "They were just selfish assholes who were more wrapped up in themselves and their petty dramas than they could ever be in their children. I don't think they ever planned on staying together, but Lucy was an oops baby and the only thing to do at the time was get married. I don't think my mom ever even wanted kids, but one thing led to another and then she had two."

Not too difficult to read between the lines. Benign neglect was one thing, but it sounded as if Becka had been reminded on a near constant basis that she wasn't wanted, that perhaps her parents' lives would be so much better if she wasn't in them. He didn't tell her he was sorry, didn't offer her sympathy she might mistake for pity. "I'm glad you had Lucy."

"Me, too." She finally looked at him. "She was always there. For nearly every game, for every important event. Even after she went to college, she was never too far or too busy to be there for me. I don't deserve her."

"She loves you." For most people, it was as simple as that. They loved someone, they showed up. At least Becka had *that* influence in her life, even if the people who should have been there for her above all others…weren't. He hesitated, but finally asked, "Have you told her yet?"

She opened her mouth as if she was going to say something, but seemed to change her mind and shook her head. "I'm getting kind of cold. Mind if we go back now?"

The opportunity slipped through his fingers like water. He couldn't force her to open up to him. The fact she'd told him even as much as she had was a small miracle. It was progress, which was a positive sign. Though it might not be enough, it was a start.

Aaron could be a patient hunter when the situation called for it and the stakes were high enough.

With Becka, they'd never been higher.

CHAPTER NINE

BECKA WAS ON edge the entire trip back to the penthouse. She kept waiting for Aaron's tension to translate to more questions or pressing her for further information, but he just walked next to her with his arm around her. He respected her emotional retreat, if not a physical one.

They walked through the front door and she had to smother her first instinct, which was to flee to her bedroom and barricade herself inside. Even if they'd danced on some of her buttons during their short walk, on the whole it'd been pleasant. More than pleasant. She liked walking down New York City's streets with Aaron's arm wrapped around her waist and the warmth of his body soaking through her sweater. She liked teasing him about his intentions. God, she even liked the reserved way he'd watched her when she spoke about her parents, as if he knew exactly how hard it was for her to confess even those small details and he didn't want to do anything to spook her.

Damn it, I like him.

And because her emotions hamstrung her retreat, she said, "You promised to ply me with drinks." When he opened his mouth, no doubt to quote some statistic about pregnant women and alcohol, she cut in, "I'll take cranberry juice."

"Cranberry juice," he repeated, as if he wasn't sure he'd heard her right.

"Yep. I picked some up yesterday. It's in the back of the fridge."

"I see." He guided her to the bar stool with his hand on the small of her back. She could feel the tiny touch even through her sweater, and it was everything she could do not to arch into his hand like a cat begging for strokes. Aaron pulled out two wineglasses, retrieved the container of cranberry juice, and poured some into both. "You know I can provide whatever you need, minx. You only have to ask."

She pressed her lips together to keep from snapping back. As a result, she sounded only mildly irritated when she said, "It's cranberry juice, not a college fund. It sounded good, so I got some on the way home. Simple as that."

"Home."

She opened her mouth, reconsidered and shut it.

Aaron nodded as if she'd spoken. "I'll try to relax. I just have more than enough money, and it's silly for you to spend your limited funds when I can take care of it." He held up a hand. "That came out wrong."

Do not yell at him. He's trying to be helpful.
High-handed.
Overbearing.
But helpful.

She hissed out a breath. "Aaron, this isn't going to work if you keep reminding me of our unequal roles financially. I've been living here a week. Believe me, I know you make a whole hell of a lot more money than I do. You don't have to whip out your wallet for every little thing to prove it." He narrowed his eyes, but she kept talking, determined not to ruin their evening. "And you know you don't have to skip alcohol on my account. I'm the only one required to be depressingly sober for the next however long. No reason for both of us to suffer."

"It's hardly suffering." He nudged her glass across the counter to her.

If she squinted just right, she might be able to pretend it was wine. Not that Becka *wanted* to drink. The thought of the *scent* of wine was enough to have her wrinkling her nose in distaste. Safe to say she wasn't going to be one of those pregnant ladies who indulged in a glass or two from time to time. That said, it would have been nice to have the option. She took a drink of her cranberry juice instead. "So, about that strip poker."

Aaron choked. "I was joking."

"I know. But it sounds fun, and if we can't drink

together and make bad life choices, we might as well go ahead with the bad life choices anyway."

"You have a strange way of looking at things."

Didn't she know it? "Strange, but compelling." She pushed to her feet and padded over to the coffee table. "Come on. I know you have cards around here somewhere." Becka sank cross-legged onto the floor next to the table and set her wineglass on a coaster. Knowing Aaron, the piece was probably painfully expensive, and she wasn't going to be the one to ruin it.

The baby won't know better, though. Babies destroy shit. It's in their genetic makeup, I'm pretty sure.

She pushed the thought away. No use working so damn hard not to ruin tonight if she was going to let herself do it despite everything. She looked up just as Aaron came back into the room, cards in hand. He sat on the other side of the table and raised his brows. "You sure?"

"You say that like I'm going to lose and you're trying to give me a gracious exit."

He laughed, the deep sound doing funny things to her stomach…and lower. The twinkle in his blue eyes didn't help her control any, either. "Aw, minx, you're cute when you're in denial."

"Denial?" She sank as much fake outrage into the word as she could.

"Denial," he repeated. "You're going to be naked and coming on my mouth inside of five hands."

Her jaw dropped even as she shifted to her knees and pressed her thighs together. As if that would be enough to stop the need his words suddenly had pulsing through her body. "Pride goeth before the fall, mister."

"And sometimes the pride is just reality." He was still smiling, the heat in his eyes barely banked as he dealt out two cards to each of them. "I'm assuming Texas Hold'em works for you."

"My favorite." She studied her cards—a king and an ace—and laid them facedown on the table. "You know, if you're trying to punish me for losing, saying I'm going to be coming on your mouth is hardly the way to go about it."

He leaned forward and propped his elbows on the coffee table. "It's not about you losing."

"Actually—"

"It's about me winning." He stared at her mouth and then lifted his gaze almost reluctantly. "You naked on my couch, your thighs spread wide, and feeling you come while I suck on that pretty little clit of yours? That's winning for me, minx. No question about it."

She couldn't quite draw a full breath. "Sounds like I'm still getting the better end of the bargain."

"Maybe." He shrugged. "But you still lose at cards."

And that was something she'd never willingly do. Becka forced herself to inhale and straighten. "In that case, when you lose—yes, I said when, not if—then *you're* going to be naked and *you're* going to be coming in *my* mouth." The shocked look on his face was almost as good as actually winning would be. She pasted an innocent expression on her face. "Sorry, is there a problem?"

Aaron cleared his throat. "No problem." He nodded at her cards. "You ready?"

"I was born ready, baby." She laughed, her stress falling away for the first time in months. Right now, in this moment, nothing outside the two of them and this game of cards mattered. She could stress about the future and she and Aaron could go back to warily circling each other in the morning. Tonight, she was going to enjoy herself.

And she was going to enjoy the fuck out of Aaron, too.

Aaron was losing. He didn't know how Becka was pulling it off, but he was down to his boxer briefs and cursing himself for not throwing on an extra layer of clothing before their date. She wore her bra and her leggings and nothing else, but she had a look in her eye for this hand that he didn't like.

As if she knew she already had the win in the bag.

He flipped over the final card and bit back a curse. His two pair was good, but he didn't think it would be good enough. Sure as shit, Becka gave him the most wicked grin and set her cards down faceup. "Full house."

"Fuck," he breathed.

"I plan on it." She pointed at his hips. "Off." And then the little minx licked her lips like she could already taste his cock. She rose to her feet, her gaze never straying from him as Aaron slid his last item of clothing off. He sat back on the sofa and let her look her fill, forcing himself to hold perfectly still as she rounded the coffee table and knelt between his thighs. Becka gripped his cock and gave him a teasing stroke. "It's not right that a gorgeous man like you is just as gorgeous here, too." Her tongue darted out and flicked the underside of his cock. "Then again, I'm not about to complain." She shot him a look. "Keep your eyes open. I want you to watch me."

No way in hell would he risk missing a moment of this. Aaron gripped the couch cushions as she slid his cock between her pretty red-painted lips and sucked him deep. She released him slowly as if savoring his taste and then smiled. "You're right. This *is* what winning feels like." Before he could digest that statement, she took him deep into her mouth and throat until her lips met his base. He kept perfectly still, letting her hold the reins, and she rewarded him for his restraint with the best fucking blow job of his life. She teased him, sucking hard and then backing off until it was everything he could do not to curse.

Finally, Becka raised her head. "Aaron?"

"Mm-hmm?"

"I have a tiny, itty-bitty request."

Considering the way she put it, he didn't know whether to be worried or so turned on he couldn't think straight. "Yeah?"

She ran a single finger the length of his cock. "I love teasing you, but what I really want right now is for you to stop holding back and fuck my mouth the way you're obviously dying to." Her smile had his heart skipping a beat. "I can take it. Promise."

He shouldn't say yes. Their first time might have been rough and deliriously good as a result, but things were different now.

Weren't they?

The answer was written across her face. Becka sat back on her heels and reached around to unsnap her bra. She slid it off and tossed it aside. "I won. Remember?" She wrapped her hand around his cock again. "This is mine until you come in my mouth. Unless you're going back on the bet."

"Not on your life." He pushed to his feet and shifted until he could stand in front of her. Seeing her on her knees, staring up at him with *that* expression in her eyes... He laced his fingers through her hair on either side of her face, pulling it back so he had a clear view and holding her tightly so he had control.

Her eyes slid half-shut. "That's it. That's exactly it." She licked the head of his cock, her gaze on his as she sucked him back into her mouth. It had been hot before. Now it was *scorching*. Heaven was the sight of Becka's red lips around his cock, a challenge in her blue eyes, daring him to do exactly what she'd commanded. *To fuck her mouth.*

He thrust lightly, testing her. But there was no panic on her face, just an eagerness as she took him deeper without effort. As if she loved this as much as he did.

Keeping a tight leash on himself, Aaron started to move. He held her head in place as he picked up his pace until she could only relax and take it. The moment she gave herself over to him completely, his knees threatened to buckle. Becka's surrender was temporary, and he wouldn't have it any other way, but it was a gift all the same. It was *more* a gift because of its fleeting nature.

Her eyes flicked open as if she heard his thoughts, and when they met his, it was too much. He orgasmed with her name on his tongue and, God help him, she drank down every drop of him.

Aaron carefully stepped back and urged her to her feet. "Come to bed with me."

Becka blinked. "What?"

He was rushing, and he didn't give a fuck. They weren't going to leave tonight half-finished, and he wanted her in his bed. Beneath him, over him and later…sleeping next to him.

He wanted it all.

He couldn't tell her as much right now. Even with desire smoothing the stress and worry from her expression, she would panic if he pushed too hard. *Damn it, think.* Aaron kissed her hard, stroking her tongue with his until she swayed against him. "You won, minx. You got your reward. Now come to bed and let me take my consolation prize."

She smiled against his lips. "Sounds like sketchy reasoning."

"Skillful negotiation." Before she could think of an argument around *that*, he scooped her into his arms and started for the bedroom.

Becka relaxed against him with a soft laugh. "Okay, I'll bite—what does your consolation prize entail?"

"Because you asked so nicely, I'm inclined to share." He nudged his bedroom door open and kicked it shut behind him. "I'm going to lay you down on my bed and spend some time enjoying your body. First with my hands. Then with my mouth. And finally with my cock."

This time her laugh bounced through the entire room. "Greedy."

"Mmm, well, I'm feeling generous, so if there's something you'd like to add in along the way, I think we can make it happen."

She looped her arms around his neck and grinned up at him. "Did I say greedy? I meant so, so generous." Her lightly mocking words didn't detract from the happiness lurking in her eyes.

Happiness he'd helped put there.

This isn't forever. This is just a reprieve in the midst of a storm.

He didn't care. He'd take it.

Aaron laid her on the bed and nudged her back until he could kneel between her thighs. The picture she painted, from her wild blue hair to her smirking lips to her rocking body... It just flat out did it for him. *She* just flat out did it for him. He traced the rose tattoo just inside her hipbone. "Why this?"

"A reminder." She didn't say more, but she didn't have to. He understood. Roses were gorgeous flowers, but their thorns were legendary. Kind of like Becka.

He pulled off her pants and underwear and tossed them aside, leaving her gloriously naked before him. "Where did you learn to play poker?" He cupped her pussy, spearing two fingers into her. "You're good."

"Bitter you lost?" She arched her back and dug her heels into the bed, trying to drive his fingers deeper, but he used his free hand to pin her hips into place. Becka fisted the sheets above her head and cursed. "I learned to play free-roll poker in high school. It's how I made extra money after I graduated."

He could see it. All she'd have to do was smile and giggle a little and men would be falling over themselves to "teach" her how to play. Then she'd clean up and walk away while they were still wondering what the hell had happened. "Tricky."

"Tactical. Thought you'd approve."

He twisted his wrist and teased her clit with his thumb. "I do. I'm going to demand a rematch, though."

Becka writhed in his grip. She grabbed his wrists and met his gaze. "Stop teasing me and let me come, Aaron. I've been aching for it ever since I had your cock in my mouth." She smiled slowly, as if she knew exactly where his thoughts had gone—to seeing himself disappear between those bright lips. She affected a pleading look. "Please."

"Since you asked so nicely." He moved, dragging her around until he leaned against the headboard and Becka was sprawled between his legs, her head at his feet. Aaron lifted her hips so he could play with her at his leisure. The blow job had barely taken the edge off for him, and the entire night stretched out before them. A promise of as much pleasure as she could handle and more. He parted her and traced her opening with a single finger, not penetrating her. Teasing.

"Aaron."

"That's right, minx. You keep saying my name like that and I might consider giving you my cock again before the end of the night."

CHAPTER TEN

BECKA'S ENTIRE EXISTENCE narrowed down to Aaron's fingers between her thighs. He teased her, doling out pleasure in waves and then drawing her back from the edge at the last possible second. She held out for longer than she could have thought possible, but then the words came. "Please, Aaron, please let me come. I need you, just please, please, *please*."

"There it is." He growled and withdrew his hands.

She barely had the space of a breath to whimper in protest when he wedged his hands beneath her ass and lifted her to his mouth. This time, he didn't mess around. After a thorough kiss that curled her toes so hard they cramped, he sucked her clit into his mouth and worked her ruthlessly. She dug her nails into her palms as she came, his name on her lips in a cry that seemed to shake the walls.

At least, it shook the walls surrounding her heart.

Aaron didn't give her a chance to recover. He set her back on the bed and then he was inside her, stretching her, filling her. The slow slide of his cock and the delicious friction it caused brought her back to herself heartbeat by heartbeat, and she became aware of his murmuring in her ear. "Beautiful minx. You're so fucking perfect and it makes me so damn crazy I can't think past my need for you." He kissed her shoulder, her neck, her jaw and then claimed her mouth.

His need called hers to the fore, and she locked her ankles at the small of his back and laced her fingers through his hair, rising up to meet him even as she met his tongue stroke for stroke. *I can't think past my need for you, either. It scares the shit out of me, and I don't know what to do with that.* He ate the words before she had a chance to give them voice, which was just as well.

She wished she could blame the sex or orgasms for the way her inner compass had failed her so spectacularly, but neither of them were the problem.

It was all Becka.

Aaron hooked a hand beneath one of her thighs and hitched it higher, allowing him deeper. The contact tore a cry from her lips, and the building pleasure reached a crescendo she couldn't have fought off if she tried. She clung to him as his strokes became less measured and he followed her over the edge, kissing her as if his next breath lay in her lungs.

Afterward, they lay tangled together, their jagged breathing a perfect match. Becka raised a shaking hand and pushed her hair back. "If that's the consolation prize, I might consider losing at poker more often."

"Mmm." He kissed the sensitive spot behind her ear. "Stay with me tonight, minx. Let me hold you."

She should say no. Having sex was one thing, but literally sleeping together crossed even more lines. She'd fought so hard to put boundaries in place, and Aaron insisted on trampling over every one he found. This was no different. If they were going to have sex, they should at least sleep in different rooms to keep things from getting messy.

But lethargy stole through her body and she couldn't quite keep her eyes open. "Just tonight."

"Sure." He answered a little too quickly, but she didn't have the energy to call him on it. Aaron shifted away, and a few seconds later, he pulled the blanket up and over them both. He tucked her against the front of his body, and she tensed in response.

Becka didn't cuddle. It muddied those boundaries she'd clung to so hard up to this point. But with his warmth soaking into her body and his slow exhales dancing across the back of her neck, she couldn't force herself to move. As sleep teased her, Aaron pressed his hand to her stomach just below her belly button.

Right where the baby currently grew.

His touch was different there, almost reverent as he explored the slight curve of her stomach that hadn't been there three months ago. He didn't say anything to break the silence, and she couldn't speak past the burning in her throat. *This isn't real. It might* feel *real, but we aren't a couple expecting our first baby. We're strangers who banged once and now are trying to figure out what the hell we're doing.*

You can't afford to forget that.

It was only for tonight. Tomorrow, she could go back to keeping precious distance between them and ensure Aaron knew that he needed to stop blurring the lines when it came to her and the baby.

Tonight…

Tonight, she just wanted to pretend for a little while. To sink into the feeling of him holding her, to luxuriate in what was probably the best date of her life. After they'd gotten past the uncomfortable topics and relaxed into being with each other, she'd had *fun* with Aaron. And she hadn't had to worry about making a clean getaway because what they had together was already so damn complicated.

Becka closed her eyes and let herself relax. Aaron responded by cuddling her a little closer, and she fell asleep to the even sounds of his breath, feeling safer than she ever had before.

Aaron woke early and put together a light breakfast for Becka while he contemplated his next step. Last night had been good—better than good—but he wanted to take steps forward. To claim ground Becka had previously held back from him. Since both pregnancy and her family seemed to be off-limits, that meant he had to find a different way to connect. He flipped the pancakes, still thinking hard.

"You're spoiling me."

He didn't jump, but it was a near thing. He turned and held out his arm, and Becka slipped under it and nestled against him. She must have noticed his surprise, because she sighed. "Last night was really nice and I'm still riding the nice vibes, so let's not think about it too hard, okay?"

Considering he'd been doing exactly the opposite just now, he didn't like his chances. "You're just drunk on power after your poker win."

"And you think you're a comedian." She leaned forward and eyed the pancakes. "I shouldn't have these before my class. They'll sit heavy on my stomach."

"Wrap them up in tinfoil and add the peanut butter later. It will be cold, but still a nice protein boost after class."

Now she really was looking at him strangely. "Thanks." She stepped away from him and snagged an apple off the counter.

Aaron could actually feel her retreating, and it made him crazy. "What do you do for fun?"

"Drink." She made a face. "Okay, that sounds bad. But happy hours are one of my favorite things. Most bars Allie and I used to hang out in have trivia or bingo or some kind of game while they pour half-priced drinks. The people-watching is superb, and we've already established that I have a competitive streak."

That, they definitely had. "Would it bother you to go for trivia night if you can't drink?"

She seemed to consider that as she took a bite of apple. "I don't know. No? I mean, we'd have to pick a place with good food, but that's easy enough to manage in this city."

We.

The fact she casually looped him into the prospective plans warmed him through. It was just a word, two simple letters that Aaron used every single damn day. But from Becka's lips, it took on a new meaning, a different mentality, making them a unit. She might not be willing to admit as much, but her thinking she was on this road alone had obviously shifted in the last week.

I'm making progress. Slowly, but surely.

He kept his body language as casual as his tone. "You free tonight?"

"Tonight?" She took another bite and chewed slowly. "I could make tonight work."

"Why don't you bring an extra set of clothes and shower at the gym? I can pick you up at…five?"

"Sure…" She grabbed her phone off the counter and backed away. "That sounds nice. Let's do that. 'Bye."

Aaron watched her run from him, but there was none of the frustration he'd grown accustomed to when it came to dealing with Becka. They'd taken a big step last night, whether she wanted to admit it or not. If she needed to retreat a little in response, he'd allow it.

But she wouldn't get far if she tried to bolt for real.

He shook his head and used a spatula to move the pancakes from the pan to a square of tinfoil he'd laid out when he started cooking. A few seconds to cool, and then he carefully rolled them up and grabbed the mini jar of peanut butter he'd picked up yesterday. The jar and the tinfoil wraps went into the lunch bag he'd found in the back of his pantry. He could hear Becka getting dressed in her room, so he poured her a cup of coffee into a thermos. Ten to one, she was about to rush out of the penthouse without worrying about her coffee or her lunch, and he didn't need her going without because he'd spooked her.

He stepped into the hallway and caught her mid-sneak. Her blue eyes went wide. "I'm going to work now."

"I see that." He passed over the bag and the thermos, and her jaw dropped when she took them. Aaron used a single finger to close her mouth and pressed a quick kiss to her lips. "I'll pick you up at five."

"At five," she parroted.

He stepped back so she had a clear escape path.

Becka blinked at him one last time and nearly sprinted to the front door. It slammed behind her, and Aaron chuckled. *That went well.* The woman obviously had been taking care of herself for a very long time. From what he knew of both her and Lucy—and what she had and *hadn't* said—he suspected Becka went without to ensure her big sister didn't feel any unnecessary guilt about their parents being shitty. He respected the hell out of that, even if he wanted to go back in time and wrap her younger self up and protect her from the ugliness she'd lived through.

He couldn't fix her past. He wouldn't even know where to start.

But if he was careful, Aaron could maneuver around her thorns to take care of her in the future.

He cleaned up the kitchen, changed and headed out for work. Becka had him entirely too distracted, but work with his new client went over well enough. The client wanted an audit of their existing computer systems and a comprehensive risk-assessment report. It was a simpler job than he normally handled. Cameron much preferred the clients who wanted cybersecurity set up from the ground up, but this particular job was a referral and not one they could subcontract.

Even though it was something he could put together in his sleep, that didn't mean he could get away without giving it all of his attention. They were paying him for the best, and that was what he needed to provide.

Cameron stood in the lobby, a scowl on his face, as Aaron walked through the door. He stopped short. "What's wrong?"

"Kim Jones walked." Cameron glared at the phone as if it was the sole responsible party. "I told her that cutting corners would undermine the integrity of our work and if she wanted a cheap option, she should have gone with one of our half-assed competitors." He glared harder. "She said that's exactly what she planned to do."

"Fuck," Aaron breathed. "I had her in the bag. Why the hell would you tell her that? We'd already agreed on the package she wanted. Our job is to give it to her—not rip her a new one because we think it's the wrong choice. That's not your call to make, Cameron."

He strode past the lobby and into his office, Cameron hot on his heels. The man's agitation rolled off him in waves. "I told you I can't do this shit, Aaron. They ask me a question and I'm not going to pussyfoot around with the answer. Honesty is supposed to be an asset."

He held on to his patience through sheer force of will. "Yes, but your brand of honesty has also driven off every single person we've hired to help manage the workload. I don't have a problem being the client-facing part of the company, but I can't do both. So, if we can't find suitable admin support, we either need to hire another tech expert or we need someone who can work under me to consult with the clients. I don't care which way we go on things, but something has to give."

"We haven't found someone qualified to fill either of those roles." Cameron frowned. "I can't even find someone qualified to man the damn front desk, and that's a simple enough job."

"You don't think *anyone* is qualified." Finding someone to work with them who could handle the job—and Cameron's surliness—was an impossible task.

"I have exacting standards."

"More like…" He caught a strange expression on Cameron's face. "What?"

"What the hell is this?" Cameron stalked over and snatched the top baby book off the pile Aaron had placed on the far side of his desk when the box showed up. He flipped through it, the book looking tiny in his massive hands. "You planning on procreating?"

He hadn't planned on sharing the information like this—or at all until strictly necessary. Aaron rubbed a hand over his face. "A girl I was, ah, seeing. She's pregnant."

"It's yours?"

He gritted his teeth. "It's mine." Becka said it was, and he had no reason to doubt her. Going down that path lay madness and ensured that any relationship blossoming between them would be dead and gone.

"Huh." Cameron set the book down. "Congrats, then, I guess. Or condolences?" He narrowed his eyes. "Which way do we fall on this?"

"I don't know yet." It was nothing more than the truth. The baby was unplanned and even with the surprise and shock wearing off, he had mixed feelings. He'd never planned on having a child with someone he wasn't married to. The whole concept was old-fashioned and he should just set it aside, but it bothered him. Things with Becka weren't buttoned up—and showed no signs of *being* buttoned up any time in the foreseeable future. They were making progress, but it was slow going. "We're keeping it, and that's enough for now."

"Guess so." Cameron scrubbed a hand over his shaved head. "Look, I'm sorry about Kim Jones. I didn't know that offering my opinion would make her freak the fuck out like that. And then she was yelling and I was yelling and…" He shrugged. "I said we'll hire someone and we will. I'll set up another round of interviews this week."

He opened his mouth, but there was no point of going round and round with this shit. He'd known who Cameron was when he went into business with the man. Aaron had made his peace with being client-facing, but he hadn't expected it to chafe quite so much. If they could get a good third in here, it would smooth over a lot of their random little issues. It just had to be someone Cameron wouldn't scare off inside of a week.

But his partner had said he'd handle it, and so he had to let it go. "Appreciate it."

"Now, get to work. Sounds like you have more mouths to feed in the near future." He grinned. "Any chance it's twins?"

"Oh, fuck right off, Cameron." He shook his head and sat behind his desk. There was plenty of work to be done, and he had to get it finished in time to pick Becka up after work. No matter what bullshit arose during the day, he wasn't going to let anything endanger another date with her.

Not when he was actually starting to make progress.

CHAPTER ELEVEN

BECKA RAN BACK to her apartment on her lunch break to grab more clothes. She stood in the middle of the living room and wrinkled her nose. Living surrounded by Aaron's understated luxury made it hard to see this place as anything other than the shithole he'd labeled it. It was home, sure… Or at least it had been. It didn't feel like much right now except for a letdown. She gave herself a shake and headed into her room to grab a bag to throw some dresses into. At some point soon she'd have to face the reality of maternity clothing, but she wasn't ready to deal with it yet.

Great job, Becka. Just avoid anything and everything related to the baby until you absolutely have to face it. That sure won't blow up in your face.

Impossible to ignore the little voice when it spoke hard-core reason at her. She'd asked Aaron for time before they got down to the nitty-gritty about baby stuff, and he'd mostly respected that in the few days since. Her reprieve wouldn't last, and she could hardly blame him for that. They were about to be responsible for another *person*, and flying by the seat of her pants might have gotten her this far in life, but his regimented scheduling and research-based personality were probably better suited for parenting than hers was.

It seemed like *everyone* was better suited to be a parent than she was, and yet look how things had turned out.

As if summoned by her thoughts, her phone rang. Becka knew who it was even before her sister's name scrolled across the screen. Lucy had been calling every couple of days for the last month, and Becka could tell her excuses for not picking up were starting to wear thin.

She had to tell Lucy the truth sooner or later. Before she could talk herself out of it, she answered. "Hey, Lucy."

"Becka! I thought for sure I'd get your voicemail again."

"I know, I've been terrible. I'm sorry." Her treacherous hormones threatened to close her throat, thickening her voice.

Lucy picked up on it. Of course she did. She'd spent too long taking care of Becka not to read her easily. "What's going on? And don't tell me that it's nothing. We both know you don't disappear like this unless you're avoiding telling me something." She lowered her voice. "Is this because of Gideon? I thought you were okay with it—"

Oh no. She should have known that her sister would jump to *that* conclusion. "No. Hell no. I am legit happy for you. I promise." There was no getting out of the truth now. Becka took a deep breath. "I'm... I'm pregnant."

"*What?*" Lucy rushed on before she could respond—not that she had a response. "Becka, if this is your idea of a joke, it's not funny."

Her stomach dropped and she closed her eyes. Disbelief in her sister's tone, yes, but also disappointment. The very reaction she'd feared. "No one's joking. You're going to be an aunt in roughly six months."

"I... Wow..." Lucy cleared her throat. "Sorry, you just caught me by surprise. I didn't realize... No, but you would have told me if you were seeing someone."

Her sister didn't mean anything by it, but every word was a knife to Becka's heart. A confirmation of what she'd always known to be the truth. She was far more like her wayward mother than she'd ever been like her responsible older sister.

Lucy finally managed to get her reaction under control. "How are you doing? Are you okay?"

Even now, even when she was obviously caught off-guard and disappointed, she still managed to set it aside and worry about Becka. "I'm fine. He's a good guy." She wasn't willing to shock Lucy further by telling her the father was Aaron. "He's pushy and determined to research this thing to death and he's constantly on my ass about making me eat, but he wants to be in the baby's life."

"It sounds like you care about him."

She pushed to her feet, but there was nowhere to run with the phone against her ear. Becka bit down on her impulse to yell that it was a one night stand and she couldn't possibly care about him because she barely knew him. It wasn't the truth. Not anymore. She swallowed hard. "I don't know how I feel about anything anymore."

"Relationships aren't always like it was with them." No need for her to ask who Lucy meant. Their parents. "Gideon and I might argue sometimes, but he's my rock. It might be nice if you had someone to be your rock, too."

"Yeah. Maybe." She glanced at the faded digital clock over her oven. "Hey, Lucy, I've got to go if I'm going to make my next appointment. Talk to you later?"

"I'm here for you, Becka. No matter what. You know you can call me anytime, right? For anything."

"I know." Damn it, now she really was going to cry. "Love you."

"Love you, too."

She hung up and stared at her phone. That had gone... *Well* wasn't the right word. Even with Lucy offering unconditional support, she couldn't shake

the fact that her DNA had outed once and for all, realizing both their worst fears.

That Becka was just their mother 2.0.

She headed for her first personal training appointment for the day, and then there was no more
time for worrying about her worst fears coming
true. Time went too fast, and it felt like seconds
later that she was in the locker room and jumping
in the shower. She pulled on a sheath dress in a brilliant pink and orange pattern that hid her growing
baby bump and slipped into simple flats and a funky
cropped jacket. Becka pulled her hair back into a
deceptively simple braid and threw some mascara
and lipstick on.

Feeling like herself for the first time in a long
time, she hurried out of the locker room just as her
phone dinged. She smiled when she saw Aaron's
text. I'm out front.

Punctual as always.

She hefted her bag more firmly on her shoulder
and strode out the doors. *It will be okay. Just because
I'm off center and scared all over again doesn't mean
I am going to ruin tonight.*

I refuse *to ruin tonight.*

Aaron had his hands in his pockets and wore a
well-fitting black suit with a dove-gray button-down
underneath. His smile dimmed when he caught sight
of her bag. "Let me carry that."

"Honey, I can bench 150 and I have arms to rival

Michelle Obama. I got it." She caught herself and sighed. "But if you're going to turn into a human storm cloud, you can take it."

"Being chivalrous is not being a human storm cloud." He took the bag easily and offered her his free arm.

No point in arguing about the damn bag further. Truth be told, her back was bothering her a little, but she'd sew her lips shut before she admitted as much to Aaron. He'd probably load her into a cab and rush her to the hospital or something in response. "And here I thought chivalry was dead."

"A nasty rumor. Nothing more."

She fell into step beside him. "You know, you're funnier than I thought when we first met. At the wedding, it was all intensity and come-fuck-me eyes, and here you are, cracking sly jokes at the drop of a hat."

"I don't know how you remember the wedding, but you didn't leave much room for jokes." He slid his arm around her waist the same way he had on the walk to the taco truck. It pressed the entire sides of their bodies together and sparked desire through her in response. Aaron, damn him, knew it.

"I was in a bad way, and you had exactly what I needed." She hadn't meant to say it aloud, to offer up even that much information, but her earlier conversation with Lucy still had her off her game. The words saturated the air between them and there was no taking them back.

Aaron kept quiet for half a block. Finally, almost reluctantly, he said, "I imagine weddings aren't your favorite thing, let alone your sister's wedding."

"I'm happy for her." The response was so automatic, it almost felt real. He shot her a look and she cursed. "Okay, fine, I was sick to my stomach from the time she told me Gideon proposed until they got in that limo and drove away. Rationally, I know that not every marriage goes down in flames, but it's hard when my heart and brain get to battling. She was engaged to a douchebag before Gideon, and he did a number on her. I *know* Gideon would rather set himself on fire than do anything to hurt her, but that doesn't stop me from worrying. What if something happens to him? She'll never recover."

"There are no guarantees in life."

Becka rolled her eyes, even though her amusement had died a terrible death at the mention of her sister's wedding. But then, she'd been in a funk all day. "Thanks for that fortune cookie–pat answer. I know that. Of course I know that. But there are enough painful moments in life without inviting the bastard to kick you in the teeth at the first available opportunity. Even you have to admit that."

He pulled her closer without missing a step. "Life is hard. It's full of all the bad stuff, sure. But it's full of good stuff, too. The difference is that sometimes you have to take a leap of faith and grab onto the good stuff with both hands. Avoiding anything that might cause you pain down the road..." He hesitated. "That's no way to live, minx."

She wanted to believe him. She wanted to so badly, she could taste the need like on the back of her tongue. It would be the simplest thing in the world to let go, to step into Aaron and let go of all her fears.

To grab onto a possible future with them together with both hands and hold it close until it became reality.

The strength of the desire startled her. Terrified her. She opened her mouth to shut down this line of conversation, but couldn't make herself do it. "Yeah, you're probably right."

Aaron had to fight to put aside their conversation as they walked into the bar. It looked like millions of other bars across the city, from the faded wood tables to the blinking neon lights of various beer signs to the half a dozen televisions positioned strategically around the room. But the floors weren't sticky and the place smelled pleasantly of something he couldn't quite place.

Becka led the way to a table near the bar where trivia was being set up. She took a paper to fill out and sat down before he could pull out her chair. Aaron repressed a sigh and took the seat diagonal from her. He picked up the menu and flipped through it. Instead of the normal bar food he expected, it was all Asian fusion. "Huh."

"The sushi is great, and so is anything stir-fry." She spoke without looking up. "There are also wings on the last page."

Strange place. He eyed the paper she was filling out. "What's our team name?"

"Cunning Linguists."

He barked out a laugh. "Clever."

"I aim to please." She smiled at the waiter that walked up. "Can I get cranberry juice and a starter of the egg rolls?"

"Sure thing." He looked expectantly at Aaron. "And for you?"

What he really wanted was a beer, but he'd been serious about not drinking in front of her for the time being, so he ordered an iced tea. "And add the wontons to the starters." He'd seen Becka eat, and he had no illusions about getting any of those egg rolls for himself.

Becka waited for the man to leave the table before sitting back to pin Aaron with a look. "I'm surprised you didn't decide to educate me on how unhealthy egg rolls are, being fried and all."

He didn't bother to hide his grin. "I figure you might dump that glass of water over my head if I did."

"Smart man."

"I have my moments." He snagged the paper to look over the categories. "Plus, you're a personal trainer. You eat better than I do most of the time.

If you want egg rolls for a starter, you can have egg rolls."

"Wow. Thanks for permission."

Aaron growled. "Don't make this into a fight, minx."

"I'm not. You—" She snapped her mouth closed and looked a little sheepish. "I might be making it into a fight. Sorry. I'm a little on edge."

Whether it was hormones or their earlier conversation made no difference. He was smart enough not to agree with her. Instead Aaron pointed at the trivia paper. "Dungeons and Dragons is one of the categories."

"Is it?" She blinked deceptively innocent eyes at him. "Did I fail to mention this was an ultimate geek trivia night?"

"Must have slipped your mind," he muttered. He glanced over the categories again. The tech gadget one he had a chance at. He was relatively well versed in Harry Potter just by virtue of living in current times and having both internet and cable. The rest might as well have been Greek for all he had a chance of deciphering it. "You like this stuff?"

"I've been known to run a campaign or two." She caught his look and laughed. "I like playing against type. Besides, it's fun if you have a good group." Something like a shadow flickered over her face, and he didn't have to ask to know that there were times when she hadn't had a good group. Knowing what little he did of geek culture and how a portion of the population treated women, he could guess how that had fallen out. Before he could ask, Becka gave him a bright smile. "Stick with me, young padawan. I'll show you the ropes."

The woman running the game stood up and introduced herself, and then they were off to the races. Despite being the weak link for their duo in this realm, Aaron found himself drawn into Becka's enthusiasm and competitive spirit. She really *did* know a whole hell of a lot in this subset of trivia, and they ended up taking second place in the competition.

After paying for their tab, he slung an arm around her waist and they headed out. She brandished their second-place sticker. "Next time, we're going for gold. You just need to brush up on about ten years' worth of knowledge in a week."

"Consider it done."

She laughed. "You took being upstaged rather well, all things considered. Most guys would have bitched and stomped out of there when the elves questions came up."

"Just because I was outmatched doesn't mean I didn't enjoy myself." He pressed a casual kiss to the top of her head. "Besides, you're into it. I had fun."

"Me, too." She sounded almost surprised by that fact. "Aaron."

"Yeah?"

"I like you."

From the way she braced as if expecting a blow, the words had taken a lot of courage to say. He stepped out of foot traffic. Aaron turned her to face him and tipped her chin up so she couldn't hide from his gaze. "I like you, too."

She worried her bottom lip. "You're right, you know. We have to talk about the baby."

This change of tone should have spelled victory for him, but he found himself reluctant to push her. He kissed her forehead and then her lips. "We can talk when you're ready—really ready."

"What if I'm never ready?" She laughed softly. "Because at this point, I don't know what I'm doing, and even thinking about it is enough to have me borderline panicking."

"You're not alone, minx. You're not facing this by yourself. I'll be there every step of the way. Never doubt that."

She smiled against his mouth. "I don't."

He didn't believe her for a second, but Aaron let it go. He was making progress, and that was all that mattered. A week of fragile peace couldn't combat an entire lifetime of living a certain way. Becka might not trust him completely, but he'd do whatever it took to win both her trust and her willingness to be in his life.

If the last few days had done anything, they'd confirmed something for him.

He didn't just want to be in the baby's life.
He wanted to be in *Becka's*.
He wanted to be *with* Becka.

CHAPTER TWELVE

BECKA LOOKED UP as the door opened and Aaron walked in. He missed a step but recovered almost immediately. "I didn't realize you'd be home before me today."

"My last appointment canceled. He's got food poisoning." She flipped through the channels for the twelfth time in the last hour. Nothing held her attention, and she'd already circled through the kitchen to stare blankly into the fridge four times before shutting it and returning to the couch. Becka didn't do well with a lack of activity, and today was no exception. She had energy to burn off and she didn't know what to do with herself. She sat up and eyed Aaron. "You in a hurry?"

He shrugged out of his jacket and hung it in the closet just inside the door. "I have some work I brought home, but it just needs to be done sometime tonight. Why? You have something in mind?"

"I do." She bounced off the couch and came

around to press a quick kiss to his lips. "Let's take a spin class."

Aaron stopped short. "That did not go where I was expecting."

"You thought I meant sex." She laughed and started down the hall. "We can bang it out later. Riding your cock is great cardio, but I didn't have a spin class today and I'm going to drive us both crazy if I don't do something about it." She pulled out her phone and paged through the app she had that gave her all the nearby gyms' schedules. It didn't take long to find one that would fit the bill.

Becka turned, but Aaron hadn't moved from his spot by the door. She stopped short and cursed herself for being an idiot. It took effort to keep her shoulders square and the disappointment from her voice. "You don't have to go, Aaron. It's okay. I just got excited."

He gave himself a shake. "No, I want to. You surprised me is all." He crossed the distance between them in two large steps and kissed her hard enough that her back hit the wall. When he finally raised his head, both their breathing had turned harsh. Aaron smiled. "I've been curious about your particular brand of spin since Roman told me about it a while back." He paused. "I'm happy you're sharing this with me, minx."

He made it sound like a much bigger deal than it should be but…

No, that wasn't fair. It *was* a big deal. She'd made plans for both of them without stopping to think about it, and she'd been disappointed when she thought he didn't want to go. Little by little, Aaron had eased into her life until she *wanted* to share parts of herself with him. Her classes and her personal training were two things important to her that she never shared with the guys she dated. She'd never *wanted* to share them.

Since she didn't know what to say to any of it, she gave him a half smile and ducked into her room to change. Fifteen minutes later, they were on their way. The gym was a trendy little boutique workout place that offered a small selection of classes, similar to Transcend, but they were open to both men and women. Becka had never been to this branch before, but she'd attended a few classes at one of the locations closer to her apartment.

After they got checked in and put on their spin shoes, she shot Aaron a look. "Uh… I know you work out, but have you ever taken spin before?" *Probably should have asked that before springing this on him.*

"Yeah, though not for a while. I prefer lifting weights and the elliptical."

She made a face before she caught herself. "Just, ah…" She put an extra dose of brightness into her tone. "It'll be fun!"

"What did you sign me up for?"

Instead of answering, she headed into the room and chose a bike in the middle row, slightly off to the side. Aaron took the one next to her and adjusted his seat without hesitating. Maybe it wouldn't be *that* bad.

As the class started, she lost herself to the bumping beat of the music and the rhythmic pedaling. The instructor didn't have as many bike pushups in his routine as Becka did, which was just as well, but he had a few fun moves she made a mental note to incorporate at some point in the future.

The hour passed in the blink of an eye, and she belatedly remembered to check on Aaron as the slow song that signaled time to stretch came on. He was just as soaked in sweat as she was, and the look he gave her when she turned to him singed her right down to her core. Becka froze. "Uh, so that was fun."

"Fun." He didn't sound totally out of breath, but he shook his head and unlocked his shoes from his bike. "I don't think that word means what you think it means."

She burst out laughing, drawing looks from the people around them. Well, at least the class was over. Becka followed him out of the room, her gaze lingering on the way his sweaty shirt clung to this muscled back. She knew working out was an aphrodisiac, of course, but she'd never done it *with* someone before. Not like this.

Suddenly, all those couples' workout videos on the internet made sense.

She grabbed Aaron's arm and towed him around the corner and down the hall, searching the signs on the doors. There were a handful of gender-neutral bathrooms and… *There.* If this gym was anything like hers, no one actually used the showers. Even if they did, there were two. She shoved Aaron into the room, cast a quick look behind them to make sure no one was paying attention and stepped in and closed the door behind her.

He was on her the second she locked the door. Aaron grabbed her hips hard enough that she had to catch herself on the door and shoved her shorts down her legs. Half a second later, his cock was there, filling her in one rough move. Her fingers scrambled over the smooth wood of the door, trying to find purchase. "Oh God."

"This is what you wanted." He pulled out for a second, looped an arm around her waist and carried her to the sink. She braced her hands on the porcelain and met his gaze in the mirror. He smoothed a hand up her back. "This is what you wanted," Aaron repeated. This time it sounded more like a question.

"Yes." He sank into her again, and she shoved back against him, taking his cock deeper yet. "Hard. Fast. Now."

He gripped her shoulder with one hand and her hip with the other and drove into her. Hard. Fast. Exactly what she needed. His expression was like a man possessed, just as out of control as Becka felt. It had never been like this, desperation clawing through her to get closer, to have more of him touching more of her. He must have felt it, too, because Aaron withdrew and lifted her onto the sink. He yanked her shorts the rest of the way off and spread her thighs wide. "Hang on to me."

She was already moving, hooking the back of his neck and dragging him down to claim his mouth as he started fucking her again. The new angle hit that sensitive spot inside her with every stroke, winding her tighter and tighter until she came with a muffled cry. He followed her seconds later, grinding hard into her as he orgasmed.

Aaron laughed softly. "I think I can get onboard with this spin thing."

"Yeah… Me, too." She shivered as his cock twitched inside her. "But we can never come back to this gym again—ever." She wasn't shy, but they'd just crossed a line, and she wasn't going to be able to look anyone in the face as they left.

"You hungry?" He pumped slightly, drawing a gasp from her lips.

She blinked. "Is that a euphemism?"

"I know a place that makes some mean peanut butter and jelly wings." He was still moving inside her, little thrusts that had her body going molten all over again. "We could pick up takeout and go home to enjoy them properly."

Becka moaned and shoved him away. "Stop that or we're going to keep fucking in this bathroom until someone comes banging on the door."

"Doesn't sound so bad." His gaze dropped to her pussy. "You're looking needy, minx. I've got just the thing."

The man went from talking about takeout to looking like he wouldn't mind giving her enough orgasms to bring down the rage of the entire staff of this gym on them. She hopped off the sink and pulled her shorts back on. "If you wanted to keep playing with me, you shouldn't have mentioned peanut butter and jelly wings."

Aaron kissed her and cupped her pussy through the thin fabric of her shorts. He circled her clit with his thumb. "I'm going to take care of you tonight." He slipped his hand into her shorts and fingered her. "Fuck, Becka, I'd think they pumped something into the air of that room if I didn't know it was all you. You make me so goddamn crazy for you." He kissed her again. "Come for me, minx. One more time to tide me over until after dinner."

Oh God. She spread her legs to give him better access even though she knew they were running out of time before someone came knocking on the door. Maybe it was that lack of time that made this whole thing hotter. It didn't matter. All that mattered was

Aaron's growl in her ear and his fingers working her pussy. He pushed two fingers into her and went back to circling her clit with his thumb. She was already on a hair trigger from coming earlier, and when he bit her neck lightly, it threw her headlong into another orgasm. He brought her down so sweetly, kissing her as he gentled his touch and finally slipped his hand out of her shorts.

Aaron readjusted her clothing and washed his hands. He pressed a quick kiss to her lips. "Let's get you those wings."

"Yeah," Becka said, more than a little dazed. "Can't forget about the wings."

"Come here." Aaron reached out to pull Becka back beneath the spray of the dual showerheads he had set up in his bathroom. They'd made it back to his penthouse in record time—with a quick stop at the wing place on the way to pick up their food—and he'd dragged her into the shower with him nearly the second they walked through the door.

She smacked his hand and bared her teeth in what was almost a grin. "Food, Livingston. Not only did we do spin class and then walk home, but you blew my mind seven ways to Sunday in the bathroom earlier. I need calories and, before you say anything, *not* the kind of calories that come from your cock." She paused in the gap leading out of the walk-in shower and surveyed him. "Though it's a mighty fine cock and I plan to use and abuse it later."

He barked out a laugh. "Noted. Go get started on your calories. I'm right behind you."

"Better enjoy the view then." She gave a little shake of her ass and hell if he didn't enjoy the view before she wrapped a towel around herself and walked out of the bathroom.

He wasted no time finishing scrubbing down and followed suit. He found her in the living room, setting up the wings on the coffee table. Aaron ducked into the kitchen to grab them glasses of water and an extra glass of cranberry juice for her, and then he joined her on the couch.

It was only then that he noticed what she was wearing.

Becka sat cross-legged, her petite body swallowed up by one of his college T-shirts. The thing was so old, it was one of the softest he owned, and the image on the front had faded away to almost nothing. Rationally, he understood why she gravitated to the shirt, but his gut said it marked her as *his*. That she was settling in for the long haul and this was a fucking relationship, not two people who happened to live together and would have a baby together in the relatively near future.

Whether her choice in clothing said that to her was another story.

She tasted the jalapeño jelly dip and made a little

moaning sound. "Oh, damn. This was such a good call."

"Glad it's hitting the spot." To keep himself from staring at her as she ate, he grabbed the remote and flicked through the channels until he landed on something that halfway caught his interest. It was an old movie, and he instantly recognized the blonde waltzing her way across the screen.

Becka obviously did, too, because she nodded. *"Gentlemen Prefer Blondes.* Good choice."

Even if he hadn't planned on keeping it there, he would have set the remote down at her interest. "I take it you like it?"

"What's not to like? Lady friendships, a smoking-hot private investigator and some killer songs thrown in for spice." She cut one of the peanut butter wings in two and dipped it into the jelly. "It's a classic, and I used to say I was Dorothy to Allie's Lorelei." She made a face. "Minus all the gold-digging stuff. That sort of thing leads to nothing but trouble."

Aaron draped his arm over the back of the couch. "You like old movies, play D&D and are a jock in your own right." He grinned. "You like to keep people guessing."

"Maybe people." She sipped her drink. "Maybe just you. Most people try to slap a label on me the second they meet me, but they never bother to dig deeper. Their loss, I guess. *My* people get me, and they don't expect me to change so they can shove me into a neat little box." She shrugged.

He should keep his damn mouth shut, but Aaron was sick of fucking around. He wanted Becka—in his bed and in his life permanently. Even if he slow-played this thing into the ground, he couldn't sit on his hands indefinitely. It wasn't fair to either of them. "I could be one of your people if you'll let me get close enough, minx."

"I know." She sighed. "Look, this is weird for me, too. I like you. It freaks me out, which is normally the part where I ghost whatever dude I'm seeing, but that's obviously not an option in our case, because where the hell am I going to run when I have to come track you down in about six months?"

"You want this to stop because it's not doing it for you, that's one thing." He watched her closely, took in the tension in her shoulders and the way she stared pointedly at her food. *Too damn bad, Becka. This is going to get said.* "But to try to run from me because you care too much? Fuck that."

"Try?"

"You heard me. I care about your contrary ass, and you care about me right back. I'm not pushing you right now, but if you bolt, I'm going to track your ass down and have a conversation like adults."

She finally twisted to face him, blue eyes flashing. "You call this not pushing?"

"That's exactly what I call this." He clenched his

jaw and worked to modulate his tone. "We have time. You need more, then you have it. But I'm not going anywhere. I'm not your commitment-phobic dad and you're sure as fuck not your flighty-ass mom. Stop using them as an excuse to keep me from getting close to you."

"You were pretty damn close to me an hour ago."

His body flashed hot at the memory, but he wasn't about to let her distract him with sex right now. "Admit that you care about me."

She threw up her hands. "Fine, asshole. I admit it. I care about you, and that scares the shit out of me in a way I'm not prepared to deal with."

"Was that so hard?"

"Yes!" She turned back to face the TV and crossed her arms over her chest.

"It spooks me, too, minx." He pressed a soft kiss to her temple. "You're not alone. Remember that when the panic gets too bad."

"I'm trying," she whispered.

CHAPTER THIRTEEN

BECKA DIDN'T MEAN to fall asleep. But the wings filling her belly and Aaron's warm thigh under her head combined with the throw blanket he'd tucked around her as they watched the movie was too compelling to resist. Her blinks became longer and longer, and when Aaron started absently running his fingers through her hair, she was lost.

Or maybe she'd been found.

She didn't know. The only thing she was sure of was that at some point, Aaron carried her into his bedroom and tucked them both into bed. He curled his body around the back of hers, as if he could shield her from the worst the world had to offer by his sheer presence alone.

Becka wasn't thinking about comfort, though. Not with her wearing only his shirt and his cock pressed against her ass. She shifted back, rubbing against him, and was rewarded by his hand spasming on her stomach. He pulled her closer, snuggling against her, and inched the shirt up, baring her from the waist down. They moved slowly, as if he was as hesitant as she to break the strange half awake, half asleep sensation of their movements.

She reached behind her and gripped the back of his neck as he pressed an openmouthed kiss to the top of her spine. Instead of touching her where she ached for him, Aaron shifted, bringing one arm under her and cupping her breasts with both hands. He squeezed gently and then pulsed his hands, creating the smallest amount of friction between his palms and her nipples. She responded by rolling her hips harder against him.

She took one of his wrists and guided his hand between her thighs. He cupped her pussy as if assuring himself that she was wet and wanting and *his*. Aaron touched her in a way she'd never experienced before. It wasn't just a touch with him.

It was a claiming.

He idly dipped a single finger into her and spread her wetness up and over her clit. The gentle sensation only heightened her desire, but she didn't want to break the spell. Not yet. She released his neck to reach back and dip her hand into his boxer briefs to stroke his cock.

"You're supposed to be asleep," he growled against her neck.

She grinned into the darkness of the room. *He*

broke first. "I am asleep." She gave his cock another pump. "So, so asleep."

"Don't think your story checks out, minx."

"You caught me." She twisted in his arms to face him and hitched her leg over his hip. A quick move shoved his boxer briefs below his hips, and she guided his cock into her. "I'm awake."

"Now the truth comes out." He rolled onto his back, taking her with him.

Instead of breaking the heightened intensity, being face-to-face with Aaron only made the whole encounter sexier. Becka kissed him as she moved over him slowly. Leisurely. Each stroke strengthened the feeling of being in a dream where nothing could touch them. Desire took hold, and she straightened to get a better angle, chasing her own pleasure.

"Ah, ah. Not yet, minx." He lifted her off his cock and up to straddle his head.

She grabbed the headboard to hold steady. Between her thighs, his face was bathed in shadows. He could have been anyone… But, no. The thought fled as soon as it rose, chased away by the slow glide of his tongue over her pussy. This was Aaron.

It will always be Aaron.

He licked and sucked at her, using his hands on her thighs to urge her to ride his mouth. Becka let the last of her worries dissolve beneath his touch. She closed her eyes and gave herself over to the pleasure building with every deep exhale that ghosted against the most private part of her.

Her orgasm rolled over her slowly, dragging her deeper than she'd ever gone before. She shuddered and slumped against the headboard, blinking into the darkness. *Ruinous. That's what Aaron Livingston is. Fucking ruinous.* She couldn't bring herself to care.

He pulled her down to spoon again and hitched her leg over his thigh so he could guide his cock into her. He stroked her clit with each slow thrust, murmuring in her ear the entire time. "I can't get enough of you, minx. I could live for another sixty years and I'd still never get enough of you." His breath hitched against her ear. "Let me keep you, Becka. Let me keep both of you."

She opened her mouth to say… She wasn't sure what. But he ground hard against her and circled her clit once, twice, a third time, and the only thing she verbalized was a breathless shriek as she came again.

Aaron flipped her onto her stomach and lifted her hips to drive into her. He moved like a man possessed, the dreamlike feeling of their encounter up to this point fading away in the feel of his cock filling her completely as he chased his own pleasure.

As he marked her as his own.

The next month passed in a blur of peaceful contentedness. Aaron came home every day to Becka. She shared his bed and gave him precious tidbits about herself and her past as they settled into what could be their life together. But she still held back part of herself, and the closer they got, the more that denied bit made him crazy. He'd promised her time, though. He'd honor it, damn it.

She met him at the door one night, looking nervous. She wore a pair of brightly colored leggings and one of the slouchy shirts she'd become fond of since moving in with him, and she was all but wringing her hands.

Aaron dropped his briefcase and carefully shut the door. "Is everything okay? Is it the baby?"

"What?" She shook her head and gave a rueful smile. "Sorry, I shouldn't have ambushed you at the door with this. I, ah…" She stared hard at the wood floor beneath their feet. "I have a doctor's appointment tomorrow. I meant to mention it to you last week, but you kind of distracted me with ice cream and that thing you do with your tongue."

Despite her obvious nerves, he grinned. "I seem to remember you liking that thing I do with my tongue."

"I do." She twisted a lock of blue hair around her finger. "I know it's last minute and I completely understand if you can't come. It's at one at a clinic close to my apartment."

He stepped closer and framed her face with his hands, guiding her to meet his gaze. "Of course I'll be there. I have a meeting, but I can reschedule. One of the perks of being the boss." She looked so unsure that he smoothed his thumbs over her cheekbones. "Unless you don't want me to go?" Aaron wanted to be in that room with her more than anything, especially since he'd missed her appointment last month. He'd only known about it because Becka mentioned it in passing, giving him a rundown as if it hadn't occurred to her to bring him and his presence there was no big deal.

It had stung. Fuck yes, it'd stung.

But ultimately having him there was her choice. If he'd learned anything in his time with Becka, it was that he couldn't badger his way into *anything* when it came to her. She'd just dig in her heels and set her jaw in that way that would be adorable if it didn't signal the start of a knock-down, drag-out fight.

She pressed her lips together. "I'd like you to be there. It just feels like a big step."

He laughed. He couldn't help it. "I hate to be the one to break it to you, minx, but having a baby is about as big a step as two people can take. We're already there."

"Correction—we'll be there in just over five months."

He bit back a sharp response to that. Her insistence at holding off talking about anything resembling the future was the one black spot on their time together. "I'll be at the appointment. Do you want me to pick you up or meet you there?"

"Might as well meet me there." She huffed out a breath. "This is silly, right? I shouldn't be so stressed out over a doctor's appointment."

It *was* a big deal. This would be the appointment with the ultrasound, the halfway point through the pregnancy. It was also the appointment when they'd get a good idea if the baby was progressing as it should—or if there were glaring problems.

Aaron pulled her into his arms and hugged her tightly. "No matter what happens, I'm there." Maybe if he said it enough times, she'd actually start to believe him. Maybe. He didn't know what the right words were. Hell, he didn't seem to *have* right words when it came to Becka. He wasn't walking on eggshells, but he was aware that one wrong step might fracture the careful peace they'd formed around themselves.

Not for the first time, it registered that things couldn't last as they stood now.

But as he looked down into her worried expression, he couldn't bring himself to pull the trigger. Not yet. Tomorrow after the doctor's appointment would be more than soon enough. They could have tonight. The real world—the future—had waited this long. It could wait another eighteen hours or so.

Aaron smoothed back her hair. "Are you hungry?"

She gave him a half smile. "Is that a trick question?"

If the baby books he'd read had taught him anything, it was that every pregnancy was different. Becka didn't seem to be suffering many of the ill effects that often showed up, but her appetite was unrelenting. It amused him even as he worried that she wasn't getting enough. With her job, she burned a significant number of calories every day, and even with her near-constant snacking and meals, it was possible she was in deficit.

He took her hand and led her into the kitchen. "Protein, veggie, carb."

"Chicken, spinach, rice." She didn't miss a beat. "Preferably with some kind of cheese on top."

Aaron laughed and dug through his fridge to find the chicken and spinach and then pulled a bag of rice from the pantry. He loved these moments with Becka. She dictated dinner, and he put it together while she sipped what had become her customary cranberry juice and they chatted about their respective days.

This is what it could be.

This is what it should *be.*

She propped her chin in her hands and watched him. "I think I have a solution to your Cameron problem. I mean, at least in theory it's a good option."

He covered the chicken breasts in wax paper and pounded them with a meat tenderizer to flatten them. "At this point, I'm about to start praying to some ancient god for patience." They'd managed to hire a secretary...and the guy lasted exactly forty-eight hours before he quit in a huff after a snarling conversation with Cameron about their differing methods of filing.

"He's the best damn security-tech expert in the country, but he is just as good at alienating people. It was never an issue when we were a different kind of company, but our workload grew and our clients changed—and Cameron didn't." It wasn't that he expected his friend to change. Cameron was Cameron, and that was one of the things Aaron had always liked about him. But something had to give, and it had to happen fast. He hadn't talked to Becka about it yet, but he fully intended to take some time off after she had the baby so he could be there to help.

So she wouldn't be alone.

So he could spend time with his new baby.

The only way he'd be able to pull that off, though, was to find the time to hire someone to handle the client-facing aspect of the company so Cameron wouldn't drive off every client they had with his inability to tolerate corporate bullshit while he was gone. He was belatedly realizing that a secretary wouldn't cut it. He needed someone with a wider skill set.

Becka laughed. "I don't think that will be necessary. Didn't you say that your little sister was looking for a job? That she was tired of living with your very wonderful parents?"

He *had* mentioned Trish more than few times over the last month. His little sister had been badgering him to let her come visit. He'd eventually told her about Becka and the pregnancy, and Trish had been asking to come check out the future mother of his child. Aaron had barely held her off. He fully expected to turn around one day in the near future and find her at his front doorstep with her sunny smile and determination.

Aaron moved to the stove and started the rice. "Trish's degree is in sales."

"Yes, you mentioned that. Three times." She smiled. "That skill set would be really useful if you want to ease back from dealing directly with clients on the level you do right now."

She had a point.

He transferred the chicken back to the pan and started lining up the cheese and spinach to fill the chicken breasts with. "It could work. Though Trish is the sweetest person I know, she's pretty damn determined. If she set out to carve a place for herself within the company, not even Cameron's surliness would be enough to stop her." He grinned. "I might actually pay to sit in on that first meeting."

"See!" Becka spread her hands and wiggled her fingers. "I'm brilliant."

"You are." He leaned over the island and pressed a quick kiss to her lips. Gratitude and happiness welled up inside him, a bolt straight to the heart with that single casual contact. Aaron rocked back on his heels as the truth settled inside him.

I love her.

He had for a while, if he was going to be honest with himself. He stared at the chicken in front of him, keeping his jaw clenched to prevent the words from escaping. If there was one thing he was sure of, it was Becka's reaction if he dropped that truth on her. She cared for him—she wouldn't act the way she did otherwise—but her fear of retreading her parents' footsteps made her so gun-shy, one wrong word was enough to close her off from him for days.

If he dropped *this* bombshell?

He might lose her forever.

Aaron cleared his throat. *Just because I love her doesn't mean I have to tell her. Not yet.* "I'll talk to Cameron tomorrow before the doctor's appointment, and call Trish after. Though we'll have to get her set up in a place, otherwise she'll move in here and take over the spare bedroom."

"My room." She rolled her eyes at his look. "Okay, fine. I haven't slept in that room in a month, so I guess it's not technically my room for the time being."

For the time being.

She kept putting qualifiers on what they were. She couldn't seem to help herself.

He set aside his frustration just like he had every other time and focused on finishing dinner. Becka was in his life and in his bed—for now. He'd do whatever it took to keep her there and ensure she didn't let the past poison the possibility of their future together.

Unfortunately, that was easier said than done.

CHAPTER FOURTEEN

BECKA COULDN'T STOP pacing as they waited for the doctor to arrive. It had been bad enough during the last appointment, sitting by herself in the consulting room with the knowledge like a rock in her gut that everything had changed and there was no going back. That was before her body had started actually showing changes. Now her stomach had a definite curve and she could actually feel the baby move regularly.

This was real.

It was happening.

She should sit down. Should be able to handle this despite feeling like she was one sharp move away from coming out of her skin. She couldn't. Nerves kept her moving despite Aaron's increasing stillness. He'd stopped watching her several minutes ago and had taken up staring at the door as if he could summon the doctor faster through sheer willpower. Knowing Aaron, it was entirely possible.

She was fucking this up, but she couldn't stop. The future sat like a weight around her neck, threatening to take her to her knees. She might be able to forget the circumstances that had brought her and Aaron back together when they were going about their lives. Playing house. There was no forgetting in that clinic room. The truth was in every diagram on the walls and the table with its thin paper laid over it. It was in the sterile hospital smell that even places like this held. It was even in the quiet murmur she could hear from beyond the walls on either side of them and in the hall as nurses led other patients through the warren of rooms.

I'm having a baby.

I'm having a baby with Aaron.

A knock on the door brought her up short. Dr. Richardson, a short Filipina lady who'd been Becka's gynecologist since she was sixteen, poked her head in and smiled warmly. "Becka, it's good to see you again." She stepped into the room and closed the door softly behind her before turning and extending a hand to Aaron. "Dr. Richardson."

"Aaron Livingston." He gave what appeared to be a firm handshake and sat back.

The doctor motioned to the table. "Shall we?"

Becka sat on the table and suffered through having her vitals taken while Dr. Richardson asked her the normal questions. No, she had no concerns. Yes, she was taking her prenatal vitamin. Yes, she was getting enough sleep. No, no weird cravings for non-food items. Unsurprisingly, her blood pressure was significantly higher than normal.

Next, she lay back as her doctor measured her uterus and felt around. Becka stared at the ceiling, just wanting the whole thing to be over. *Until next month when I have to come in again.* She held her breath as Dr. Richardson brought out the machine to listen to the baby's heartbeat.

This was it. The moment when there was no denying how real this whole fucked-up situation was.

But as the seconds ticked by, Dr. Richardson's dark brows drew together. "Your little one is being difficult today."

"Is that normal?" Aaron hadn't moved from his chair, but his question sliced through the air and made Becka wince.

The doctor gave a reassuring smile. "The baby can be in certain positions that make finding the heartbeat challenging, but we'll do an ultrasound just in case."

In case the baby's heart isn't beating.

Becka's breath hitched in her lungs, and she couldn't seem to find the strength to exhale. She blinked blindly at the ceiling as her doctor wiped the slimy shit off her stomach and helped her sit up. Dr. Richardson squeezed her hand. "Don't panic, Becka. I'm sure everything's fine."

The world snapped back into focus, and she

wheezed out a breath. She latched onto the doctor's hand. "I need my baby to be okay."

"I know. Just give me a few minutes to see when we can slot you in for the ultrasound." She slipped out of the room, leaving Becka staring after her.

She turned to Aaron. "I need our baby to be okay," she repeated.

Instantly, he was on his feet and before her. He pulled her into his arms and hugged her tightly. "Like she said—listening to the heartbeat with that machine is an imperfect system. The ultrasound will tell us more."

But there was no guarantee that it would deliver good news.

She buried her face in Aaron's chest and listened to the beat of his heart. Too fast, a perfect match to her own. "I didn't think I wanted this baby. I mean, obviously I did because I kept it, but I didn't *really* want it. I wasn't excited. I was just dealing with it and pretending I wasn't pregnant because I don't know what I'm doing." She fisted her hands in Aaron's shirt. "I want this baby. I want *our* baby."

"I know." He smoothed a hand over her hair and down her back. Over and over again. "I know. I want our baby, too."

She didn't know how long they sat like that, her trying and failing not to cry, him whispering words that ceased to have meaning as he rubbed her back.

A knock on the door signaled Dr. Richardson's

return. Her expression was perfectly placid as she took them in. "There was a last-minute cancellation, so we can get you in right now, if that will work?"

"It does," Aaron answered for her, which was fine by her.

The doctor nodded. "This way." She led them deeper into the clinic, to a darkened room where she introduced them to the ultrasound tech. Dr. Richardson hesitated. "The nurse will bring you back to a room once you're finished and then we'll go over the results."

Because the technician wasn't allowed to tell them anything.

Becka managed a nod.

And then it began again. The cold lube stuff on her lower stomach. The wand pressing into her sensitive skin.

She couldn't bring herself to look at the static-filled screen for more than a few seconds, for fear of what she might see. Instead, she turned to Aaron. He held her hand, his gaze glued to the screen as if he had suddenly acquired the knowledge to decipher it. Hell, knowing the man, it was possible he'd found and read a book about ultrasounds along with every other aspect of pregnancy he'd researched.

The ultrasound tech clicked things on her computer and typed in other things, but she didn't say a word until she removed the wand and handed Becka a handful of tissues. The woman gave a soft smile.

"You don't have to be worried." Her smile became less tentative. "Do you want to know if you're having a boy or a girl?"

How could you ask me that if I don't know if my baby is okay?

Aaron squeezed her hand, grounding her. "It's up to you, Becka."

She swallowed hard. "I'd like to know."

The nurse's smile widened. "You have a beautiful baby girl."

Even as joy suffused her, an insidious little voice in the back of her mind murmured, *A little girl. You really* are *repeating history, aren't you?*

Aaron kept a grip on Becka's hand as much for his benefit as for hers. *A little girl. Is she okay?* The nurse led them back to the room, and they spent ten agonizing minutes waiting for the doctor to return. Becka didn't say anything, so he kept his silence. There would be plenty of time to talk once they had the verdict.

Rationally, he knew from his reading that people lost babies all the time. Miscarriages were significantly more common than Aaron could have imagined, and there were a number of factors that went into them—but the overwhelming consensus was that it was rarely the mother's fault.

Becka would blame herself, though. He saw that truth written across her face.

Dr. Richardson arrived and closed the door behind her. She gave them both a bright smile. "Good news. The baby is perfectly fine and measuring right on track for where she should be. The mischievous little one just decided to be difficult earlier." She walked over and patted Becka's knee. "You're doing wonderfully. Just keep it up and let me know if anything changes or if you have any concerns."

"Thanks, Doc." Becka's smile didn't quite banish the worried expression in her eyes.

After assuring her that they had no further questions, the appointment ended and Aaron trailed behind Becka as she strode out of the clinic. The baby might be fine, but the adrenaline still coursed through his system. So many things had raced through his mind as they waited through the ultrasound, but chief among them was the knowledge that if they lost the baby, he'd lose Becka in the process. There was nothing tying her to him. She'd only contacted him again because she was pregnant. If that hadn't happened, she would have moved on with her life and left him to do the same.

Without the baby in the picture, no doubt she'd do exactly that again.

There would be no more shared meals. No more nights spent wrapped up in each other. No more of her lively presence brightening up his home and his life.

He'd lose her—for good this time.

Aaron drove them back to his building and cupped her elbow as they took the elevator up. But as soon as he shut the front door behind him, he couldn't keep the words inside any longer. "Marry me."

Becka spun around and would have tripped if he hadn't caught her. She shook her head. "I'm sorry. I thought you just said 'marry me,' but there's no way you actually said that, because that would be *crazy*."

"As crazy as moving you in here and realizing we'd actually be good together." The brakes that had kept him quiet up to this point were long gone, and the sheer horror on her face only spurred him to keep talking. He'd only get one chance to convince her of this. Aaron clasped her shoulders. "Becka, I love you. I think if you weren't so scared, you could admit that you love me, too. And today more than proved that we both already love this baby. We're not your parents. We're not going to make those same mistakes, no matter what you think. Trust me."

"Trust you." A laugh burst from her that edged toward hysterical. "How can I trust you when you just turned around and did everything you promised you wouldn't? You *promised* to give me time."

Frustration ignited into fury. "I have given you time. I've respected your childish desire to hide under the covers and ignore what's happening instead of planning accordingly and facing it. I've sat back and watched you play pretend for six fucking weeks, Becka. That ends now."

"I see." She nodded and stepped back, out of his reach. "I wasn't the only one playing pretend, though, was I? You had this idea of what the future was supposed to look like, and you've systematically ignored any piece of evidence that doesn't line up with that plan. I'm not some perfect little wifey who's going to fall into line just because you will it to happen. I'm only me, Aaron. I've only ever been me. And you've been asking too much from the very beginning."

The floor seemed to tilt beneath his feet, but he was too angry to care. This was the truth he hadn't wanted to face, the thread running through her that he didn't have the words to combat. Even if he had, Becka possessed a singular ability to tune out anything that didn't fit with her worldview. Just like she was doing right goddamn now.

He crossed his arms over his chest and strove to keep his tone even and not yell at her. If he could just get her to *listen*, they could talk their way through this. "I'd rather shoot for the stars than be content to live in the dirt just because I'm too afraid of repeating my parents' mistake. The last month has more than proven that you're not like them—like her. Why can everyone see that but you?"

Her blue eyes flashed. "Really? I'm the one who's letting my parents' lives get in the way of reality? Because your happy home that you grew up in has given you a wicked case of rose-tinted glasses. Wake up. Life isn't like that for most people. More than half the people who get married turn around and get divorced again within seven years. *That* is a fact you can hang your hat on—not this fantasy future you've created in your head. You and I?" She motioned between them. "We would never work. Not outside this fucked-up situation, and sure as hell not in a marriage." Becka shook her head. "I should leave."

He'd fought so fucking hard to make her see, and he might as well have been yelling into a hurricane. Both actions accomplished a grand total of jack shit. She had her reality, and she fought tooth and nail to stay there. Aaron knew a thing or two about fear, but he'd always faced that emotion down until he conquered it. It was the only way forward. Her flat-out refusal to even try…

It's over.

"No need for you to leave. I will." He turned for the door but paused. "It doesn't have to be like this, Becka. All you have to do is take a leap with me and trust in us." Aaron found himself holding his breath as he waited for her answer.

But she only shook her head again, her eyes shining. "We won't fly, Aaron. The free fall might feel like it for a little while, but the landing will ruin us both."

He searched for something more to say, but in the end it wouldn't change anything. "I'll be at the next appointment."

She hesitated like she wanted to tell him to fuck

off but finally gave a short nod. "Wouldn't expect anything different."

This was it. It was really over.

Aaron turned without another word and walked out of the penthouse.

Becka barely had the energy to walk down the hallway to collapse on her bed. She buried her face in her cold pillow, hating that it wasn't the one on Aaron's bed that smelled like him, and hating herself even more for wanting that in the first place. She screamed into the offending pillow, but it didn't make her feel the least bit better.

Why would it?

Aaron had left.

Not only left—left because *she'd* freaked out on him and kept yelling until he couldn't stand to be in the same space as her. Just like her parents.

No, that wasn't fair…

But Becka didn't feel much like being fair right then. He threw that marriage proposal—if someone could even call it that—at her like it was the most logical step to take. And when she—understandably—freaked out, he cut and ran.

He *left* her.

She rolled onto her back and stared at the white ceiling. "Okay. Okay, he left. Which is a shitty way to end an argument. But this is Aaron we're talking about. Maybe he just needs to walk it off a little bit and then he'll be back here with some kind of plan and we'll figure this out in a way that doesn't involve a shotgun wedding." She took a shuddering breath. "And then I will put my issues on hold and *talk* to him instead of freaking out." Not an easy task by any means, but she could make an effort. She *would* make an effort.

She might not be ready to marry him, but she *did* care about him and she didn't want to be *without* him. Becka scrubbed a hand over her face. Trust their first real fight to be one for the record books. She rolled over to get more comfortable and stared at the clock. An hour—two, tops—and he'd be back there. She just had to smother her instinct to flee the penthouse until then. She curled her legs and hugged the second pillow on the bed.

Just a little longer…

CHAPTER FIFTEEN

TWENTY-FOUR HOURS LATER, Becka ran out of excuses. Aaron hadn't come home last night, and though she'd called in to both her jobs because she wanted to be here when he *did* come back…he didn't. She checked her phone, but her single text had gone unanswered.

He left me.

No, stop that. Maybe something happened. This is Aaron. *He wouldn't have just left. Not like that.*

She scrolled through her contacts to find the one Aaron had given her when she'd first moved in. There might be times when she needed to get ahold of him and wasn't able to, and so he wanted her to have Cameron's number. She held her breath as she pressed dial.

An unfamiliar voice answered almost immediately. "Cameron O'Clery."

"Hi, Cameron. This is Becka. I'm, ah, Aaron's… Whatever. I was wondering if you've seen him?"

Please say he's okay. I wouldn't be able to stand it if something happened to him.

"Yeah, he's in his office right now."

She stared at the wall, her breath leaving her in a whoosh. It had been bad to think that Aaron might be hurt in some hospital in the city and unable to contact her. Knowing that he was fine, that he'd *chosen* not to call her or come home…

It was worse. So much worse.

"Thank you," she said through numb lips and hung up.

Becka looked around the room that had ceased to be hers the second she'd ended up in Aaron's bed a month ago. She'd built this fiction around the idea that Aaron was different from her father—that being with him was different from every relationship her mother had ever been in. From every relationship *Becka* had been in. She'd believed him when he said they were in this together, when he claimed she wasn't alone. That declaration had only lasted as long as their honeymoon period had. The second things got rough—and they *had* gotten rough—he'd bailed.

He *left*.

She shoved to her feet and rushed to the closet. He wanted in the baby's life? Fine. She might feel like he'd ripped her heart out of her chest and thrown it into a wood chipper, but she wasn't completely delusional. He loved the baby as much as she did.

He just didn't love *her*. If he really had, he wouldn't have pulled a cheap stunt like this.

Maybe he's clearing the way for me to move out without him having to deal with me again.

She threw her clothes onto the bed and had to lean over to wait for the lurching of her stomach to pass. A lie. It had all been a lie. Becka packed as fast as she could. She had things in *his* room, but she couldn't bear the thought of crossing that threshold and being assaulted by all the good memories they'd made there.

All that mattered was getting the hell out. She could go back to her apartment. The thought brought her up short. Just because he obviously didn't want anything to do with her didn't mean he'd back down from his ridiculous condition of her not living in that apartment. He couldn't have it both ways.

Unless he calls my bluff and hauls me back here to live in the spare room and then we have to see each other on a daily basis while he holds himself apart.

No. She couldn't do it. The pain in her chest was so sharp, she could barely breathe past it *now*. Seeing him and trying to function as if she wasn't emotionally bleeding out at his feet? She'd rather actually bleed out.

Becka fumbled for her phone and dialed. Allie answered almost immediately. "Hey, girl. What's up?"

"Are you home?" Her voice cracked in the middle of the sentence.

Instantly, all happiness was gone from Allie's tone. "I can be there in fifteen. Is everything okay? Is it the baby?"

The baby. She pressed her hand to her stomach. The doctor said the baby was fine, but this level of stress had to be releasing all sorts of crazy hormones that couldn't be good. She took a slow breath and tried to calm her racing heart. "It's nothing like that. I just... Remember when you offered to let me crash at your place? Does that still stand?"

"Of course." Allie, bless her soul, didn't hesitate. "Meet you there?"

"Yeah, I'm getting in a cab in two minutes." She'd have to offer an explanation, but at least her friend was willing to wait until they were face-to-face.

It took Becka forty minutes to cab it to the new apartment Roman and Allie had bought together last year. They'd compromised on location, so it was roughly an equal distance between her gym and his office. Allie buzzed her up, and she walked into an apartment smelling of peanut butter cookies.

It was too much. She dropped her bag on the floor and the burning in her eyes got the best of her. This apartment practically reeked of love and happiness from Roman and Allie living here. It was there in the little details—the table next to the door with a key bowl and a little notepad where they wrote notes to each other; the framed picture of them just down the hall, staring at each other with such love in their eyes that it made Becka want to cry. She could have had that. She almost *did* have that.

No longer.

She wrapped her arms around herself as Allie poked her head out of the doorway leading to the kitchen. Her friend took one look at her, and her expression fell. "Oh, honey. What did he do?" She rushed to Becka and pulled her into a hug. It was a good hug.

She clung to Allie. "Why do you assume he did something and not me?"

"Because that's not guilt on your face. That's heartbreak." She rubbed soothing circles on Becka's back. "And I talked to you two days ago, and you were all giddy and very much in love."

Becka blinked. "I'm not…" But there was no point in hiding from the truth anymore. Only love could feel like a spiked arrow through her chest, digging in deeper with each heartbeat that dragged her into a future that didn't have Aaron in it. "Shit, I love him."

"I know." Allie huffed out a laugh. "Come sit down. I grabbed the cookie dough and some cranberry juice on the way here. Eat your sorrows and we'll see if I need to go key Aaron's car by the end of this conversation."

Becka gave her a look. "While that might be satisfying, that's also a little criminal."

"Worth it." Allie ushered her into a chair at the small nook table and placed a plate of cookies and a glass of cranberry juice in front of her. "Now, spill."

And she did. Every little detail of the nightmarish doctor's appointment and the ensuing marriage proposal that resulted in the fight that broke them. She broke the cookie she hadn't managed to take a bite of and set it back on the table. "He left, Allie. I overreacted maybe—probably—but he just...walked out. And didn't come back."

"Which triggered every single issue you have." Allie reached over and covered her hand with her own. "Why don't you plan on staying here at least a couple days? Roman adores you, and it'd be nice to spend some more time with you."

She was too devastated to make a swinger joke, which more than anything told her just how screwed up this situation was. She tried for a smile. "Thanks."

"If you don't want to see Aaron while you're here, you don't have to. We'll keep him away until you're ready to deal with him."

The burning in her throat got worse, but she managed to whisper. "I don't think that's going to be a problem, Allie. He made his choice. Now I just have to learn to live with it."

"Fuck that."

She jerked back. "What?"

"If you're done with him, that's fine. I know you were kind of cagey about living with him in the first place." Allie narrowed her eyes. "But if you're retreating because you're scared of getting hurt or rejected... Fuck that, Becka. Sometimes you have to be the one to take the lead and fight for what you want." She held up her hand. "Not today. Not even tomorrow. But when the smoke clears and you can think again, you need to decide what *you* want. If that's to keep going without him, then fine. If what you want is Aaron, then you need to fight for him."

"Not today," she said.

"Not today," Allie agreed. She came around the table and gave her another hug. "Roman's going to be working late, so why don't we order in and watch a movie? Something mindless and no pressure."

"That sounds good." Her voice was thick with unshed tears. "What did I do to deserve such a great best friend?"

"Takes one to know one." Allie tugged her to her feet, grabbed the plate of cookies and nudged her out of the kitchen and into the living room. "Besides, I seem to remember someone dragging me to a tropical island paradise not too long ago, and look how that turned out."

She'd met the love of her life there.

Becka managed a smile. "Someone should make that someone more cookies."

"On it!"

She settled into the couch and grabbed a throw blanket to wrap around her. While she waited for Allie, she replayed her friend's words through her head.

Fight for him.

The very thought was laughable. How could she fight a losing battle? Aaron had made his choice. Not only had he left, but he'd stayed gone and iced her out. She couldn't fight if there was no one there to fight with.

Becka swallowed hard. It was too soon to think about it. She could barely draw a breath without pain lancing her chest, and all she wanted to do was curl up with this plate of cookies under a blanket and cry for the next twelve hours. After that?

After that, she'd figure out what she was going to do.

Aaron stared at his computer screen, the letters blurring together the same way they had for the last thirty-odd hours. He couldn't focus, too distracted by replaying his fight with Becka over and over again. Her outright refusal to talk about the future and willingness to stick her head in the sand when it came to every single future subject still made him see red. But beneath the surface-level anger was a fear he didn't know how to deal with.

She didn't want him.

Or, rather, she wanted to cling to her walls and keep him at a distance more than she wanted to actually be with him.

A knock on his office door brought his head up. Aaron minimized the screen and sat back. "Yeah?"

Cameron walked in and dropped into the chair

on the other side of his desk. "Think it's about time we had a talk."

"Did we lose another client?" He couldn't even work up the energy to be pissed about it. Becka's solution for bringing his sister in to work as a junior consultant was still hanging in the wind. He had been too twisted up inside over Becka to worry about work, which was ironic, because he'd been at the office since their fight.

His partner laced his fingers behind his head and stared hard at him. "Doesn't sound like you'd care if we did."

He didn't in that moment, but he *would*. Aaron straightened in his seat and tried to focus. "I can get them back, whoever they were."

"Probably, but there's no crisis to deal with." Cameron raised a single eyebrow. "Except the one I'm looking at right now. What the fuck is going on with you and your woman? You're walking around here like a zombie, and judging from the state of the couch over there, you slept here last night."

He glanced at the couch, guilt flaring. The thought of going back to his penthouse and fighting with Becka more, of having her layer rejection upon rejection over him had been...too much. Cowardly didn't begin to cover camping out here for the night, but he wasn't ready to be done and he hadn't figured out a plan to keep it from happening. He *would* figure it out if he could just *think*. "You have a point. Get to it."

"My *point* is that you're fucking it up. I don't do relationships and even I can see that." Cameron shook his head. "She called earlier and sounded just as messed up as you do. Go home. Fix your shit. Don't come back to the office until you have it taken care of."

Aaron frowned. "What are you talking about? She didn't call here." He would have heard the phone. She *had* texted yesterday, but it was so damn confrontational, he'd set his phone aside without responding. *A plan. I just need a damn plan.*

"No, she didn't call the office. She called *me*." Cameron leaned forward and propped his elbows on his knees. "Seems she couldn't get ahold of you, which is confusing as fuck to me because you're sitting right here with two phones on your desk and yet it looks like you walked out of a fight and have been acting like an asshole ever since." He gave Aaron a disgusted look. "She wanted to make sure you were okay. Didn't say as much, but the relief and hurt practically radiated through the phone, and if leaving her hanging like that isn't some bullshit, I don't know what is."

She'd called Cameron.

Horror flooded Aaron. He hadn't responded to her text. Hadn't called. Hadn't done anything to let her know where he was or where his head was at.

For her to call Cameron, she had to have been in a bad place, worried about him, and he hadn't done a single thing to stop that. He'd let his own hurt get in the way of everything. He'd *promised* her that he would be in her corner no matter what, and the first time she got truly skittish on him, he acted like a dick and left her.

He shoved to his feet so fast, he tipped his chair over. "I'm an asshole."

"Finally." Cameron sat back. "Took you long enough to figure it out."

He rushed out of the office, barely pausing long enough to grab his phone and his keys, and then took the stairs down to the street because he didn't want to wait for the elevator. The trip to his penthouse took on a nightmarish quality. No matter how fast he moved, it wasn't fast enough.

He should have taken a walk around the block and immediately come back after the fight.

Fuck, he shouldn't have left in the first place.

It would have played on every single insecurity and fear Becka had. And then to leave her hanging…

He was well and truly an asshole.

Aaron raced through the doors of his building and took the elevator up to his floor. He burst through the door. "Becka? Becka, where are you?"

Silence greeted him.

I'm too late.

He closed the door behind him and stalked through

the penthouse. The answers he sought lay in the spare bedroom. The closet doors hung open, all her clothing gone, along with her suitcases. Even knowing it was a lost cause, Aaron walked to the bedroom they'd begun sharing together and opened the door.

It looked exactly like it had when he'd left for work two days ago. A pair of Becka's shoes had been tossed in the approximate direction of the closet. Her towel still lay in a pile on the dresser where she'd set it while she was getting dressed. There was even the slightest indent on the pillow she'd claimed as her own.

Aaron leaned against the wall and closed his eyes. It was worse seeing evidence of her here compared to the searing lack in the other room. It meant she hadn't been able to force herself through the door. He'd hurt her that much.

Fuck.

He didn't know how to make this right. There wasn't a single plan that would work—he knew, because he'd labored over countless ones while he sat in his office and didn't work. Becka was *gone*. He was to blame.

Each second ticked by, a reminder of the way he'd failed her. Aaron pushed off the wall and rushed back through the penthouse, looking for some indication of where she'd gone.

Nothing.

No note, no convenient piece of evidence that would lead him to her.

Think, damn it. You can't go running down the street bellowing her name.

Even though that was exactly what he wanted to do.

Aaron dug his phone out of his pocket and called Lucy. It barely rang once before he hung up. What was he thinking? She might have told her sister she was pregnant, but showing up there would just reinforce her incorrect belief that she was somehow failing Lucy. Becka wouldn't go to Lucy.

No, she'd go to Allie and Roman.

He started to call his friend, but Aaron paused. If there was one truth when it came to Roman, it was that the man loved Allie beyond all reasonable doubt. If Becka was there, he would stand sentry over her and Allie if it was what the women wanted. An admirable quality, but it would put them directly at odds, and Aaron couldn't risk the possibility of being kept from her.

He couldn't make this right if he couldn't see her.

What do you think you're going to do? That you'll show up and she'll be so relieved you decided to stop being a dick that she'll fall at your feet in gratitude? Not likely.

The odds were Becka would throw something at his head rather than sit still long enough to hear him apologize. He deserved it. There was no doubt about *that*.

He reached the ground floor and headed out onto

the street. He had no plan. No guarantee that she wouldn't kick him to the curb the second she saw him. Nothing.

Nothing but his love and an apology he didn't even know how to put into words.

It didn't matter.

He would make it right.

The alternative—a future with Becka moving peripherally through his life—was too heartbreaking to even consider. If he fucked this up, they'd share a child and nothing else. He'd have to stand by and watch her move on. She might avoid relationships like a plague right now, but eventually she'd come across a man determined enough to get past her barriers, who would be patient with her skittishness, and who would earn her love as a result.

Fuck. That.

Aaron wanted to be that man. Aaron *was* that man.

He just had to prove it to her.

CHAPTER SIXTEEN

BECKA COULDN'T SETTLE into the movie. It was more than her bladder crying foul every fifteen minutes or the fact that too many peanut butter cookies had upset her stomach. She kept running over Allie's words, and every repeat put her more on edge. She sat up. "I *did* fight for him."

"Hmm?" Allie turned to look at her. "What's that?"

"Aaron." She pushed to her feet and pressed a knuckle to the small of her back, where an ache had started. "I moved in with him. I went on dates with him. I shared his damn bed. I was making an effort."

"Uh-huh."

She paced back and forth, energy snapping through her limbs. "You know what I need to do?" Becka continued before her friend could respond. "I need to go down to his office and say what I need to say. He can't just ice me out and expect me to fade quietly into the night." She spun around. "I love that asshole, and people that love each other don't have a single fight and break up. That's bullshit. He can't ghost me. I'm having his freaking baby."

Allie cleared her throat. "Well, technically, he *could* ghost you." She held up her hands when Becka growled. "I mean, this is Aaron, and obviously he's not going to because he's Aaron. But just wanted to point that out."

"You're not helping." She snatched up her phone and headed for the door. "I'm going to track that jerk down and figure this out."

"Go get 'em, tiger."

Considering Becka had said almost the same thing to Allie after she and Roman had their bumpy start, she didn't growl at her friend again. "I'll call you later." She stalked to the door and threw it open.

And almost plowed right into Aaron.

He stood there, one hand raised to knock. "Becka."

She froze. "Aaron." Now that they were face-to-face, her anger drained away as if it'd never been, leaving only the hurt and heartbreak behind. She stepped back and wrapped her arms around herself. "What are you doing here?" He shifted, and she zeroed in on the plastic containers in his free hand. They looked familiar... "Are those peanut butter and jelly wings?"

He slowly lowered his hand. "I figured my best chance of getting you to sit still long enough to hear me apologize was if I provided your favorite food." He motioned to the containers. "And if it brought up some of the good memories to combat what an asshole I've been, I wouldn't complain about that, either."

It was right about then that she realized they still stood half in the hallway outside the apartment. "How did you get up here?"

Guilt flared in his blue eyes. "One of my old clients lives on the floor below. I asked him to buzz me up."

Shady. He obviously didn't want to project his arrival for fear of how she'd react, which was enough to tell her that Allie had no idea he was coming. Becka shot a glance over her shoulder, but if her friend was eavesdropping, she was being subtle about it. After a quick internal debate, she stepped back. "Why don't you come in?" Allie had set her up in their spare bedroom, so she led Aaron there.

He didn't speak as she shut the door behind him, but he did set the food on the dresser. Becka opened her mouth, but she didn't know what to say. The fear rose again, the instinctive desire to retreat behind her shell to avoid being vulnerable. Letting Aaron in had *hurt*, and if he had showed up just to reject her…

Have a little faith.

She cleared her throat. "I overreacted. You startled me with the marriage thing, and instead of talking it out like a reasonable adult, I flipped my shit and unloaded a couple decades' worth of issues on you. That wasn't fair." She pressed her lips together.

"But I still think marriage isn't the answer. Not like this—not in response to being pregnant."

Aaron sank onto the bed and looked up at her. Her pain was reflected in his eyes, and it struck her that these two days apart hadn't been any easier on him than they had been on her. He scrubbed a hand over his face. "After the doctor's appointment… After that scare…" He shook his head. "All I could think about was that if we lost the baby for some reason, I could survive it. I'd be upset and sad because I've gotten used to the idea of being a father, but I'd survive. But losing the baby meant that I'd lose you in the process. You made it more than clear that the only reason you got back in contact with me again was because you were pregnant. The thought of losing *you*…"

He'd proposed because he wanted a way to link her to him, an assurance that she wouldn't leave him.

Becka crossed the room to sit on the bed next to him. "You know, you could have just asked me if I planned on bolting if that happened." As soon as the words were out of her mouth, she winced. "Then again, I probably could have been more forthcoming with the fact that I'm in love with you."

"You're in love with me." He went so still next to her, she didn't think he drew breath.

She stared hard at the door—anything was easier than looking at him in that moment. "Yeah, well, I don't know if you noticed, but you're kind of the greatest guy I've ever met and I'd have to be crazy not to fall for you." The next part was harder to get out. "I have issues, Aaron. They aren't going to magically disappear because of the love of a good man, but I'm trying to work on them. But you can't leave like that. I sat in that penthouse for over twenty-four hours wondering if you'd left me, or if something had happened to you and... We're going to fight. I don't know a couple that *doesn't* fight—even Lucy and Gideon—and I need to know that you aren't going to hurt me like that again. I can deal with the arguing. I can't deal with you disappearing on me."

"I'm so fucking sorry." He lifted her into his lap and wrapped his arms around her. "I promise I'll never do it again."

She leaned her head against his shoulder. "Good. Because next time I'm liable to hunt your ass down and cause a scene."

"That won't be necessary." He pressed a soft kiss to her temple. "Come home, minx. I promise not to throw you over my shoulder and sprint to the nearest courthouse."

She laughed, though the sound faded almost as soon as she'd given it voice. "I don't know where we go from here. I was kind of hoping you had a plan."

"I don't." He cuddled her closer. "Turns out, plans don't save you from fucking up from time to time. I love you. You love me. We're going to have a baby together. Maybe we don't have to have every little detail ironed out right now."

God, she loved this man. But he wasn't the only one who would be making compromises. Becka looked up at him. "I'm not ready to rush into marriage or anything but…maybe let's not take it completely off the table?"

"If you're sure."

She laughed and, this time, it was downright joyous. "Oh, I'm sure. You're stuck with me, Aaron Livingston." She leaned up and kissed him. "But I'll be honest—I'm going to go balls out when I propose to you. Think those crazy prom proposals, but just downright extra."

He grinned against her mouth. "I can get onboard with this plan."

EPILOGUE

"Get ready to push."

Aaron braced himself behind Becka and tried not to wince as she clasped his fingers in a death grip. Her entire body went tense, little ripples making waves in the birthing pool they sat in. He couldn't help her. He couldn't step in and take away the pain radiating from every pore of her body as she tried to bring their daughter into the world. All he could do was hold her and let her crush his fingers and breathe the way they'd been taught in their birthing classes.

As the contraction passed, Becka slumped against him. "Ouch."

"You're doing wonderfully," Lucy said as she mopped Becka's brow. She had her dark hair tied back and a look of concentration on her face, as if she could will Becka to have an uncomplicated labor.

"You are," the midwife confirmed. "The baby's in position and engaged. A few more pushes and you'll get to hold your daughter."

Aaron smoothed back the damp hair from Becka's forehead. "I love you. You're amazing."

Becka huffed out a strained laugh. "I'm thinking murderous thoughts about *you* right now."

"You can tell me all about them if it would help." He reached between them and gently massaged the small of her back. The contractions were coming fast now, and they had less than twenty seconds before the next one by his count.

"No energy." She drew in a long breath. "Here we go."

"You've got this, Becka. Almost there." Lucy mimicked the breathing pattern they'd been taught to use.

The battle to bring their daughter into the world was exactly that—a battle. Becka bore down with a determined silence that scared the shit out of him. There was no screaming. No yelling. None of the things he'd read about and tried to emotionally prepare for so he could support her. Nothing but a focus that left him totally and completely in awe of her.

"This is it, you're doing great. Don't stop. Harder, Becka. Push harder. You can do it!" The midwife's commanding tone had Aaron biting back a snarl; Lucy held her breath in utter stillness, but Becka let loose a muted shriek and the midwife crowed in delight. "Here she is!"

He barely got a glimpse of a wrinkled pink face

before their baby let loose a scream to shake the rafters. The midwife grinned. "Healthy set of lungs."

Things moved quickly after that. Aaron could barely process that the event had finally happened—that they were parents—in the midst of all the insanity. Lucy fielding the news out to Allie and their men. Nurses coming and going. Becka being checked out and pronounced perfectly fine.

Both Aaron and Becka changed into dry clothing while their daughter was weighed and measured and underwent all manner of poking and prodding.

Finally—*finally*—the last nurse shut the door and they were alone.

He pushed out of the chair he'd been relegated to and crossed over to sink onto the edge of the bed. Becka lay with her eyes half-closed, their daughter lying against her naked chest. Aaron carefully stroked the baby's downy-soft hair. "She's here."

"She is." Becka smiled, and a tear escaped the corner of her eye. "She's perfect. More perfect than I ever dared dream."

"You both are." He pressed a soft kiss to their daughter's head and then another to Becka's lips. "What do you think? Is she a Summer or an Evangeline?" The two names they'd finally settled on after months of rigorous debate and even a fight or two.

She looked down into the baby's sleeping face. "Summer. Definitely Summer. She's been in this world a grand total of two hours and she's already brightened everyone's life she touched." Becka made a face. "Oh God, motherhood is going to turn me into one of *those* people, isn't it? I'm so happy I can't even think straight, and if I had my phone, I'd already be sending pictures to everyone in my contact list."

He chuckled. "I already texted a picture of her, along with her weight, length and time of birth, to all our friends and family." He'd restrained himself to a single picture, but he already had half a dozen in his phone. Aaron grinned. "How long do you think it will be before Roman stages an intervention?"

"Two months—tops." She smiled back. Becka reached out and covered his hand with her own. "Hey, Aaron?"

"Yes, minx?"

She nodded at the bag they'd packed and repacked three separate times in the last month, convinced that they'd forgotten something important every time. "Can you grab my purse out of there?"

Curious, he dug through the bag until he found the tiny clutch that she'd insisted on. He handed it over and watched as Becka used her free hand to dig inside it. She paused. "Okay, so in my head, this would be all soft lighting and I wouldn't be feeling like I've just been ripped in half and look like day-old roadkill, but squint a little and pretend with me." She pressed her lips together. "Aaron Livingston, you are the best man I've ever met. Better than I deserve, and I damn well know it. I can't promise that your organization and borderline compulsive need to re-search things won't drive me to drink sometimes, but I *do* promise that I'll love you for the rest of our lives.

"There's no one else but you for me. I want a life with you. I want to fill our home with a couple more kids. I want meandering walks to delicious food trucks and old movie marathons and the early-morning talks over breakfast and the nights spent wrapped up in each other."

She glanced at Summer and laughed. "Though I suspect we'll both be too exhausted for the next however many months to do more than sleep in that bed. But the point stands—I want a future with you. With *us*." Becka leveraged open the tiny box in her hand and turned it to face him. "Will you do me the immeasurable honor of being my husband, Aaron?"

He lifted the ring out of the box. It was a dark gray that he suspected was titanium and had a faint ab-stract pattern etched on the outside. "You proposed."

"Well, yeah. I did say I was going to."

He left the bed long enough to grab a nearly iden-tical ring box from the side pocket of the bag. Aaron returned to her, smiling so hard his face hurt. "You beat me to it, minx." He opened the box and showed her the princess-cut diamond he'd had commissioned over a month ago. "The answer is yes, Becka. I'll be your husband if you'll be my wife."

She touched the ring, smiling as hard as he was. "I was thinking three kids, but that might be the left-over adrenaline making me loopy, so that is completely open to negotiation."

They both glanced down at Summer. Aaron shifted to drop a lingering kiss to Becka's mouth. "I love you. I love you so much it makes me crazy in the best way possible."

"The feeling is very much mutual." She smiled against his lips. "Do you want to hold her?"

He carefully took Summer from her and cradled their daughter in his arms. Aaron's chest hurt with how *right* it was to have this right here, right now, with this woman. "Welcome to the world, princess."

* * * * *

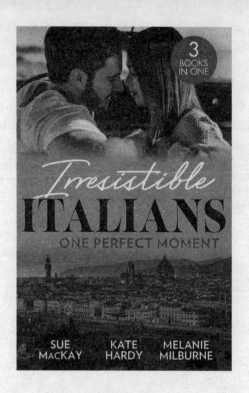

LET'S TALK

Romance

For exclusive extracts, competitions
and special offers, find us online:

f facebook.com/millsandboon

𝕏 @MillsandBoon

◎ @MillsandBoonUK

♪ @MillsandBoonUK

Get in touch on 01413 063 232

MILLS & BOON

THE HEART OF ROMANCE

A ROMANCE FOR EVERY READER

MODERN
Prepare to be swept off your feet by sophisticated, sexy and seductive heroes, in some of the world's most glamourous and romantic locations, where power and passion collide.

HISTORICAL
Escape with historical heroes from time gone by. Whether your passion is for wicked Regency Rakes, muscled Vikings or rugged Highlanders, awaken the romance of the past.

MEDICAL
Set your pulse racing with dedicated, delectable doctors in the high-pressure world of medicine, where emotions run high and passion, comfort and love are the best medicine.

True Love
Celebrate true love with tender stories of heartfelt romance, from the rush of falling in love to the joy a new baby can bring, and a focus on the emotional heart of a relationship.

Desire
Indulge in secrets and scandal, intense drama and sizzling hot action with heroes who have it all: wealth, status, good looks…everything but the right woman.

HEROES
The excitement of a gripping thriller, with intense romance at its heart. Resourceful, true-to-life women and strong, fearless men face danger and desire - a killer combination!

To see which titles are coming soon, please visit

millsandboon.co.uk/nextmonth

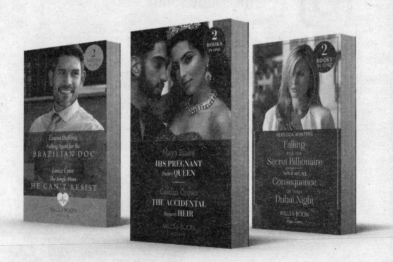

GET YOUR ROMANCE FIX!

Get the latest romance news,
exclusive author interviews, story
extracts and much more!

MILLS & BOON
MODERN
Power and Passion

Prepare to be swept off your feet by
sophisticated, sexy and seductive heroes, in some of
the world's most glamourous and romantic
locations, where power and passion collide.